FORD MADOX FORD was born Ford Hermann Hueffer in Merton, Surrey, in 1873, the eldest son of Francis Hueffer, a German emigré, musicologist and music critic for *The Times*, and Catherine, the daughter of Ford Madox Brown, the Pre-Raphaelite painter. Christina and Dante Gabriel Rossetti were his aunt and uncle by marriage. Ford was a prolific writer, producing some eighty books in a variety of genres: novels, poems, criticism, memoirs, and impressionist accounts of English, European, and American culture.

Ford published his first book—a fairy-tale—when he was seventeen. He collaborated with Joseph Conrad from 1898 to 1909 on two novels and a novella. He became a central figure in the Modernist movement, founding *The English Review* in 1908, publishing established writers such as his friends Henry James and H. G. Wells alongside his new discoveries D. H. Lawrence, Wyndham Lewis, and Ezra Pound, who became another close friend. Ford is best known for his novels, especially *The Fifth Queen* trilogy (1906–8), *The Good Soldier* (1915), and the four 'Tietjens' novels making up *Parade's End* (1924–8).

Ford served as an officer in the Welch Regiment during the First World War, getting concussed by a nearby shell-explosion during the Battle of the Somme. After the war he changed his name to Ford Madox Ford and moved to France. In Paris he founded the *transatlantic review*, taking on Ernest Hemingway as a sub-editor, discovering Jean Rhys and Basil Bunting, and publishing Gertrude Stein and James Joyce. In the 1920s and 1930s he moved between Paris, New York, and Provence. He died in Deauville in June 1939.

MAX SAUNDERS is Director of the Arts and Humanities Research Institute, Professor of English, and Co-Director of the Centre for Life-Writing Research at King's College London, where he teaches modern literature. He is the author of *Ford Madox Ford: A Dual Life*, 2 vols. (Oxford University Press, 1996) and *Self Impression: Life-Writing, Autobiografiction, and the Forms of Modern Literature* (Oxford University Press, 2010), and editor of four other volumes of Ford's writing, including an annotated critical edition of the first novel of the *Parade's End* sequence about the First World War, *Some Do Not . . .* (Carcanet, 2010).

OXFORD WORLD'S CLASSICS

FORD MADOX FORD

The Good Soldier
A Tale of Passion

Edited with an Introduction and Notes by
MAX SAUNDERS

OXFORD
UNIVERSITY PRESS

OXFORD

UNIVERSITY PRESS

Great Clarendon Street, Oxford, OX2 6DP,
United Kingdom

Oxford University Press is a department of the University of Oxford.
It furthers the University's objective of excellence in research, scholarship,
and education by publishing worldwide. Oxford is a registered trade mark of
Oxford University Press in the UK and in certain other countries

Editorial material © Max Saunders 2012

The moral rights of the author have been asserted

First published as a World's Classics paperback 1990
Reissued as an Oxford World's Classics paperback 1999, 2008
New edition 2012

Impression: 3

British Library Cataloguing in Publication Data
Data available

Library of Congress Cataloging in Publication Data
Data available

ISBN 978-0-19-958594-6

Printed in Great Britain by
Clays Ltd, St Ives plc

INTRODUCTION

[Readers who are unfamiliar with the plot may prefer to treat the Intro-duction as an Afterword.]

FORD MADOX FORD referred to *The Good Soldier* (1915) as his 'one novel'—though he had written eighteen before it, and twenty-four of his eventual thirty or more when he made that comment in 1931.[1] 'I have always regarded this as my best book', he says in the Dedica-tory Letter (written for a second edition in 1927 and included here); and many critics have echoed that judgement. It is an extraordinary achievement. The intricate first-person narration manages the rare feat of pulling off a virtuoso technical performance while remaining powerfully engaging. It is an exemplary modernist text in its use of unreliable narration, the 'time-shift', and its play with interpretative enigma. From its arresting first sentence to its bitterly ironic last, it sustains its intensity, its compelling intimacy, and its disconcerting but irresistible mix of pathos and humour. It can divide opinions, but rarely leaves readers cold. *The Good Soldier* is amongst the handful of Ford's eighty or so books to have remained in print constantly since the 1940s; it has gone through more editions and translations than any of his other works; and it is one of only two of his works to have been filmed for television.[2]

Rebecca West wrote that *The Good Soldier* had 'set the pattern for perhaps half the novels which have been written since'.[3] But Ford's transatlantic theme and presentation of the sexual intrigues and duplicities of a civilized elite show his own debt to the work of his friend Henry James; as *The Good Soldier*'s technical virtuosity owes much to a decade of collaboration with a closer friend, Joseph Conrad. Its influence on later modernist and post-modernist fiction has indeed

1 Ford, *Return to Yesterday* (London: Gollancz, 1931), 417, 429.

2 *The Good Soldier* was adapted for British television by Julian Mitchell and broadcast by Granada in 1981, directed by Kevin Billington and starring Jeremy Brett and Susan Fleetwood as the Ashburnhams, and Robin Ellis and Vickery Turner as the Dowells. *Parade's End* has been adapted twice for the BBC; once in 1964, and again in 2012 with a screenplay by Tom Stoppard.

3 West, 'Unlucky Eccentric's Private World', *Sunday Telegraph* (17 June 1962), 6. An exaggeration, certainly: she was perhaps thinking of its influence on her own *The Return of the Soldier* (1916).

been profound. Works like F. Scott Fitzgerald's *The Great Gatsby* (1925), Jean Rhys's *Quartet* (published as *Postures* in 1928), Graham Greene's *The End of the Affair* (1951), Anthony Burgess's *Earthly Powers* (1980), Julian Barnes's *Flaubert's Parrot* (1984), or Kazuo Ishiguro's *The Remains of the Day* (1989) are unlikely to have taken the form they did without Ford's example. Indeed, Ford has found champions among the best modern writers, including Ezra Pound, W. H. Auden, Robert Lowell, William Carlos Williams, Gore Vidal, Malcolm Bradbury, A. S. Byatt, Edmund White, and Tom Stoppard.

There was little in his previous work to prepare *The Good Soldier*'s first readers for its formal brilliance and psychological resonance. The books for which Ford was known throughout the Edwardian years were very different—criticism and reminiscences of the Pre-Raphaelites; a trilogy of poignant books about *England and the English* (1905–7); a trilogy of historical novels about Henry VIII and his *Fifth Queen* (1906–8); and a spirited historical romance with a modern twist, *Ladies Whose Bright Eyes* (1911). He had some cachet as a literary critic and editor, founding the *English Review* in 1908, and publishing prestigious established writers such as James, Conrad, H. G. Wells, and Arnold Bennett alongside his new discoveries—Pound, D. H. Lawrence, and Wyndham Lewis. But he felt he had not really shown what he could do himself. *The Good Soldier* was subtitled 'A Tale of Passion', and passion had always been the predominant theme of his fiction. But only *A Call: The Tale of Two Passions* (1910) had dealt with it with comparable intensity, setting the story in the contemporary world and dealing frankly with desire, adultery, psychoanalysis, and modern technologies of communication such as the telegraph and telephone. Otherwise, his most powerful evocations of desire and obsession were to be found in his historical fantasies such as *Ladies Whose Bright Eyes* or the novel he had published just before starting *The Good Soldier*, *The Young Lovell* (1913). He could turn an elegant comic novel too, whether historical, as with *The Portrait* (1910), or contemporary, as with *The Panel* (1912). And he could equally turn a deft satire: of the media and celebrity in *Mr. Apollo* (1908), or of political manipulation in *Mr. Fleight* (1913). In *The Good Soldier* all these strengths came together for the first time in his work: the pitiless satirical analysis of the codes of behaviour of the upper-class English, 'good people', and of the naivety of the American narrator; the vivid historical sense, reaching back through Victorian sentimentality, to the Reformation, and, earlier still, to the invention of romance in medieval Provence; the registering of modern anxieties about problems such as sexuality, class, 'the condition of England', degeneration, imperial decline, the rise of America, and the fate of Europe on the verge of war.

Modernism, Impressionism, and the Unreliable Narrator

The Good Soldier is most often placed now in the context of modern- ism. Ford was closely involved with three major modernist networks: the circle of James, Conrad, Stephen Crane, and Wells, in Kent and Sussex around 1900; then the avant-garde in London before the war, including Lawrence, May Sinclair, Dorothy Richardson, West, Pound, and Lewis; and third, the expatriates in postwar Paris, espe- cially Joyce, Hemingway, Jean Rhys, and Gertrude Stein. While Parade's End—the coruscating sequence of novels he wrote in the 1920s about British Society through the First World War—responds to the experiments of these last, it is the first two groups which pro- vide crucial contexts for The Good Soldier. Where Parade's End has been juxtaposed with works by Proust, Musil, and the Joyce of Ulysses, The Good Soldier needs to be situated alongside both the early modernism of James and Conrad and also contemporary high- modernist works reinventing the representation of consciousness, time, memory, and narration, such as the early volumes of A la recherche, A Portrait of the Artist as a Young Man, and 'The Love Song of J. Alfred Prufrock'.

Ford was very much at the heart of the modernist rethinking of the poetics of verse and prose. The Good Soldier is the culmination of an astonishing burst of critical activity over the previous five years: founding the English Review, and furiously writing literary journal- ism refining the critical theories elaborated with Conrad. His cham- pioning of younger modernist talents, and his English Review editorials, later collected as The Critical Attitude (1911), arguing for a technical self-consciousness and critical rigour in the writing of fic- tion, had already marked him as a key contributor to the avant-garde. Wyndham Lewis included the opening of The Good Soldier, under its original title of 'The Saddest Story', in the first number of his aggres- sively modern 'Vorticist' magazine Blast in June 1914. In pre-war

London Ford moved in the world of aesthetic coteries—Imagists, Futurists, Vorticists. Though they saw themselves as 'modern', and occasionally wrote of 'modernism' in the arts, they were not seen as a coherent single movement. Nor did Ford call himself modernist. He saw his method as 'impressionism'; and it was as he began *The Good Soldier* that he started to define it in two major essays. One— 'Impressionism—Some Speculations'—became the preface to his 1913 *Collected Poems*: a document that, channelled by Pound, had a profound influence on English poetics.[4] The other—'On Impressionism'—has more to say about prose, and is reprinted here in full, in an annotated version that brings out its profound interplay with *The Good Soldier*.

Impressionism was of course first taken as the name for a move- ment by the French group of artists—including Monet, Renoir, and Pissarro—who began exhibiting in Paris from 1874. Ford certainly knew of these painters. But his allegiance to the Pre-Raphaelites of his beloved grandfather Ford Madox Brown's circle perhaps made him reluctant at first to identify himself with their successors. He only started to do that as he was poised to write *The Good Soldier*, though he had written much about 'impressions' through the Edwardian years; and his verse and prose of that period could well be described as 'impressionist'. The application of the term to literature has always been controversial; but literary impressionism has recently been undergoing a rehabilitation as a crucial, if ambiguous, category.[5] It describes both a historical phase of writing, coming between real- ism and modernism; and also a style or method with a rather longer span, identifiable within realist and modernist works as well. Earlier writers in English—John Ruskin, Walter Pater, Henry James—had made the 'impression' central to their aesthetics. But Ford is argu- ably the foremost critic who argued for impressionism as both a tech- nical approach and a literary tradition. He is certainly one of the most prolific writers on impressionism in literature.

When Ford writes of impressionism he is not thinking primarily of the French painters. Nor is he thinking of the British aesthetes of the turn of the century—such as Pater, George Moore, or Arthur

⁴ See Brita Lindberg-Seyersted (ed.), *Pound/Ford: The Story of a Literary Friendship* (London: Faber & Faber, 1982).

⁵ See the works cited in the Select Bibliography by Paul Armstrong, Jesse Matz, John Peters, Tamar Katz, and others.

Symons—who had sought to translate impressionism into literature. Instead, he identifies a line of what he calls 'conscious art',[6] coming to maturity with the French writers Gustave Flaubert and Guy de Maupassant, and the Russian Ivan Turgenev; and then passing into English through the Americans James and Crane, and the Polish émigré Conrad. That Ford knew these last three, and could remember as a young child offering Turgenev a chair on a visit to Madox Brown's studio, gave him a strong personal connection with these figures. James and Conrad themselves probably would not have seen themselves as part of an impressionist movement. But Ford's view of impressionism was more capacious still: he saw it as continuing into, and helping to shape, the contemporary work he admired most, by writers such as Pound, Lawrence, Joyce, Hemingway, and Jean Rhys. Like impressionism in painting, then, literary impressionism starts in the late nineteenth century, and moves away from realism's claims to objectivity and omniscience. But what is distinctive about Ford's account is that impressionism does not end with modernism (as art-historians see pictorial impressionism ending with post-impressionism and cubism). Instead, rather than trying to theorize a literary impressionism that never caught on, Ford was using that term to describe the main currents of experimental writing that did catch on, from the nineteenth century into the twentieth: the writing that develops into what we now term modernism.

What, then, did Ford understand the method to be that could unite such diverse writers? Impressionism is sometimes described in ways that make it sound like a mere refinement of realism: moving realism from its fascination with the detail of the material world closer to the interior world of individual consciousness, perception, thought, and feeling; and thus a step on the road to the modernist stream-of-consciousness novel. But *The Good Soldier*'s narration, modelled on speaking rather than thinking, can all too often be made to seem essentially realist: ultimately a study of character and situation. Such an approach is a necessary part of a full response to the text; but it is only a part. Certainly all the four main characters are interesting *as* characters. But part of their interest is that they do not stay true to their character in the way that realist characters are supposed to do. And the fact that they are all presented to us by

[6] See for example Ford, *The March of Literature* (London: Allen and Unwin, 1939), 639, 800–1.

Dowell means that we never know whether that indeterminacy is due to the other three characters being unstable, or whether it is Dowell who keeps changing. Fordian impressionism, that is, proceeds by a duality which is at once a form and a doubt. As he puts it in the essay 'On Impressionism':

I suppose that Impressionism exists to render those queer effects of real life that are like so many views seen through bright glass—through glass so bright that whilst you perceive through it a landscape or a backyard, you are aware that, on its surface, it reflects a face of a person behind you. For the whole of life is really like that; we are almost always in one place with our minds somewhere quite other.[1]

Impressionist 'views' are thus both of a world and a person. The formal doubleness means that we can read each episode as about a situation or about a psychology. The doubt is that we can never be sure how much the situation is shaped by that psychology. Doubt is a leitmotiv of *The Good Soldier*. Dowell is continually abstaining from judgement; lamenting that 'It is all a darkness'; asking 'For who in this world can give anyone a character? Who in this world knows anything of any other heart—or of his own?' (p. 122); and telling us: 'I don't know.' The doubt is important to Ford, though, because it is the sign of our perplexity when faced with the enigmas of character and perception. Our perceptions are always incomplete and never infallible, whether of landscapes or of persons. And Ford's impressionism accords doubt its prominent place in our dealings with the world.

One of the striking things about the essay 'On Impressionism' is how similar its cadences are to Dowell's—as when the second paragraph begins 'I do not know', and then echoes the disclaimer twice within a few lines. That might be taken as a sign that *The Good Soldier* is an especially personal book, written in Ford's own manner. In one sense this is true. He does impressionism in whatever genre he takes up: not just the novel, but poems, memoirs, conversations, even criticism. And his criticism is a novelist's; novelistic, even. Nowhere is this truer than in his memoir, *Joseph Conrad: A Personal Remembrance*, which Ford provocatively described as a novel rather than a biography, and in one section of which—effectively a manual of impressionism—he sets out the techniques he and Conrad developed

---

[1] 'On Impressionism', *Poetry and Drama*, 2 (June and December 1914), 167–75, 323–34 (p. 74). See Appendix B, p. 197.

in their quest for a new form for the novel. But to say that is to suggest not so much that the criticism is written in his own voice, against which we can gauge the novels, as rather that his novelistic imagination comes into play even in the criticism, and is as liable to start fictionalizing his positions and tones. Hugh Kenner wrote memorably about Joyce's use of 'shadow-selves', roles he would act out 'that he might better write them. To make Bloom an authentic parody of himself, Joyce turned himself for long periods into a par-ody of Bloom.' So, with Ford, to make Dowell an authentic impres-sion of himself, he turned himself into an impression of Dowell. As with Bloom and Joyce though, Dowell is an impression of only part of Ford's self. If Ford could sound as despondently baffled as Dowell at times, more often what struck people was the opposite: his Olympian pose of omniscience. Conrad referred to the 'characteristic-ally casual and omniscient manner' of the friend who told him the anarchist story that was the germ for *The Secret Agent*.[8] Wyndham Lewis described him at a country house party in Scotland at the end of July 1914, at which Ford read from 'The Saddest Story' in *Blast*. Lewis and Mary Borden Turner, their host, argued that Britain's Liberal government could not possibly declare war; but 'omniscient, bored, sleepy Ford', as Lewis called him, insisted that 'it has always been the Liberals who have gone to war. It is *because* it is a Liberal Government that it *will* declare war.'[9] If that note of ennui is echoed by Dowell, Ford's knowledge of the ways of the world, his political *nous*, is certainly not. For that you need to listen to Ford's characters based on his friend Arthur Marwood: Mr Blood in the political satire *Mr. Fleight*; or the hyper-intelligent Christopher Tietjens in *Parade's End*.

If we work it the other way, one of the striking things about Dowell's narration is how much he sounds like an impressionist critic or novelist. He is extremely self-conscious, that is, about how a story should be narrated; about the precise effects he is trying to produce. (Compare 'On Impressionism': 'I am a perfectly self-conscious writer; I know exactly how I get my effects, as far as those effects go.') When Dowell says: 'I am, at any rate, trying to get you to see what sort of life it was I led with Florence and what Florence was like', we

8 Conrad, 'Author's Note' to *The Secret Agent*, ed. John Lyon (Oxford: Oxford University Press, 2004), 230.
9 Lewis, *Blasting and Bombardiering*, revised edition (London: John Calder; and New York: Riverrun Press, 1982), 58–9.

can hear Ford echoing Conrad's profoundly impressionist credo: 'My task which I am trying to achieve is, by the power of the written word, to make you hear, to make you feel—it is, before all, to make you *see*.'[10] But Dowell is continually anxious he is failing in the attempt: 'I have given you a wrong impression if I have not made you see.' 'It is very difficult to give an all-round impression of any man,' he says: 'I wonder how far I have succeeded with Edward Ashburnham. I dare say I haven't succeeded at all'; and adds: 'It is even very difficult to see how such things matter' (p. 119). But they keep mattering to him. He worries that the detailed history he has given us of Ashburnham's philandering has blown it out of proportion: 'Because, until the very last, the amount of time taken up by his various passions was relatively small [. . .] But I guess I have made it hard for you, O silent listener, to get that impression' (p. 119). Or, worse still: 'looking over what I have written, I see that I have unintentionally misled you when I said that Florence was never out of my sight. Yet that was the impression that I really had until just now. When I come to think of it she was out of my sight most of the time' (p. 72).

The question of how to give an impression of someone matters to Ford too, but differently. Where Dowell is puzzling out how to tell his own story, Ford is writing a novel about someone puzzling out how to tell his own story. What may be unintentional for an obtuse narrator–character is intentional for the conscious impressionist. The critical tradition of discussing *The Good Soldier* in terms of knowledge, epistemology, and doubt sometimes attempts to recuperate uncertainty back to psychological realism: the characters keep appearing different because that is what our experience of others is like; we think we know where we are, then some revelation disorientates us. But Ford's turning of these anxieties into a theme in the novel shows him to be doing something different, and which instead looks forward, to postmodernism. Dowell's fussing about story is an element of what might be seen as Ford's metafiction. If literary impressionism shares realism's aim of seeking a more accurate, candid account of life, it does so by stripping away false certainties so as to reach the real questions; and in the process strips away the very certainties on which realism relies: the knowability of character; the intelligibility of a character's destiny. Ford's book on Conrad gives a vivid example

[10] Preface to *The Nigger of the 'Narcissus'*; first printed as an 'Author's Note' after the serialization in the *New Review*, 17 (December 1897), 628–31.

of how this difficulty in the subject matter—knowing what to make of people—required a corresponding difficulty in the presentation:

You meet an English gentleman at your golf club. He is beefy, full of health, the moral of the boy from an English Public School of the finest type. You discover, gradually, that he is hopelessly neurasthenic, dishonest in matters of small change, but unexpectedly self-sacrificing, a dreadful liar but a most painfully careful student of lepidoptera and, finally, from the public prints, a bigamist who was once, under another name, hammered on the Stock Exchange. . . . Still, there he is, the beefy, full-fed fellow, moral of an English Public School product. To get such a man in fiction you could not begin at his beginning and work his life chronologically to the end. You must first get him in with a strong impression, and then work backwards and forwards over his past. . . . That theory at least we gradually evolved.[11]

This was written soon after Conrad's death, and a decade after *The Good Soldier*. But Ford had then been working on a French translation of the novel (which he said he had begun during the Battle of the Somme).[12] He was presumably thinking, in part, of the novel, since this describes its structure precisely: the narrator, John Dowell, gives a detailed strong first impression of Edward Ashburnham when the two couples meet in Germany in August 1904, and then completes their story with vertiginous 'time-shifts'.[13] Dowell says, 'That question of first impressions has always bothered me a good deal [. . .]' (p. 120). But it is also a question of the impossibility of ever arriving at a last impression, because the earlier ones keep coming back in a disturbed, and disturbing, order.' To make the point unmistakably, in *The Good Soldier* Dowell's most devastating revelations of the extent to which his wife Florence had betrayed him with his best friend Edward Ashburnham are still coming even after they have both committed suicide. The novel is Ford's greatest attainment of what Ann Snitow has called 'the voice of uncertainty'.[14] Fordian uncertainty, though, is not the static impasse the critics can make it sound. As here, it is a dynamic process; the experience of multiply-shifting perspectives, jumps in time and space and understanding. This process

11 Ford, *Joseph Conrad: A Personal Remembrance* (London: Duckworth, 1924), 129–30.
12 See explanatory note to p. 4 of the novel.
13 On the 'time-shift' see for example *It Was the Nightingale*, 143.
14 See Ann Barr Snitow, *Ford Madox Ford and the Voice of Uncertainty* (Baton Rouge and London: Louisiana State University Press, 1984).

does not just unsettle the narrative, or our grasp of that narrative; does not just make us feel, as soon as we have finished reading the book, that if only we were to reread it we might at last know what we thought about its characters. As Frank Kermode said of its interpretative conundrum: 'the illusion of the single right reading is possible no longer.'[15] It makes us wonder whether the reason why the characters do not stand still is not because character itself is a fiction. Since the novel is regularly explicit about character, personality, stories, novels, we need to consider its metafictional aspects—the ways in which it plays with, and undermines, rather than just resting upon, conventional assumptions about character, psychology, and narrative. Chief among these is the use of an unreliable narrator, who makes us as uncertain about him as he is about others. But such metafictional moves have other consequences. One is to risk collapsing the distance between narrator and author. The more Dowell talks about telling a story, the more he sounds like a novelist, like his author. Too close, and our trust in Dowell as a fully-realized character (rather than a mouthpiece) would be jeopardized, as would our trust in Ford as an author. Ford's revisions to the manuscript show him adjusting this fine balance, excising some of Dowell's comments about novels, so as to make him sound less literary. When Dowell worries that he has 'unintentionally misled' us we might feel reassured: Ford is making it clear that Dowell is inept but honest. But if Dowell sounds too close to a novelist for such moments to maintain the distance between narrator and author, then instead of Ford intending to have Dowell mislead us, we might have Dowell (and by extension, Ford too) intending to mislead. A novelist might purposely mislead us for some of the time, so as to make the revelation of truth more effective. And to some extent that is Dowell's purpose too. He was deceived by Florence, Edward, and Leonora for over nine years. So he may feel his narrative needs to mislead us at first, to re-create his experience of deceit. But in that case, his misleading is not always unintentional. And once he admits to misleading us, we are likely to suspect that his assurance that it was unintentional might itself be misleading.

That might sound merely like a way of re-describing narratorial unreliability. But narrators can be unreliable in different ways. Many novelists before Ford had used narrators whose reliability is called

[15] Kermode, *Essays on Fiction* (London: Routledge and Kegan Paul, 1983), 102.

into question. Most often what may be unreliable is their under-standing of the events they narrate. Whether they are eccentric or mad, like Sterne's Tristram Shandy, or self-interested or amoral like Defoe's Robinson Crusoe or Moll Flanders, we do not suspect them of intentionally misleading us. It is not that they give a dubious account of events; what is unreliable is not what they narrate but how they interpret it. They generally display a limitation—whether of character or understanding—which hinders them from grasping the full implications of their story or attaining full self-knowledge. We can always know or suspect things about them of which they would be unconscious. Henry James, in works such as *The Aspern Papers*, 'The Turn of the Screw', *The Sacred Fount*, or 'The Figure in the Carpet', experimented with clever narrators who reveal themselves as (at least, possibly) possessed by their own ideas to the point of insanity. But even with these knowing figures, the question is whether they are deceiving *themselves*, not us. Ford takes this to the next level. In certain key scenes—when Dowell describes being embraced by Florence as they are eloping; or when Florence touches Ashburnham's wrist while showing him the 'Protest' documents—Dowell's responses seem so obtuse as to suggest (and not just to us, but to the other characters) that he is incapable of grasping what is happening around him. He seems surprised that his bride-to-be expects him to be more passionate; he seems not to realize that she is later flirting with Ashburnham. Yet such blindness is hard to square with his per-ceptive descriptions and sensitivity to impressions. We can put down the disparity to the gap between his ignorance while Florence and Edward were deceiving him, and his subsequent knowledge as the affair comes to light after their deaths. But some of his statements arouse a greater degree of doubt, such as his claim:

Of the question of the sex-instinct I know very little and I do not think that it counts for very much in a really great passion. It can be aroused by such nothings—by an untied shoelace, by a glance of the eye in passing—that I think it might be left out of the calculation. (p. 92)

We may wish to grant him his ignorance of 'the sex-instinct'; and may find moving the implication that he has felt 'a really great pas-sion' without it, as he may for Nancy—or even arguably for Edward. Yet he seems knowing enough about how it can be aroused, which appears to contradict his claim for ignorance. He may know such things from books. But even if they may be left out of the calculation for him, his own experience should have taught him (if the books did not) that they cannot be for most others—given that it was because he left it out of the calculation that he has so miscalculated his life. In short, statements like this, or his claim that 'nothing happened' between 1904 and 1913, raise more serious doubts about his truthfulness. (We later learn that what was happening during those nine years was his wife and best friend cuckolding him.) When he says: 'from time to time I have wondered whether it were or were not best to trust to one's first impressions in dealing with people' (p. 120), the novel makes us wonder how far to trust our first—and indeed our subsequent—impressions of him. One way of describing this is to say Ford uses our relation to Dowell as an analogue to his relation to the other characters. Our uncertainties about whether to trust his stories correlate to his experience of trusting too much in the stories they were telling him. But where that analogy leads is to implying that he should not be trusted either.[16] What is innovative about Ford's use of the unreliable narrator, then, is the way he keeps making us wonder whether Dowell is not actually lying to us, or trying to conceal things. People often used to wonder that about Ford himself (especially during the time he was with Violet Hunt, whom Florence often resembles in her flirtatious talkativeness). It was a tightrope he seemed to enjoy walking in his own life, often exaggerating his stories to see how far he could go and still be believed. In *The Good Soldier* he found a form which makes the technique mesmerizingly effective. Any doubt we have about Dowell might seem to undermine what he tells us about the others; but simultaneously, it makes him a more complex and intriguing character, and thus draws us further into his world, and his entanglements with those same other characters. And Dowell's voice is so distinctive—Ford's grip on his way of thinking and talking is so sure—that despite the doubt, and even *through* it, the reality of his story becomes utterly convincing. If Ford's creation of his narrator's uncertainties is a tribute to his own technical certainty, that certainty involves disturbing our sense of the boundaries between life and fictionality.

---

16 For a fuller discussion of this question of trust see Max Saunders, 'Ford, Impressionism, and Trust in *The Good Soldier*', in John Attridge and Rod Rosenquist (eds.), *Incredible Modernism—Literature, Trust and Deception* (Farnham: Ashgate, forthcoming).

The Stories Behind 'The Saddest Story'

Graham Greene wrote of *The Good Soldier* that 'the impression which will be left most strongly on the reader is the sense of Ford's involvement', adding: 'one cannot help wondering what agonies of frustration and error lay behind *The Saddest Story*.'[17] Ford's biographers have found much in his life to relate to his 'Tale of Passion'. Like Ashburnham, Ford had married young, to Elsie Martindale. They left London, and settled in the Romney Marsh, on the borders of Kent and Sussex. Again like Edward, he had betrayed her; first in what appears to have been a disastrous brief affair with her sister, undermining not only their marriage but also his mental stability. The novel draws on this fraught period a decade earlier, when Ford underwent a severe agoraphobic nervous breakdown in the summer of 1904—the date on which the Ashburnhams and Dowells meet; and, like them, he visited German spa resorts for a 'cure'.

Then, in 1908, estranged from Elsie, and now living in London and setting up the *English Review*, he got to know the racy novelist Violet Hunt. By the following year he had embarked on an equally disastrous affair with her. Friends like James and Conrad, who had known him with Elsie and were still her neighbours, became markedly colder. Though Ford was a—nominal—Catholic, he sought a divorce, but Elsie—who was not Catholic, unlike Leonora Ashburnham—refused (Leonora's hardness is thought to be modelled on hers). Then Ford was told that another of his closest friends, Arthur Marwood, had 'made advances' towards Elsie. Marwood was ill with tuberculosis, and the story was perhaps implausible. He may have been trying to console her rather than seduce her—as Dowell wonders about Ashburnham's embracing the girl on a train in the 'Kilsyte case'. But there were letters which Ford's solicitor saw, and which seemed to confirm that something untoward had happened. Marwood was also Ford's business partner in publishing the *English Review*, and a rift between them during the magazine's first few months proved catastrophic. As the *Review*'s finances worsened, Ford fell out with friends like Wells whom he had persuaded to join his altruistic profit-sharing scheme instead of receiving payment for contributions. A rescue package was worked out, but the result was to oust Ford from the editor's chair after little more than a year. The novel's sense of a world collapsing; intimacies turning out to have been betrayed; one's closest friends proving to be unreliable; and of a man destroying himself in the effort to stop himself doing further damage to those around him, all seem to draw on this second period of personal crisis too, four or five years before Ford wrote the novel.

By the end of 1913, when he said he began *The Good Soldier*, the strain was also beginning to tell on his relationship with Hunt. They had hoped to be able to marry if Ford could acquire German national-ity (his father, Francis Hueffer, having been a German émigré), and then get a divorce under German law. He went to live in Giessen, near Marburg (the town of 'M——' the Ashburnhams and Dowells visit to see the castle where Protestantism was argued out), and when Violet came over they spent time at Nauheim, the spa the novel's 'good people' frequent. The divorce plan failed when Ford was refused German nationality. When he returned to London he and Hunt nonetheless claimed they had got married abroad. But when she was referred to in print as 'Mrs Ford Madox Hueffer', Elsie sued, and the resulting court case scandalized Violet's society friends and humiliated both her and Ford. His vignette of the English gentleman you meet at a golf club, but then hear scandalous rumours about, also registers his anxiety about how he had himself appeared at this time. Ashburnham-like, his response to these pressures was to fall in love with someone else: the young Irish beauty Brigit Patmore, who had become a regular at Violet's Kensington home, South Lodge. Patmore wrote—much later—that 'People have said that Ford was slightly in love with me, but he never attracted me. I admired his intellect, but that was all.' Violet may have felt, like Leonora Ashburnham arranging for Maisie Maidan to accompany them to Nauheim, that if Ford was prone to infatuations, they would do less damage if she could manage them her-self. She invited Patmore to stay in her seaside cottage at Selsey. It was during her visit that Ford wrote his best-known poem, 'On Heaven', ostensibly addressed to Hunt, but clearly inspired by his feelings for Patmore. And, despite Patmore's denial, Hunt noted in 1917 that she had 'succumbed from the flattery of his suit—his plausibility . . .'.[18]

[18] Patmore, *My Friends When Young* (London: Heinemann, 1968), 52–3. Hunt, entry for 20 April 1917: *The Return of the Good Soldier: Ford Madox Ford and Violet Hunt's 1917 Diary*, ed. Robert and Marie Secor (University of Victoria, BC, 1983), 57.

Hunt's diary for 1914, which only emerged into the public domain in 1995, gives a poignant account of the affair over the following months.[19] Brigit was married, and when her husband came to collect her on 12 April Hunt assumed he knew 'what she had been up to'. If the parallel here seems to be with the married women Ashburnham takes up with—Maisie Maidan or Mrs Basil—it is hard not to see what happened next as suggesting Ashburnham's last passion, for his wife's ward Nancy Rufford, devastating not just for its force, but because of his determination to try to resist it. On the 16th Hunt wrote that Ford went to stay near the Conrads: 'his idea of a rest cure & get over Bridgit [*sic*]'. 'I think he really was trying to give her up', she added. Then, on 8 May she noted (presumably, as she often did, annotating the diary in retrospect): 'Brigit came & went? Is this the day they sat & cried all day silently & I left them alone.' The sadness of 'The Saddest Story' surely owes much to such scenes (though the heartbreaking parting at the end of *The Good Soldier* gets its poignancy from the terrible suppression of any such demonstrativeness). It makes a difference to how we read the novel to know that the beginning was actually dictated to Patmore, who was acting as what Hunt called Ford's 'play secretary' at Selsey;[20] that when Dowell imagines a 'sympathetic soul' listening silently to him telling the story across 'the fireplace of a country cottage', this was also how the novel was coming into existence.[21]

And yet. The beginning of the novel, which already knows its end, was dictated well before the sad visit in May. This might mean that Ashburnham's passion for Nancy draws upon other sources. The quasi-incestuous relationship might recall Ford's affair with his sister-in-law. Ford later said Conrad had wanted to write a story about incest showing not 'the consummation of forbidden desires', but 'the emotions of a shared passion that by its nature must be most hopeless of all'.[22] Much of the novel's sadness comes from the hopelessness of Edward trying not to succumb to his passion for the young woman living in the position of his ward or daughter. Alternatively, in *The Spirit of the People* (1907), the third volume of

¹⁹ The diary is now in the Ford collection of the Carl A. Kroch Library, Cornell University, and quoted here with the Library's kind permission.

²⁰ Hunt, *The Flurried Years* (London: Hurst and Blackett, 1926), 215.

²¹ p. 17.

²² Ford, 'Tiger, Tiger': Being a Commentary on Conrad's *The Sisters*, *Bookman*, 66:5 (January 1928), 495–8 (p. 497).

his trilogy about Englishness, Ford relates a story which many have seen as the 'germ' of 'The Saddest Story'. Though here Ford casts himself in Dowell's role of witnessing other people acting out an unbearably sad station farewell very like that between Edward and Nancy:

I stayed, too, at the house of a married couple one summer. Husband and wife were both extremely nice people—'good people', as the English phrase is. There was also living in the house a young girl, the ward of the husband, and between him and her—in another of those singularly expressive phrases—an attachment had grown up. P—— had not only never 'spoken to' his ward; his ward, I fancy, had spoken to Mrs. P——. At any rate the situation had grown impossible, and it was arranged that Miss W—— would take a trip round the world [. . .] The only suspicion that things were not of their ordinary train was that the night before the parting P—— had said to me: 'I wish you'd drive to the station with us to-morrow morning.' He was, in short, afraid of a 'scene.' [. . .] the parting at the station was too surprising, too really superhuman not to give one, as the saying is, the jumps. For P—— never even shook her by the hand; touching the flap of his cloth cap sufficed for leave-taking. Probably he was choking too badly to say even 'Good-bye' [. . .] as the train drew out of the station P—— turned suddenly on his heels, went through the booking-office to pick up a parcel of fish that was needed for lunch, got into his trap and drove off. He had forgotten me—but he had kept his end up [. . .] Miss W—— died at Brindisi on the voyage out, and P—— spent the next three years at various places on the Continent where nerve cures are attempted.[23]

Ford varied some of the details for Nancy's leave-taking in *The Good Soldier*: she is being sent to her father in India rather than taking a trip round the world. Whereas Miss W—— died at Brindisi, it is from Brindisi that Nancy sends the telegram which causes Edward to kill himself. Rather than the man having a breakdown, it is she who goes mad, when she reads of Edward's suicide. That suicide is the most significant alteration, since 'P——' survives for at least the three years he spends taking Continental nerve-cures. Ford says in the Dedicatory Letter that he had the story 'hatching' within himself for a decade, and that 'the story is a true story', adding: 'I had it from Edward Ashburnham himself and I could not write it till all the others were dead.' According to that chronology, Ashburnham's inconsummable passion for Nancy may have been based on someone quite

23 Ford, *The Spirit of the People* (London: Alston Rivers, 1907), 148–50.

CONTENTS

THE GOOD SOLDIER

other whom Ford met during his own nerve cure in Germany in 1904. If so, his feelings for Brigit Patmore may have made him feel that his life was beginning to take the shape of that story; and that now he was in a position to write it out. According to this view, rather than the novel drawing on his affair with Patmore, that affair was drawing upon the story for the novel. Hunt wrote in her 1917 diary that Patmore had told her Ford 'must always pose'; that he was 'never real—histrionic to his fingertips . . . Dreaming—*not* dreaming true—false to himself.'[24] She may have been trying to reassure Violet that whatever had happened had not signified. But she may also have picked up how Ford was living himself into the Ashburnham role as he was preparing to write it. Or perhaps the way such things develop is a more complex, reciprocal process: his feelings for Patmore reminding him of the earlier story, and stirring him to begin the novel; but then, in the heat of composition, the novel's situation getting reflected onto his affair with Brigit.

But even that version would be too reductive, assuming a novel is made only from biographical sources. The Dedicatory Letter also says that Ford had an ambition 'to do for the English novel what in *Fort Comme la Mort*, Maupassant had done for the French'. The context makes it sound like a matter of importing French style and technique, as when Ford quotes his friend John Rodker calling *The Good Soldier* 'the finest French novel in the English language'. But the plot and the effect of Maupassant's novel, published in 1889, contribute much to Ford's text.[25] Maupassant's is also a 'Tale of Passion'. Olivier Bertin, a fashionable middle-aged artist, has been carrying on an adulterous affair with the Countess de Guilleroy for many years. When the Countess brings her daughter, Annette, back from the provinces where she has been living with her grandmother, Bertin, who has not seen the girl for years, is struck by her resemblance to her mother when younger. He finds himself entranced by her and invigorated by her presence. It dawns on the Countess that Bertin has fallen in love with her daughter. At first Bertin denies it, thinking that what he was feeling was a rejuvenation of his feelings for the mother. But, overcome by his jealousy of Annette's fiancé, he is

---

[24] Hunt, entry for 20 April 1917: *The Return of the Good Soldier*, 57.

[25] See W. B. Hutchings, 'Ford and Maupassant', in Robert Hampson and Max Saunders (eds.), *Ford Madox Ford's Modernity* (Amsterdam and New York: Rodopi, 2003), 257–70.

forced to recognize that the Countess is right. The passion here too is quasi-incestuous—Bertin is so often at the Guilleroys' house as to be treated almost as a member of the family. Realizing the hopelessness of his passion on this score; and because it has not even occurred to Annette; and also because he still loves the Countess, he attempts to fight it, walking off into the night and becoming so exhausted that he gets run over and fatally injured.

Unusually for the cynical Maupassant, *Fort Comme la Mort* does not ironize its melodrama as *The Good Soldier* does. But the effect it works for, continually tightening the screw with the gradual intensification of effect that Ford advocated, using Flaubert's term '*progression d'effet*', is one of overwhelming sadness, as first the Countess, then Bertin, grasp the hopelessness of their situation, and even manage to find a form of solidarity in it as they both feel their lives being devastated by age, passion, and suffering. If the portrayal of the social elites is comparable, Ford's plot is different. Neither Ashburnham nor Dowell is an artist. Nancy is not Leonora Ashburnham's daughter (though the novel has made some wonder whether she is not Edward's).[26] So the device on which Maupassant's story turns—the echo of the Countess's youthful appearance in the daughter—has no counterpart in *The Good Soldier*. But the theme and feeling of sadness resounding through the ending of Maupassant's novel is what Ford sought to emulate.

Sex, Polygamous Desire, and the Unconscious

As we have glimpsed already, it is sexuality that most disturbs Dowell's narrative. Ford was to write later:

The trouble is that, at any rate in Anglo-Saxondom, the moment a man of distinction gets hold of an unorthodox idea—be it connected with politics or religion or sex—straight-way he loses most of his sense of proportion and nearly all his power of putting things.[27]

'Things' are what Ford remembered being told not to discuss with a young lady, by the young lady's mother. He was 'bewildered' because he 'did not know just what "things" were': 'Nowadays', he continued:

---

[26] See below, pp. xxix–xxx.
[27] Ford, 'Declined with Thanks', *New York Herald Tribune Books* (24 June 1928), 1, 6.

I know very well what 'things' are; they include, in fact, religious topics, questions of the relations of the sexes, the conditions of poverty-stricken districts—every subject from which one can digress into anything moving.[28]

Dowell certainly worries obsessively about 'proportion' and about his 'power of putting things'; especially where questions of religion or sex are concerned.

The Good Soldier's explicitness about sex is one of the main things that marked it out as modern. If Dowell's hesitant talk about 'the sex-instinct' sounds slightly staid now, the story it tells of Edward's and Florence's affairs was shocking to many contemporary reviewers. Ford's progressive friends like Rebecca West were enthusiastic, but the notices in the more conservative press were not.[29] One complained of the book's 'distorted, sex-morbid atmosphere'. Another mused: 'we can well imagine that the work will prove of some value to the specialist in pathology'. The plot was deemed 'most unsavoury', 'sordid', 'a chronicle of sordid treachery and vice', and 'simply detestable'; Ford's imagination was called 'unpleasant'.[30] Some reviewers were still incandescing the following year, when a storm erupted in the paper *The New Witness* (edited by G. K. Chesterton's brother Cecil) over a book Ford published with Violet Hunt called *Zeppelin Nights*. The editor's wife reviewed the book pseudonymously, accusing Ford of cowardice, unpatriotism, and being 'not exactly of pure European extraction' (by which she meant to insinuate that Mr Hueffer—he did not change his surname to Ford till 1919—was not only German but Jewish, which he was not).[31] In the correspondence that ensued she dragged in *The Good Soldier*—'a novel centering round a particularly brutal type of sensualist'—and a later anonymous letter echoed her outrage that Ford's title seemed a slur on the military:

'The Perfect Stallion' would have been an appropriate title for a book which none of Mr. Hueffer's admirers can have read without wondering what necessity he saw, in this hour when men have so gloriously fought

[28] Ford, *The Spirit of the People*, 146.

[29] West reviewed the novel in the *Daily News* (2 April 1915), 6, commenting on its 'magnificence' and 'extreme beauty'.

[30] Quotations from, respectively, the *Boston Evening Transcript* (17 March 1915), 24; *Bookman* (London), 48 (July 1915), 117; *Outlook*, 35 (17 April 1915), 507–8; *Athenaeum*, no. 4563 (10 April 1915), 334; *Saturday Review*, 119 (19 June 1915), iv; *Morning Post* (5 April 1915), 2; *Independent*, 81 (22 March 1915), 432.

[31] 'J. K. Prothero', *New Witness*, 7 (6 January 1916), 293.

xxvi   *Introduction*

for and entered into their Kingdom, to portray them in such a despicable light.[32]

Ford, of course, had not seen any necessity in the title. His publisher, John Lane, told him his salesmen thought 'The Saddest Story' a difficult title to sell. Ford replied:

My Dear Lane/ I should have thought that you publishers had had eye-openers enough about monkeying with authors' titles, at the request of travellers. 'The Saddest Story'—I say it in all humility—is about the best book you ever published and the title is about the best title. Still, I make it a principle never to interfere with my publisher, but to take it out in calling him names. Why not call the book 'The Roaring Joke'? Or call it anything you like, or perhaps it would be better to call it 'A Good Soldier'—that might do. At any rate it is all I can think of.[33]

The 'Dedicatory Letter' makes it clear Lane thought 'the darkest days of the war' meant people wouldn't want to read a story of sadness; and perhaps Ford tried to address this by suggesting a military title. He moved the phrase 'the saddest story' into a new, provocative first sentence, making it more effective as it becomes part of the presentation of Dowell. 'The Good Soldier' makes a more evidently ironic title; though the irony may have been lost on the reviewers who had attacked the subject-matter—perhaps because they too thought the title a slur on the wartime Army. But their responses also show how even as measured (and un-pornographic) an account of sex as Ford's could scandalize an Edwardian readership. Perhaps they protested too much because they knew he was right. Ford had to write another letter to Lane when a circulating library in Liverpool objected to the book's 'lewdness'.

You see, that work is as serious an analysis of the polygamous desires that underlie all men—except perhaps the members of the Publishers' Association—as 'When Blood is Their Argument' is an analysis of Prussian Culture.[34]

When Blood is Their Argument was the first of two wartime propaganda

[32] Ibid. (20 January 1916), 352. 'M. F.', *New Witness*, 7 (10 February 1916), 449.
[33] Ford to John Lane, 17 December 1914: *The Ford Madox Ford Reader*, ed. Sondra J. Stang (Manchester: Carcanet, 1986), 477. Though the 'Dedicatory Letter to Stella Ford', p. 4, describes this exchange as taking place via letters and telegrams, this letter bears out the substance of the story.
[34] 28 March 1915: *Reader*, 477–8.

books Ford wrote for the British government (at the request of his friend, the Liberal Cabinet Minister C. F. G. Masterman): an extensively documented diagnosis of German militarism. Ford offers *The Good Soldier* as a psychological study of comparable depth. The claim that 'polygamous desires [. . .] underlie all men' might sound odd in relation to the novel, as it puts the sex-instinct decidedly back into the calculation, even for the apparently sex-blind Dowell—though even he appears to have had unconscious desires for Nancy before the death of his wife. But the novel certainly explores polygamous desires, not only in all the main characters, but even in its version of history—as when 'Florence started to tell us how Ludwig the Courageous wanted to have three wives at once—in which he differed from Henry VIII, who wanted them one after the other, and this caused a good deal of trouble [. . .]' (p. 36). This tangles up sexuality with that other troubling 'thing', religion.

That concept of desire as multiple, ('three [. . .] at once'), omnipotent and omnipresent, is also our later, post-Freudian view. Dowell writes of 'that mysterious and unconscious self that underlies most people' (p. 85). Like many writers of the period, Ford was deeply ambivalent about psychoanalytic ideas. He had been subjected to them, or their sexological forerunners, during his German 'nerve cure' of 1904. 'Those were the early days of that mania that has since beset the entire habitable globe', he wrote, saying of one of the specialists he was assigned to:

In the effort to prove that my troubles had an obscure sexual origin he would suddenly produce from his desk and flash before my eyes indecent photographs of a singular banality. He expected me to throw fits or faint. I didn't.[35]

When Ford saw the German spa of Nauheim in 1910–11 it had recently been rebuilt into the imposing *Jugendstil* complex that can still be seen today. It provided the perfect setting for so much of the novel's tangle of affairs: a resort offering to cure sufferers from possibly sexual maladies, while providing them with opportunities for new liaisons. In 1912 the Vienna Psychoanalytic Society focused its attention on the habitués of spas. During a discussion of the psychoanalysis of travel, one speaker related 'travel' (in German *reisen*) to 'tearing (free)' (*reissen*):

---

[35] *Return to Yesterday*, 269, 267–8.

Freud thought this plausible: he spoke of his own travelling as tearing himself away from a repressive background. Freud then spoke of taking the waters. Some neurotics, he stated, transfer their inner conflicts onto a place such as a spa: 'There are types—obsessional neurotics, in particular, are such people—who have a much more solid relation with space than with time. In other persons, one sees clearly how they transfer their complexes onto other fields; they copy over their affects, for instance, onto localities—as do those who visit watering places.'[36]

Had Dowell been Freud's patient, obsessional neurosis would perhaps have been the diagnosis. Dowell certainly has a disturbed relation to time; and his obsessive counting of the paces between the different spaces at Nauheim does indeed suggest a displacement of affect. *The Good Soldier* has most often been read in terms of character—whether either Dowell or Ashburnham warrant our sympathy; or in terms of Ford's biography. But such readings can obscure Ford's up-to-the-minute sense of sexuality as newly problematic in an era of campaigns for female emancipation (and what that meant for contemporary masculinity), for birth control and sex education, and for divorce law reform.

The most fraught psycho-sexual issue in the novel is the love between Edward and Nancy. What is it about it that makes Dowell describe it as 'monstrously wicked' (p. 91), Leonora as 'the most atrocious thing you have done' (p. 162), and determines Edward uncharacteristically to resist at all costs? When Dowell tells us that Nancy's mother writes to her something like: 'How do you know that you are even Colonel Rufford's daughter?' (p. 172) we understand her to be hinting at her life of prostitution. Nancy, says Dowell,

was Leonora's only friend's only child, and Leonora was her guardian, if that is the correct term. She had lived with the Ashburnhams ever since she had been of the age of thirteen, when her mother was said to have committed suicide owing to the brutalities of her father.

But the mother's letter proves the suicide story a lie. It may not be a lie that Leonora was her friend, though it seems unlikely; and the note of doubt about what is the 'correct term' for Nancy's relation to

---

[36] These proceedings are cited in a caption at the Freud Museum, London. See Herman Nunberg and Ernst Federn (eds.), *Minutes of the Vienna Psychoanalytic Society*, Vol. 4: 1912–18 (New York: International Universities Press, 1975), 67; minuting the scientific meeting of 6 March 1912. I'm grateful to the Museum's former Director, Michael Molnar for this reference.

the Ashburnhams seems designed to make us wonder exactly what she is doing living with them. As a magistrate Edward was 'always trying to put prostitutes into respectable places—and he was a perfect maniac about children' (p. 50). His motives for looking after Nancy appear equally altruistic. But 'perfect maniac' sounds another worrying note, and these comments have made some readers wonder whether there is any possibility Nancy might actually be Edward's illegitimate daughter.[37] Ford cut several passages from the manuscript which showed Ashburnham more as a dangerous libertine; in one of them he had fathered bastards: 'every one of his illegitimate offspring must be sent to Eton or to the convent at Roehampton'.[38] Perhaps he felt such details would lose Ashburnham all sympathy; or worried that the book might have been censored. (D. H. Lawrence's *The Rainbow* was prosecuted for obscenity later in 1915, and all copies were ordered to be seized and burnt. It could not be bought in Britain for another eleven years.) Or perhaps Ford specifically wanted to exclude any suggestion that Nancy might have been one of Edward's children. Yet the text subtly insinuates that possibility: 'there was the further complication that both Edward and Leonora really regarded the girl as their daughter' (p. 99). How should we read Dowell's comment that 'it had not even come into [Edward's] head that the tabu which extended around her was not inviolable'? Is the taboo not inviolable because Nancy is not his daughter? (Or because, having just come of age, she is no longer a ward?)[39] Or has the possibility of violating it not come into Edward's head because she is? The anthropological use of 'taboo' (dating from Captain Cook's visit to Tonga in 1777) pre-dates the psychoanalytic. But

[37] Dewey Ganzel asserts this reading categorically in 'What the Letter Said: Fact and Inference in *The Good Soldier*', *Journal of Modern Literature*, 11 (July 1984), 277–90; but his argument ignores the ambiguity of much of his evidence.

[38] 'The Saddest Story', 88, 88A, 88B: Cornell. This passage was revised into the one on pp. 68–70 of the published text (from 'Yes, they quarrelled bitterly' to 'You see, she was childless herself'). Dowell's comment in the revision—'I trust that I have not, in talking of his liabilities, given the impression that poor Edward was a promiscuous libertine'—could thus stand for Ford's feeling that he *had* given that impression. See *The Good Soldier*, ed. Martin Stannard (New York: Norton, 1995), 184. Other cuts included a mention of 'the girls he ruined', and the suggestion that if he were to be allowed to become destitute he would be 'committing rapes'.

[39] In 1913 Leonora says: 'I think the girl ought to have the appearance of being chaperoned with Edward in these places. I think the time has come.' Nancy came to live with them when she was 13 and has remained for eight years; Dowell says she was 'rising twenty-two' in August 1913.

XXX   *Introduction*

Freud's *Totem und Tabu*, with its first chapter on 'The Horror of Incest', was published in German in 1913. Shock, catatonia, horror, amnesia—extreme reactions we would now describe as traumatic—abound in *The Good Soldier*, and imply a profoundly disturbing cause. Could it have been the suggestion of incest rather than—or as well as—the explicit polygamous desire which so disturbed the reviewers?

We cannot be certain whether Edward is actually Nancy's father or not. But the thought of a relationship between them *feels* incestuous even if biologically it is not. Again, 'he had regarded her exactly as he would have regarded a daughter' (p. 90). That is why Edward assures Dowell that if he had been conscious of his passion for her, 'he would have fled from it as from a thing accursed' (p. 90); but also why he says Edward felt 'the immense temptation to do the unthinkable thing' (p. 184). Perhaps the most hauntingly poignant suggestion comes when Leonora tells Nancy Edward is dying because of her, and Nancy 'looked past her at the panels of the half-closed door' (the perfect image for a repression of the almost unthinkable) and says, twice, 'My poor father' (pp. 247–8). Horror of the even quasi-incestuous (such as a passion of guardian—or guardian's husband—and ward) could account for both the terror and devastation in the novel. In a review written soon after he had begun it, Ford wrote: 'I am not sure that there is not something after all in the English-German idea that if one saw the whole truth of things—being English-German oneself—one would go mad.'[40] Once Edward becomes conscious of his passion for Nancy he destroys himself; and she goes mad. *The Good Soldier* has been read as anticipating Freud's later great essays *Beyond the Pleasure Principle* (1920) and *Civilisation and its Discontents* (1930); especially the latter in its exploration of the destructive cost of repression.[41] The civilized life the two couples live seems like an elegant 'minuet', but underneath they are 'a prison full of screaming hysterics' (p. 13).

The style Ford developed to express both polygamous desire and

[40] Ford, 'Literary Portraits—XIX.: Gerhart Hauptmann and "Atlantis"', *Outlook*, 33 (17 January 1914), 77–9. Compare *The New Humpty-Dumpty* (published under the pseudonym 'Daniel Chaucer': London: John Lane, The Bodley Head, 1912), 83: 'He had never really learnt that the truth is a dangerous thing.'

[41] As Sondra Stang noted, 'The novel and the essays most startlingly illuminate each other': 'A Reading of *The Good Soldier*', *Modern Language Quarterly*, 30:4 (1969), 545–63 (p. 545).

its repression is one of sustained innuendo. Florence's maiden
aunts—'the Misses Hurlbird'—hint darkly that there is some reason
why Dowell should not marry Florence: 'We ought to tell you more.
But she's our dear sister's child' (p. 68). On a first reading this sounds
like it refers to her affair with her uncle's minder, Jimmy; possibly to
other affairs. But then that evening Florence disappears. Dowell
tracks her down at her uncle's:

> The old man received me with a stony, husky face. I was not to see Flor-
> ence; she was ill; she was keeping her room. And, from something that he
> let drop—an odd Biblical phrase that I have forgotten—I gathered that all
> that family simply did not intend her to marry ever in her life. (p. 68)

This may just be a fanatical Puritanism; or an anxiety that Florence
is sexually too voracious to be a faithful wife. But the lying about her
health, the determination she should never marry, the mysterious
biblical phrase, are all troubling, suggesting a more sinister reason.
Dowell wonders whether they were worried lest the heart defect they
(wrongly) thought Uncle John suffered from might be hereditary.
But we might wonder why Florence, the niece of the Misses Hurlbird,
is also named Hurlbird. If her mother had married, would she not
have had a different married name? Is Florence illegitimate, and the
family don't want it known? Has she taken the Hurlbird name because
they brought her up (perhaps because she had no other legitimate
name)? Or is it that her mother married another Hurlbird—perhaps
a cousin? Might that be grounds for an anxiety about degeneracy of
some kind (even of a sexual kind) due to inbreeding? Or is there
another explanation for Uncle John's protectiveness? Is there a possibility he might actually be Florence's father, and Florence the
product of an incestuous union with his sister? (Is some suggestion
of incest what was 'odd' about the Biblical phrase?) Or even that
he might himself desire his niece—whether or not she is also his
daughter?

Such speculations may seem prurient; but the text's insinuations
and suppressions incite prurience. Take the Ashburnham marriage.
It is fairly clear that Dowell's marriage to Florence is not consum-
mated: she elaborates her fictional 'heart' excuse as they elope to
Europe. But what about Edward and Leonora? Dowell says Edward
denied his philandering to her because 'He wanted to preserve
the virginity of his wife's thoughts' (p. 49). Does that imply the

virginity of her body? 'His marriage with Leonora had been arranged by his parents and, though he always admired her immensely, he had hardly ever pretended to be much more than tender to her' (p. 50). That 'hardly ever' does not mean he never appeared more than tender. But 'pretended'? Even if we knew what being 'more than tender' actually entailed, we could not be sure Edward meant it, or had any desire to consummate the marriage. Nothing they actually did produced any children, but that does not mean they did not do it. Dowell keeps us guessing. After the two couples meet (in 1904), he says Edward seemed 'about that time to have conceived the naïve idea that he might become a polygamist', and that 'it certainly appears that at about that date Edward cared more for Leonora than he had ever done before—or, at any rate, for a long time' (p. 149). In other words, it was only after he began his adulteries with Florence (perhaps because he had learned from her about his own desire) that he began to desire Leonora; though the last characteristic hesitation leaves us unclear whether he had ever thus desired her before.

Here too, Ford's picture of desire is close to the psychoanalytic one: a desire which drives our infatuations, obsessions, and identifications but never coincides with them. A desire which incites a curiosity about the sexuality of others; a curiosity which is itself insatiable because we can never know what we would need to know for it to be satisfied: what it feels like to be the other person. Dowell's trouble with knowledge is inescapably carnal. Once we grant that unconscious desire underlies our thoughts, our ability to know anything is troubled. The opening of *The Good Soldier* turns on the distinction noted by Henry James's brother, the philosopher William James, between '*knowledge of acquaintance*' (as in the French *connaître*) and '*knowledge-about*' (as in the French *savoir*): 'We had known the Ashburnhams for nine seasons of the town of Nauheim with an extreme intimacy—or, rather, with an acquaintanceship as loose and easy and yet as close as a good glove's with your hand.'[42] Dowell has learnt that however well acquainted you are with people you still cannot say you know about them. But his terms all bristle with insinuations: *extreme* intimacy? Loose? Easy? Close? Hand in glove? The thing that he cannot know about is their sexuality. That is the knowledge *The Good Soldier* has which William James's account lacks: that

[42] William James, *The Principles of Psychology*, Vol. 1 (New York: Henry Holt and Company, 1890), 221.

sense of knowledge of people being profoundly troubled by the sense of sexuality, of desire and its repression, of the unconscious. Innuendo serves as a way of sounding knowing about what you cannot know. Ford was fond of quoting the proverb 'The heart of another is a dark forest'.[43] Having 'a heart' is the other main innuendo in *The Good Soldier*. When Ford's father dropped dead aged only 43 after contracting erysipelas, the family were told that 'The heart was wrong'. Ford worried his own heart might be wrong, though, like Florence's and Ashburnham's, it did not fail. A 'heart' can denote a physical illness or passion. Passion and its repression can cause mental illness too, which can manifest itself physically. Ford was intensely preoccupied with death during his breakdown, as if his state of mind could destroy his body. The psychosomatic is itself a form of innuendo.

Ford's term 'passion' is carefully poised between love and sex. One reason the new sexology was so disturbing, especially to writers, was that it challenged what was known about love, and how love stories could be told. In one of the most lyrical passages of the novel, Dowell ruminates on passion:

With each new woman that a man is attracted to there appears to come a broadening of the outlook, or, if you like, an acquiring of new territory. A turn of the eye-brow, a tone of the voice, a queer characteristic gesture—all these things, and it is these things that cause to arise the passion of love— all these things are like so many objects on the horizon of the landscape that tempt a man to walk beyond the horizon, to explore. He wants to get, as it were, behind those eye-brows with the peculiar turn, as if he desired to see the world with the eyes that they overshadow. He wants to hear that voice applying itself to every possible proposition, to every possible topic; he wants to see those characteristic gestures against every possible background. (p. 92)

It is at this point he disavows the importance of the 'sex-instinct'; though he characteristically doubles back, conceding: 'I don't mean to say that any great passion can exist without a desire for consummation.' That goes without saying, he says, making us wonder whether it has not gone without saying in his account of his own feelings.

---

[43] The title page of Ford's *The New Humpty-Dumpty* attributes the saying to 'Tambov', which, as Moser says (p. 105), is the name of the place the Russian in *Heart of Darkness* comes from (Thomas C. Moser, *The Life in the Fiction of Ford Madox Ford* (Princeton: Princeton University Press, 1980). The quotation is in fact from W. R. S. Ralston's translation of Turgenev's 'Lisa'. Ford also alludes to it in *Ancient Lights*, p. xi.

But he returns to the idea that what is important in passion is not sexuality but identification:

But the real fierceness of desire, the real heat of a passion long continued and withering up the soul of a man is the craving for identity with the woman that he loves. He desires to see with the same eyes, to touch with the same sense of touch, to hear with the same ears, to lose his identity, to be enveloped, to be supported. For, whatever may be said of the relation of the sexes, there is no man who loves a woman that does not desire to come to her for the renewal of his courage, for the cutting asunder of his difficulties. And that will be the mainspring of his desire for her. We are all so afraid, we are all so alone, we all so need from the outside the assurance of our own worthiness to exist. (p. 93)

This is deeply paradoxical. The man desires to lose his identity in the other; to experience the world as the other does. But the move outside the self enables a view of the self from outside. It is seeing himself as the other sees him that assures him of his worthiness to exist. One of the many striking things about this passage is that it aligns passion with writing. Ford's definition of passion, that is, is also his manifesto of impressionism: a mode of writing that tries to get inside its characters' heads so that the reader can experience as closely as possible the impressions of those characters. Ford's first volume of memoirs, *Ancient Lights*, says of one of his earliest childhood memories: 'I seem to be looking at myself from outside'; and he uses the clause as the caption for an illustration of his grandfather Madox Brown's painting of young Ford as *William Tell's Son*.[44] *The Good Soldier* complicates the idea when Dowell asserts—both surprisingly and unsurprisingly—that the person with whom he most identifies is not a woman but his closest male friend: 'For I can't conceal from myself the fact that I loved Edward Ashburnham—and that I love him because he was just myself' (p. 192).

'I can't conceal from myself'. . . . Dowell's phrase stands for the way so many of the important things in this novel are not simply declared, but have been concealed, and either need to be inferred, or get blurted out when the strain of repressing them becomes intolerable. Garrulous Dowell values a stiff-upper-lip reserve. He admires Edward who 'naturally never spoke of his affair with my wife' (p. 143) over Leonora who succumbs out of loneliness to her 'desire for communicativeness'

---

[44] Ford, *Ancient Lights* (London: Chapman & Hall, 1911), facing p. vii.

(pp. 149). Florence's relentless talk spurs Leonora to answer back; then Edward's silence also provokes her speech:

And, indeed, in speaking of it afterwards, she has said several times: "I said a great deal more to him than I wanted to, just because he was so silent." She talked, in fact, in the endeavour to sting him into speech. (p. 163)

The 'speaking of it afterwards' is part of the same trouble, and reminds us of how Dowell opens his narrative as if he were speaking. The novel is good on motives for silence and speech; the silences and speeches *in* the novel within the speeches and silences that *are* the novel. Language, as Sondra Stang argued, is represented here as dangerous.[45] When Edward does 'the most monstrously wicked thing', letting slip to Nancy, in the dark park outside the Casino, that she is 'the person he cared most for in the world' (p. 91), his language is saying more than he knows:

And, in speaking to her on that night, he wasn't, I am convinced, committing a baseness. It was as if his passion for her hadn't existed; as if the very words that he spoke, without knowing that he spoke them, created the passion as they went along. Before he spoke, there was nothing; afterwards, it was the integral fact of his life. Well, I must get back to my story. (p. 93)

At the end of the story the Ashburnhams summon Dowell to Branshaw to witness their sending off of Nancy to India. It is as if they hope his presence will stop them from talking. But again Edward's words speak despite himself:

"I am so desperately in love with Nancy Rufford that I am dying of it."
    Poor devil—he hadn't meant to speak of it. But I guess he just had to speak to somebody and I appeared to be like a woman or a solicitor. He talked all night. (p. 189)

Here too, once uttered, the words have an irresistible power over him. Once he says that he is dying for love, his death becomes an inevitable reality. A world of so much unconsciousness or concealment produces what Paul Ricoeur called a hermeneutics of suspicion: an assumption that what we observe whether we are reading people or books are merely symptoms of something else; underlying desires, secret motives, repressed thoughts, concealed ideologies.[46]

---

[45] Stang, 'A Reading of *The Good Soldier*', 547–9.
[46] Paul Ricoeur, *Freud and Philosophy*, trans. D. Savage (New Haven: Yale University Press, 1977).

Ford ingeniously lights on a stylistic device to express these processes of repression and unwitting expression. In *The Good Soldier* he develops an extraordinary use of negative metaphors. During the 'Protest' scene, the moment Florence 'laid one finger upon Captain Ashburnham's wrist', Dowell says:

I was aware of something treacherous, something frightful, something evil in the day. I can't define it and can't find a simile for it. It wasn't as if a snake had looked out of a hole. (p. 40)

He can't find a simile for it, but he can find a simile for what it is not. Or at least: though he goes on to find two similes, the snake has already been let out of the hole, and it is hard to stop thinking of it. When Dowell denies 'the beginnings of a trace of what is called the sex instinct' towards Leonora, his explanation bizarrely conjures up the desire it is denying, even to the point of imagining kissing her:

As far as I am concerned I think it was those white shoulders that did it. I seemed to feel when I looked at them that, if ever I should press my lips upon them that they would be slightly cold—not icily, not without a touch of human heat, but, as they say of baths, with the chill off. I seemed to feel chilled at the end of my lips when I looked at her . . . (p. 31)

Dowell says that Edward 'was very careful to assure me that at that time there was no physical motive about his declaration' to Nancy. But, as Freud argued in his masterly paper on 'Negation', such denials are often the sign of the repression of underlying desires.[47] 'He said that he never had the slightest notion to enfold her in his arms or so much as to touch her hand', Dowell assures us. But would he have needed to deny these things if he had not desired them? The effect of such negations is to summon up all the things being fended off. 'Oh, I'm not thinking of saying that he is not the best of husbands, or that he is not very fond of the girl', Leonora tells Dowell. Yet she is thinking of the thing she is not thinking of saying. Indeed, to say you are not thinking of saying something is to say you are thinking of it, and to think of saying it, and even to say it, and to suggest it might be true, however hedged with negatives.

These underlying or unconscious desires, repressions, and negations return us to the question of the reliability of the narration.

[47] Freud, 'Negation' (1925), *Pelican Freud Library*, Vol. 11: *On Metapsychology*, ed. Angela Richards (Harmondsworth: Penguin, 1984), 435–42.

Arguably the unconscious renders all narrative unreliable: something that can no longer be taken on trust, but must be suspected, interrogated, diagnosed, interpreted for slips of the Freudian kind. This approach poses a special problem for an editor, especially in the case of a first-person narrative like *The Good Soldier*. When Dowell makes a slip, we have to consider whether Ford meant him to, and meant us to notice.

Chronology

It is with the book's chronology that this question of slips is most perplexing. The chronological order of events is so disturbed in the telling as to have stirred several critics to produce lists of the key events in chronological order. A new, fuller version is also provided here, in Appendix C. There are four main oddities about the novel's chronology. The first, obvious to any reader, is Florence's—and thus also Dowell's—obsession about dates. The fact that most of her key life-events occur on 4 August is strange enough to suggest either that her superstitiousness has driven her to act out her fate; or that Dowell is distorting or at least impressionistically exaggerating. Here too, the insistence of the realistic—the obsessive time-markers—pulls Fordian impressionism away from realism. Instead, it places him with other moderns—Proust, Woolf, Joyce, Bergson, or Heidegger—reimagining the experience of temporality. Second, the coincidence of that '4 August' date with the start of the First World War raises the question of when Ford hit on the date, and how far he intended a parallel between Dowell's story and the war. The other two points become easier to see once the chronology is tabulated. Third, Ford dates the climax of the novel—the 'four crashing days' after Dowell has come to Branshaw, and learns that he has been living a lie—in late 1913 or early 1914—around the time he began writing the novel. And he also includes time-markers to indicate how long Dowell takes in the writing. This dramatization of the process of writing the narration is another of the novel's modern traits. According to these time-markers, the earliest possible date by which he can have finished the novel is early 1916. This does more than bring the novel right up to date, as opposed to the Victorian novels characteristically set twenty or thirty years back, since *The Good Soldier* was published on 17 March 1915. The more perceptive or chronophiliac of its first readers would surely have been puzzled to find its ending apparently set a year in the future.

The fourth oddity is the most problematic. One of the most important dates given in the text is 4 August 1904. It is when the Dowells and Ashburnhams make their daytime excursion together to the town of 'M——' and the 'Protest' scene takes place. Yet it is also the date on which the couples are said to have met for the first time that evening at dinner. Clearly both events cannot have occurred on the same day. Most critics have assumed that the plotting became too complicated and Ford muddled the chronology. There are several other such inconsistencies, as the chronology provided here makes clear; though none of them is so crucial to the book's structure. But again, we have to entertain the possibility that Ford consciously wanted Dowell to be as unreliable about time as about anything else—as he is the first to point out:

When one discusses an affair—a long, sad affair—one goes back, one goes forward. One remembers points that one has forgotten and one explains them all the more minutely since one recognizes that one has forgotten to mention them in proper places and that one may have given, by omitting them, a false impression.[48]

Dowell's anxiety about time manifests itself in his anxiety about how to narrate time:

You are to remember that all this happened a month before Leonora went into the girl's room at night. I have been casting back again; but I cannot help it. It is so difficult to keep all these people going. I tell you about Leonora and bring her up to date; then about Edward, who has fallen behind. And then the girl gets hopelessly left behind. I wish I could put it down in diary form. (p. 169)

He says he did keep a diary—'I find, on looking at my diaries, that on September the fourth, 1904, Edward accompanied Florence and myself to Paris, where we put him up till the twenty-first of that month' (p. 79)—which ought perhaps to have saved him from the confusion. Yet he also asserts his certainty over the date of the 'Protest' scene in such a way as to suggest that he is having to work it out from memory:

And that enables me to fix exactly the day of our going to the town of

M——. For it was the very day poor Mrs. Maidan died. We found her dead when we got back—pretty awful, that, when you come to figure out what it all means. . . . (p. 55)

Elsewhere he takes a more impressionistic view of temporality:

I had expected to find the Misses Hurlbird excessively old—in the nineties or thereabouts. The time had passed so slowly that I had the impression that it must have been thirty years since I had been in the United States. It was only twelve years. (p. 152)

These inconsistencies could indicate that Ford wanted Dowell to appear—like most people—unable to recall the exact sequence of events over several years. In metafictional vein, Ford even has Dowell highlight his uncertainty over the date of the M—— excursion:

I can't remember whether it was in our first year—the first year of us four at Nauheim, because, of course, it would have been the fourth year of Florence and myself—but it must have been in the first or second year. And that gives the measure at once of the extraordinariness of our discussion and of the swiftness with which intimacy had grown up between us. On the one hand we seemed to start out on the expedition so naturally and with so little preparation, that it was as if we must have made many such excursions before; and our intimacy seemed so deep. . . .

Yet the place to which we went was obviously one to which Florence at least would have wanted to take us quite early, so that you would almost think we should have gone there together at the beginning of our intimacy. (p. 35)

But there is evidence for thinking Ford changed his mind about the chronology in at least two respects, and the confusion probably arose as a result of unsystematic revision. First, Dowell says that 'by the time [Florence] was sick of Jimmy—which happened in the year 1903—she had taken on Edward Ashburnham' (p. 73). So Ford may originally have meant the meeting of the two couples to have occurred in August 1903, not 1904 (so that by the excursion to 'M——', on what would then be the anniversary of their meeting, Florence and Edward could already have begun their affair); but then realized that this dating was impossible since the Ashburnhams are said to have been in India until 1904; so he may have shifted the meeting to the following year. That would not necessarily in itself have introduced the impossible dating, since, as Martin Stannard has shown, the first 'August' date in the novel was in fact the result of a double revision.

Chapter III begins: 'It was a very hot summer, in August, 1904' (p. 24). Originally, 'in August, 1904' read 'in 1906'. A first correction was made by an amanuensis, who inserted the word 'July' before '1906'. Ford then later revised the date altogether to 'August 1904'.[49] This suggests that he had originally thought of a meeting in July followed by an excursion in August. It's clear from what Dowell says of Leonora's response to the 'Protest' scene that the couples are supposed to have known each other for some time before the excursion:

She knew that that gaze meant that those two had had long conversations of an intimate kind—about their likes and dislikes, about their natures, about their views of marriage. She knew what it meant that she, when we all four walked out together, had always been with me ten yards ahead of Florence and Edward. (p. 147)

One might think Ford changed the date after the outbreak of war on 4 August 1914. But this first 'August' date appears in the version published in *Blast* the previous June. The 4 August date doesn't enter until the first sentence of Part II, several chapters after the *Blast* instalment ended. There too there is revision: '1904' has been revised from '1903' (another trace, perhaps, of a superseded chronology in which Florence takes up with Edward in the earlier year).[50] But the day of the month is unrevised. If Ford began the novel in late 1913 or early 1914, he probably got much further than this by August. Stannard notes that there is a similar case in Part III where '4th of August, 1900' appears, unrevised, in the original holograph, supporting what he calls the 'amazing coincidence' theory.[51] Though he notes that at this point there is also a revision 'establishing the date 4th August as [the] spine of [the] novel's diffuse chronology'. It appears that, after the war started, Ford then built on the coincidence to foreground 4 August, and make that date central to his novel too, suggesting a parallel between the death of his 'good soldier' and his company, and the disaster striking the heart of European civilization. The revision in Chapter III of Part I from 'July' to 'August' may then have been of this kind, and may suggest how the impossible combination of the afternoon 'Protest' excursion and the first meeting later in the evening of the same day may have come about.

Ford told his friend the American poet Allen Tate in 1929 that 'he had had the entire novel—every sentence—in his head before he

---

[49] See ibid. 197.   [50] Ibid. 203.   [51] Ibid. 82.

began to write it in 1913': a claim which did not surprise Tate, who commented: 'He had the most prodigious memory I have encountered in any man. And *The Good Soldier* is not only his masterpiece, but in my view the masterpiece of British fiction in this century.'[52] Stannard calls Ford's claim 'disingenuous' in the light of the extensive revisions, which technically is right in that he cannot have premeditated every sentence of the published text. But he might have had much of the first version by heart (or have meant, with impressionist exaggeration, that it felt like he had). Either way, he must have had a powerful imaginative grasp of the whole 'affair'—an unusually vivid sense of each episode, and how it interconnected with all the others—to be able to write it so tautly and confidently. Such a complex narrative as *The Good Soldier*'s 'intricate tangle of references and cross-references' would be unlikely to escape some confusion. When Ford started revising the dates during the composition process, confusion became inevitable. He tended to produce his best work when under greatest stress—from his memories as well as from his present circumstances. While this raised the temperature of the creative furnace, it did not conduce to careful checking and proof-correcting.

The fault-line in the chronology at 4 August 1904 was given a very different, provocative reading by Roger Poole.[53] Arguing that an artist so self-conscious about his effects as Ford, and such an eloquent advocate of the importance of fictional architectonics, should be given the benefit of the doubt, he wonders what it would mean if Ford had consciously planted the incompatible chronologies for readers to notice (as some have). He sees the contradiction not as evidence of Ford's carelessness or Dowell's incompetence, but as evidence that Dowell is covering something up. Marshalling other episodes which stretch our credulity, Poole suggests ingeniously that the novel could be given a reading deriving from, but entirely counter to Dowell's, in which he and Leonora, rather than being victims of the others' egotistical passions, have in fact murdered them, acquiring large fortunes each as a result. (*The Good Soldier* is one of

[52] Tate, *Memories and Essays* (Manchester: Carcanet, 1976), 58.
[53] See Poole, 'The Real Plot Line of Ford Madox Ford's *The Good Soldier*: An Essay in Applied Deconstruction', *Textual Practice*, 4:3 (Winter 1990), 391–427; and 'The Unknown Ford Madox Ford', in Hampson and Saunders (eds.), *Ford Madox Ford's Modernity*, 117–36.

the best modern novels about the psycho-sexual power of money. As
Dowell says, 'I had, in fact, forgotten that there was such a thing as a
dollar and that a dollar can be extremely desirable if you don't happen to possess one', p. 120.) Poole makes a persuasive case for suspi-
cious circumstances in the case of Florence's death; and Ashburnham's
too, narrated by the last man to see him alive, and who has revealed
himself as perfectly capable of assault in the case of his defenceless
African-American servant Julius. Ford enjoyed murder and detective stories, and wrote some of the latter, so it is plausible he might
have tried his hand at a novel-length murder. Ultimately, there are
two objections to this stimulating reading. First, Poole's argument
combines two methods of dispensing with any evidence that might
stand in its way: either it is a mark of Ford's anti-realism so its existence can be denied; or Dowell is lying. Second, it misses an essential
aspect of the novel: why Dowell tells his story at all. If he really were
a murderer, he would be mad to risk incriminating himself by narrating at such length. Furthermore, if we suppose him cunning enough
to have committed murder and concealed it so elaborately, why does
he not notice the problem with the dates?

It is impossible to prove that the chronological confusion should
not be attributed to Dowell rather than to Ford. Dowell, after all, has
reason enough to be confused and disturbed by the losses and shocks
he has suffered; and, as we have seen, admits to the possibility of
muddle. He introduces his narrative as the 'saddest story' he has
'ever heard', as if it hadn't happened to him. But it has, and its sadness is his, as much as it is Edward's, or Nancy's, or Maisie's, or
Leonora's—or even Florence's. Ford's 'Tale of Passion' is about
Dowell's passions too. For ultimately *The Good Soldier* is a love story.
Denis Donoghue has observed that the narrative changes key after
Nancy loses her reason; and suggests that that event accounts for
Dowell's shift from describing the book as spoken to a 'sympathetic
soul' listening to him, to discussing the painful process of writing his
narrative down.[54] According to that view, it is Dowell's love for
Nancy that motivates the story, and that seals its tragedy. But what
comes across even more powerfully, for most readers, is Dowell's
love for Edward; even, for the group:

[54] See p. 18. Donoghue, 'Listening to the Saddest Story', *Sewanee Review*, 88:4 (Fall
1980), 557–71; rptd. Sondra J. Stang (ed.), *The Presence of Ford Madox Ford* (Philadelphia:
University of Pennsylvania Press, 1981), 44–54.

They were three to one—and they made me happy. Oh, God, they made me so happy that I doubt if even paradise, that shall smooth out all temporal wrongs, shall ever give me the like. And what could they have done better, or what could they have done that could have been worse? I don't know. . . . (p. 58)

The 'three' are presumably Edward, Leonora, and Florence, though Dowell has also just mentioned 'the girl'. As readers or editors we may not have the authority to smooth out all the temporal wrinkles in the narrative. But we can recognize the power of that happiness and its destruction; and see that unless we acknowledge that power, Dowell's need to narrate is scarcely comprehensible. It is, after all, love that etches Dowell's first impressions into the memory, and makes him hold fast to them despite all that follows. His is a case of love at first impression.

NOTE ON THE TEXT

THERE are two complete manuscripts of the novel. The first (MS) is a mixture of autograph manuscripts written by three amanuenses, thought to be Brigit Patmore, and the Imagist poets and friends of Pound and Ford, H.D. [Hilda Doolittle] and her husband Richard Aldington; plus typescript sections probably typed by Ford; the whole manuscript corrected in Ford's hand. The second is the 'printer's copy' (TS); a typescript, not by Ford, but corrected in his and another's hand. There is also a typescript fragment, falling chronologically between these two, and corresponding to the opening chapters of the novel published in *Blast* (20 June 1914), 87–97. All three manuscripts, and the *Blast* instalment, are titled 'The Saddest Story'. The manuscripts were studied thoroughly by Thomas Moser, who identified the amanuenses; and have been brilliantly analysed by Martin Stannard in his excellent critical edition of the novel (New York: Norton, 1995).

The first edition of the complete book came out on 17 March 1915, published by John Lane in London, and simultaneously in New York. The two editions are apparently identical apart from their title-pages. As the second issue of *Blast* did not appear till after this, in July 1915, the serialization was discontinued. A second US edition was published in 1927 by A. and C. Boni, one of several of Ford's books they issued as an 'Avignon Edition'. This was the first edition to include the 'Dedicatory Letter to Stella Ford', reprinted here. A second UK edition was issued by John Lane in 1928, also including the Dedicatory Letter.

The copy-text for the present edition of the novel is the UK first edition (UK), on the grounds that this is the edition Ford was most involved with; it provided the version that entered literary history; and remained the basis of all the reissues of the novel before 1995, such as the orange Penguin edition of 1948; the Vintage paperback of 1951; or the text in the first volume of the *Bodley Head Ford Madox Ford* in 1963.

Stannard's critical edition collates the three manuscripts and UK. He took the defensible but controversial decision to use UK as copy-text, but to repunctuate it using the punctuation of TS, on the grounds that Ford revised the punctuation in both MS and TS, but that an editorial 'house style' appears to have been imposed on UK, heavily punctuating Dowell's more conversational syntax. He also makes emendations to two of the names in the text, including altering the first half of the name of the Ashburnhams' house from 'Branshaw' to 'Bramshaw', on the grounds that that was what MS has, but it got mistranscribed early in TS, which then caused the compositor to start setting it wrongly, and to continue with the wrong form. As he says of the name-changes, 'One might argue that the corrupt forms received Ford's tacit approval at proof stage' (p. 192), though he thinks inertia and publishing economics the more decisive factors. The problem is that with no proofs having survived or having been traced, we cannot know which changes were Ford's and which he tacitly approved or missed; and that argument applies to the punctuation as well. Another possible counter-argument is that Ford had the opportunity to restore the names or the punctuation for the 1927 edition, but did not. That edition contains some minor revisions, mostly aimed at an American readership. Though some editors have wondered whether the revisions might be Ford's, none has included them, and as Stannard says (p. 180), there is no evidence Ford had a hand in them. Indeed, his comment to Stella Bowen that one of its publishers, Charles Boni, was 'so ashamed of the ed. deluxe of the *Good Soldier* that he wd. not show me a copy' suggests otherwise.[1]

Stannard's edition is a magnificent work of scholarship, and I am grateful to be able to read the repunctuated version and his analysis of the variants. But it seems to me that it complements rather than replaces the UK text, and that there are equally cogent reasons for reading the version that Ford's contemporaries and later admirers read.

One feature of Ford's style that presents particular problems to a textual editor is his liberal use of suspension dots. The number of dots can vary widely in manuscript (those for *Parade's End*, say, use from three to eight). Publishers generally standardized these to three or four; though not always consistently. In *The Good Soldier* UK uses either three or four dots. The general principle appears to be the conventional one of using a space followed by three dots when a

---

[1] Ford to Bowen, 14 October 1927: *The Correspondence of Ford Madox Ford and Stella Bowen*, ed. Sondra J. Stang and Karen Cochran (Bloomington and Indianapolis: Indiana University Press, 1994), 330.

sentence is left incomplete, and no space and four dots when it is complete (the first dot functioning as the full-stop). However, UK sometimes uses the three dots after sentences that seem grammatically complete. Given that the manuscript evidence is that Ford thought of the number of dots as rather like the notation of dynamics in music, the distinctions should be preserved; even though we cannot be sure whether the anomalies are expressive devices or errors. So that when, for example, Dowell watches Florence go off to her baths (p. 25) he ends two paragraphs with a space and three dots. Both dwell on her attraction: 'her complexion had a perfect clearness, a perfect smoothness . . .'; 'the eyes flashed very blue—dark pebble blue . . .'. The repetitions in each case suggest Dowell dwelling distractedly on the image of Florence's physical presence. The dots here seem to suggest he could go on in the same vein; so that although the sentences would not be grammatically awry if they ended with full-stops, they are not necessarily complete; or one might say his thought-process is incomplete but suppressed. Of course the four-dot pause might function in the same way; though it may also suggest a pause between different thoughts.

As indicated in the Introduction, Ford's use of an unreliable narrator presents editors with a particular problem regarding errors. Are they Ford's, in which case they might warrant emending? Or are they Dowell's, in which case they would be intentional on Ford's part? The policy in this edition has been not to correct errors (except in a handful of cases of incoherence inexplicable except as error; all of which are tabulated in Appendix A), on the grounds that it is impossible to be sure whether they are Dowell's or Ford's; but instead to comment on them in the Explanatory Notes.

SELECT BIBLIOGRAPHY

Biography

Bowen, Stella, *Drawn from Life* (London: Collins, 1941).

Goldring, Douglas, *The Last Pre-Raphaelite: A Record of the Life and Writings of Ford Madox Ford* (London: Macdonald, 1948).

—— *South Lodge: Reminiscences of Violet Hunt, Ford Madox Ford and the English Review Circle* (London: Constable, 1943).

Hunt, Violet, *The Flurried Years* (London: Hurst & Blackett, [1926]).

—— *The Return of the Good Soldier: Ford Madox Ford and Violet Hunt's 1917 Diary*, ed. Robert and Marie Secor, English Literary Studies Monograph no. 30 (University of Victoria, BC, 1983).

Judd, Alan, *Ford Madox Ford* (London: Collins, 1990).

MacShane, Frank, *The Life and Work of Ford Madox Ford* (London: Routledge & Kegan Paul, 1965).

Mizener, Arthur, *The Saddest Story: A Biography of Ford Madox Ford* (New York: Harper & Row, 1971; London: The Bodley Head, 1972).

Moser, Thomas C., *The Life in the Fiction of Ford Madox Ford* (Princeton: Princeton University Press, 1980).

Saunders, Max, *Ford Madox Ford: A Dual Life*, 2 vols. (Oxford: Oxford University Press, 1996).

Wiesenfarth, Joseph, *Ford Madox Ford and the Regiment of Women: Violet Hunt, Jean Rhys, Stella Bowen, Janice Biala* (Madison: University of Wisconsin Press, 2003).

Letters

Lindberg-Seyersted, Brita (ed.), *Pound/Ford: The Story of a Literary Friendship: The Correspondence between Ezra Pound and Ford Madox Ford and Their Writings About Each Other* (London: Faber & Faber, 1982).

Ludwig, Richard M. (ed.), *Letters of Ford Madox Ford* (Princeton: Princeton University Press, 1965).

Stang, Sondra J., and Cochran, Karen (eds.), *The Correspondence of Ford Madox Ford and Stella Bowen* (Bloomington and Indianapolis: Indiana University Press, 1994).

Bibliography

Harvey, David Dow, *Ford Madox Ford: 1873–1939: A Bibliography of Works and Criticism* (Princeton: Princeton University Press, 1962).

Saunders, Max, 'Ford Madox Ford: Further Bibliographies', *English Literature in Transition 1880–1920*, 43:2 (2000), 131–205.

Other works by Ford of particular relevance to The Good Soldier

Ancient Lights (London: Chapman & Hall, 1911).

Antwerp (London: The Poetry Bookshop, 1915).

Between St. Dennis and St. George: A Sketch of Three Civilisations (London: Hodder and Stoughton, 1915).

A Call (London: Chatto & Windus, 1910).

Collected Poems (London: Max Goschen, 1913).

The Critical Attitude (London: Duckworth, 1911).

Critical Essays, ed. Max Saunders and Richard Stang (Manchester: Carcanet Press, 2002).

Critical Writings of Ford Madox Ford, ed. Frank MacShane (Lincoln: University of Nebraska Press, 1964).

The Desirable Alien, with Violet Hunt (London: Chatto and Windus, 1913).

England and the English—collecting Ford's trilogy on Englishness, comprising: *Soul of London* (London: Alston Rivers, 1905); *The Heart of the Country* (Alston Rivers, 1906); and *The Spirit of the People* (London: Alston Rivers, 1907)—(New York: McClure, Phillips, 1907); new edition, ed. Sara Haslam (Manchester: Carcanet, 2003).

The English Novel (Philadelphia: J. B. Lippincott, 1929; London: Constable, 1930).

The Ford Madox Ford Reader, ed. Sondra J. Stang, with Foreword by Graham Greene (Manchester: Carcanet, 1986).

Henry James (London: Martin Secker, 1913).

Hans Holbein the Younger (London: Duckworth, 1905; New York: Dutton, 1905).

High Germany (London: Duckworth, 1912).

The Inheritors (with Joseph Conrad) (New York: McClure, Phillips, 1901; London: Heinemann, 1901).

It Was the Nightingale (Philadelphia: J. B. Lippincott, 1933; London: William Heinemann, 1934).

Joseph Conrad (London: Duckworth, 1924; Boston: Little, Brown, 1924).

Ladies Whose Bright Eyes (London: Constable, 1911; revised version, Philadelphia: J. B. Lippincott, 1935).

Last Post (London: Duckworth, 1928), fourth of the Tietjens novels; annotated critical edition, ed. Paul Skinner (Manchester: Carcanet, 2011).

A Man Could Stand Up (London: Duckworth, 1926), third of the Tietjens novels; annotated critical edition, ed. Sara Haslam (Manchester: Carcanet, 2011)

The March of Literature (New York: Dial Press, 1938; London: Allen & Unwin, 1939).

Mr. Fleight (London: Howard Latimer, 1913).

The New Humpty-Dumpty, pseud. 'Daniel Chaucer' (London and New York: John Lane, 1912).

No More Parades (London: Duckworth, 1925), second of the Tietjens novels; annotated critical edition, ed. Joseph Wiesenfarth (Manchester: Carcanet, 2011).

On Heaven and Poems Written on Active Service (London: John Lane, 1918).

Parade's End (one-volume edition of all the Tietjens novels: *Some Do Not . . .*, *No More Parades*, *A Man Could Stand Up –*, and *Last Post*; see under separate titles for publication details) (New York: Alfred A. Knopf, 1950).

Return to Yesterday (London: Victor Gollancz, 1931).

Some Do Not . . . (London: Duckworth, 1924), first of the Tietjens novels; annotated critical edition, ed. Max Saunders (Manchester: Carcanet, 2010).

This Monstrous Regiment of Women (London: Women's Freedom League, [1913]).

'Tiger, Tiger: Being a Commentary on Conrad's *The Sisters*', *Bookman*, 66:5 (January 1928), 495–8.

When Blood is Their Argument (New York and London: Hodder & Stoughton, 1915).

Women & Men (Paris: Three Mountains Press, 1923).

The Young Lovell (London: Chatto & Windus, 1913).

Zeppelin Nights, with Violet Hunt (London: John Lane, 1915).

Critical books discussing The Good Soldier

Armstrong, Paul B., *The Challenge of Bewilderment: Understanding and Representation in James, Conrad, and Ford* (Ithaca and London: Cornell University Press, 1987).

Brown, Dennis, and Plastow, Jenny (eds.), *Ford Madox Ford and Englishness*, International Ford Madox Ford Studies, Vol. 5 (Amsterdam and New York, 2006).

Brown, Nicholas, *Utopian Generations: The Political Horizon of Twentieth-Century Literature* (Princeton: Princeton University Press, 2005).

Cassell, Richard A., *Critical Essays on Ford Madox Ford* (Boston: G. K. Hall, 1987).

—— *Ford Madox Ford: Modern Judgements* (London: Macmillan, 1972).

Colombino, Laura, *Ford Madox Ford: Vision, Visuality and Writing* (Oxford: Peter Lang, 2008).

Fortunati, Vita, and Lamberti, Elena (eds.), *Ford Madox Ford and 'The Republic of Letters'* (Bologna: CLUEB [Cooperativa Libraria Universitaria Editrice Bologna], 2002).

Gallix, François, *The Good Soldier / Ford Madox Ford*, introduction de Max Saunders, préface de Julian Barnes (Paris: Ellipses, 2005).

Gasiorek, Andrzej, and Moore, Daniel (eds.), *Ford Madox Ford: Literary Networks and Cultural Transformations*, International Ford Madox Ford Studies, Vol. 7 (Amsterdam and New York, 2008).

Green, Robert, *Ford Madox Ford: Prose and Politics* (Cambridge: Cambridge University Press, 1981).

Hampson, Robert, and Saunders, Max (eds.), *Ford Madox Ford's Modernity*, International Ford Madox Ford Studies, Vol. 2 (Amsterdam and New York, 2003).

Haslam, Sara, *Fragmenting Modernism: Ford Madox Ford, the Novel and the Great War* (Manchester: Manchester University Press, 2002).

—— 'The Good Soldier', in David Bradshaw and Kevin J. H. Dettmar (eds.), *A Companion to Modernist Literature and Culture* (Oxford: Blackwell, 2006), 350–7.

Hynes, Samuel, *Edwardian Occasions: Essays on English Writing in the Early Twentieth Century* (London: Routledge & Kegan Paul, 1972).

Jacobs, Carol, *Telling Time: Lévi-Strauss, Ford, Lessing, Benjamin, de Man, Wordsworth, Rilke* (Baltimore: Johns Hopkins University Press, 1992).

Katz, Tamar, *Impressionist Subjects: Gender, Interiority, and Modernist Fiction in England* (Urbana and Chicago: University of Illinois Press, 2000).

Lemarchal, Dominique, *Première Leçon Sur The Good Soldier de Ford Madox Ford* (Paris: Ellipses, 2005).

Levenson, Michael, *Modernism and the Fate of Individuality: Character and Novelistic Form from Conrad to Woolf* (Cambridge: Cambridge University Press, 1991).

Lid, Richard W., *Ford Madox Ford: The Essence of His Art* (Berkeley and Los Angeles: University of California Press, 1964).

MacShane, Frank (ed.), *Ford Madox Ford: The Critical Heritage* (London: Routledge and Kegan Paul, 1972).

Meixner, John Albert, *Ford Madox Ford's Novels: A Critical Study* (Minneapolis: University of Minnesota Press, 1962).

Saunders, Max, *Ford Madox Ford: A Dual Life* (Oxford: Oxford University Press, 1996), i. 399–460.

—— 'Ford Madox Ford, Impressionism, and Trust in *The Good Soldier*', in John Attridge and Rod Rosenquist (eds.), *Incredible Modernism—Literature, Trust and Deception* (Farnham: Ashgate, forthcoming).

Snitow, Ann Barr, *Ford Madox Ford and the Voice of Uncertainty* (Baton Rouge and London: Louisiana State University Press, 1984).

Stang, Sondra J., *Ford Madox Ford* (New York: Frederick Ungar, 1977).

—— (ed.), *The Presence of Ford Madox Ford* (Philadelphia: University of Pennsylvania Press, 1981).

Stannard, Martin (ed.), *The Good Soldier*, Norton Critical Edition (New York and London: W. W. Norton & Company, 1995; second edition, 2012).

Sutherland, John, *Can Jane Eyre Be Happy? More Puzzles in Classic Fiction* (Oxford: Oxford University Press, 1997), chapter on 'Whose Daughter is Nancy', pp. 210–14.

Articles on The Good Soldier

Adams, James T., 'Discrepancies in the Time-Scheme of *The Good Soldier*', *English Literature in Transition*, 34:2 (1991), 153–64.

Barnes, Julian, 'The Saddest Story', *Guardian Review* (7 June 2008), 2–3.

Cheng, Vincent J., 'A Chronology of *The Good Soldier*', *English Language Notes*, 24:1 (Sept. 1986), 91–7.

Fleishmann, Avrom, 'The Genre of *The Good Soldier*: Ford's Comic Mastery', *Studies in the Literary Imagination*, 13:1 (Spring 1980), 31–42; rptd. in Jack I. Biles (ed.), *British Novelists Since 1900* (New York: AMS Press, 1987), 41–53.

Foss, Chris, 'Abjection and Appropriation: Male Subjectivity in *The Good Soldier*', *Lit: Literature, interpretation, theory*, 9:3 (1998), 225–44.

Ganzel, Dewey, 'What the Letter Said: Fact and Inference in *The Good Soldier*', *Journal of Modern Literature*, 11 (July 1984), 277–90.

Goodheart, Eugene, 'The Art of Ambivalence: *The Good Soldier*', *Sewanee Review*, 106 (1998), 619–29.

—— 'What Dowell Knew: A Reading of *The Good Soldier*', in Sondra J. Stang (ed.), *Antaeus*, no. 56 (Spring 1986), 70–80.

Greene, Graham, 'Introduction', *The Bodley Head Ford Madox Ford*, Vol. 1 (London: The Bodley Head, 1962), 7–12.

Hoffmann, Karen A., ' "Am I no better than a eunuch?": Narrating Masculinity and Empire in Ford Madox Ford's *The Good Soldier*', *Journal of Modern Literature*, 27:3 (Winter 2004), 30–46.

Hood, Richard A., ' "Constant Reduction": Modernism and the Narrative Structure of *The Good Soldier*', *Journal of Modern Literature*, 14:4 (1988), 460.

Jacobs, Carol, 'The (Too) Good Soldier: "A Real Story" ', in *Glyph 3: Johns Hopkins Textual Studies* (Baltimore: Johns Hopkins University Press, 1978), 32–51.

Kermode, Frank, 'Novels: Recognition and Deception', *Critical Inquiry*, 1:1 (Sept. 1974), 103–21; rptd. in *Essays on Fiction: 1971–82* (London, Melbourne, and Henley: Routledge and Kegan Paul, 1983) as 'Recognition and Deception'.

McCarthy, Jeffrey Mathes, '*The Good Soldier* and the War for British Modernism', *Modern Fiction Studies*, 45:2 (1999), 303–39.

Poole, Roger, 'The Real Plot Line of Ford Madox Ford's *The Good Soldier*:
   An Essay in Applied Deconstruction', *Textual Practice*, 4:3 (Winter
   1990), 391–427; also see 'The Unknown Ford Madox Ford', in Hampson
   and Saunders (eds.), *Ford Madox Ford's Modernity*, 117–36.

Sanders, Wilbur, 'Polishing the Bright Stars: Ford's Drama of Narration',
   Agenda, 27:4–28:1 (Winter 1989–Spring 1990), 85–92.

Saunders, Max, 'Modernism, Impressionism, and Ford Madox Ford's *The
   Good Soldier*', *Études Anglaises*, 57:4 (Oct.–Dec. 2004), 421–37.

Stang, Sondra J., 'A Reading of Ford's *The Good Soldier*', *Modern Language
   Quarterly*, 30:4 (1969), 545–63.

Stannard, Martin, '*The Good Soldier*: Editorial Problems', in Hampson
   and Saunders (eds.), *Ford Madox Ford's Modernity*, 137–48.

——— 'Cutting Remarks: What Went Missing From *The Good Soldier*?', in
   Jason Harding (ed.), *Ford Madox Ford: Modernist Magazines and Editing*
   (Amsterdam and New York: Rodopi, 2010), 229–42.

Tóibín, Colm, 'The Art of Being Found Out', *London Review of Books* (20
   Mar. 2008), 24–7; expanded, annotated version: 'Outsiders in England
   and the Art of Being Found Out', in Andrzej Gasiorek and Daniel
   Moore (eds.), *Ford Madox Ford: Literary Networks and Cultural
   Transformations*, International Ford Madox Ford Studies, Vol. 7
   (Amsterdam and New York: Rodopi, 2008), 61–80.

General Background

Armstrong, Paul B., 'The Hermeneutics of Literary Impressionism:
   Interpretation and Reality in James, Conrad and Ford', *Centennial
   Review*, 27:4 (Fall 1983), 244–69.

Conrad, Joseph, Preface to *The Nigger of the 'Narcissus'*; first printed as an
   'Author's Note' after the serialization in the *New Review*, 17 (Dec. 1897),
   628–31.

Fortunati, Vita, and Lamberti, Elena (eds.), *Ford Madox Ford and 'The
   Republic of Letters'* (Bologna: CLUEB, 2002).

Freud, Sigmund, 'Negation' (1925), *Pelican Freud Library*, Vol. 11: *On
   Metapsychology*, ed. Angela Richards (Harmondsworth: Penguin, 1984),
   435–42.

Hynes, Samuel, *The Edwardian Turn of Mind* (Princeton: Princeton
   University Press, 1968).

James, William, *The Principles of Psychology*, Vol. 1 (New York: Henry Holt
   and Company, 1890).

Lewis, P. Wyndham, *Blasting and Bombardiering*, revised edition (London:
   John Calder; and New York: Riverrun Press, 1982).

Matz, Jesse, *Literary Impressionism and Modernist Aesthetics* (Cambridge:
   Cambridge University Press, 2001).

Patmore, Brigit, *My Friends When Young* (London: Heinemann, 1968).

Peters, John G., *Conrad and Impressionism* (Cambridge: Cambridge University Press, 2001).

Rau, Petra, *English Modernism, National Identity and the Germans, 1890–1950* (Aldershot: Ashgate, 2009).

Ricoeur, Paul, *Freud and Philosophy*, trans. D. Savage (New Haven: Yale University Press, 1977).

Saunders, Max, 'From Pre-Raphaelism to Impressionism', in Laura Colombino (ed.), *Ford Madox Ford and Visual Culture*, International Ford Madox Ford Studies, Vol. 8 (Amsterdam and New York: Rodopi, 2009), 51–70.

—— 'Literary Impressionism', in David Bradshaw and Kevin J. H. Dettmar (eds.), *A Companion to Modernist Literature and Culture* (Oxford: Blackwell, 2006), 204–11.

Tate, Allen, *Memories and Essays* (Manchester: Carcanet, 1976).

Trotter, David, *Paranoid Modernism: Literary Experiment, Psychosis, and the Professionalization of English Society* (Oxford: Oxford University Press, 2001).

Wollaeger, Mark, *Modernism, Media, and Propaganda: British Narrative from 1900 to 1945* (Princeton: Princeton University Press, 2006).

A CHRONOLOGY OF FORD MADOX FORD

1873 17 December: born Ford Hermann Hueffer, Merton, Surrey (now in Greater London). The eldest of three children, with siblings Oliver (1876–1931), novelist and journalist; and Juliet (1880–1943), translator of Russian poetry.

1881 Enters modern, co-educational Praetorius School, Folkestone, Kent.

1889 Death of Ford's father, Dr Francis Hueffer, music critic of *The Times*, Provençal scholar, and champion of Wagner. Ford goes to live with his grandfather, Ford Madox Brown, the Pre-Raphaelite painter, at 1 St Edmund's Terrace, Regent's Park. Attends University College School, London, for less than a year.

1891 Publishes first book, a children's fairy-tale, *The Brown Owl*.

1892 Received into the Roman Catholic Church. Publishes first novel, *The Shifting of the Fire*; also *The Feather*, another fairy-tale.

1893 Death of Ford Madox Brown. First volume of poems, *The Questions at the Well*.

1894 7 May: elopes with and marries his childhood sweetheart, Elsie Martindale. They move to southern Kent. *The Queen Who Flew* (fairy-tale).

1896 *Ford Madox Brown* (biography).

1897 Birth of first daughter, Christina.

1898 Meets Joseph Conrad. They decide to collaborate, producing three books: *The Inheritors* (1901), *Romance* (1903), and *The Nature of a Crime* (1909/1924).

1900 Birth of second daughter, Katharine. *Poems for Pictures*, *The Cinque Ports* (history).

1901 Moves near Martindale family at Winchelsea, Sussex.

1902 *Rossetti: A Critical Essay on his Art*.

?1903 Begins affair with sister-in-law, Mary Martindale.

1904 March: onset of protracted agoraphobic breakdown. August to December: seeks cure in Germany. *The Face of the Night* (poems).

?1905 Meets Arthur Marwood, who becomes a close friend, and a model for aspects of Edward Ashburnham in *The Good Soldier* and

Christopher Tietjens in *Parade's End*. *The Soul of London* (city impressions: first volume of the *England and the English* trilogy), *The Benefactor* (novel), *Hans Holbein* (art criticism).

1906 Daughters received into the Roman Catholic Church. Visits United States with Elsie. *The Fifth Queen* (historical romance about Henry VIII and Katharine Howard), *The Heart of the Country* (rural impressions: second volume of the *England and the English* trilogy), *Christina's Fairy Book* (fairy-stories).

1907 Moves to London, separating from Elsie. Meets Violet Hunt. *Privy Seal* (historical romance: second volume of the *Fifth Queen* trilogy), *From Inland* (poems), *An English Girl* (novel), *The Pre-Raphaelite Brotherhood* (art criticism), *The Spirit of the People* (third volume of impressionist survey of *England and the English*).

1908 Founds and edits the *English Review*. *The Fifth Queen Crowned* (historical romance: concluding volume of the *Fifth Queen* trilogy), *Mr. Apollo* (fantasy).

1909 Quarrels with Conrad and Marwood. Leaves Elsie Hueffer for Violet Hunt. Later, collaborates with her on *The Desirable Alien* (1913) and *Zeppelin Nights* (1915). *The 'Half Moon'* (historical romance). Meets D. H. Lawrence, Ezra Pound, and Wyndham Lewis.

1910 Loses editorship of *The English Review*. *A Call* (novel), *Songs from London* (poems), *The Portrait* (historical romance).

1911 Loses custody of his daughters. Reconciled with Conrad and Marwood. 21 October: marriage to Violet Hunt claimed in a report in the D*aily Mirror*; Ford's wife sues *Mirror*. *The Simple Life Limited* (satirical novel, published under pseudonym 'Daniel Chaucer'), *Ancient Lights* (his first volume of reminiscences), *Ladies Whose Bright Eyes* (historical fantasy), *The Critical Attitude* (criticism).

1912 *High Germany* (poems), *The Panel* (comic novel), *The New Humpty-Dumpty* (second satirical novel published under pseudonym 'Daniel Chaucer').

1913 7 February: damages awarded to Ford's wife in highly publicized *Throne* magazine case. Ford in Bankruptcy Court. Begins involvement with Brigit Patmore. *Mr. Fleight* (satirical novel), *The Young Lovell* (historical romance), *Collected Poems*, *Henry James*.

1914 Begins writing war propaganda.

1915 August: commissioned Second Lieutenant, the Welch Regiment, and based first at Tenby then Cardiff. *The Good Soldier* (novel), *When Blood is Their Argument* (war propaganda), *Between St. Dennis and St. George* (war propaganda).

1916 July: sees daughters for the last time, in London. Attached to First Line Transport, 9th Battalion, Welch Regiment; under fire for ten days of the Battle of the Somme in late July. Concussed by shell-explosion; sent to Casualty Clearing Station.

1916 August: rejoins his regiment, now stationed in the Ypres Salient near Kemmel Hill.

1916 September: ill and diagnosed as suffering from shell-shock, reassigned to North Wales. Late November: returned to France; stationed in the regiment's base camp at Rouen, assigned to bureaucratic jobs and guarding German prisoners. Falls ill again in December and is hospitalized.

1917 January: transferred to Lady Michelham's convalescent hospital at Menton, on the Riviera. February: sent back to Rouen, assigned to a Canadian Casual Battalion; put in charge of a hospital tent of German prisoners at Abbeville.

1917 15 March: invalided home to England to serve in training capacity. Meets Stella Bowen.

1918 *On Heaven: and Poems Written on Active Service*.

1919 January: resigns commission. April: moves to Sussex farmhouse called 'Red Ford', found by Bowen. June: joined by Bowen and changes name to Ford Madox Ford.

1920 Birth of third daughter, Julia.

1921 *A House* (long poem), *Thus to Revisit* (reminiscences).

1922 November: Ford and Bowen spend a month in Paris, then travel to Cap Ferrat for the winter. They decide to stay in France, alternating between Paris and Provence.

1923 Autumn: back in Paris, Ford establishes the *transatlantic review*, published throughout 1924. *The Marsden Case* (novel), *Mr Bosphorus and the Muses* (parodic pantomime in verse and prose), *Women & Men* (essays, written in 1911).

1924 Takes on Hemingway as sub-editor of *transatlantic*. Begins affair with Jean Rhys. May: makes first of many postwar trips to United States. Demise of *transatlantic review*. *Some Do Not . . .* (novel, first of the Tietjens tetralogy, later called *Parade's End*), *Joseph Conrad* (memoir and criticism).

1925 *No More Parades* (second Tietjens novel).

1926 *A Mirror to France* (essays), *A Man Could Stand Up—* (third Tietjens novel).

1927 Separation from Stella Bowen. *New Poems*, *New York is Not America* (essays), *New York Essays* (criticism and reminiscences).

1928 *Last Post* (fourth Tietjens novel), *A Little Less Than Gods* (historical romance).

1929 *The English Novel* (literary history and criticism), *No Enemy* (fictionalized autobiography, largely written in 1919).

1930 May: meets Janice Biala, Polish-American painter. Lives with her in Provence, Paris, and America until his death.

1931 *When the Wicked Man* (novel), *Return to Yesterday* (reminiscences, 1894–1914).

1933 *The Rash Act* (novel), *It Was the Nightingale* (reminiscences from 1919 to the Wall Street Crash).

1934 *Henry for Hugh* (novel, sequel to *The Rash Act*).

1935 *Provence* (culture, history, and travel book).

1936 *Vive Le Roy* (detective novel), *Collected Poems*.

1937 Appointed writer and critic in residence, Olivet College, Michigan. *Great Trade Route* (culture, history, and travel book), *Portraits from Life* (reminiscences and criticism, published in England in 1938 as *Mightier than the Sword*).

1938 *The March of Literature* (literary history and criticism).

1939 26 June: dies in Deauville, France.

1988 *A History of Our Own Times* (history of Western Europe, England, and the United States, 1870–5; finished by 1930, as the first of three planned volumes).

THE GOOD SOLDIER

DEDICATORY LETTER To STELLA FORD*

My dear Stella,

I have always regarded this as my best book*—at any rate as the best book of mine of a pre-war period; and between its writing and the appearance of my next novel nearly ten years must have elapsed, so that whatever I may have since written may be regarded as the work of a different man—as the work of *your* man. For it is certain that without the incentive to live that you offered me I should scarcely have survived the war-period and it is more certain still that without your spurring me again to write I should never have written again. And it happens that, by a queer chance, the *Good Soldier* is almost alone amongst my books in being dedicated to no one: Fate must have elected to let it wait the ten years that it waited—for this dedication.

What I am now I owe to you: what I was when I wrote the *Good Soldier* I owed to the concatenation of circumstances of a rather purposeless and wayward life. Until I sat down to write this book—on the 17th December, 1913—I had never attempted to extend myself, to use a phrase of race-horse training. Partly because I had always entertained very fixedly the idea that—whatever may be the case with other writers—I at least should not be able to write a novel by which I should care to stand before reaching the age of forty; partly because I very definitely did not want to come into competition with other writers whose claim or whose need for recognition and what recognitions bring were greater than my own. I had never really tried to put into any novel of mine *all* that I knew about writing. I had written rather desultorily a number of books—a great number—but they had all been in the nature of *pastiches*, of pieces of rather precious writing, or of *tours de force*. But I have always been mad about writing—about the way writing should be done and partly alone, partly with the companionship of Conrad,* I had even at that date made exhaustive studies into how words should be handled and novels constructed.

So, on the day I was forty I sat down to show what I could do—and the *Good Soldier* resulted. I fully intended it to be my last book. I used to think—and I do not know that I do not think the same now—that one book was enough for any man to write, and, at the date when the *Good Soldier* was finished, London at least and possibly the world appeared to be passing under the dominion of writers newer and much more vivid. Those were the passionate days of the literary Cubists, Vorticists, Imagistes* and the rest of the tapageur* and riotous Jeunes* of that young decade. So I regarded myself as the Eel which, having reached the deep sea brings forth its young and dies— or as the Great Auk* I considered that, having reached my allotted I had laid my one egg and might as well die. So I took a formal farewell of Literature in the columns of a magazine called the *Thrush**—which also, poor little auk that it was, died of the effort. Then I prepared to stand aside in favour of our good friends—yours and mine—Ezra, Eliot, Wyndham Lewis, H. D.* and the rest of the clamorous young writers who were then knocking at the door.

But greater clamours beset London and the world which till then had seemed to lie at the proud feet of those conquerors; Cubism, Vorticism, Imagism and the rest never had their fair chance amid the voices of the cannon and so I have come out of my hole again and beside your strong, delicate and beautiful works have taken heart to lay some work of my own.

The Good Soldier, however, remains my great auk's egg for me as being something of a race that will have no successors and as it was written so long ago I may not seem over-vain if I consider it for a moment or two. No author, I think, is deserving of much censure for vanity if, taking down one of his ten year old books, he exclaims: "Great Heavens, did I write as well as that then?" for the implication always is that one does not any longer write so well and few are so envious as to censure the complacencies of an extinct volcano.

Be that as it may, I was lately forced into the rather close examination of this book, for I had to translate it into French,* that forcing me to give it much closer attention than would be the case in any reading however minute. And I will permit myself to say that I was astounded at the work I must have put into the construction of the book, at the intricate tangle of references and cross-references. Nor is that to be wondered at for, though I wrote it with comparative rapidity, I had it hatching within myself for fully another decade. That was because the story is a true story and because I had it from Edward Ashburnham himself and I could not write it till all the others were dead. So I carried it about with me all those years, thinking about it from time to time.

I had in those days an ambition: that was to do for the English novel what in *Fort Comme la Mort*, Maupassant* had done for the French. One day I had my reward, for I happened to be in a company where a fervent young admirer exclaimed: "By Jove, the *Good Soldier* is the finest novel in the English language!" whereupon my friend Mr. John Rodker* who has always had a properly tempered admiration for my work remarked in his clear, slow drawl: "Ah yes. It is, but you have left out a word. It is the finest French novel in the English language!"*

With that—which is my tribute to my masters and betters of France—I will leave the book to the reader. But I should like to say a word about the title. This book was originally called by me *The Saddest Story*, but since it did not appear till the darkest days of the war were upon us, Mr. Lane* importuned me with letters and tele-grams—I was by that time engaged in other pursuits!*—to change the title which he said would at that date render the book unsaleable. One day, when I was on parade, I received a final wire of appeal from Mr. Lane, and the telegraph being reply-paid I seized the reply-form and wrote in hasty irony: "Dear Lane, Why not *The Good Soldier?*" ... To my horror six months later the book appeared under that title.

I have never ceased to regret it but, since the War I have received so much evidence that the book has been read under that name that I hesitate to make a change for fear of causing confusion. Had the chance occurred during the War I should not have hesitated to make the change for I had only two evidences that anyone had ever heard of it. On one occasion I met the adjutant of my regiment just come off leave and looking extremely sick. I said: "Great Heavens, man, what is the matter with you?" He replied: "Well, the day before yesterday I got engaged to be married and today I have been reading *The Good Soldier*."

On the other occasion I was on parade again, being examined in drill, on the Guards' Square at Chelsea. And, since I was petrified with nervousness, having to do it before a half dozen elderly gentle-men with red hatbands* I got my men about as hopelessly boxed as it is possible to do with the gentlemen privates of H.M. Coldstream Guards. Whilst I stood stiffly at attention one of the elderly red hat-bands walked close behind my back and said distinctly in my ear, "Did you say *The* Good *Soldier?*" So no doubt Mr. Lane was avenged. At any rate I have learned that irony may be a two-edged sword.

You, my dear Stella, will have heard me tell these stories a great many times. But the seas now divide us and I put them in this, your letter, which you will read before you see me in the hope that they may give you some pleasure with the illusion that you are hearing familiar—and very devoted—tones. And so I subscribe myself in all truth and in the hope that you will accept at once the particular dedication of this book and the general dedication of the edition.

Your
F. M. F.

NEW YORK, *January* 9, 1927.

THE
GOOD SOLDIER

A TALE OF PASSION

BY

FORD MADOX HUEFFER

AUTHOR OF "THE FIFTH QUEEN," ETC.

*"Beati Immaculati"**

LONDON : JOHN LANE, THE BODLEY HEAD
NEW YORK : JOHN LANE COMPANY
MCMXV

PART I

I

THIS is the saddest story I have ever heard. We had known the Ashburnhams for nine seasons of the town of Nauheim* with an extreme intimacy—or, rather, with an acquaintanceship as loose and easy and yet as close as a good glove's with your hand. My wife and I knew Captain and Mrs. Ashburnham as well as it was possible to know anybody, and yet, in another sense, we knew nothing at all about them. This is, I believe, a state of things only possible with English people of whom, till to-day, when I sit down to puzzle out what I know of this sad affair, I knew nothing whatever. Six months ago I had never been to England, and, certainly, I had never sounded the depths of an English heart. I had known the shallows.

I don't mean to say that we were not acquainted with many English people. Living, as we perforce lived, in Europe, and being, as we perforce were, leisured Americans, which is as much as to say that we were un-American, we were thrown very much into the society of the nicer English. Paris, you see, was our home. Somewhere between Nice and Bordighera* provided yearly winter quarters for us, and Nauheim always received us from July to September. You will gather from this statement that one of us had, as the saying is, a "heart", and, from the statement that my wife is dead, that she was the sufferer.

Captain Ashburnham also had a heart. But, whereas a yearly month or so at Nauheim tuned him up to exactly the right pitch for the rest of the twelvemonth, the two months or so were only just enough to keep poor Florence alive from year to year. The reason for his heart was, approximately, polo, or too much hard sportsmanship in his youth. The reason for poor Florence's broken years was a storm at sea upon our first crossing to Europe, and the immediate reasons for our imprisonment in that continent were doctors' orders. They said that even the short Channel crossing might well kill the poor thing.

When we all first met, Captain Ashburnham, home on sick leave from an India to which he was never to return, was thirty-three; Mrs. Ashburnham—Leonora—was thirty-one. I was thirty-six and poor Florence thirty. Thus to-day Florence would have been thirty-nine and Captain Ashburnham forty-two; whereas I am forty-five and Leonora forty. You will perceive, therefore, that our friendship has been a young-middle-aged affair, since we were all of us of quite quiet dispositions, the Ashburnhams being more particularly what in England it is the custom to call "quite good people".

They were descended, as you will probably expect, from the Ashburnham* who accompanied Charles I to the scaffold, and, as you must also expect with this class of English people, you would never have noticed it. Mrs. Ashburnham was a Powys; Florence was a Hurlbird of Stamford, Connecticut, where, as you know, they are more old-fashioned than even the inhabitants of Cranford,* England, could have been. I myself am a Dowell of Philadelphia, Pa., where, it is historically true, there are more old English families than you would find in any six English counties taken together. I carry about with me, indeed—as if it were the only thing that invisibly anchored me to any spot upon the globe—the title deeds of my farm, which once covered several blocks between Chestnut and Walnut Streets.* These title deeds are of wampum,* the grant of an Indian chief to the first Dowell, who left Farnham in Surrey in company with William Penn.* Florence's people, as is so often the case with the inhabitants of Connecticut, came from the neighbourhood of Fordingbridge,* where the Ashburnhams' place is. From there, at this moment, I am actually writing.

You may well ask why I write. And yet my reasons are quite many. For it is not unusual in human beings who have witnessed the sack of a city or the falling to pieces of a people to desire to set down what they have witnessed for the benefit of unknown heirs or of generations infinitely remote; or, if you please, just to get the sight out of their heads.

Some one has said that the death of a mouse from cancer is the whole sack of Rome by the Goths,* and I swear to you that the breaking up of our little four-square coterie was such another unthinkable event. Supposing that you should come upon us sitting together at one of the little tables in front of the club house, let us say, at Homburg,* taking tea of an afternoon and watching the miniature golf, you would have said that, as human affairs go, we were an extraordinarily safe castle. We were, if you will, one of those tall ships with the white sails upon a blue sea, one of those things that seem the proudest and the safest of all the beautiful and safe things that God has permitted the mind of men to frame. Where better could one take refuge? Where better?

Permanence? Stability! I can't believe it's gone. I can't believe that that long, tranquil life, which was just stepping a minuet,* vanished in four crashing days at the end of nine years and six weeks.* Upon my word, yes, our intimacy was like a minuet, simply because on every possible occasion and in every possible circumstance we knew where to go, where to sit, which table we unanimously should choose; and we could rise and go, all four together, without a signal from any one of us, always to the music of the Kur orchestra,* always in the temperate sunshine, or, if it rained, in discreet shelters. No, indeed, it can't be gone. You can't kill a minuet de la cour. You may shut up the music-book, close the harpsichord; in the cupboard and presses the rats may destroy the white satin favours.* The mob may sack Versailles; the Trianon may fall, but surely the minuet—the minuet itself is dancing itself away into the furthest stars, even as our minuet of the Hessian bathing places must be stepping itself still. Isn't there any heaven where old beautiful dances, old beautiful intimacies prolong themselves? Isn't there any Nirvana* pervaded by the faint thrilling of instruments that have fallen into the dust of wormwood but that yet had frail, tremulous, and everlasting souls?

No, by God, it is false! It wasn't a minuet that we stepped; it was a prison—a prison full of screaming hysterics, tied down so that they might not outsound the rolling of our carriage wheels as we went along the shaded avenues of the Taunus Wald.*

And yet I swear by the sacred name of my creator that it was true. It was true sunshine; the true music; the true splash of the fountains from the mouth of stone dolphins. For, if for me we were four people with the same tastes, with the same desires, acting—or, no, not acting—sitting here and there unanimously, isn't that the truth? If for nine years I have possessed a goodly apple that is rotten at the core and discover its rottenness only in nine years and six months less four days, isn't it true to say that for nine years I possessed a goodly apple? So it may well be with Edward Ashburnham, with Leonora his wife and with poor dear Florence. And, if you come to think of it, isn't it a little odd that the physical rottenness of at least two pillars of our four-square house never presented itself to my mind as a menace to its security? It doesn't so present itself now though the two of them are actually dead. I don't know . . .

I know nothing—nothing in the world—of the hearts of men. I only know that I am alone—horribly alone. No hearthstone will ever again witness, for me, friendly intercourse. No smoking-room will ever be other than peopled with incalculable simulacra amidst smoke wreaths. Yet, in the name of God, what should I know if I don't know the life of the hearth and of the smoking-room, since my whole life has been passed in those places? The warm hearthside!—Well, there was Florence: I believe that for the twelve years her life lasted, after the storm that seemed irretrievably to have weakened her heart—I don't believe that for one minute she was out of my sight, except when she was safely tucked up in bed and I should be downstairs, talking to some good fellow or other in some lounge or smoking-room or taking my final turn with a cigar before going to bed. I don't, you understand, blame Florence. But how can she have known what she knew? How could she have got to know it? To know it so fully. Heavens! There doesn't seem to have been the actual time. It must have been when I was taking my baths, and my Swedish exercises,* being manicured. Leading the life I did, of the sedulous, strained nurse, I had to do something to keep myself fit. It must have been then! Yet even that can't have been enough time to get the tremendously long conversations full of worldly wisdom that Leonora has reported to me since their deaths. And is it possible to imagine that during our prescribed walks in Nauheim and the neighbourhood she found time to carry on the protracted negotiations which she did carry on between Edward Ashburnham and his wife? And isn't it incredible that during all that time Edward and Leonora never spoke a word to each other in private? What is one to think of humanity?

For I swear to you that they were the model couple. He was as devoted as it was possible to be without appearing fatuous. So well set up, with such honest blue eyes, such a touch of stupidity, such a warm goodheartedness! And she—so tall, so splendid in the saddle, so fair! Yes, Leonora was extraordinarily fair and so extraordinarily the real thing that she seemed too good to be true. You don't, I mean, as a rule, get it all so superlatively together. To be the county family,* to look the county family, to be so appropriately and perfectly wealthy; to be so perfect in manner—even just to the saving touch of insolence that seems to be necessary. To have all that and to be all that! No, it was too good to be true. And yet, only this afternoon, talking over the whole matter she said to me: "Once I tried to have a lover but I was so sick at the heart, so utterly worn out that I had to send him away." That struck me as the most amazing thing I had ever heard. She said "I was actually in a man's arms. Such a nice chap! Such a dear fellow! And I was saying to myself, fiercely, hissing it between my teeth, as they say in novels—and really clenching them together: I was saying to myself: 'Now, I'm in for it and I'll really have a good time for once in my life—for once in my life!' It was in the dark, in a carriage, coming back from a hunt ball. Eleven miles we had to drive! And then suddenly the bitterness of the endless poverty, of the endless acting—it fell on me like a blight, it spoilt everything. Yes, I had to realize that I had been spoilt even for the good time when it came. And I burst out crying and I cried and I cried for the whole eleven miles. Just imagine *me* crying! And just imagine me making a fool of the poor dear chap like that. It certainly wasn't playing the game, was it now?"

I don't know; I don't know; was that last remark of hers the remark of a harlot, or is it what every decent woman, county family or not county family, thinks at the bottom of her heart? Or thinks all the time for the matter of that? Who knows?

Yet, if one doesn't know that at this hour and day, at this pitch of civilisation to which we have attained, after all the preachings of all the moralists, and all the teachings of all the mothers to all the daughters *in saeculum saeculorum** . . . but perhaps that is what all mothers teach all daughters, not with lips but with the eyes, or with heart whispering to heart. And, if one doesn't know as much as that about the first thing in the world, what does one know and why is one here?

I asked Mrs. Ashburnham whether she had told Florence that and what Florence had said and she answered:—"Florence didn't offer any comment at all. What could she say? There wasn't anything to be said. With the grinding poverty we had to put up with to keep up appearances, and the way the poverty came about—*you* know what I mean—any woman would have been justified in taking a lover and presents too. Florence once said about a very similar position—she was a little too well-bred, too American, to talk about mine—that it was a case of perfectly open riding and the woman could just act on the spur of the moment. She said it in American of course, but that was the sense of it. I think her actual words were:—'That it was up to her to take it or leave it . . .'"

I don't want you to think that I am writing Teddy Ashburnham
down a brute. I don't believe he was. God knows, perhaps all men are
like that. For as I've said what do I know even of the smoking-room?
Fellows come in and tell the most extraordinarily gross stories*—so
gross that they will positively give you a pain. And yet they'd be
offended if you suggested that they weren't the sort of person you
could trust your wife alone with. And very likely they'd be quite
properly offended—that is if you can trust anybody alone with anybody. But that sort of fellow obviously takes more delight in listening
to or in telling gross stories—more delight than in anything else in
the world. They'll hunt languidly and dress languidly and dine languidly and work without enthusiasm and find it a bore to carry on
three minutes' conversation about anything whatever and yet, when
the other sort of conversation begins, they'll laugh and wake up and
throw themselves about in their chairs. Then, if they so delight in the
narration, how is it possible that they can be offended—and properly
offended at the suggestion that they might make attempts upon your
wife's honour? Or again: Edward Ashburnham was the cleanest looking sort of chap;—an excellent magistrate, a first rate soldier, one of
the best landlords, so they said, in Hampshire, England. To the poor
and to hopeless drunkards, as I myself have witnessed, he was like a
painstaking guardian. And he never told a story that couldn't have
gone into the columns of the *Field** more than once or twice in all the
nine years of my knowing him. He didn't even like hearing them; he
would fidget and get up and go out to buy a cigar or something of that
sort. You would have said that he was just exactly the sort of chap
that you could have trusted your wife with. And I trusted mine—and
it was madness.

And yet again you have me. If poor Edward was dangerous because
of the chastity of his expressions—and they say that that is always the
hall-mark of a libertine—what about myself? For I solemnly avow
that not only have I never so much as hinted at an impropriety in my
conversation in the whole of my days; and more than that, I will
vouch for the cleanness of my thoughts and the absolute chastity of
my life. At what, then, does it all work out? Is the whole thing a folly
and a mockery? Am I no better than a eunuch or is the proper man—
the man with the right to existence—a raging stallion forever neighing after his neighbour's womenkind?*

I don't know. And there is nothing to guide us. And if everything is so nebulous about a matter so elementary as the morals of sex, what is there to guide us in the more subtle morality of all other personal contacts, associations, and activities? Or are we meant to act on impulse alone? It is all a darkness.

II

I DON'T know how it is best to put this thing down—whether it would be better to try and tell the story from the beginning, as if it were a story; or whether to tell it from this distance of time, as it reached me from the lips of Leonora or from those of Edward himself.

So I shall just imagine myself for a fortnight or so at one side of the fireplace of a country cottage, with a sympathetic soul opposite me. And I shall go on talking, in a low voice while the sea sounds in the distance and overhead the great black flood of wind polishes the bright stars. From time to time we shall get up and go to the door and look out at the great moon and say:— "Why, it is nearly as bright as in Provence!"* And then we shall come back to the fireside, with just the touch of a sigh because we are not in that Provence where even the saddest stories are gay. Consider the lamentable history of Peire Vidal.* Two years ago Florence and I motored from Biarritz to Las Tours, which is in the Black Mountains.* In the middle of a tortuous valley there rises up an immense pinnacle and on the pinnacle are four castles—Las Tours, the Towers. And the immense mistral* blew down that valley which was the way from France into Provence so that the silver grey olive leaves appeared like hair flying in the wind, and the tufts of rosemary crept into the iron rocks that they might not be torn up by the roots.

It was, of course, poor dear Florence who wanted to go to Las Tours. You are to imagine that, however much her bright personality came from Stamford, Connecticut, she was yet a graduate of Poughkeepsie.* I never could imagine how she did it—the queer, chattery person that she was. With the far-away look in her eyes—which wasn't, however, in the least romantic—I mean that she didn't look as if she were seeing poetic dreams, or looking through you, for she hardly ever did look at you!—holding up one hand as if she wished to silence any objection—or any comment for the matter of that—she would talk. She would talk about William the Silent, about Gustave the Loquacious, about Paris frocks, about how the poor dressed in 1337, about Fantin Latour,* about the Paris-Lyons-Mediterranée train-de-luxe, about whether it would be worth while to get off at Tarascon and go across the windswept suspension-bridge, over the Rhone to take another look at Beaucaire.*

We never did take another look at Beaucaire, of course—beautiful Beaucaire, with the high, triangular white tower, that looked as thin as a needle and as tall as the Flatiron,* between Fifth and Broadway—Beaucaire with the grey walls on the top of the pinnacle surrounding an acre and a half of blue irises, beneath the tallness of the stone pines. What a beautiful thing the stone pine is! . . .

No, we never did go back anywhere. Not to Heidelberg, not to Hamelin, not to Verona, not to Mont Majour*—not so much as to Carcassonne* itself. We talked of it, of course, but I guess Florence got all she wanted out of one look at a place. She had the seeing eye.

I haven't, unfortunately, so that the world is full of places to which I want to return—towns with the blinding white sun upon them; stone pines against the blue of the sky; corners of gables, all carved and painted with stags and scarlet flowers and crowstepped gables with the little saint at the top; and grey and pink palazzi* and walled towns a mile or so back from the sea, on the Mediterranean, between Leghorn* and Naples. Not one of them did we see more than once, so that the whole world for me is like spots of colour in an immense canvas. Perhaps if it weren't so I should have something to catch hold of now.

Is all this digression or isn't it digression? Again I don't know. You, the listener, sit opposite me. But you are so silent. You don't tell me anything. I am, at any rate, trying to get you to see what sort of life it was I led with Florence and what Florence was like. Well, she was bright; and she danced. She seemed to dance over the floors of castles and over seas and over and over the salons of modistes* and over the *plages** of the Riviera—like a gay tremulous beam, reflected from water upon a ceiling. And my function in life was to keep that bright thing in existence. And it was almost as difficult as trying to catch with your hand that dancing reflection. And the task lasted for years.

Florence's aunts used to say that I must be the laziest man in Philadelphia. They had never been to Philadelphia and they had the New England conscience. You see, the first thing they said to me when I called in on Florence in the little ancient, colonial, wooden house beneath the high, thin-leaved elms—the first question they asked me was not how I did but what did I do. And I did nothing.

I suppose I ought to have done something, but I didn't see any call to do it. Why does one do things? I just drifted in and wanted Florence. First I had drifted in on Florence at a Browning tea,* or something of the sort in Fourteenth Street,* which was then still residential. I don't know why I had gone to New York; I don't know why I had gone to the tea. I don't see why Florence should have gone to that sort of spelling bee.* It wasn't the place at which, even then, you expected to find a Poughkeepsie graduate. I guess Florence wanted to raise the culture of the Stuyvesant crowd* and did it as she might have gone in slumming. Intellectual slumming, that was what it was. She always wanted to leave the world a little more elevated than she found it. Poor dear thing, I have heard her lecture Teddy Ashburnham by the hour on the difference between a Frantz Hals and a Woovermans* and why the Pre-Mycenaic* statues were cubical with knobs on the top. I wonder what he made of it? Perhaps he was thankful.

I know I was. For do you understand my whole attentions, my whole endeavours were to keep poor dear Florence on to topics like the finds at Gnossos* and the mental spirituality of Walter Pater.* I had to keep her at it, you understand, or she might die. For I was solemnly informed that if she became excited over anything or if her emotions were really stirred her little heart might cease to beat. For twelve years I had to watch every word that any person uttered in any conversation and I had to head it off what the English call "things"*— off love, poverty, crime, religion and the rest of it. Yes, the first doctor that we had when she was carried off the ship at Havre assured me that this must be done. Good God, are all these fellows monstrous idiots, or is there a freemasonry between all of them from end to end of the earth? . . . That is what makes me think of that fellow Peire Vidal.

Because, of course, his story is culture and I had to head her towards culture and at the same time it's so funny and she hadn't got to laugh, and it's so full of love and she wasn't to think of love. Do you know the story? Las Tours of the Four Castles had for chatelaine Blanche Somebody-or-other* who was called as a term of commendation, La Louve—the She-Wolf. And Peire Vidal the Troubadour* paid his court to La Louve. And she wouldn't have anything to do with him. So, out of compliment to her—the things people do when they're in love!—he dressed himself up in wolfskins and went up into the Black Mountains. And the shepherds of the Montagne Noire and their dogs mistook him for a wolf and he was torn with the fangs and beaten with clubs. So they carried him back to Las Tours and La Louve wasn't at all impressed. They polished him up and her husband remonstrated seriously with her. Vidal was, you see, a great poet and it was not proper to treat a great poet with indifference.

So Peire Vidal declared himself Emperor of Jerusalem or somewhere and the husband had to kneel down and kiss his feet though La Louve wouldn't. And Peire set sail in a rowing boat with four companions to redeem the Holy Sepulchre.* And they struck on a rock somewhere, and, at great expense, the husband had to fit out an expedition to fetch him back. And Peire Vidal fell all over the Lady's bed while the husband, who was a most ferocious warrior, remonstrated some more about the courtesy that is due to great poets. But I suppose La Louve was the more ferocious of the two. Anyhow, that is all that came of it. Isn't that a story?

You haven't an idea of the queer old-fashionedness of Florence's aunts—the Misses Hurlbird,* nor yet of her uncle. An extraordinarily lovable man, that Uncle John. Thin, gentle, and with a "heart" that made his life very much what Florence's afterwards became. He didn't reside at Stamford; his home was in Waterbury* where the watches come from. He had a factory there which, in our queer American way, would change its functions almost from year to year. For nine months or so it would manufacture buttons out of bone. Then it would suddenly produce brass buttons for coachmen's liveries.* Then it would take a turn at embossed tin lids for candy boxes. The fact is that the poor old gentleman, with his weak and fluttering heart, didn't want his factory to manufacture anything at all. He wanted to retire. And he did retire when he was seventy. But he was so worried at having all the street boys in the town point after him and exclaim:—"There goes the laziest man in Waterbury!" that he tried taking a tour round the world. And Florence and a young man called Jimmy went with him. It appears from what Florence told me that Jimmy's function with Mr. Hurlbird was to avoid exciting topics for him. He had to keep him, for instance, out of political discussions. For the poor old man was a violent Democrat in days when you might travel the world over without finding anything but a Republican.* Anyhow, they went round the world.

I think an anecdote is about the best way to give you an idea of what the old gentleman was like. For it is perhaps important that you should know what the old gentleman was; he had a great deal of influence in forming the character of my poor dear wife.

Just before they set out from San Francisco for the South Seas old Mr. Hurlbird said he must take something with him to make little presents to people he met on the voyage. And it struck him that the things to take for that purpose were oranges—because California is the orange country—and comfortable folding chairs. So he bought I don't know how many cases of oranges—the great cool California oranges, and half-a-dozen folding chairs in a special case that he always kept in his cabin. There must have been half a cargo of fruit.

For, to every person on board the several steamers that they employed—to every person with whom he had so much as a nodding acquaintance, he gave an orange every morning. And they lasted him right round the girdle of this mighty globe of ours. When they were at North Cape,* even, he saw on the horizon, poor dear thin man that he was, a lighthouse. "Hello," says he to himself, "these fellows must be very lonely. Let's take them some oranges." So he had a boatload of his fruit out and had himself rowed to the lighthouse on the horizon. The folding-chairs he lent to any lady that he came across and liked or who seemed tired and invalidish on the ship. And so, guarded against his heart and, having his niece with him, he went round the world . . .

He wasn't obtrusive about his heart. You wouldn't have known he had one. He only left it to the physical laboratory at Waterbury for the benefit of science, since he considered it to be quite an extraordinary kind of heart. And the joke of the matter was that, when, at the age of eighty-four, just five days before poor Florence, he died of bronchitis there was found to be absolutely nothing the matter with that organ. It had certainly jumped or squeaked or something just sufficiently to take in the doctors, but it appears that that was because of an odd formation of the lungs. I don't much understand about these matters.

I inherited his money because Florence died five days after him. I wish I hadn't. It was a great worry. I had to go out to Waterbury just after Florence's death because the poor dear old fellow had left a good many charitable bequests and I had to appoint trustees. I didn't like the idea of their not being properly handled.

Yes, it was a great worry. And just as I had got things roughly settled I received the extraordinary cable from Ashburnham begging me to come back and have a talk with him. And immediately afterwards came one from Leonora saying, "Yes, please do come. You could be so helpful." It was as if he had sent the cable without consulting her and had afterwards told her. Indeed, that was pretty much what had happened, except that he had told the girl and the girl told the wife. I arrived, however, too late to be of any good if I could have been of any good. And then I had my first taste of English life. It was amazing. It was overwhelming. I never shall forget the polished cob that Edward, beside me, drove; the animal's action, its high-stepping, its skin that was like satin. And the peace! And the red cheeks! And the beautiful, beautiful old house.

Just near Branshaw Teleragh* it was and we descended on it from the high, clear, windswept waste of the New Forest.* I tell you it was amazing to arrive there from Waterbury. And it came into my head— for Teddy Ashburnham, you remember, had cabled to me to "come and have a talk" with him—that it was unbelievable that anything essentially calamitous could happen to that place and those people. I tell you it was the very spirit of peace. And Leonora, beautiful and smiling, with her coils of yellow hair stood on the top doorstep, with a butler and footman and a maid or so behind her. And she just said:—"So glad you've come," as if I'd run down to lunch from a town ten miles away, instead of having come half the world over at the call of two urgent telegrams.

The girl was out with the hounds, I think.

And that poor devil beside me was in an agony. Absolute, hopeless, dumb agony such as passes the mind of man to imagine.

III

It was a very hot summer, in August, 1904; and Florence had already been taking the baths for a month. I don't know how it feels to be a patient at one of those places. I never was a patient anywhere. I daresay the patients get a home feeling and some sort of anchorage in the spot. They seem to like the bath attendants, with their cheerful faces, their air of authority, their white linen. But, for myself, to be at Nauheim gave me a sense—what shall I say?—a sense almost of nakedness—the nakedness that one feels on the sea-shore or in any great open space.* I had no attachments, no accumulations. In one's own home it is as if little, innate sympathies draw one to particular chairs that seem to enfold one in an embrace, or take one along particular streets that seem friendly when others may be hostile. And, believe me, that feeling is a very important part of life. I know it well, that have been for so long a wanderer upon the face of public resorts. And one is too polished up. Heaven knows I was never an untidy man. But the feeling that I had when, whilst poor Florence was taking her morning bath, I stood upon the carefully swept steps of the Englischer Hof, looking at the carefully arranged trees in tubs upon the carefully arranged gravel whilst carefully arranged people walked past in carefully calculated gaiety, at the carefully calculated hour, the tall trees of the public gardens, going up to the right; the reddish stone of the baths—or were they white half-timber châlets? Upon my word I have forgotten, I who was there so often. That will give you the measure of how much I was in the landscape. I could find my way blindfolded to the hot rooms, to the douche rooms, to the fountain in the centre of the quadrangle where the rusty water gushes out. Yes, I could find my way blindfolded. I know the exact distances. From the Hotel Regina* you took one hundred and eighty-seven paces, then, turning sharp, lefthanded, four hundred and twenty took you straight down to the fountain. From the Englischer Hof, starting on the sidewalk, it was ninety-seven paces and the same four hundred and twenty, but turning lefthanded this time.*

And now you understand that, having nothing in the world to do—but nothing whatever! I fell into the habit of counting my footsteps. I would walk with Florence to the baths. And, of course, she entertained me with her conversation. It was, as I have said, wonderful what she could make conversation out of. She walked very lightly, and her hair was very nicely done, and she dressed beautifully and very expensively. Of course she had money of her own, but I shouldn't have minded. And yet you know I can't remember a single one of her dresses. Or I can remember just one, a very simple one of blue figured silk—a Chinese pattern—very full in the skirts and broadening out over the shoulders. And her hair was copper-coloured, and the heels of her shoes were exceedingly high, so that she tripped upon the points of her toes. And when she came to the door of the bathing place and, when it opened to receive her, she would look back at me with a little coquettish smile, so that her cheek appeared to be caressing her shoulder.

I seem to remember that, with that dress, she wore an immensely broad Leghorn hat*—like the Chapeau de Paille of Rubens,* only very white. The hat would be tied with a lightly knotted scarf of the same stuff as her dress. She knew how to give value to her blue eyes. And round her neck would be some simple pink, coral beads. And her complexion had a perfect clearness, a perfect smoothness . . .

Yes, that is how I most exactly remember her, in that dress, in that hat, looking over her shoulder at me so that the eyes flashed very blue—dark pebble blue . . .

And, what the devil! For whose benefit did she do it? For that of the bath attendant? of the passers-by? I don't know. Anyhow, it can't have been for me, for never, in all the years of her life, never on any possible occasion, or in any other place did she so smile to me, mockingly, invitingly. Ah, she was a riddle; but then, all other women are riddles. And it occurs to me that some way back I began a sentence that I have never finished . . . It was about the feeling that I had when I stood on the steps of my hotel every morning before starting out to fetch Florence back from the bath. Natty, precise, well-brushed, conscious of being rather small amongst the long English, the lank Americans, the rotund Germans, and the obese Russian Jewesses, I should stand there, tapping a cigarette on the outside of my case, surveying for a moment the world in the sunlight. But a day was to come when I was never to do it again alone. You can imagine, therefore, what the coming of the Ashburnhams meant to me.

I have forgotten the aspect of many things but I shall never forget the aspect of the dining-room of the Hotel Excelsior* on that evening—and on so many other evenings. Whole castles have vanished from my memory, whole cities that I have never visited again, but that white room, festooned with papier-maché fruits and flowers; the tall windows; the many tables; the black screen round the door with three golden cranes flying upward on each panel; the palm-tree in the centre of the room; the swish of the waiter's feet; the cold expensive elegance; the mien of the diners as they came in every evening—their air of earnestness as if they must go through a meal prescribed by the Kur authorities and their air of sobriety as if they must seek not by any means to enjoy their meals—those things I shall not easily forget. And then, one evening, in the twilight, I saw Edward Ashburnham lounge round the screen into the room. The head waiter, a man with a face all grey—in what subterranean nooks or corners do people cultivate those absolutely grey complexions?— went with the timorous patronage of these creatures towards him and held out a grey ear to be whispered into. It was generally a disagreeable ordeal for newcomers but Edward Ashburnham bore it like an Englishman and a gentleman. I could see his lips form a word of three syllables—remember I had nothing in the world to do but to notice these niceties—and immediately I knew that he must be Edward Ashburnham, Captain, Fourteenth Hussars,* of Branshaw House, Branshaw Teleragh. I knew it because every evening just before dinner, whilst I waited in the hall, I used, by the courtesy of Monsieur Schontz, the proprietor, to inspect the little police reports that each guest was expected to sign upon taking a room.

The head waiter piloted him immediately to a vacant table, three away from my own—the table that the Grenfalls of Falls River, N. J., had just vacated. It struck me that that was not a very nice table for the newcomers, since the sunlight, low though it was, shone straight down upon it, and the same idea seemed to come at the same moment into Captain Ashburnham's head. His face hitherto had, in the wonderful English fashion, expressed nothing whatever. Nothing. There was in it neither joy nor despair; neither hope nor fear; neither boredom nor satisfaction. He seemed to perceive no soul in that crowded room; he might have been walking in a jungle. I never came across such a perfect expression before and I never shall again. It was insolence and not insolence; it was modesty and not modesty. His hair was fair, extraordinarily, ordered in a wave, running from the left temple to the right; his face was a light brick-red, perfectly uniform in tint up to the roots of the hair itself; his yellow moustache was as stiff as a toothbrush and I verily believe that he had his black smoking jacket thickened a little over the shoulder-blades so as to give himself the air of the slightest possible stoop. It would be like him to do that; that was the sort of thing he thought about. Martingales, Chiffney bits,* boots; where you got the best soap, the best brandy, the name of the chap who rode a plater down the Khyber* cliffs; the spreading power of number three shot before a charge of number four powder . . . by heavens, I hardly ever heard him talk of anything else. Not in all the years that I knew him did I hear him talk of anything but these subjects. Oh, yes, once he told me that I could buy my special shade of blue ties cheaper from a firm in Burlington Arcade* than from my own people in New York. And I have bought my ties from that firm ever since. Otherwise I should not remember the name of the Burlington Arcade. I wonder what it looks like. I have never seen it. I imagine it to be two immense rows of pillars, like those of the Forum at Rome, with Edward Ashburnham striding down between them. But it probably isn't in the least like that. Once also he advised me to buy Caledonian Deferred,* since they were due to rise. And I did buy them and they did rise. But of how he got the knowledge I haven't the faintest idea. It seemed to drop out of the blue sky.

And that was absolutely all that I knew of him until a month ago—that and the profusion of his cases, all of pigskin and stamped with his initials, E. F. A. There were guncases, and collar cases, and shirt cases, and letter cases and cases each containing four bottles of medicine; and hat cases and helmet cases. It must have needed a whole herd of the Gadarene swine* to make up his outfit. And, if I ever penetrated into his private room it would be to see him standing, with his coat and waistcoat off and the immensely long line of his perfectly elegant trousers from waist to boot heel. And he would have a slightly reflective air and he would be just opening one kind of case and just closing another.

Good God, what did they all see in him; for I swear that was all there was of him, inside and out; though they said he was a good soldier. Yet, Leonora adored him with a passion that was like an agony, and hated him with an agony that was as bitter as the sea. How could he arouse anything like a sentiment, in anybody?

What did he even talk to them about—when they were under four eyes?—Ah, well, suddenly, as if by a flash of inspiration, I know. For all good soldiers are sentimentalists—all good soldiers of that type. Their profession, for one thing is full of the big words, courage, loyalty, honour, constancy. And I have given a wrong impression of Edward Ashburnham if I have made you think that literally never in the course of our nine years of intimacy did he discuss what he would have called "the graver things." Even before his final outburst to me, at times, very late at night, say, he has blurted out something that gave an insight into the sentimental view of the cosmos that was his. He would say how much the society of a good woman could do towards redeeming you, and he would say that constancy was the finest of the virtues. He said it very stiffly, of course, but still as if the statement admitted of no doubt.

Constancy! Isn't that the queer thought? And yet, I must add that poor dear Edward was a great reader—he would pass hours lost in novels of a sentimental type—novels in which typewriter girls married Marquises and governesses Earls. And in his books, as a rule, the course of true love ran as smooth as buttered honey. And he was fond of poetry, of a certain type—and he could even read a perfectly sad love story. I have seen his eyes filled with tears at reading of a hopeless parting. And he loved, with a sentimental yearning, all children, puppies, and the feeble generally . . .

So, you see, he would have plenty to gurgle about to a woman—with that and his sound common sense about martingales and his—still sentimental—experiences as a county magistrate; and with his intense, optimistic belief that the woman he was making love to at the moment was the one he was destined, at last, to be eternally constant to . . . Well, I fancy he could put up a pretty good deal of talk when there was no man around to make him feel shy. And I was quite astonished, during his final burst out to me—at the very end of things, when the poor girl was on her way to that fatal Brindisi* and he was trying to persuade himself and me that he had never really cared for her—I was quite astonished to observe how literary and how just his expressions were. He talked like quite a good book—a book not in the least cheaply sentimental. You see, I suppose he regarded me not so much as a man. I had to be regarded as a woman or a solicitor. Anyhow, it burst out of him on that horrible night. And then, next morning, he took me over to the Assizes* and I saw how, in a perfectly calm and business-like way he set to work to secure a verdict of not guilty for a poor girl, the daughter of one of his tenants who had been accused of murdering her baby. He spent two hundred pounds on her defence . . . Well, that was Edward Ashburnham.

I had forgotten about his eyes. They were as blue as the sides of a certain type of box of matches. When you looked at them carefully you saw that they were perfectly honest, perfectly straightforward, perfectly, perfectly stupid. But the brick pink of his complexion, running perfectly level to the brick pink of his inner eyelids, gave them a curious, sinister expression—like a mosaic of blue porcelain set in pink china. And that chap, coming into a room, snapped up the gaze of every woman in it, as dexterously as a conjurer pockets billiard balls. It was most amazing. You know the man on the stage who throws up sixteen balls at once and they all drop into pockets all over his person, on his shoulders, on his heels, on the inner side of his sleeves; and he stands perfectly still and does nothing. Well, it was like that. He had rather a rough, hoarse voice.

And, there he was, standing by the table. I was looking at him, with my back to the screen. And, suddenly, I saw two distinct expressions flicker across his immobile eyes. How the deuce did they do it, those unflinching blue eyes with the direct gaze? For the eyes themselves never moved, gazing over my shoulder towards the screen. And the gaze was perfectly level and perfectly direct and perfectly unchanging. I suppose that the lids really must have rounded themselves a little and perhaps the lips moved a little too, as if he should be saying:—"There you are, my dear." At any rate, the expression was that of pride, of satisfaction, of the possessor. I saw him once afterwards, for a moment, gaze upon the sunny fields of Branshaw and say:—"All this is my land!"

And then again, the gaze was perhaps more direct, harder if possible—hardy too. It was a measuring look; a challenging look. Once when we were at Wiesbaden* watching him play in a polo match against the Bonner Hussaren* I saw the same look come into his eyes, balancing the possibilities, looking over the ground. The German Captain, Count Baron Idigon von Lelöffel,* was right up by their goal posts, coming with the ball in an easy canter in that tricky German fashion. The rest of the field were just anywhere. It was only a scratch sort of affair. Ashburnham was quite close to the rails not five yards from us and I heard him saying to himself:—"Might just be done!" And he did it. Goodness! he swung that pony round with all its four legs spread out, like a cat dropping off a roof. . . .

Well, it was just that look that I noticed in his eyes:—"It might," I seem even now to hear him muttering to himself, "just be done."

I looked round over my shoulder and saw, tall, smiling brilliantly and buoyant—Leonora. And, little and fair, and as radiant as the track of sunlight along the sea—my wife.

That poor wretch! to think that he was at that moment in a perfect devil of a fix, and there he was, saying at the back of his mind:—"It might just be done." It was like a chap in the middle of the eruption of a volcano, saying that he might just manage to bolt into the tumult and set fire to a haystack. Madness? Predestination? Who the devil knows?

Mrs. Ashburnham exhibited at that moment more gaiety than I have ever since known her to show. There are certain classes of English people—the nicer ones when they have been to many spas, who seem to make a point of becoming much more than usually animated when they are introduced to my compatriots. I have noticed this often. Of course, they must first have accepted the Americans. But that once done, they seem to say to themselves: "Hallo, these women are so bright. We aren't going to be outdone in brightness." And for the time being they certainly aren't. But it wears off. So it was with Leonora—at least until she noticed me. She began, Leonora did—and perhaps it was that that gave me the idea of a touch of insolence in her character, for she never afterwards did any one single thing like it—she began by saying in quite a loud voice and from quite a distance:

"Don't stop over by that stuffy old table, Teddy. Come and sit by these nice people!"

And that was an extraordinary thing to say. Quite extraordinary. I couldn't for the life of me refer to total strangers as nice people. But, of course, she was taking a line of her own in which I at any rate—and no one else in the room, for she too had taken the trouble to read through the list of guests—counted any more than so many clean, bull terriers. And she sat down rather brilliantly at a vacant table, beside ours—one that was reserved for the Guggenheimers. And she just sat absolutely deaf to the remonstrances of the head waiter with his face like a grey ram's. That poor chap was doing his steadfast duty too. He knew that the Guggenheimers of Chicago, after they had stayed there a month and had worried the poor life out of him, would give him two dollars fifty and grumble at the tipping system. And he knew that Teddy Ashburnham and his wife would give him no trouble whatever except what the smiles of Leonora might cause in his apparently unimpressionable bosom—though you never can tell what may go on behind even a not quite spotless plastron!*—And every week Edward Ashburnham would give him a solid, sound, golden English sovereign. Yet this stout fellow was intent on saving that table for the Guggenheimers of Chicago. It ended in Florence saying:

"Why shouldn't we all eat out of the same trough?—that's a nasty New York saying. But I'm sure we're all nice quiet people and there can be four seats at our table. It's round."

Then came, as it were, an appreciative gurgle from the Captain and I was perfectly aware of a slight hesitation—a quick sharp motion in Mrs. Ashburnham, as if her horse had checked. But she put it at the fence all right, rising from the seat she had taken and sitting down opposite me, as it were, all in one motion.

I never thought that Leonora looked her best in evening dress. She seemed to get it too clearly cut, there was no ruffling. She always affected black and her shoulders were too classical. She seemed to stand out of her corsage* as a white marble bust might out of a black Wedgwood vase. I don't know.

I loved Leonora always and, to-day, I would very cheerfully lay down my life, what is left of it, in her service. But I am sure I never had the beginnings of a trace of what is called the sex instinct towards her. And I suppose—no I am certain that she never had it towards me. As far as I am concerned I think it was those white shoulders that did it. I seemed to feel when I looked at them that, if ever I should press my lips upon them that they would be slightly cold—not icily, not without a touch of human heat, but, as they say of baths, with the chill off. I seemed to feel chilled at the end of my lips when I looked at her . . .

No, Leonora always appeared to me at her best in a blue tailor-made.* Then her glorious hair wasn't deadened by her white shoulders. Certain women's lines guide your eyes to their necks, their eyelashes, their lips, their breasts. But Leonora's seemed to conduct your gaze always to her wrist. And the wrist was at its best in a black or a dog-skin glove and there was always a gold circlet with a little chain supporting a very small golden key to a dispatch box. Perhaps it was that in which she locked up her heart and her feelings.

Anyhow, she sat down opposite me and then, for the first time, she paid any attention to my existence. She gave me, suddenly, yet deliberately, one long stare. Her eyes too were blue and dark and the eyelids were so arched that they gave you the whole round of the irises. And it was a most remarkable, a most moving glance, as if for a moment a lighthouse had looked at me. I seemed to perceive the swift questions chasing each other through the brain that was behind them. I seemed to hear the brain ask and the eyes answer with all the simpleness of a woman who was a good hand at taking in qualities of a horse—as indeed she was. "Stands well; has plenty of room for his oats behind the girth. Not so much in the way of shoulders," and so on. And so her eyes asked: "Is this man trustworthy in money matters; is he likely to try to play the lover; is he likely to let his women be troublesome? Is he, above all, likely to babble about my affairs?"

And, suddenly, into those cold, slightly defiant, almost defensive china blue orbs, there came a warmth, a tenderness, a friendly recognition . . . oh, it was very charming and very touching—and quite mortifying. It was the look of a mother to her son, of a sister to her brother. It implied trust; it implied the want of any necessity for barriers. By God, she looked at me as if I were an invalid—as any kind woman may look at a poor chap in a bath chair. And, yes, from that day forward she always treated me and not Florence as if I were the invalid. Why, she would run after me with a rug upon chilly days. I suppose, therefore, that her eyes had made a favourable answer. Or, perhaps, it wasn't a favourable answer. And then Florence said: "And so the whole round table* is begun." Again Edward Ashburnham gurgled slightly in his throat; but Leonora shivered a little, as if a goose had walked over her grave. And I was passing her the nickel-silver basket of rolls. Avanti! . . .*

IV

So began those nine years of uninterrupted tranquillity. They were characterised by an extraordinary want of any communicativeness on the part of the Ashburnhams to which, we on our part replied by leaving out quite as extraordinarily, and nearly as completely, the personal note. Indeed, you may take it that what characterised our relationship was an atmosphere of taking everything for granted. The given proposition was, that we were all "good people." We took for granted that we all liked beef underdone but not too underdone; that both men preferred a good liqueur brandy after lunch; that both women drank a very light Rhine wine qualified with Fachingen water*—that sort of thing. It was also taken for granted that we were both sufficiently well off to afford anything that we could reasonably want in the way of amusements fitting to our station—that we could take motor cars and carriages by the day; that we could give each other dinners and dine our friends and we could indulge if we liked in economy. Thus, Florence was in the habit of having the *Daily Telegraph* sent to her every day from London. She was always an Anglo-maniac, was Florence; the Paris edition of the New York *Herald* was always good enough for me. But when we discovered that the Ashburnhams' copy of the London paper followed them from England, Leonora and Florence decided between them to suppress one subscription one year and the other the next. Similarly it was the habit of the Grand Duke* of Nassau Schwerin, who came yearly to the baths, to dine once with about eighteen families of regular Kur guests. In return he would give a dinner of all the eighteen at once. And, since these dinners were rather expensive (you had to take the Grand Duke and a good many of his suite and any members of the diplomatic bodies that might be there)—Florence and Leonora, putting their heads together, didn't see why we shouldn't give the Grand Duke his dinner together. And so we did. I don't suppose the Serenity minded that economy, or even noticed it. At any rate, our joint dinner to the Royal Personage gradually assumed the aspect of a yearly function. Indeed, it grew larger and larger, until it became a sort of closing function for the season, at any rate as far as we were concerned.

I don't in the least mean to say that we were the sort of persons who aspired to mix "with royalty." We didn't; we hadn't any claims; we were just "good people." But the Grand Duke was a pleasant, affable sort of royalty, like the late King Edward VII, and it was pleasant to hear him talk about the races and, very occasionally, as a bonne bouche,* about his nephew, the Emperor; or to have him pause for a moment in his walk to ask after the progress of our cures or to be benignantly interested in the amount of money we had put on Lelöffel's hunter for the Frankfurt Welter Stakes.

But upon my word, I don't know how we put in our time. How does one put in one's time? How is it possible to have achieved nine years and to have nothing whatever to show for it? Nothing whatever, you understand. Not so much as a bone penholder, carved to resemble a chessman and with a hole in the top through which you could see four views of Nauheim. And, as for experience, as for knowledge of one's fellow beings—nothing either. Upon my word, I couldn't tell you offhand whether the lady who sold the so expensive violets at the bottom of the road that leads to the station, was cheating me or no; I can't say whether the porter who carried our traps* across the station at Leghorn was a thief or no when he said that the regular tariff was a lire* a parcel. The instances of honesty that one comes across in this world are just as amazing as the instances of dishonesty. After forty-five years of mixing with one's kind, one ought to have acquired the habit of being able to know something about one's fellow beings. But one doesn't.

I think the modern civilized habit—the modern English habit of taking every one for granted is a good deal to blame for this. I have observed this matter long enough to know the queer, subtle thing that it is; to know how the faculty, for what it is worth, never lets you down.

Mind, I am not saying that this is not the most desirable type of life in the world; that it is not an almost unreasonably high standard. For it is really nauseating, when you detest it, to have to eat every day several slices of thin, tepid, pink india rubber, and it is disagreeable to have to drink brandy when you would prefer to be cheered up by warm, sweet Kummel.* And it is nasty to have to take a cold bath in the morning when what you want is really a hot one at night. And it stirs a little of the faith of your fathers that is deep down within you to have to have it taken for granted that you are an Episcopalian when really you are an old-fashioned Philadelphia Quaker.

But these things have to be done; it is the cock that the whole of this society owes to Æsculapius.*

And the odd, queer thing is that the whole collection of rules applies to anybody—to the anybodies that you meet in hotels, in railway trains, to a less degree, perhaps, in steamers, but even, in the end, upon steamers. You meet a man or a woman and, from tiny and intimate sounds, from the slightest of movements, you know at once whether you are concerned with good people or with those who won't do. You know, this is to say, whether they will go rigidly through with the whole programme from the underdone beef to the Anglicanism. It won't matter whether they be short or tall; whether the voice squeak like a marionette or rumble like a town bull's; it won't matter whether they are Germans, Austrians, French, Spanish, or even Brazilians—they will be the Germans or Brazilians who take a cold bath every morning and who move, roughly speaking, in diplomatic circles.

But the inconvenient—well, hang it all, I will say it—the damnable nuisance of the whole thing is, that with all the taking for granted, you never really get an inch deeper than the things I have catalogued.

I can give you a rather extraordinary instance of this. I can't remember whether it was in our first year—the first year of us four at Nauheim, because, of course, it would have been the fourth year of Florence and myself—but it must have been in the first or second year. And that gives the measure at once of the extraordinariness of our discussion and of the swiftness with which intimacy had grown up between us. On the one hand we seemed to start out on the expedition so naturally and with so little preparation, that it was as if we must have made many such excursions before; and our intimacy seemed so deep. . . .

Yet the place to which we went was obviously one to which Florence at least would have wanted to take us quite early, so that you would almost think we should have gone there together at the beginning of our intimacy. Florence was singularly expert as a guide to archæological exceptions* and there was nothing she liked so much as taking people round ruins and showing you the window from which some one looked down upon the murder of some one else. She only did it once; but she did it quite magnificently. She could find her way, with the sole help of Baedeker,* as easily about any old

monument as she could about any American city where the blocks
are all square and the streets all numbered, so that you can go perfectly easily from Twenty-fourth to Thirtieth.

Now it happens that fifty minutes away from Nauheim, by a good
train, is the ancient city of M——,* upon a great pinnacle of basalt,
girt with a triple road running sideways up its shoulder like a scarf.
And at the top there is a castle—not a square castle like Windsor—
but a castle all slate gables and high peaks with gilt weathercocks
flashing bravely—the castle of St. Elizabeth of Hungary.* It has the
disadvantage of being in Prussia;* and it is always disagreeable to go
into that country; but it is very old and there are many double-spired
churches and it stands up like a pyramid out of the green valley of the
Lahn.* I don't suppose the Ashburnhams wanted especially to go
there and I didn't especially want to go there myself. But, you understand, there was no objection. It was part of the cure to make an
excursion three or four times a week. So that we were all quite unani-
mous in being grateful to Florence for providing the motive power.
Florence, of course, had a motive of her own. She was at that time
engaged in educating Captain Ashburnham—oh, of course, quite
pour le bon motif!* She used to say to Leonora: "I simply can't
understand how you can let him live by your side and be so ignorant!" Leonora herself always struck me as being remarkably well
educated. At any rate, she knew beforehand all that Florence had to
tell her. Perhaps she got it up out of Baedeker before Florence was up
in the morning. I don't mean to say that you would ever have known
that Leonora knew anything, but if Florence started to tell us how
Ludwig the Courageous* wanted to have three wives at once—in
which he differed from Henry VIII, who wanted them one after the
other, and this caused a good deal of trouble—if Florence started to
tell us this, Leonora would just nod her head in a way that quite
pleasantly rattled my poor wife.

She used to exclaim: "Well, if you knew it, why haven't you told it
all already to Captain Ashburnham? I'm sure he finds it interesting!"
And Leonora would look reflectively at her husband and say: "I have
an idea that it might injure his hand—the hand, you know, used in
connection with horses' mouths . . ." And poor Ashburnham would
blush and mutter and would say: "That's all right. Don't you bother
about me."

I fancy his wife's irony did quite alarm poor Teddy; because one evening he asked me seriously in the smoking-room if I thought that having too much in one's head would really interfere with one's quickness in polo. It struck him, he said, that brainy Johnnies generally were rather muffs* when they got on to four legs. I reassured him as best I could. I told him that he wasn't likely to take in enough to upset his balance. At that time the Captain was quite evidently enjoying being educated by Florence. She used to do it about three or four times a week under the approving eyes of Leonora and myself. It wasn't, you understand, systematic. It came in bursts. It was Florence clearing up one of the dark places of the earth,* leaving the world a little lighter than she had found it. She would tell him the story of Hamlet; explain the form of a symphony, humming the first and second subjects to him, and so on; she would explain to him the difference between Armenians and Erastians;* or she would give him a short lecture on the early history of the United States. And it was done in a way well calculated to arrest a young attention. Did you ever read Mrs. Markham?* Well, it was like that . . .

But our excursion to M—— was a much larger, a much more full dress affair. You see, in the archives of the Schloss* in that city there was a document which Florence thought would finally give her the chance to educate the whole lot of us together. It really worried poor Florence that she couldn't, in matters of culture, ever get the better of Leonora. I don't know what Leonora knew or what she didn't know, but certainly she was always there whenever Florence brought out any information. And she gave, somehow, the impression of really knowing what poor Florence gave the impression of having only picked up. I can't exactly define it. It was almost something physical. Have you ever seen a retriever dashing in play after a greyhound? You see the two running over a green field, almost side by side, and suddenly the retriever makes a friendly snap at the other. And the greyhound simply isn't there. You haven't observed it quicken its speed or strain a limb; but there it is, just two yards in front of the retriever's outstretched muzzle. So it was with Florence and Leonora in matters of culture.

But on this occasion I knew that something was up. I found Florence some days before, reading books like Ranke's *History of the Popes*, Symonds' *Renaissance*, Motley's *Rise of the Dutch Republic*, and Luther's *Table Talk.**

I must say that, until the astonishment came, I got nothing but pleasure out of the little expedition. I like catching the two-forty; I like the slow, smooth roll of the great big trains—and they are the best trains in the world! I like being drawn through the green country and looking at it through the clear glass of the great windows. Though, of course, the country isn't really green. The sun shines, the earth is blood red and purple and red and green and red. And the oxen in the ploughlands are bright varnished brown and black and blackish purple; and the peasants are dressed in the black and white of magpies; and there are great flocks of magpies too. Or the peasants' dresses in another field where there are little mounds of hay that will be grey-green on the sunny side and purple in the shadows*—the peasants' dresses are vermilion with emerald green ribbons and purple skirts and white shirts and black velvet stomachers.* Still, the impression is that you are drawn through brilliant green meadows that run away on each side to the dark purple fir-woods; the basalt pinnacles; the immense forests. And there is meadow-sweet* at the edge of the streams, and cattle. Why, I remember on that afternoon I saw a brown cow hitch its horns under the stomach of a black and white animal and the black and white one was thrown right into the middle of a narrow stream. I burst out laughing. But Florence was imparting information so hard and Leonora was listening so intently that no one noticed me. As for me, I was pleased to be off duty; I was pleased to think that Florence for the moment was indubitably out of mischief—because she was talking about Ludwig the Courageous (I think it was Ludwig the Courageous but I am not an historian) about Ludwig the Courageous of Hessen* who wanted to have three wives at once and patronised Luther—something like that!—I was so relieved to be off duty, because she couldn't possibly be doing anything to excite herself or set her poor heart a-fluttering—that the incident of the cow was a real joy to me. I chuckled over it from time to time for the whole rest of the day. Because it does look very funny, you know, to see a black and white cow land on its back in the middle of a stream. It is so just exactly what one doesn't expect of a cow.

I suppose I ought to have pitied the poor animal; but I just didn't. I was out for enjoyment. And I just enjoyed myself. It is so pleasant to be drawn along in front of the spectacular towns with the peaked castles and the many double spires. In the sunlight gleams come from the city—gleams from the glass of windows; from the gilt signs of apothecaries; from the ensigns of the student corps* high up in the mountains; from the helmets of the funny little soldiers moving their stiff little legs in white linen trousers. And it was pleasant to get out in the great big spectacular Prussian station with the hammered bronze ornaments and the paintings of peasants and flowers and cows; and to hear Florence bargain energetically with the driver of an ancient droschka* drawn by two lean horses. Of course, I spoke German much more correctly than Florence, though I never could rid myself quite of the accent of the Pennsylvania Duitsch* of my childhood. Anyhow, we were drawn in a sort of triumph, for five marks without any trinkgeld,* right up to the castle. And we were taken through the museum and saw the firebacks,* the old glass, the old swords and the antique contraptions. And we went up winding corkscrew staircases and through the Rittersaal,* the great painted hall where the Reformer* and his friends met for the first time under the protection of the gentleman that had three wives at once and formed an alliance with the gentleman that had six wives, one after the other (I'm not really interested in these facts but they have a bearing on my story). And we went through chapels, and music rooms, right up immensely high in the air to a large old chamber, full of presses,* with heavily-shuttered windows all round. And Florence became positively electric. She told the tired, bored custodian what shutters to open; so that the bright sunlight streamed in palpable shafts into the dim old chamber. She explained that this was Luther's bedroom and that just where the sunlight fell had stood his bed. As a matter of fact, I believe that she was wrong* and that Luther only stopped, as it were, for lunch, in order to evade pursuit. But, no doubt, it would have been his bedroom if he could have been persuaded to stop the night. And then, in spite of the protest of the custodian, she threw open another shutter and came tripping back to a large glass case.

"And there," she exclaimed with an accent of gaiety, of triumph, and of audacity. She was pointing at a piece of paper, like the half-sheet of a letter with some faint pencil scrawls that might have been a jotting of the amounts we were spending during the day. And I was extremely happy at her gaiety, in her triumph, in her audacity. Captain Ashburnham had his hands upon the glass case. "There it is—the Protest." And then, as we all properly stage-managed our bewilderment, she continued: "Don't you know that is why we were all called Protestants? That is the pencil draft of the Protest* they drew up. You can see the signatures of Martin Luther, and Martin Bucer, and Zwingli,* and Ludwig the Courageous . . ."

I may have got some of the names wrong, but I know that Luther and Bucer were there. And her animation continued and I was glad. She was better and she was out of mischief. She continued, looking up into Captain Ashburnham's eyes: "It's because of that piece of paper that you're honest, sober, industrious, provident, and clean-lived. If it weren't for that piece of paper you'd be like the Irish or the Italians or the Poles, but particularly the Irish . . ."

And she laid one finger upon Captain Ashburnham's wrist.

I was aware of something treacherous, something frightful, something evil in the day. I can't define it and can't find a simile for it. It wasn't as if a snake had looked out of a hole. No, it was as if my heart had missed a beat. It was as if we were going to run and cry out; all four of us in separate directions, averting our heads. In Ashburnham's face I know that there was absolute panic. I was horribly frightened and then I discovered that the pain in my left wrist was caused by Leonora's clutching it:

"I can't stand this," she said with a most extraordinary passion; "I must get out of this."

I was horribly frightened. It came to me for a moment, though I hadn't time to think it, that she must be a madly jealous woman—jealous of Florence and Captain Ashburnham, of all people in the world! And it was a panic in which we fled! We went right down the winding stairs, across the immense Rittersaal to a little terrace that overlooks the Lahn, the broad valley and the immense plain into which it opens out.

"Don't you see?" she said, "don't you see what's going on?" The panic again stopped my heart. I muttered, I stuttered—I don't know how I got the words out:

"No! What's the matter? Whatever's the matter?"

She looked me straight in the eyes; and for a moment I had the feeling that those two blue discs were immense, were overwhelming, were like a wall of blue that shut me off from the rest of the world. I know it sounds absurd; but that is what it did feel like.

"Don't you see," she said, with a really horrible bitterness, with a really horrible lamentation in her voice, "Don't you see that that's the cause of the whole miserable affair; of the whole sorrow of the world? And of the eternal damnation of you and me and them . . ."

I don't remember how she went on; I was too frightened; I was too amazed. I think I was thinking of running to fetch assistance—a doctor, perhaps, or Captain Ashburnham. Or possibly she needed Florence's tender care, though, of course, it would have been very bad for Florence's heart. But I know that when I came out of it she was saying: "Oh, where are all the bright, happy, innocent beings in the world? Where's happiness? One reads of it in books!"

She ran her hand with a singular clawing motion upwards over her forehead. Her eyes were enormously distended; her face was exactly that of a person looking into the pit of hell and seeing horrors there. And then suddenly she stopped. She was, most amazingly, just Mrs. Ashburnham again. Her face was perfectly clear, sharp and defined; her hair was glorious in its golden coils. Her nostrils twitched with a sort of contempt. She appeared to look with interest at a gypsy caravan that was coming over a little bridge far below us.

"Don't you know," she said, in her clear hard voice, "don't you know that I'm an Irish Catholic?"

V

THOSE words gave me the greatest relief that I have ever had in my life. They told me, I think, almost more than I have ever gathered at any one moment—about myself. I don't think that before that day I had ever wanted anything very much except Florence. I have, of course, had appetites, impatiences . . . Why, sometimes at a table d'hôte, when there would be, say, caviare handed round, I have been absolutely full of impatience for fear that when the dish came to me there should not be a satisfying portion left over by the other guests. I have been exceedingly impatient at missing trains. The Belgian State Railway has a trick of letting the French trains miss their connections at Brussels. That has always infuriated me. I have written about it letters to the *Times* that the *Times* never printed; those that I wrote to the Paris edition of the New York *Herald* were always printed, but they never seemed to satisfy me when I saw them. Well, that was a sort of frenzy with me.

It was a frenzy that now I can hardly realise. I can understand it intellectually. You see, in those days I was interested in people with "hearts." There was Florence, there was Edward Ashburnham—or, perhaps, it was Leonora that I was more interested in. I don't mean in the way of love. But, you see, we were both of the same profession—at any rate as I saw it. And the profession was that of keeping heart patients alive.

You have no idea how engrossing such a profession may become. Just as the blacksmith says: "By hammer and hand all Art doth stand,"* just as the baker thinks that all the solar system revolves around his morning delivery of rolls, as the postmaster general believes that he alone is the preserver of society—and surely, surely, these delusions are necessary to keep us going—so did I and, as I believed, Leonora, imagine that the whole world ought to be arranged so as to ensure the keeping alive of heart patients. You have no idea how engrossing such a profession may become—how imbecile, in view of that engrossment, appear the ways of princes, of republics, of municipalities. A rough bit of road beneath the motor tyres, a couple of succeeding "thank'ee-marms"* with their quick jolts would be enough to set me grumbling to Leonora against the Prince or the

Grand Duke or the Free City* through whose territory we might be passing. I would grumble like a stockbroker whose conversations over the telephone are incommoded by the ringing of bells from a city church. I would talk about mediæval survivals, about the taxes being surely high enough. The point, by the way, about the missing of the connections of the Calais boat trains at Brussels was that the shortest possible sea journey is frequently of great importance to sufferers from the heart. Now, on the Continent, there are two special heart cure places, Nauheim and Spa,* and to reach both of these baths from England if in order to ensure a short sea passage, you come by Calais—you have to make the connection at Brussels. And the Belgian train never waits by so much the shade of a second for the one coming from Calais or from Paris. And even if the French trains are just on time, you have to run—imagine a heart patient running!— along the unfamiliar ways of the Brussels station and to scramble up the high steps of the moving train. Or, if you miss connection, you have to wait five or six hours. . . . I used to keep awake whole nights cursing that abuse.

My wife used to run—she never, in whatever else she may have misled me, tried to give me the impression that she was not a gallant soul. But, once in the German Express, she would lean back, with one hand to her side and her eyes closed. Well, she was a good actress. And I would be in hell. In hell, I tell you. For in Florence I had at once a wife and an unattained mistress—that is what it comes to— and in the retaining of her in this world I had my occupation, my career, my ambition. It is not often that these things are united in one body. Leonora was a good actress too. By Jove she was good! I tell you, she would listen to me by the hour, evolving my plans for a shock-proof world. It is true that, at times, I used to notice about her an air of inattention as if she were listening, a mother, to the child at her knee, or as if, precisely, I were myself the patient.

You understand that there was nothing the matter with Edward Ashburnham's heart—that he had thrown up his commission and had left India and come half the world over in order to follow a woman who had really had a "heart" to Nauheim. That was the sort of sentimental ass he was. For, you understand, too, that they really needed to live in India, to economise, to let the house at Branshaw Teleragh.

Of course, at that date, I had never heard of the Kilsyte case.

Ashburnham had, you know, kissed a servant girl in a railway train, and it was only the grace of God, the prompt functioning of the communication cord and the ready sympathy of what I believe you call the Hampshire Bench, that kept the poor devil out of Winchester Gaol for years and years. I never heard of that case until the final stages of Leonora's revelations . . .

But just think of that poor wretch . . . I, who have surely the right, beg you to think of that poor wretch. Is it possible that such a luckless devil should be so tormented by blind and inscrutable destiny? For there is no other way to think of it. None. I have the right to say it, since for years he was my wife's lover, since he killed her, since he broke up all the pleasantnesses that there were in my life. There is no priest that has the right to tell me that I must not ask pity for him, from you, silent listener beyond the hearth-stone, from the world, or from the God who created in him those desires, those madnesses . . .

Of course, I should not hear of the Kilsyte case. I knew none of their friends; they were for me just good people—fortunate people with broad and sunny acres in a southern county. Just good people! By heavens, I sometimes think that it would have been better for him, poor dear, if the case had been such a one that I must needs have heard of it—such a one as maids and couriers and other Kur guests whisper about for years after, until gradually it dies away in the pity that there is knocking about here and there in the world. Supposing he had spent his seven years in Winchester Gaol or whatever it is that inscrutable and blind justice allots to you for following your natural but ill-timed inclinations—there would have arrived a stage when nodding gossips on the Kursaal* terrace would have said, "Poor fellow," thinking of his ruined career. He would have been the fine soldier with his back now bent . . . Better for him, poor devil, if his back had been prematurely bent.

Why, it would have been a thousand times better. . . . For, of course, the Kilsyte case, which came at the very beginning of his finding Leonora cold and unsympathetic, gave him a nasty jar. He left servants alone after that.

It turned him, naturally, all the more loose amongst women of his own class. Why, Leonora told me that Mrs. Maidan—the woman he followed from Burma* to Nauheim—assured her he awakened her attention by swearing that when he kissed the servant in the train he was driven to it. I daresay he was driven to it, by the mad passion to find an ultimately satisfying woman. I daresay he was sincere enough. Heaven help me, I daresay he was sincere enough in his love for Mrs. Maidan. She was a nice little thing, a dear little dark woman with long lashes, of whom Florence grew quite fond. She had a lisp and a happy smile. We saw plenty of her for the first month of our acquaintance, then she died, quite quietly—of heart trouble.

But you know, poor little Mrs. Maidan—she was so gentle, so young. She cannot have been more than twenty-three and she had a boy husband out in Chitral* not more than twenty-four, I believe. Such young things ought to have been left alone. Of course Ashburnham could not leave her alone. I do not believe that he could. Why, even I, at this distance of time am aware that I am a little in love with her memory. I can't help smiling when I think suddenly of her—as you might at the thought of something wrapped carefully away in lavender, in some drawer, in some old house that you have long left. She was so—so submissive. Why, even to me she had the air of being submissive—to me that not the youngest child will ever pay heed to. Yes, this is the saddest story . . .

No, I cannot help wishing that Florence had left her alone—with her playing with adultery, I suppose it was; though she was such a child that one has the impression that she would hardly have known how to spell such a word. No, it was just submissiveness—to the importunities, to the tempestuous forces that pushed that miserable fellow on to ruin. And I do not suppose that Florence really made much difference. If it had not been for her that Ashburnham left his allegiance for Mrs. Maidan, then it would have been some other woman. But still, I do not know. Perhaps the poor young thing would have died—she was bound to die, anyhow, quite soon—but she would have died without having to soak her noonday pillow with tears whilst Florence, below the window talked to Captain Ashburnham about the Constitution of the United States . . . Yes, it would have left a better taste in the mouth if Florence had let her die in peace . . .

Leonora behaved better in a sense. She just boxed Mrs. Maidan's ears—yes, she hit her, in an uncontrollable access* of rage, a hard blow on the side of the cheek, in the corridor of the hotel, outside Edward's room. It was that, you know, that accounted for the sudden, odd intimacy that sprang up between Florence and Mrs. Ashburnham.

Because it was, of course, an odd intimacy. If you look at it from the outside nothing could have been more unlikely than that Leonora, who is the proudest creature on God's earth, would have struck up an acquaintanceship with two casual Yankees whom she could not really have regarded as being much more than a carpet beneath her feet. You may ask what she had to be proud of. Well, she was a Powys married to an Ashburnham—I suppose that gave her the right to despise casual Americans as long as she did it unostentatiously. I don't know what anyone has to be proud of. She might have taken pride in her patience, in her keeping her husband out of the bank-ruptcy court. Perhaps she did.

At any rate that was how Florence got to know her. She came round a screen at the corner of the hotel corridor and found Leonora with the gold key that hung from her wrist caught in Mrs. Maidan's hair just before dinner. There was not a single word spoken. Little Mrs. Maidan was very pale, with a red mark down her left cheek and the key would not come out of her black hair. It was Florence who had to disentangle it, for Leonora was in such a state that she could not have brought herself to touch Mrs. Maidan without growing sick.

And there was not a word spoken. You see, under those four eyes—her own and Mrs. Maidan's—Leonora could just let herself go as far as to box Mrs. Maidan's ears. But the moment a stranger came along she pulled herself wonderfully up. She was at first silent and then, the moment the key was disengaged by Florence she was in a state to say: "So awkward of me . . . I was just trying to put the comb straight in Mrs. Maidan's hair . . ."

Mrs Maidan, however, was not a Powys married to an Ashburnham; she was a poor little O'Flaherty whose husband was a boy of country parsonage origin. So there was no mistaking the sob she let go as she went desolately away along the corridor. But Leonora was still going to play up. She opened the door of Ashburnham's room quite osten-tatiously, so that Florence should hear her address Edward in terms of intimacy and liking. "Edward," she called. But there was no Edward there.

You understand that there was no Edward there. It was then, for the only time of her career that Leonora really compromised her-self—She exclaimed . . . "How frightful! . . . Poor little Maisie! . . ."

She caught herself up at that, but of course it was too late. It was a queer sort of affair . . .

I want to do Leonora every justice. I love her very dearly for one thing and in this matter, which was certainly the ruin of my small household cockle-shell,* she certainly tripped up. I do not believe— and Leonora herself does not believe that poor little Maisie Maidan* was ever Edward's mistress. Her heart was really so bad that she would have succumbed to anything like an impassioned embrace. That is the plain English of it, and I suppose plain English is best. She was really what the other two, for reasons of their own, just pretended to be. Queer, isn't it? Like one of those sinister jokes that Providence plays upon one. Add to this that I do not suppose that Leonora would much have minded, at any other moment, if Mrs. Maidan had been her husband's mistress. It might have been a relief from Edward's sentimental gurglings over the lady and from the lady's submissive acceptance of those sounds. No, she would not have minded.

But, in boxing Mrs. Maidan's ears Leonora was just striking the face of an intolerable universe. For, that afternoon she had had a frightfully painful scene with Edward.

As far as his letters went, she claimed the right to open them when she chose. She arrogated to herself that right because Edward's affairs were in such a frightful state and he lied so about them that she claimed the privilege of having his secrets at her disposal. There was not, indeed, any other way, for the poor fool was too ashamed of his lapses ever to make a clean breast of anything. She had to drag these things out of him.

It must have been a pretty elevating job for her. But that afternoon, Edward being on his bed for the hour and a half prescribed by the Kur authorities, she had opened a letter that she took to come from a Colonel Hervey. They were going to stay with him in Linlithgowshire* for the month of September and she did not know whether the date fixed would be the eleventh or the eighteenth. The address on this letter was, in handwriting, as like Colonel Hervey's as one blade of corn is like another. So she had at the moment no idea of spying on him.

But she certainly was. For she discovered that Edward Ashburnham was paying a blackmailer of whom she had never heard something like three hundred pounds a year . . . It was a devil of a blow; it was like death; for she imagined that by that time she had really got to the bottom of her husband's liabilities. You see, they were pretty heavy.

What had really smashed them up had been a perfectly commonplace affair at Monte Carlo—an affair with a cosmopolitan harpy who passed for the mistress of a Russian Grand Duke. She exacted a twenty thousand pound pearl tiara from him as the price of her favours for a week or so. It would have pipped* him a good deal to have found so much, and he was not in the ordinary way a gambler. He might, indeed, just have found the twenty thousand and the not slight charges of a week at an hotel with the fair creature. He must have been worth at that date five hundred thousand dollars* and a little over.

Well, he must needs go to the tables and lose forty thousand pounds* . . . Forty thousand solid pounds, borrowed from sharks! And even after that he must—it was an imperative passion—enjoy the favours of the lady. He got them, of course, when it was a matter of solid bargaining, for far less than twenty thousand, as he might, no doubt have done from the first. I daresay ten thousand dollars covered the bill.

Anyhow, there was a pretty solid hole in a fortune of a hundred thousand pounds or so. And Leonora had to fix things up; he would have run from money lender to money lender. And that was quite in the early days of her discovery of his infidelities—if you like to call them infidelities. And she discovered that one from public sources. God knows what would have happened if she had not discovered it from public sources. I suppose he would have concealed it from her until they were penniless. But she was able, by the grace of God, to get hold of the actual lenders of the money, to learn the exact sums that were needed. And she went off to England.

Yes, she went right off to England to her attorney and his while he was still in the arms of his Circe—at Antibes,* to which place they had retired. He got sick of the lady quite quickly, but not before Leonora had had such lessons in the art of business from her attorney that she had her plan as clearly drawn up as was ever that of General Trochu* for keeping the Prussians out of Paris in 1870. It was about as effectual at first, or it seemed so.

That would have been, you know, in 1895, about nine years before the date of which I am talking—the date of Florence's getting her hold over Leonora; for that was what it amounted to . . . Well, Mrs. Ashburnham had simply forced Edward to settle all his property upon her. She could force him to do anything; in his clumsy, good-natured, inarticulate way he was as frightened of her as of the devil. And he admired her enormously, and he was as fond of her as any man could be of any woman. She took advantage of it to treat him as if he had been a person whose estates are being managed by the Court of Bankruptcy. I suppose it was the best thing for him.

Anyhow, she had no end of a job for the first three years or so. Unexpected liabilities kept on cropping up—and that afflicted fool did not make it any easier. You see, along with the passion of the chase went a frame of mind that made him be extraordinarily ashamed of himself. You may not believe it, but he really had such a sort of respect for the chastity of Leonora's imagination that he hated—he was positively revolted at the thought that she should know that the sort of thing that he did existed in the world. So he would stick out in an agitated way against the accusation of ever having done anything. He wanted to preserve the virginity of his wife's thoughts. He told me that himself during the long walks we had at the last—while the girl was on the way to Brindisi.

So, of course, for those three years or so, Leonora had many agitations. And it was then that they really quarrelled.

Yes, they quarrelled bitterly. That seems rather extravagant. You might have thought that Leonora would be just calmly loathing and he lachrymosely contrite. But that was not it a bit . . . Along with Edward's passions and his shame for them went the violent conviction of the duties of his station—a conviction that was quite unreasonably expensive. I trust I have not, in talking of his liabilities, given the impression that poor Edward was a promiscuous libertine. He was not; he was a sentimentalist. The servant girl in the Kilsyte case had been pretty, but mournful of appearance. I think that, when he had kissed her, he had desired rather to comfort her. And, if she had succumbed to his blandishments I daresay he would have set her up in a little house in Portsmouth or Winchester and would have been faithful to her for four or five years. He was quite capable of that.

No, the only two of his affairs of the heart that cost him money were that of the Grand Duke's mistress and that which was the subject of the blackmailing letter that Leonora opened. That had been a quite passionate affair with quite a nice woman. It had succeeded the one with the Grand Ducal Lady. The lady was the wife of a brother officer and Leonora had known all about the passion, which had been quite a real passion and had lasted for several years. You see, poor

Edward's passions were quite logical in their progression upwards. They began with a servant, went on to a courtesan and then to a quite nice woman, very unsuitably mated. For she had a quite nasty husband who, by means of letters and things, went on blackmailing poor Edward to the tune of three or four hundred a year—with threats of the divorce court. And after this lady came Maisie Maidan, and after poor Maisie only one more affair and then—the real passion of his life. His marriage with Leonora had been arranged by his parents and, though he always admired her immensely, he had hardly ever pretended to be much more than tender to her, though he desperately needed her moral support, too . . .

But his really trying liabilities were mostly in the nature of generosities proper to his station. He was, according to Leonora, always remitting his tenants' rents and giving the tenants to understand that the reduction would be permanent; he was always redeeming drunkards who came before his magisterial bench; he was always trying to put prostitutes into respectable places—and he was a perfect maniac about children. I don't know how many ill-used people he did not pick up and provide with careers—Leonora has told me, but I daresay she exaggerated and the figure seems so preposterous that I will not put it down. All these things, and the continuance of them seemed to him to be his duty—along with impossible subscriptions to hospitals and boy scouts and to provide prizes at cattle shows and anti-vivisection societies . . .

Well, Leonora saw to it that most of these things were not continued. They could not possibly keep up Branshaw Manor at that rate after the money had gone to the Grand Duke's mistress. She put the rents back at their old figures; discharged the drunkards from their homes, and sent all the societies notice that they were to expect no more subscriptions. To the children, she was more tender; nearly all of them she supported till the age of apprenticeship or domestic service. You see, she was childless herself.

She was childless herself, and she considered herself to be to blame. She had come of a penniless branch of the Powys family, and they had forced upon her poor dear Edward without making the stipulation that the children should be brought up as Catholics. And that, of course, was spiritual death to Leonora. I have given you a wrong impression if I have not made you see that Leonora was a woman of a strong, cold conscience, like all English Catholics.

(I cannot, myself, help disliking this religion; there is always, at the bottom of my mind, in spite of Leonora, the feeling of shuddering at the Scarlet Woman,* that filtered in upon me in the tranquillity of the little old Friends' Meeting House in Arch Street,* Philadelphia.) So I do set down a good deal of Leonora's mismanagement of poor dear Edward's case to the peculiarly English form of her religion. Because, of course, the only thing to have done for Edward would have been to let him sink down until he became a tramp of gentlemanly address, having, maybe, chance love affairs upon the highways. He would have done so much less harm; he would have been much less agonised too. At any rate, he would have had fewer chances of ruining and of remorse. For Edward was great at remorse.

But Leonora's English Catholic conscience, her rigid principles, her coldness, even her very patience, were, I cannot help thinking, all wrong in this special case. She quite seriously and naïvely imagined that the Church of Rome disapproves of divorce; she quite seriously and naïvely believed that her church could be such a monstrous and imbecile institution as to expect her to take on the impossible job of making Edward Ashburnham a faithful husband. She had, as the English would say, the Nonconformist* temperament. In the United States of North America we call it the New England conscience. For, of course, that frame of mind has been driven in on the English Catholics. The centuries that they have gone through—centuries of blind and malignant oppression, of ostracism from public employment, of being, as it were, a small beleaguered garrison in a hostile country, and therefore having to act with great formality—all these things have combined to perform that conjuring trick. And I suppose that Papists in England are even technically Nonconformists.

Continental Papists are a dirty, jovial and unscrupulous crew. But that, at least, lets them be opportunists. They would have fixed poor dear Edward up all right. (Forgive my writing of these monstrous things in this frivolous manner. If I did not I should break down and cry.) In Milan, say, or in Paris, Leonora would have had her marriage dissolved in six months for two hundred dollars paid in the right quarter. And Edward would have drifted about until he became a tramp of the kind I have suggested. Or he would have married a barmaid who would have made him such frightful scenes in public places and would so have torn out his moustache and left visible signs upon his face that he would have been faithful to her for the rest of his days. That was what he wanted to redeem him. . . .

For, along with his passions and his shames there went the dread of scenes in public places, of outcry, of excited physical violence; of publicity, in short. Yes, the barmaid would have cured him. And it would have been all the better if she drank; he would have been kept busy looking after her.

I know that I am right in this. I know it because of the Kilsyte case. You see, the servant girl that he then kissed was nurse in the family of the Nonconformist head of the county—whatever that post may be called. And that gentleman was so determined to ruin Edward, who was the chairman of the Tory caucus, or whatever it is*—that the poor dear sufferer had the very devil of a time. They asked questions about it in the House of Commons; they tried to get the Hampshire magistrates degraded;* they suggested to the War Ministry that Edward was not the proper person to hold the King's commission. Yes, he got it hot and strong.

The result you have heard. He was completely cured of philandering amongst the lower classes. And that seemed a real blessing to Leonora. It did not revolt her so much to be connected—it is a sort of connection—with people like Mrs. Maidan, instead of with a little kitchenmaid.

In a dim sort of way, Leonora was almost contented when she arrived at Nauheim, that evening. . . .

She had got things nearly straight by the long years of scraping in little stations in Chitral and Burma*—stations where living is cheap in comparison with the life of a county magnate, and where, moreover, liaisons of one sort or another are normal and inexpensive too. So that, when Mrs. Maidan came along—and the Maidan affair might have caused trouble out there because of the youth of the husband—Leonora had just resigned herself to coming home. With pushing and scraping and with letting Branshaw Teleragh, and with selling a picture and a relic of Charles I or so, she had got—and, poor dear, she had never had a really decent dress to her back in all those years and years—she had got, as she imagined, her poor dear husband back into much the same financial position as had been his before the mistress of the Grand Duke had happened along. And, of course, Edward himself had helped her a little on the financial side. He was a fellow that many men liked. He was so presentable and quite ready to lend you his cigar puncher—that sort of thing. So, every now and then some financier whom he met about would give him a good, sound, profitable tip. And Leonora was never afraid of a bit of a gamble— English Papists seldom are, I do not know why.

So nearly all her investment turned up trumps, and Edward was really in fit case to reopen Branshaw Manor and once more to assume his position in the county. Thus Leonora had accepted Maisie Maidan almost with resignation—almost with a sigh of relief. She really liked the poor child—she had to like somebody. And, at any rate, she felt she could trust Maisie—she could trust her not to rook* Edward for several thousands a week, for Maisie had refused to accept so much as a trinket ring from him. It is true that Edward gurgled and raved about the girl in a way that she had never yet experienced. But that, too, was almost a relief. I think she would really have welcomed it if he could have come across the love of his life. It would have given her a rest.

And there could not have been anyone better than poor little Mrs. Maidan; she was so ill she could not want to be taken on expensive jaunts. . . . It was Leonora herself who paid Maisie's expenses to Nauheim. She handed over the money to the boy husband, for Maisie would never have allowed it; but the husband was in agonies of fear. Poor devil!

I fancy that, on the voyage from India, Leonora was as happy as ever she had been in her life. Edward was wrapped up, completely, in his girl—he was almost like a father with a child, trotting about with rugs and physic and things, from deck to deck. He behaved, however, with great circumspection, so that nothing leaked through to the other passengers. And Leonora had almost attained to the attitude of a mother towards Mrs. Maidan. So it had looked very well— the benevolent, wealthy couple of good people, acting as saviours to the poor, dark-eyed, dying young thing. And that attitude of Leonora's towards Mrs. Maidan no doubt partly accounted for the smack in the face. She was hitting a naughty child who had been stealing chocolates at an inopportune moment.

It was certainly an inopportune moment. For, with the opening of that blackmailing letter from that injured brother officer, all the old terrors had redescended upon Leonora. Her road had again seemed to stretch out endless; she imagined that there might be hundreds and hundreds of such things that Edward was concealing from her—that they might necessitate more mortgagings, more pawnings of bracelets, more and always more horrors. She had spent an excruciating afternoon. The matter was one of a divorce case, of course, and she wanted to avoid publicity as much as Edward did, so that she saw the necessity of continuing the payments. And she did not so much mind that. They could find three hundred a year. But it was the horror of there being more such obligations.

She had had no conversation with Edward for many years—none that went beyond the mere arrangements for taking trains or engaging servants. But that afternoon she had to let him have it. And he had been just the same as ever. It was like opening a book after a decade to find the words the same. He had the same motives. He had not wished to tell her about the case because he had not wished her to sully her mind with the idea that there was such a thing as a brother officer who could be a blackmailer—and he had wanted to protect the credit of his old light of love. That lady was certainly not concerned with her husband. And he swore, and swore, and swore, that there was nothing else in the world against him. She did not believe him.

He had done it once too often—and she was wrong for the first time, so that he acted a rather creditable part in the matter. For he went right straight out to the post-office and spent several hours in coding a telegram to his solicitor, bidding that hard-headed man to threaten to take out at once a warrant against the fellow who was on his track. He said afterwards that it was a bit too thick on poor old Leonora to be ballyragged* any more. That was really the last of his outstanding accounts, and he was ready to take his personal chance of the Divorce Court if the blackmailer turned nasty. He would face it out—the publicity, the papers, the whole bally show. Those were his simple words. . . .

He had made, however, the mistake of not telling Leonora where he was going, so that, having seen him go to his room to fetch the code for the telegram, and seeing, two hours later, Maisie Maidan come out of his room, Leonora imagined that the two hours she had spent in silent agony Edward had spent with Maisie Maidan in his arms. That seemed to her to be too much.

As a matter of fact, Maisie's being in Edward's room had been the result, partly of poverty, partly of pride, partly of sheer innocence. She could not, in the first place, afford a maid; she refrained as much as possible from sending the hotel servants on errands, since every penny was of importance to her, and she feared to have to pay high tips at the end of her stay. Edward had lent her one of his fascinating cases containing fifteen different sizes of scissors, and, having seen from her window, his departure for the post-office, she had taken the opportunity of returning the case. She could not see why she should not, though she felt a certain remorse at the thought that she had kissed the pillows of his bed. That was the way it took her.

But Leonora could see that, without the shadow of a doubt, the incident gave Florence a hold over her. It let Florence into things and Florence was the only created being who had any idea that the Ashburnhams were not just good people with nothing to their tails. She determined at once, not so much to give Florence the privilege of her intimacy—which would have been the payment of a kind of blackmail—as to keep Florence under observation until she could have demonstrated to Florence that she was not in the least jealous of poor Maisie. So that was why she had entered the dining-room arm in arm with my wife, and why she had so markedly planted herself at our table. She never left us, indeed, for a minute that night, except just to run up to Mrs. Maidan's room to beg her pardon and to beg her also to let Edward take her very markedly out into the gardens that night. She said herself, when Mrs. Maidan came rather wistfully down into the lounge where we were all sitting: "Now, Edward, get up and take Maisie to the Casino. I want Mrs. Dowell to tell me all about the families in Connecticut who came from Fordingbridge." For it had been discovered that Florence came of a line that had actually owned Branshaw Teleragh for two centuries before the Ashburnhams came there. And there she sat with me in that hall, long after Florence had gone to bed, so that I might witness her gay reception of that pair. She could play up.

And that enables me to fix exactly the day of our going to the town of M——. For it was the very day poor Mrs. Maidan died. We found her dead when we got back—pretty awful, that, when you come to figure out what it all means. . . .

At any rate the measure of my relief when Leonora said that she was an Irish Catholic gives you the measure of my affection for that couple. It was an affection so intense that even to this day I cannot think of Edward without sighing. I do not believe that I could have gone on any more with them. I was getting too tired. And I verily believe, too, if my suspicion that Leonora was jealous of Florence had been the reason she gave for her outburst I should have turned upon Florence with the maddest kind of rage. Jealousy would have been incurable. But Florence's mere silly jibes at the Irish and at the Catholics could be apologised out of existence. And that I appeared to fix up in two minutes or so.

She looked at me for a long time rather fixedly and queerly while I was doing it. And at last I worked myself up to saying:

"Do accept the situation. I confess that I do not like your religion. But I like you so intensely. I don't mind saying that I have never had anyone to be really fond of, and I do not believe that anyone has ever been fond of me, as I believe you really to be."

"Oh, I'm fond enough of you," she said. "Fond enough to say that I wish every man was like you. But there are others to be considered." She was thinking, as a matter of fact, of poor Maisie. She picked a little piece of pellitory* out of the breast-high wall in front of us. She chafed it for a long minute between her finger and thumb, then she threw it over the coping.

"Oh, I accept the situation," she said at last, "if you can."

VI

I REMEMBER laughing at the phrase, "accept the situation", which she seemed to repeat with a gravity too intense. I said to her something like:

"It's hardly as much as that. I mean, that I must claim the liberty of a free American citizen to think what I please about your co-religionists. And I suppose that Florence must have liberty to think what she pleases and to say what politeness allows her to say."

"She had better," Leonora answered, "not say one single word against my people or my faith."

It struck me at the time, that there was an unusual, an almost threatening, hardness in her voice. It was almost as if she were trying to convey to Florence, through me, that she would seriously harm my wife if Florence went to something that was an extreme. Yes, I remember thinking at the time that it was almost as if Leonora were saying, through me to Florence:

"You may outrage me as you will; you may take all that I personally possess, but do not you care to say one single thing in view of the situation that that will set up—against the faith that makes me become the doormat for your feet."

But obviously, as I saw it, that could not be her meaning. Good people, be they ever so diverse in creed, do not threaten each other. So that I read Leonora's words to mean just no more than:

"It would be better if Florence said nothing at all against my co-religionists, because it is a point that I am touchy about."

That was the hint that, accordingly, I conveyed to Florence when, shortly afterwards, she and Edward came down from the tower. And I want you to understand that, from that moment until after Edward and the girl* and Florence were all dead together, I had never the remotest glimpse, not the shadow of a suspicion, that there was anything wrong, as the saying is. For five minutes, then, I entertained the possibility that Leonora might be jealous; but there was never another flicker in that flame-like personality. How in the world should I get it?

For, all that time, I was just a male sick nurse. And what chance had I against those three hardened gamblers, who were all in league to conceal their hands from me? What earthly chance? They were three to one—and they made me happy. Oh God, they made me so happy that I doubt if even paradise, that shall smooth out all temporal wrongs, shall ever give me the like. And what could they have done better, or what could they have done that could have been worse? I don't know. . . .

I suppose that, during all that time I was a deceived husband and that Leonora was pimping for Edward. That was the cross that she had to take up during her long Calvary of a life. . . .

You ask how it feels to be a deceived husband. Just Heavens, I do not know. It feels just nothing at all. It is not Hell, certainly it is not necessarily Heaven. So I suppose it is the intermediate stage. What do they call it? Limbo. No, I feel nothing at all about that. They are dead; they have gone before their Judge who, I hope, will open to them the springs of His compassion. It is not my business to think about it. It is simply my business to say, as Leonora's people say: "*Requiem aeternam dona eis, domine, et lux perpetua luceat per eis. In memoriam aeternam erit. . . .*"* But what were they? The just? The unjust? God knows! I think that the pair of them were only poor wretches, creeping over this earth in the shadow of an eternal wrath. It is very terrible. . . .

It is almost too terrible, the picture of that judgment, as it appears to me sometimes, at nights. It is probably the suggestion of some picture that I have seen somewhere.* But upon an immense plain, suspended in mid-air, I seem to see three figures, two of them clasped close in an intense embrace, and one intolerably solitary. It is in black and white, my picture of that judgment, an etching, perhaps; only I cannot tell an etching from a photographic reproduction. And the immense plain is the hand of God, stretching out for miles and miles, with great spaces above it and below it. And they are in the sight of God, and it is Florence that is alone. . . .

And, do you know, at the thought of that intense solitude I feel an overwhelming desire to rush forward and comfort her. You cannot, you see, have acted as nurse to a person for twelve years without wishing to go on nursing them, even though you hate them with the hatred of the adder, and even in the palm of God. But, in the nights, with that vision of judgment before me, I know that I hold myself back. For I hate Florence. I hate Florence with such a hatred that I would not spare her an eternity of loneliness. She need not have done what she did. She was an American, a New Englander. She had not the hot passions of these Europeans. She cut out that poor imbecile of an Edward—and I pray God that he is really at peace, clasped close in the arms of that poor, poor girl! And, no doubt, Maisie Maidan will find her young husband again, and Leonora will burn, clear and serene, a northern light* and one of the archangels of God. And me. . . . Well, perhaps, they will find me an elevator to run. . . . But Florence. . . .

She should not have done it. She should not have done it. It was playing it too low down. She cut out poor dear Edward from sheer vanity; she meddled between him and Leonora from a sheer, imbecile spirit of district visiting.* Do you understand that, whilst she was Edward's mistress, she was perpetually trying to reunite him to his wife? She would gabble on to Leonora about forgiveness—treating the subject from the bright, American point of view. And Leonora would treat her like the whore she was. Once she said to Florence in the early morning:

"You come to me straight out of his bed to tell me that that is my proper place. I know it, thank you."

But even that could not stop Florence. She went on saying that it was her ambition to leave this world a little brighter by the passage of her brief life, and how thankfully she would leave Edward, whom she thought she had brought to a right frame of mind, if Leonora would only give him a chance. He needed, she said, tenderness beyond anything.

And Leonora would answer—for she put up with this outrage for years—Leonora, as I understand, would answer something like:

"Yes, you would give him up. And you would go on writing to each other in secret, and committing adultery in hired rooms. I know the pair of you, you know. No. I prefer the situation as it is."

Half the time Florence would ignore Leonora's remarks. She would think they were not quite ladylike. The other half of the time she would try to persuade Leonora that her love for Edward was quite spiritual—on account of her heart. Once she said:

"If you can believe that of Maisie Maidan, as you say you do, why cannot you believe it of me?"

Leonora was, I understand, doing her hair at that time in front of the mirror in her bedroom. And she looked round at Florence, to whom she did not usually vouchsafe a glance,—she looked round coolly and calmly, and said:

"Never do you dare to mention Mrs. Maidan's name again. You

murdered her. You and I murdered her between us. I am as much a scoundrel as you. I don't like to be reminded of it."

Florence went off at once into a babble of how could she have hurt a person whom she hardly knew, a person whom with the best intentions, in pursuance of her efforts to leave the world a little brighter, she had tried to save from Edward. That was how she figured it out to herself. She really thought that. . . . So Leonora said patiently:

"Very well, just put it that I killed her and that it's a painful subject. One does not like to think that one had killed someone. Naturally not. I ought never to have brought her from India."

And that, indeed, is exactly how Leonora looked at it. It is stated a little baldly, but Leonora was always a great one for bald statements.

What had happened on the day of our jaunt to the ancient city of M—— had been this:

Leonora, who had been even then filled with pity and contrition for the poor child, on returning to our hotel had gone straight to Mrs. Maidan's room. She had wanted just to pet her. And she had perceived at first only, on the clear, round table covered with red velvet, a letter addressed to her. It ran something like:

"Oh, Mrs. Ashburnham, how could you have done it? I trusted you so. You never talked to me about me and Edward, but I trusted you. How could you buy me from my husband? I have just heard how you have—in the hall they were talking about it, Edward and the American lady. You paid the money for me to come here. Oh, how could you? How could you? I am going straight back to Bunny. . . ."

Bunny was Mrs. Maidan's husband.

And Leonora said that, as she went on reading the letter, she had, without looking round her, a sense that that hotel room was cleared, that there were no papers on the table, that there were no clothes on the hooks, and that there was a strained silence—a silence, she said, as if there were something in the room that drank up such sounds as there were. She had to fight against that feeling, whilst she read the postscript of the letter.

"I did not know you wanted me for an adulteress," the postscript began. The poor child was hardly literate. "It was surely not right of you and I never wanted to be one. And I heard Edward call me a poor little rat to the American lady. He always called me a little rat in private, and I did not mind. But, if he called me it to her, I think he does not love me any more. Oh, Mrs. Ashburnham, you knew the world and I knew nothing. I thought it would be all right if you thought it could, and I thought you would not have brought me if you did not, too. You should not have done it, and we out of the same convent. . . ."

Leonora said that she screamed when she read that.

And then she saw that Maisie's boxes were all packed, and she began a search for Mrs. Maidan herself—all over the hotel. The manager said that Mrs. Maidan had paid her bill, and had gone up to the station to ask the Reiseverkehrsbureau* to make her out a plan for her immediate return to Chitral. He imagined that he had seen her come back, but he was not quite certain. No one in the large hotel had bothered his head about the child. And she, wandering solitarily in the hall, had no doubt sat down beside a screen that had Edward and Florence on the other side. I never heard then or after what had passed between that precious couple. I fancy Florence was just about beginning her cutting out of poor dear Edward by addressing to him some words of friendly warning as to the ravages he might be making in the girl's heart. That would be the sort of way she would begin. And Edward would have sentimentally assured her that there was nothing in it; that Maisie was just a poor little rat whose passage to Nauheim his wife had paid out of her own pocket. That would have been enough to do the trick.

For the trick was pretty efficiently done. Leonora, with panic growing and with contrition very large in her heart, visited every one of the public rooms of the hotel—the dining-room, the lounge, the *Schreibzimmer*, the winter garden.* God knows what they wanted with a winter garden in an hotel that is only open from May till October. But there it was. And then Leonora ran—yes, she ran up the stairs—to see if Maisie had not returned to her rooms. She had determined to take that child right away from that hideous place. It seemed to her to be all unspeakable. I do not mean to say that she was not quite cool about it. Leonora was always Leonora. But the cold justice of the thing demanded that she should play the part of mother to this child who had come from the same convent. She figured it out to amount to that. She would leave Edward to Florence—and to me—and she would devote all her time to providing that child with an atmosphere of love until she could be returned to her poor young husband. It was naturally too late.

She had not cared to look round Maisie's rooms at first. Now, as soon as she came in, she perceived, sticking out beyond the bed, a small pair of feet in high-heeled shoes. Maisie had died in the effort to strap up a great portmanteau. She had died so grotesquely that her little body had fallen forward into the trunk, and it had closed upon her, like the jaws of a gigantic alligator. The key was in her hand. Her dark hair, like the hair of a Japanese, had come down and covered her body and her face.

Leonora lifted her up—she was the merest featherweight—and laid her on the bed with her hair about her. She was smiling, as if she had just scored a goal in a hockey match. You understand she had not committed suicide. Her heart had just stopped. I saw her, with the long lashes on the cheeks, with the smile about the lips, with the flowers all about her. The stem of a white lily rested in her hand so that the spike of flowers was upon her shoulder. She looked like a bride in the sunlight of the mortuary candles that were all about her, and the white coifs of the two nuns that knelt at her feet with their faces hidden might have been two swans that were to bear her away to kissing-kindness land, or wherever it is. Leonora showed her to me. She would not let either of the others see her. She wanted, you know, to spare poor dear Edward's feelings. He never could bear the sight of a corpse. And, since she never gave him an idea that Maisie had written to her, he imagined that the death had been the most natural thing in the world. He soon got over it. Indeed, it was the one affair of his about which he never felt much remorse.

PART II

I

THE death of Mrs. Maidan occurred on the 4th of August, 1904. And then nothing happened until the 4th of August, 1913. There is the curious coincidence of dates, but I do not know whether that is one of those sinister, as if half-jocular and altogether merciless proceedings on the part of a cruel Providence that we call a coincidence. Because it may just as well have been the superstitious mind of Florence that forced her to certain acts, as if she had been hypnotised. It is, however, certain that the fourth of August always proved a significant date for her. To begin with, she was born on the fourth of August. Then, on that date, in the year 1899, she set out with her uncle for the tour round the world in company with a young man called Jimmy. But that was not merely a coincidence. Her kindly old uncle, with the supposedly damaged heart, was in his delicate way, offering her, in this trip, a birthday present to celebrate her coming of age. Then, on the fourth of August, 1900, she yielded to an action that certainly coloured her whole life—as well as mine. She had no luck. She was probably offering herself a birthday present that morning. . . .

On the fourth of August, 1901, she married me, and set sail for Europe in a great gale of wind—the gale that affected her heart. And no doubt there, again, she was offering herself a birthday gift—the birthday gift of my miserable life. It occurs to me that I have never told you anything about my marriage. That was like this: I have told you, as I think, that I first met Florence at the Stuyvesants, in Fourteenth Street. And, from that moment, I determined with all the obstinacy of a possibly weak nature, if not to make her mine, at least to marry her. I had no occupation—I had no business affairs. I simply camped down there in Stamford, in a vile hotel, and just passed my days in the house, or on the verandah of the Misses Hurlbird. The Misses Hurlbird, in an odd, obstinate way, did not like my presence. But they were hampered by the national manners of these occasions. Florence had her own sitting-room. She could ask to it whom she liked, and I simply walked into that apartment. I was as timid as you will, but in that matter I was like a chicken that is determined to get across the road in front of an automobile. I would walk into Florence's pretty, little, old-fashioned room, take off my hat, and sit down.

Florence had, of course, several other fellows, too—strapping young New Englanders, who worked during the day in New York and spent only the evenings in the village of their birth. And, in the evenings, they would march in on Florence with almost as much determination as I myself showed. And I am bound to say that they were received with as much disfavour as was my portion—from the Misses Hurlbird. . . .

They were curious old creatures, those two. It was almost as if they were members of an ancient family under some curse—they were so gentlewomanly, so proper, and they sighed so. Sometimes I would see tears in their eyes. I do not know that my courtship of Florence made much progress at first. Perhaps that was because it took place almost entirely during the daytime, on hot afternoons, when the clouds of dust hung like fog, right up as high as the tops of the thin-leaved elms. The night, I believe, is the proper season, for the gentle feats of love, not a Connecticut July afternoon, when any sort of proximity is an almost appalling thought. But, if I never so much as kissed Florence, she let me discover very easily, in the course of a fortnight, her simple wants. And I could supply those wants. . . .

She wanted to marry a gentleman of leisure; she wanted a European establishment. She wanted her husband to have an English accent, an income of fifty thousand dollars a year from real estate and no ambitions to increase that income. And—she faintly hinted—she did not want much physical passion in the affair. Americans, you know, can envisage such unions without blinking.

She gave out this information in floods of bright talk—she would pop a little bit of it into comments over a view of the Rialto,* Venice, and, whilst she was brightly describing Balmoral Castle, she would say that her ideal husband would be one who could get her received at the British Court. She had spent, it seemed, two months in Great Britain—seven weeks in touring from Stratford to Strathpeffer,* and one as paying guest in an old English family near Ledbury,* an impoverished, but still stately family, called Bagshawe. They were to have spent two months more in that tranquil bosom, but inopportune events, apparently in her uncle's business, had caused their rather hurried return to Stamford. The young man called Jimmy had remained in Europe to perfect his knowledge of that continent. He certainly did: he was most useful to us afterwards.

But the point that came out—that there was no mistaking—was that Florence was coldly and calmly determined to take no look at any man who could not give her a European settlement. Her glimpse of English home life had effected this. She meant, on her marriage, to have a year in Paris, and then to have her husband buy some real estate in the neighbourhood of Fordingbridge, from which place the Hurlbirds had come in the year 1688.* On the strength of that she was going to take her place in the ranks of English county society. That was fixed.

I used to feel mightily elevated when I considered these details, for I could not figure out that, amongst her acquaintances in Stamford there was any fellow that would fill the bill. The most of them were not as wealthy as I, and those that were were not the type to give up the fascinations of Wall Street even for the protracted companionship of Florence. But nothing really happened during the month of July. On the first of August Florence apparently told her aunts that she intended to marry me.

She had not told me so, but there was no doubt about the aunts, for, on that afternoon, Miss Florence Hurlbird, Senior, stopped me on my way to Florence's sitting-room and took me, agitatedly, into the parlour. It was a singular interview, in that old-fashioned colonial room, with the spindle-legged furniture, the silhouettes, the miniatures, the portrait of General Braddock, and the smell of lavender. You see, the two poor maiden ladies were in agonies—and they could not say one single thing direct. They would almost wring their hands and ask if I had considered such a thing as different temperaments. I assure you they were almost affectionate, concerned for me even, as if Florence were too bright for my solid and serious virtues.

For they had discovered in me solid and serious virtues. That might have been because I had once dropped the remark that I preferred General Braddock to General Washington.* For the Hurlbirds had backed the losing side in the War of Independence, and had been seriously impoverished and quite efficiently oppressed for that reason. The Misses Hurlbird could never forget it.

Nevertheless they shuddered at the thought of a European career for myself and Florence. Each of them really wailed when they heard that that was what I hoped to give their niece. That may have been partly because they regarded Europe as a sink of iniquity, where strange laxities prevailed. They thought the Mother Country as

Erastian as any other. And they carried their protests to extraordinary lengths, for them. . . .

They even, almost, said that marriage was a sacrament; but neither Miss Florence nor Miss Emily could quite bring herself to utter the word. And they almost brought themselves to say that Florence's early life had been characterised by flirtations—something of that sort.

I know I ended the interview by saying:

"I don't care. If Florence has robbed a bank I am going to marry her and take her to Europe."

And at that Miss Emily wailed and fainted. But Miss Florence, in spite of the state of her sister, threw herself on my neck and cried out:

"Don't do it, John. Don't do it. You're a good young man," and she added, whilst I was getting out of the room to send Florence to her aunt's rescue:

"We ought to tell you more. But she's our dear sister's child."

Florence, I remember, received me with a chalk-pale face and the exclamation:

"Have those old cats been saying anything against me?" But I assured her that they had not and hurried her into the room of her strangely afflicted relatives. I had really forgotten all about that exclamation of Florence's until this moment. She treated me so very well—with such tact—that, if I ever thought of it afterwards I put it down to her deep affection for me.

And that evening, when I went to fetch her for a buggy-ride, she had disappeared. I did not lose any time. I went into New York and engaged berths on the "Pocahontas",* that was to sail on the evening of the fourth of the month, and then, returning to Stamford, I tracked out,* in the course of the day, that Florence had been driven to Rye Station.* And there I found that she had taken the cars to Waterbury. She had, of course, gone to her uncle's. The old man received me with a stony, husky face. I was not to see Florence; she was ill; she was keeping her room. And, from something that he let drop—an odd Biblical phrase that I have forgotten—I gathered that all that family simply did not intend her to marry ever in her life.

I procured at once the name of the nearest minister and a rope ladder—you have no idea how primitively these matters were arranged in those days in the United States. I daresay that may be so still. And, at one o'clock in the morning of the fourth of August I was standing in Florence's bedroom. I was so one-minded in my purpose that it never struck me there was anything improper in being, at one o'clock in the morning, in Florence's bedroom. I just wanted to wake her up. She was not, however, asleep. She expected me, and her relatives had only just left her. She received me with an embrace of a warmth . . . Well, it was the first time I had ever been embraced by a woman—and it was the last when a woman's embrace has had in it any warmth for me. . . .

I suppose it was my own fault, what followed. At any rate, I was in such a hurry to get the wedding over, and was so afraid of her relatives finding me there, that I must have received her advances with a certain amount of absence of mind. I was out of that room and down the ladder in under half a minute. She kept me waiting at the foot an unconscionable time—it was certainly three in the morning before we knocked up that minister. And I think that that wait was the only sign Florence ever showed of having a conscience as far as I was concerned, unless her lying for some moments in my arms was also a sign of conscience. I fancy that, if I had shown warmth then, she would have acted the proper wife to me, or would have put me back again. But, because I acted like a Philadelphia gentleman, she made me, I suppose, go through with the part of a male nurse. Perhaps she thought that I should not mind.

After that, as I gather, she had not any more remorse. She was only anxious to carry out her plans. For, just before she came down the ladder, she called me to the top of that grotesque implement that I went up and down like a tranquil jumping-jack. I was perfectly collected. She said to me with a certain fierceness:

"It is determined that we sail at four this afternoon? You are not lying about having taken berths?"

I understood that she would naturally be anxious to get away from the neighbourhood of her apparently insane relatives, so that I readily excused her for thinking that I should be capable of lying about such a thing. I made it, therefore, plain to her that it was my fixed determination to sail by the "Pocahontas". She said then—it was a moonlit morning, and she was whispering in my ear whilst I stood on the ladder. The hills that surround Waterbury showed, extraordinarily tranquil, around the villa. She said, almost coldly:

"I wanted to know, so as to pack my trunks." And she added: "I may be ill, you know. I guess my heart is a little like Uncle Hurlbird's. It runs in families."

I whispered that the "Pocahontas" was an extraordinarily steady boat. . . .

Now I wonder what had passed through Florence's mind during the two hours that she had kept me waiting at the foot of the ladder. I would give not a little to know. Till then, I fancy she had had no settled plan in her mind. She certainly never mentioned her heart till that time. Perhaps the renewed sight of her Uncle Hurlbird had given her the idea. Certainly her Aunt Emily, who had come over with her to Waterbury, would have rubbed into her, for hours and hours, the idea that any accentuated discussions would kill the old gentleman. That would recall to her mind all the safeguards against excitement with which the poor silly old gentleman had been hedged in during their trip round the world. That, perhaps, put it into her head. Still, I believe there was some remorse on my account, too. Leonora told me that Florence said there was—for Leonora knew all about it, and once went so far as to ask her how she could do a thing so infamous. She excused herself on the score of an overmastering passion. Well, I always say that an overmastering passion is a good excuse for feelings. You cannot help them. And it is a good excuse for straight actions—she might have bolted with the fellow, before or after she married me. And, if they had not enough money to get along with, they might have cut their throats, or sponged on her family, though, of course, Florence wanted such a lot that it would have suited her very badly to have for a husband a clerk in a dry-goods store, which was what old Hurlbird would have made of that fellow. He hated him. No, I do not think that there is much excuse for Florence.

God knows. She was a frightened fool, and she was fantastic, and I suppose that, at that time, she really cared for that imbecile. He certainly didn't care for her. Poor thing. . . . At any rate, after I had assured her that the "Pocahontas" was a steady ship, she just said:

"You'll have to look after me in certain ways—like Uncle Hurlbird is looked after. I will tell you how to do it." And then she stepped over the sill, as if she were stepping on board a boat. I suppose she had burnt hers!

I had, no doubt, eye-openers enough. When we re-entered the Hurlbird mansion at eight o'clock the Hurlbirds were just exhausted.

Florence had a hard, triumphant air. We had got married about four in the morning and had sat about in the woods above the town till then, listening to a mocking-bird imitate an old tom-cat. So I guess Florence had not found getting married to me a very stimulating process. I had not found anything much more inspiring to say than how glad I was, with variations. I think I was too dazed. Well, the Hurlbirds were too dazed to say much. We had breakfast together, and then Florence went to pack her grips and things. Old Hurlbird took the opportunity to read me a full-blooded lecture, in the style of an American oration, as to the perils for young American girlhood lurking in the European jungle. He said that Paris was full of snakes in the grass, of which he had had bitter experience. He concluded, as they always do, poor, dear old things, with the aspiration that all American women should one day be sexless—though that is not the way they put it. . . .

Well, we made the ship all right by one-thirty—and there was a tempest blowing. That helped Florence a good deal. For we were not ten minutes out from Sandy Hook* before Florence went down into her cabin and her heart took her. An agitated stewardess came running up to me, and I went running down. I got my directions how to behave to my wife. Most of them came from her, though it was the ship's doctor who discreetly suggested to me that I had better refrain from manifestations of affection. I was ready enough.

I was, of course, full of remorse. It occurred to me that her heart was the reason for the Hurlbirds' mysterious desire to keep their youngest and dearest unmarried. Of course, they would be too refined to put the motive into words. They were old stock New Englanders. They would not want to have to suggest that a husband must not kiss the back of his wife's neck. They would not like to suggest that he might, for the matter of that. I wonder, though, how Florence got the doctor to enter the conspiracy—the several doctors.

Of course her heart squeaked a bit—she had the same configuration of the lungs as her Uncle Hurlbird. And, in his company, she must have heard a great deal of heart talk from specialists. Anyhow, she and they tied me pretty well down—and Jimmy, of course, that dreary boy—what in the world did she see in him? He was lugubrious, silent, morose. He had no talent as a painter. He was very sallow and dark, and he never shaved sufficiently. He met us at Havre, and he proceeded to make himself useful for the next two years, during which he lived in our flat in Paris, whether we were there or not. He studied painting at Julien's,* or some such place. . . .

That fellow had his hands always in the pockets of his odious, square-shouldered, broad-hipped, American coats, and his dark eyes were always full of ominous appearances. He was, besides, too fat. Why, I was much the better man. . . .

And I daresay Florence would have given me the better. She showed signs of it. I think, perhaps, the enigmatic smile with which she used to look back at me over her shoulder when she went into the bathing place was a sort of invitation. I have mentioned that. It was as if she were saying: "I am going in here. I am going to stand so stripped and white and straight—and you are a man. . . ." Perhaps it was that . . .

No, she cannot have liked that fellow long. He looked like sallow putty. I understand that he had been slim and dark and very graceful at the time of her first disgrace. But, loafing about in Paris, on her pocket-money and on the allowance that old Hurlbird made him to keep out of the United States, had given him a stomach like a man of forty, and dyspeptic irritation on top of it.

God, how they worked me! It was those two between them who really elaborated the rules. I have told you something about them— how I had to head conversations, for all those eleven years off such topics as love, poverty, crime, and so on. But, looking over what I have written, I see that I have unintentionally misled you when I said that Florence was never out of my sight. Yet that was the impression that I really had until just now. When I come to think of it she was out of my sight most of the time.

You see, that fellow impressed upon me that what Florence needed most of all were sleep and privacy. I must never enter her room without knocking, or her poor little heart might flutter away to its doom. He said these things with his lugubrious croak, and his black eyes like a crow's, so that I seemed to see poor Florence die ten times a day—a little, pale, frail corpse. Why, I would as soon have thought of entering her room without her permission as of burgling a church. I would sooner have committed that crime. I would certainly have done it if I had thought the state of her heart demanded the sacrilege. So at ten o'clock at night the door closed upon Florence, who had gently, and, as if reluctantly, backed up that fellow's recommendations; and she would wish me good night as if she were a *cinque cento** Italian lady saying good-bye to her lover. And at ten o'clock of the next morning there she would come out the door of her room as fresh as Venus rising from any of the couches that are mentioned in Greek legends.*

Her room door was locked because she was nervous about thieves; but an electric contrivance on a cord was understood to be attached to her little wrist. She had only to press a bulb to raise the house. And I was provided with an axe—an axe!—great gods, with which to break down her door in case she ever failed to answer my knock, after I knocked really loud several times. It was pretty well thought out, you see.

What wasn't so well thought out were the ultimate consequences—our being tied to Europe. For that young man rubbed it so well into me that Florence would die if she crossed the Channel—he impressed it so fully on my mind that, when later Florence wanted to go to Fordingbridge, I cut the proposal short—absolutely short, with a curt no. It fixed her and it frightened her. I was even backed up by all the doctors. I seemed to have had endless interviews with doctor after doctor, cool, quiet men, who would ask, in reasonable tones, whether there was any reason for our going to England—any special reason. And since I could not see any special reason, they would give the verdict: "Better not, then." I daresay they were honest enough, as things go. They probably imagined that the mere associations of the steamer might have effects on Florence's nerves. That would be enough, that and a conscientious desire to keep our money on the Continent.

It must have rattled poor Florence pretty considerably, for you see, the main idea—the only main idea of her heart, that was otherwise cold—was to get to Fordingbridge and be a county lady in the home of her ancestors. But Jimmy got her, there: he shut on her the door of the Channel; even on the fairest day of blue sky, with the cliffs of England shining like mother of pearl in full view of Calais, I would not have let her cross the steamer gangway to save her life. I tell you it fixed her.

It fixed her beautifully, because she could not announce herself as cured, since that would have put an end to the locked bedroom arrangements. And, by the time she was sick of Jimmy—which happened in the year 1903—she had taken on Edward Ashburnham. Yes, it was a bad fix for her, because Edward could have taken her to Fordingbridge, and, though he could not give her Branshaw Manor, that home of her ancestors being settled on his wife, she could at least have pretty considerably queened it there or thereabouts, what with our money and the support of the Ashburnhams. Her uncle, as soon as he considered that she had really settled down with me—and I sent him only the most glowing accounts of her virtue and constancy—made over to her a very considerable part of his fortune for which he had no use. I suppose that we had, between us, fifteen thousand a year in English money, though I never quite knew how much of hers went to Jimmy. At any rate, we could have shone in Fordingbridge.

I never quite knew, either, how she and Edward got rid of Jimmy. I fancy that fat and disreputable raven must have had his six golden front teeth knocked down his throat by Edward one morning whilst I had gone out to buy some flowers in the Rue de la Paix, leaving Florence and the flat in charge of those two. And serve him very right, is all that I can say. He was a bad sort of blackmailer; I hope Florence does not have his company in the next world.

As God is my Judge, I do not believe that I would have separated those two if I had known that they really and passionately loved each other. I do not know where the public morality of the case comes in, and, of course, no man really knows what he would have done in any given case. But I truly believe that I would have united them, observing ways and means as decent as I could. I believe that I should have given them money to live upon and that I should have consoled myself somehow. At that date I might have found some young thing, like Maisie Maidan, or the poor girl, and I might have had some peace. For peace I never had with Florence, and I hardly believe that I cared for her in the way of love after a year or two of it. She became for me a rare and fragile object, something burdensome, but very frail. Why, it was as if I had been given a thin-shelled pullet's egg to carry on my palm from Equatorial Africa to Hoboken.* Yes, she became for me, as it were, the subject of a bet—the trophy of an athlete's achievement, a parsley crown that is the symbol of his chastity, his soberness, his abstentions, and of his inflexible will. Of intrinsic value as a wife, I think she had none at all for me. I fancy I was not even proud of the way she dressed.

But her passion for Jimmy was not even a passion, and, mad as the suggestion may appear, she was frightened for her life. Yes, she was afraid of me. I will tell you how that happened.

I had, in the old days, a darky servant, called Julius, who valeted me, and waited on me, and loved me, like the crown of his head. Now, when we left Waterbury to go to the "Pocahontas", Florence intrusted to me one very special and very precious leather grip. She told me that her life might depend on that grip, which contained her drugs against heart attacks. And, since I was never much of a hand at carrying things, I intrusted this, in turn, to Julius, who was a grey-haired chap of sixty or so, and very picturesque at that. He made so much impression on Florence that she regarded him as a sort of father, and absolutely refused to let me take him to Paris. He would have inconvenienced her.

Well, Julius was so overcome with grief at being left behind that he must needs go and drop the precious grip. I saw red, I saw purple. I flew at Julius. On the ferry, it was, I filled up one of his eyes; I threatened to strangle him. And, since an unresisting negro can make a deplorable noise and a deplorable spectacle, and, since that was Florence's first adventure in the married state, she got a pretty idea of my character. It affirmed in her the desperate resolve to conceal from me the fact that she was not what she would have called "a pure woman".* For that was really the mainspring of her fantastic actions. She was afraid that I should murder her. . . .

So she got up the heart attack, at the earliest possible opportunity, on board the liner. Perhaps she was not so very much to be blamed. You must remember that she was a New Englander, and that New England had not yet come to loathe darkies as it does now. Whereas, if she had come from even so little south as Philadelphia, and had been of an oldish family, she would have seen that for me to kick Julius was not so outrageous an act as for her cousin, Reggie Hurlbird, to say—as I have heard him say to his English butler—that for two cents he would bat him on the pants. Besides, the medicine-grip did not bulk as largely in her eyes as it did in mine, where it was the symbol of the existence of an adored wife of a day. To her it was just a useful lie. . . .

Well, there you have the position, as clear as I can make it—the husband an ignorant fool, the wife a cold sensualist with imbecile fears—for I was such a fool that I should never have known what she was or was not—and the blackmailing lover. And then the other lover came along. . . .

Well, Edward Ashburnham was worth having. Have I conveyed

to you the splendid fellow that he was—the fine soldier, the excellent landlord, the extraordinarily kind, careful and industrious magistrate, the upright, honest, fair-dealing, fair-thinking, public character? I suppose I have not conveyed it to you. The truth is, that I never knew it until the poor girl came along—the poor girl who was just as straight, as splendid and as upright as he. I swear she was. I suppose I ought to have known. I suppose that was, really, why I liked him so much—so infinitely much. Come to think of it, I can remember a thousand little acts of kindliness, of thoughtfulness for his inferiors, even on the Continent. Look here, I know of two families of dirty, unpicturesque, Hessian paupers that that fellow, with an infinite patience, rooted up, got their police reports, set on their feet, or exported to my patient land. And he would do it quite inarticulately, set in motion by seeing a child crying in the street. He would wrestle with dictionaries, in that unfamiliar tongue. . . . Well, he could not bear to see a child cry. Perhaps he could not bear to see a woman and not give her the comfort of his physical attractions.

But, although I liked him so intensely, I was rather apt to take these things for granted. They made me feel comfortable with him, good towards him; they made me trust him. But I guess I thought it was part of the character of any English gentleman. Why, one day he got it into his head that the head waiter at the Excelsior had been crying—the fellow with the grey face and grey whiskers. And then he spent the best part of a week, in correspondence and up at the British consul's, in getting the fellow's wife to come back from London and bring back his girl baby. She had bolted with a Swiss scullion.* If she had not come inside the week he would have gone to London himself to fetch her. He was like that.

Edward Ashburnham was like that, and I thought it was only the duty of his rank and station. Perhaps that was all that it was—but I pray God to make me discharge mine as well. And, but for the poor girl, I daresay that I should never have seen it, however much the feeling might have been over me. She had for him such enthusiasm that, although even now I do not understand the technicalities of English life, I can gather enough. She was with them during the whole of our last stay at Nauheim.

Nancy Rufford was her name; she was Leonora's only friend's only child, and Leonora was her guardian, if that is the correct term. She had lived with the Ashburnhams ever since she had been of the age of thirteen, when her mother was said to have committed suicide owing to the brutalities of her father. Yes, it is a cheerful story. . . .

Edward always called her "the girl," and it was very pretty, the evident affection he had for her and she for him. And Leonora's feet she would have kissed—those two were for her the best man and the best woman on earth—and in heaven. I think that she had not a thought of evil in her head—the poor girl. . . .

Well, anyhow, she chanted Edward's praises to me for the hour together, but, as I have said, I could not make much of it. It appeared that he had the D. S. O.,* and that his troop loved him beyond the love of men. You never saw such a troop as his. And he had the Royal Humane Society's* medal with a clasp. That meant, apparently, that he had twice jumped off the deck of a troopship to rescue what the girl called "Tommies," who had fallen overboard in the Red Sea and such places. He had been twice recommended for the V. C.,* whatever that might mean, and, although owing to some technicalities he had never received that apparently coveted order, he had some special place about his sovereign at the coronation. Or perhaps it was some post in the Beefeaters'.* She made him out like a cross between Lohengrin* and the Chevalier Bayard.* Perhaps he was. . . . But he was too silent a fellow to make that side of him really decorative. I remember going to him at about that time and asking him what the D. S. O. was, and he grunted out:

"It's a sort of a thing they give grocers who've honourably supplied the troops with adulterated coffee in war-time"—something of that sort. He did not quite carry conviction to me, so, in the end, I put it directly to Leonora. I asked her fully and squarely—prefacing the question with some remarks, such as those that I have already given you, as to the difficulty one has in really getting to know people when one's intimacy is conducted as an English acquaintanceship—I asked her whether her husband was not really a splendid fellow— along at least the lines of his public functions. She looked at me with a slightly awakened air—with an air that would have been almost startled if Leonora could ever have been startled.

"Didn't you know?" she asked. "If I come to think of it there is not a more splendid fellow in any three counties, pick them where you will—along those lines." And she added, after she had looked at me reflectively for what seemed a long time:

"To do my husband justice there could not be a better man on the earth. There would not be room for it—along those lines."

"Well," I said, "then he must really be Lohengrin and the Cid* in one body. For there are not any other lines that count."

Again she looked at me for a long time.

"It's your opinion that there are no other lines that count?" she asked slowly.

"Well," I answered gaily, "you're not going to accuse him of not being a good husband, or of not being a good guardian to your ward?"

She spoke then, slowly, like a person who is listening to the sounds in a sea-shell held to her ear—and, would you believe it?—she told me afterwards that, at that speech of mine, for the first time she had a vague inkling of the tragedy that was to follow so soon—although the girl had lived with them for eight years or so:

"Oh, I'm not thinking of saying that he is not the best of husbands, or that he is not very fond of the girl."

And then I said something like:

"Well, Leonora, a man sees more of these things than even a wife. And, let me tell you, that in all the years I've known Edward he has never, in your absence, paid a moment's attention to any other woman—not by the quivering of an eyelash. I should have noticed. And he talks of you as if you were one of the angels of God."

"Oh," she came up to the scratch, as you could be sure Leonora would always come up to the scratch, "I am perfectly sure that he always speaks nicely of me."

I daresay she had practice in that sort of scene—people must have been always complimenting her on her husband's fidelity and adoration. For half the world—the whole of the world that knew Edward and Leonora believed that his conviction in the Kilsyte affair had been a miscarriage of justice—a conspiracy of false evidence, got together by Nonconformist adversaries. But think of the fool that I was. . . .

II

Let me think where we were. Oh, yes . . . that conversation took place on the fourth of August, 1913. I remember saying to her that, on that day, exactly nine years before, I had made their acquaintance, so that it had seemed quite appropriate and like a birthday speech to utter my little testimonial to my friend Edward. I could quite confidently say that, though we four had been about together in all sorts of places, for all that length of time, I had not, for my part, one single complaint to make of either of them. And I added, that that was an unusual record for people who had been so much together. You are not to imagine that it was only at Nauheim that we met. That would not have suited Florence.

I find, on looking at my diaries, that on September the fourth, 1904, Edward accompanied Florence and myself to Paris, where we put him up till the twenty-first of that month. He made another short visit to us in December of that year—the first year of our acquaintance. It must have been during this visit that he knocked Mr. Jimmy's teeth down his throat. I daresay Florence had asked him to come over for that purpose. In 1905 he was in Paris three times—once with Leonora, who wanted some frocks. In 1906 we spent the best part of six weeks together at Mentone, and Edward stayed with us in Paris on his way back to London. That was how it went.

The fact was that in Florence the poor wretch had got hold of a Tartar, compared with whom Leonora was a sucking kid.* He must have had a hell of a time. Leonora wanted to keep him for—what shall I say—for the good of her church, as it were, to show that Catholic women do not lose their men. Let it go at that, for the moment. I will write more about her motives later, perhaps. But Florence was sticking on to the proprietor of the home of her ancestors. No doubt he was also a very passionate lover. But I am convinced that he was sick of Florence within three years of even interrupted companionship and the life that she led him. . . .

If ever Leonora so much as mentioned in a letter that they had had a woman staying with them—or, if she so much as mentioned a woman's name in a letter to me—off would go a desperate cable in cipher to that poor wretch at Branshaw, commanding him on pain of an instant and horrible disclosure to come over and assure her of his fidelity. I daresay he would have faced it out; I daresay he would have thrown over Florence and taken the risk of exposure. But there he had Leonora to deal with. And Leonora assured him that, if the minutest fragment of the real situation ever got through to my senses, she would wreak upon him the most terrible vengeance that she could think of. And he did not have a very easy job. Florence called for more and more attentions from him as the time went on. She would make him kiss her at any moment of the day; and it was only by his making it plain that a divorced lady could never assume a position in the county of Hampshire that he could prevent her from making a bolt of it with him in her train. Oh, yes, it was a difficult job for him.

For Florence, if you please, gaining in time a more composed view of nature, and overcome by her habits of garrulity, arrived at a frame of mind in which she found it almost necessary to tell me all about it—nothing less than that. She said that her situation was too unbearable with regard to me.

She proposed to tell me all, secure a divorce from me, and go with Edward and settle in California. . . . I do not suppose that she was really serious in this. It would have meant the extinction of all hopes of Branshaw Manor for her. Besides she had got it into her head that Leonora, who was as sound as a roach, was consumptive. She was always begging Leonora, before me, to go and see a doctor. But, none the less, poor Edward seems to have believed in her determination to carry him off. He would not have gone; he cared for his wife too much. But, if Florence had put him at it,* that would have meant my getting to know of it, and his incurring Leonora's vengeance. And she could have made it pretty hot for him in ten or a dozen different ways. And she assured me that she would have used every one of them. She was determined to spare my feelings. And she was quite aware that, at that date, the hottest she could have made it for him would have been to refuse, herself, ever to see him again. . . .

Well, I think I have made it pretty clear. Let me come to the fourth of August, 1913, the last day of my absolute ignorance—and, I assure you, of my perfect happiness. For the coming of that dear girl only added to it all.

On that fourth of August I was sitting in the lounge with a rather odious Englishman called Bagshawe, who had arrived that night, too late for dinner. Leonora had just gone to bed and I was waiting for

Florence and Edward and the girl to come back from a concert at the Casino. They had not gone there all together. Florence, I remember, had said at first that she would remain with Leonora and me and Edward and the girl had gone off alone. And then Leonora had said to Florence with perfect calmness:

"I wish you would go with those two. I think the girl ought to have the appearance of being chaperoned with Edward in these places. I think the time has come." So Florence, with her light step had slipped out after them. She was all in black for some cousin or other. Americans are particular in those matters.

We had gone on sitting in the lounge till towards ten, when Leonora had gone up to bed. It had been a very hot day, but there it was cool. The man called Bagshawe had been reading the *Times* on the other side of the room, but then he moved over to me with some trifling question as a prelude to suggesting an acquaintance. I fancy he asked me something about the poll-tax on Kur-guests, and whether it could not be sneaked out of. He was that sort of person.

Well, he was an unmistakable man, with a military figure, rather exaggerated, with bulbous eyes that avoided your own, and a pallid complexion that suggested vices practised in secret along with an uneasy desire for making acquaintance at whatever cost . . . The filthy toad. . . .

He began by telling me that he came from Ludlow Manor, near Ledbury. The name had a slightly familiar sound, though I could not fix it in my mind. Then he began to talk about a duty on hops, about Californian hops, about Los Angeles, where he had been. He was fencing for a topic with which he might gain my affection.

And then, quite suddenly, in the bright light of the street, I saw Florence running. It was like that—I saw Florence running with a face whiter than paper and her hand on the black stuff over her heart. I tell you, my own heart stood still; I tell you I could not move. She rushed in at the swing doors. She looked round that place of rush chairs, cane tables and newspapers. She saw me and opened her lips. She saw the man who was talking to me. She stuck her hands over her face as if she wished to push her eyes out. And she was not there any more.

I could not move; I could not stir a finger. And then that man said:

"By Jove: Florry Hurlbird." He turned upon me with an oily and uneasy sound meant for a laugh. He was really going to ingratiate himself with me. "Do you know who that is?" he asked. "The last time I saw that girl she was coming out of the bedroom of a young man called Jimmy at five o'clock in the morning. In my house at Ledbury. You saw her recognise me." He was standing on his feet, looking down at me. I don't know what I looked like. At any rate, he gave a sort of gurgle and then stuttered:

"Oh, I say . . ." Those were the last words I ever heard of Mr. Bagshawe's. A long time afterwards I pulled myself out of the lounge and went up to Florence's room. She had not locked the door—for the first night of our married life. She was lying, quite respectably arranged, unlike Mrs. Maidan, on her bed. She had a little phial that rightly should have contained nitrate of amyl, in her right hand. That was on the fourth of August, 1913.

PART III

I

THE odd thing is that what sticks out in my recollection of the rest of that evening was Leonora's saying:

"Of course you might marry her," and, when I asked whom, she answered:

"The girl."

Now that is to me a very amazing thing—amazing for the light of possibilities that it casts into the human heart. For I had never had the slightest conscious idea of marrying the girl; I never had the slightest idea even of caring for her. I must have talked in an odd way, as people do who are recovering from an anæsthetic. It is as if one had a dual personality, the one I being entirely unconscious of the other. I had thought nothing; I had said such an extraordinary thing.

I don't know that analysis of my own psychology matters at all to this story. I should say that it didn't or, at any rate, that I had given enough of it. But that odd remark of mine had a strong influence upon what came after. I mean, that Leonora would probably never have spoken to me at all about Florence's relations with Edward if I hadn't said, two hours after my wife's death:

"Now I can marry the girl."

She had, then, taken it for granted that I had been suffering all that she had been suffering, or, at least, that I had permitted all that she had permitted. So that, a month ago,— about a week after the funeral of poor Edward she could say to me in the most natural way in the world—I had been talking about the duration of my stay at Branshaw—she said with her clear, reflective intonation:

"O stop here for ever and ever if you can." And then she added, "You couldn't be more of a brother to me, or more of a counsellor, or more of a support. You are all the consolation I have in the world. And isn't it odd to think that if your wife hadn't been my husband's mistress, you would probably never have been here at all?"

That was how I got the news—full in the face, like that. I didn't say anything and I don't suppose I felt anything, unless maybe it was with that mysterious and unconscious self that underlies most people. Perhaps one day when I am unconscious or walking in my sleep I may go and spit upon poor Edward's grave. It seems about the most unlikely thing I could do; but there it is.

No, I remember no emotion of any sort, but just the clear feeling that one has from time to time when one hears that some Mrs. So-and-So is *au mieux** with a certain gentleman. It made things plainer, suddenly, to my curiosity. It was as if I thought, at that moment, of a windy November evening, that, when I came to think it over afterwards, a dozen unexplained things would fit themselves into place. But I wasn't thinking things over then. I remember that distinctly. I was just sitting back, rather stiffly, in a deep arm-chair. That is what I remember. It was twilight.

Branshaw Manor lies in a little hollow with lawns across it and pine-woods on the fringe of the dip. The immense wind, coming from across the forest, roared overhead. But the view from the window was perfectly quiet and grey. Not a thing stirred, except a couple of rabbits on the extreme edge of the lawn. It was Leonora's own little study that we were in and we were waiting for the tea to be brought. I, as I have said, was sitting in the deep chair, Leonora was standing in the window twirling the wooden acorn at the end of the window-blind cord desultorily round and round. She looked across the lawn and said, as far as I can remember:

"Edward has been dead only ten days and yet there are rabbits on the lawn."

I understand that rabbits do a great deal of harm to the short grass in England. And then she turned round to me and said without any adornment at all, for I remember her exact words:

"I think it was stupid of Florence to commit suicide."

I cannot tell you the extraordinary sense of leisure that we two seemed to have at that moment. It wasn't as if we were waiting for a train, it wasn't as if we were waiting for a meal—it was just that there was nothing to wait for. Nothing.

There was an extreme stillness with the remote and intermittent sound of the wind. There was the grey light in that brown, small room. And there appeared to be nothing else in the world.

I knew then that Leonora was about to let me into her full confidence. It was as if—or no, it was the actual fact that—Leonora with an odd English sense of decency had determined to wait until Edward had been in his grave for a full week before she spoke. And with some vague motive of giving her an idea of the extent to which she must permit herself to make confidences, I said slowly—and these words too I remember with exactitude—

"Did Florence commit suicide? I didn't know."

I was just, you understand, trying to let her know that, if she were going to speak she would have to talk about a much wider range of things than she had before thought necessary.

So that that was the first knowledge I had that Florence had committed suicide. It had never entered my head. You may think that I had been singularly lacking in suspiciousness; you may consider me even to have been an imbecile. But consider the position.

In such circumstances of clamour, of outcry, of the crash of many people running together, of the professional reticence of such people as hotel-keepers, the traditional reticence of such "good people" as the Ashburnhams—in such circumstances it is some little material object, always, that catches the eye and that appeals to the imagination. I had no possible guide to the idea of suicide and the sight of the little flask of nitrate of amyl in Florence's hand suggested instantly to my mind the idea of the failure of her heart. Nitrate of amyl, you understand, is the drug that is given to relieve sufferers from angina pectoris.*

Seeing Florence, as I had seen her, running with a white face and with one hand held over her heart, and seeing her, as I immediately afterwards saw her, lying upon her bed with the so familiar little brown flask clenched in her fingers, it was natural enough for my mind to frame the idea. As happened now and again, I thought, she had gone out without her remedy and, having felt an attack coming on whilst she was in the gardens, she had run in to get the nitrate in order, as quickly as possible, to obtain relief. And it was equally inevitable my mind should frame the thought that her heart, unable to stand the strain of the running, should have broken in her side. How could I have known that, during all the years of our married life, that little brown flask had contained, not nitrate of amyl, but prussic acid?* It was inconceivable.

Why, not even Edward Ashburnham, who was, after all more intimate with her than I was, had an inkling of the truth. He just thought that she had dropped dead of heart disease. Indeed, I fancy that the only people who ever knew that Florence had committed suicide were Leonora, the Grand Duke, the head of the police and the hotel-keeper. I mention these last three because my recollection of that night is only the sort of pinkish effulgence from the electric-lamps in the hotel lounge. There seemed to bob into my consciousness, like floating globes, the faces of those three. Now it would be the bearded, monarchical, benevolent head of the Grand Duke; then the sharp-featured, brown, cavalry-moustached features of the chief of police; then the globular, polished and high-collared vacuousness that represented Monsieur Schontz, the proprietor of the hotel. At times one head would be there alone, at another the spiked helmet of the official would be close to the healthy baldness of the prince; then M. Schontz's oiled locks would push in between the two. The sovereign's soft, exquisitely trained voice would say, "Ja, ja, ja!" each word dropping out like so many soft pellets of suet; the subdued rasp of the official would come: "Zum Befehl Durchlaucht,"* like five revolver-shots; the voice of M. Schontz would go on and on under its breath like that of an unclean priest reciting from his breviary in the corner of a railway-carriage. That was how it presented itself to me.

They seemed to take no notice of me; I don't suppose that I was even addressed by one of them. But, as long as one or the other, or all three of them were there, they stood between me as if, I being the titular possessor of the corpse, had a right to be present at their conferences. Then they all went away and I was left alone for a long time.

And I thought nothing; absolutely nothing. I had no ideas; I had no strength. I felt no sorrow, no desire for action, no inclination to go upstairs and fall upon the body of my wife. I just saw the pink effulgence, the cane tables, the palms, the globular match-holders, the indented ash-trays. And then Leonora came to me and it appears that I addressed to her that singular remark:

"Now I can marry the girl."

But I have given you absolutely the whole of my recollection of that evening, as it is the whole of my recollection of the succeeding three or four days. I was in a state just simply cataleptic. They put me to bed and I stayed there; they brought me my clothes and I dressed; they led me to an open grave and I stood beside it. If they had taken me to the edge of a river, or if they had flung me beneath a railway train, I should have been drowned or mangled in the same spirit. I was the walking dead.

Well, those are my impressions.

What had actually happened had been this. I pieced it together afterwards. You will remember I said that Edward Ashburnham and the girl had gone off, that night, to a concert at the Casino* and that Leonora had asked Florence, almost immediately after their departure, to follow them and to perform the office of chaperone. Florence, you may also remember, was all in black, being the mourning that she wore for a deceased cousin, Jean Hurlbird. It was a very black night and the girl was dressed in cream-coloured muslin, that must have glimmered under the tall trees of the dark park like a phosphorescent fish in a cupboard. You couldn't have had a better beacon.

And it appears that Edward Ashburnham led the girl not up the straight allée that leads to the Casino, but in under the dark trees of the park. Edward Ashburnham told me all this in his final outburst. I have told you that, upon that occasion, he became deucedly vocal. I didn't pump him. I hadn't any motive. At that time I didn't in the least connect him with my wife. But the fellow talked like a cheap novelist.—Or like a very good novelist for the matter of that, if it's the business of a novelist to make you see things clearly.* And I tell you I see that thing as clearly as if it were a dream that never left me. It appears that, not very far from the Casino, he and the girl sat down in the darkness upon a public bench. The lights from that place of entertainment must have reached them through the tree-trunks, since, Edward said, he could quite plainly see the girl's face—that beloved face with the high forehead, the queer mouth, the tortured eye-brows, and the direct eyes. And to Florence, creeping up behind them, they must have presented the appearance of silhouettes. For I take it that Florence came creeping up behind them over the short grass to a tree that, as I quite well remember, was immediately behind that public seat. It was a not very difficult feat for a woman instinct with jealousy. The Casino orchestra was, as Edward remembered to tell me, playing the Rakocsy march,* and although it was not loud enough, at that distance, to drown the voice of Edward Ashburnham it was certainly sufficiently audible to efface, amongst the noises of the night, the slight brushings and rustlings that might have been made by the feet of Florence or by her gown in coming over the short grass. And that miserable woman must have got it in the face, good and strong. It must have been horrible for her. Horrible! Well, I suppose she deserved all that she got.

Anyhow, there you have the picture, the immensely tall trees, elms most of them, towering and feathering away up into the black

mistiness that trees seem to gather about them at night; the silhouettes of those two upon the seat; the beams of light coming from the
Casino, the woman all in black peeping with fear behind the tree-
trunk. It is melodrama; but I can't help it.

And then, it appears, something happened to Edward Ashburnham.
He assured me—and I see no reason for disbelieving him—that until
that moment he had had no idea whatever of caring for the girl. He
said that he had regarded her exactly as he would have regarded a
daughter. He certainly loved her, but with a very deep, very tender
and very tranquil love. He had missed her when she went away to her
convent-school; he had been glad when she had returned. But of
more than that he had been totally unconscious. Had he been conscious of it, he assured me, he would have fled from it as from a thing
accursed. He realized that it was the last outrage upon Leonora. But
the real point was his entire unconsciousness. He had gone with her
into that dark park with no quickening of the pulse, with no desire for
the intimacy of solitude. He had gone, intending to talk about polo-
ponies, and tennis-racquets; about the temperament of the reverend
Mother at the convent she had left and about whether her frock for a
party when they got home should be white or blue. It hadn't come
into his head that they would talk about a single thing that they hadn't
always talked about; it had not even come into his head that the tabu
which extended around her was not inviolable. And then, suddenly,
that——

He was very careful to assure me that at that time there was no
physical motive about his declaration. It did not appear to him to be
a matter of a dark night and a propinquity and so on. No, it was simply of her effect on the moral side of his life that he appears to have
talked. He said that he never had the slightest notion to enfold her in
his arms or so much as to touch her hand. He swore that he did not
touch her hand. He said that they sat, she at one end of the bench, he
at the other; he leaning slightly towards her and she looking straight
towards the light of the Casino, her face illuminated by the lamps.
The expression upon her face he could only describe as "queer".

At another time, indeed, he made it appear that he thought she was
glad. It is easy to imagine that she was glad, since at that time she
could have had no idea of what was really happening. Frankly,
she adored Edward Ashburnham. He was for her, in everything that
she said at that time, the model of humanity, the hero, the athlete, the

father of his country, the law-giver. So that for her, to be suddenly, intimately and overwhelmingly praised must have been a matter for mere gladness, however overwhelming it were. It must have been as if a god had approved her handiwork or a king her loyalty. She just sat still and listened, smiling.

And it seemed to her that all the bitterness of her childhood, the terrors of her tempestuous father, the bewailings of her cruel-tongued mother were suddenly atoned for. She had her recompense at last. Because, of course, if you come to figure it out, a sudden pouring forth of passion by a man whom you regard as a cross between a pastor and a father might, to a woman, have the aspect of mere praise for good conduct. It wouldn't, I mean, appear at all in the light of an attempt to gain possession. The girl, at least, regarded him as firmly anchored to his Leonora. She had not the slightest inkling of any infidelities. He had always spoken to her of his wife in terms of reverence and deep affection. He had given her the idea that he regarded Leonora as absolutely impeccable* and as absolutely satisfying. Their union had appeared to her to be one of those blessed things that are spoken of and contemplated with reverence by her church.

So that, when he spoke of her as being the person he cared most for in the world, she naturally thought that he meant to except Leonora and she was just glad. It was like a father saying that he approved of a marriageable daughter . . . And Edward, when he realised what he was doing, curbed his tongue at once. She was just glad and she went on being just glad.

I suppose that that was the most monstrously wicked thing that Edward Ashburnham ever did in his life. And yet I am so near to all these people that I cannot think any of them wicked. It is impossible for me to think of Edward Ashburnham as anything but straight, upright and honourable. That, I mean, is, in spite of everything, my permanent view of him. I try at times by dwelling on some of the things that he did to push that image of him away, as you might try to push aside a large pendulum. But it always comes back—the memory of his innumerable acts of kindness, of his efficiency, of his unspiteful tongue. He was such a fine fellow.

So I feel myself forced to attempt to excuse him in this as in so many other things. It is, I have no doubt, a most monstrous thing to attempt to corrupt a young girl just out of a convent. But I think Edward had no idea at all of corrupting her. I believe that he simply loved her. He said that that was the way of it and I, at least, believe him and I believe too that she was the only woman he ever really loved. He said that that was so; and he did enough to prove it. And Leonora said that it was so and Leonora knew him to the bottom of his heart.

I have come to be very much of a cynic in these matters; I mean that it is impossible to believe in the permanence of man's or woman's love. Or, at any rate, it is impossible to believe in the permanence of any early passion. As I see it, at least, with regard to man, a love affair, a love for any definite woman—is something in the nature of a widening of the experience. With each new woman that a man is attracted to there appears to come a broadening of the outlook, or, if you like, an acquiring of new territory. A turn of the eye-brow, a tone of the voice, a queer characteristic gesture—all these things, and it is these things that cause to arise the passion of love—all these things are like so many objects on the horizon of the landscape that tempt a man to walk beyond the horizon, to explore. He wants to get, as it were, behind those eye-brows with the peculiar turn, as if he desired to see the world with the eyes that they overshadow. He wants to hear that voice applying itself to every possible proposition, to every possible topic; he wants to see those characteristic gestures against every possible background. Of the question of the sex-instinct I know very little and I do not think that it counts for very much in a really great passion. It can be aroused by such nothings—by an untied shoelace, by a glance of the eye in passing—that I think it might be left out of the calculation. I don't mean to say that any great passion can exist without a desire for consummation. That seems to me to be a commonplace and to be therefore a matter needing no comment at all. It is a thing, with all its accidents, that must be taken for granted, as, in a novel, or a biography, you take it for granted that the characters have their meals with some regularity. But the real fierceness of desire, the real heat of a passion long continued and withering up the soul of a man is the craving for identity with the woman that he loves. He desires to see with the same eyes, to touch with the same sense of touch, to hear with the same ears, to lose his identity, to be enveloped, to be supported. For, whatever may be said of the relation of the sexes, there is no man who loves a woman that does not desire to come to her for the renewal of his courage, for the cutting asunder of his difficulties. And that will be the mainspring of his desire for her.

We are all so afraid, we are all so alone, we all so need from the outside the assurance of our own worthiness to exist.

So, for a time, if such a passion come to fruition, the man will get what he wants. He will get the moral support, the encouragement, the relief from the sense of loneliness, the assurance of his own worth. But these things pass away; inevitably they pass away as the shadows pass across sun-dials. It is sad, but it is so. The pages of the book will become familiar; the beautiful corner of the road will have been turned too many times. Well, this is the saddest story.

And yet I do believe that for every man there comes at last a woman—or, no, that is the wrong way of formulating it. For every man there comes at last a time of life when the woman who then sets her seal upon his imagination has set her seal for good. He will travel over no more horizons; he will never again set the knapsack over his shoulders; he will retire from those scenes. He will have gone out of the business.

That at any rate was the case with Edward and the poor girl. It was quite literally the case. It was quite literally the case that his passions—for the mistress of the grand-duke, for Mrs. Basil, for little Mrs. Maidan, for Florence, for whom you will—these passions were merely preliminary canters compared to his final race with death for her. I am certain of that. I am not going to be so American as to say that all true love demands some sacrifice. It doesn't. But I think that love will be truer and more permanent in which self-sacrifice has been exacted. And, in the case of the other women, Edward just cut in and cut them out as he did with the polo-ball from under the nose of Count Baron von Lelöffel. I don't mean to say that he didn't wear himself as thin as a lath in the endeavour to capture the other women; but over her he wore himself to rags and tatters and death—in the effort to leave her alone.

And, in speaking to her on that night, he wasn't, I am convinced, committing a baseness. It was as if his passion for her hadn't existed; as if the very words that he spoke, without knowing that he spoke them, created the passion as they went along. Before he spoke, there was nothing; afterwards, it was the integral fact of his life. Well, I must get back to my story.

And my story was concerning itself with Florence—with Florence, who heard those words from behind the tree. That of course is only conjecture, but I think the conjecture is pretty well justified.

You have the fact that those two went out, that she followed them almost immediately afterwards through the darkness and, a little later, she came running back to the hotel with that pallid face and the hand clutching her dress over her heart. It can't have been only Bagshawe. Her face was contorted with agony before ever her eyes fell upon me or upon him beside me. But I dare say Bagshawe may have been the determining influence in her suicide. Leonora says that she had that flask, apparently of nitrate of amyl, but actually of prussic acid, for many years and that she was determined to use it if ever I discovered the nature of her relationship with that fellow Jimmy. You see, the mainspring of her nature must have been vanity. There is no reason why it shouldn't have been; I guess it is vanity that makes most of us keep straight, if we do keep straight, in this world.

If it had been merely a matter of Edward's relations with the girl I dare say Florence would have faced it out. She would no doubt have made him scenes, have threatened him, have appealed to his sense of honour, to his promises. But Mr. Bagshawe and the fact that the date was the 4th of August must have been too much for her superstitious mind. You see, she had two things that she wanted. She wanted to be a great lady, installed in Branshaw Teleragh. She wanted also to retain my respect.

She wanted, that is to say, to retain my respect for as long as she lived with me. I suppose, if she had persuaded Edward Ashburnham to bolt* with her she would have let the whole thing go with a run. Or perhaps she would have tried to exact from me a new respect for the greatness of her passion on the lines of all for love and the world well lost.* That would be just like Florence.

In all matrimonial associations there is, I believe, one constant factor—a desire to deceive the person with whom one lives as to some weak spot in one's character or in one's career. For it is intolerable to live constantly with one human being who perceives one's small meannesses. It is really death to do so—that is why so many marriages turn out unhappily.

I, for instance, am a rather greedy man; I have a taste for good cookery and a watering tooth at the mere sound of the names of certain comestibles. If Florence had discovered this secret of mine I should have found her knowledge of it so unbearable that I never could have supported all the other privations of the régime that she extracted from me. I am bound to say that Florence never discovered this secret.

Certainly she never alluded to it; I dare say she never took sufficient interest in me.

And the secret weakness of Florence—the weakness that she could not bear to have me discover, was just that early escapade with the fellow called Jimmy. Let me, as this is in all probability the last time I shall mention Florence's name,* dwell a little upon the change that had taken place in her psychology. She would not, I mean, have minded if I had discovered that she was the mistress of Edward Ashburnham. She would rather have liked it. Indeed, the chief trouble of poor Leonora in those days was to keep Florence from making, before me, theatrical displays, on one line or another, of that very fact. She wanted, in one mood, to come rushing to me, to cast herself on her knees at my feet and to declaim a carefully arranged, frightfully emotional, outpouring as to her passion. That was to show that she was like one of the great erotic women of whom history tells us. In another mood she would desire to come to me disdainfully and to tell me that I was considerably less than a man and that what had happened was what must happen when a real male came along. She wanted to say that in cool, balanced and sarcastic sentences. That was when she wished to appear like the heroine of a French comedy. Because of course she was always play-acting.

But what she didn't want me to know was the fact of her first escapade with the fellow called Jimmy. She had arrived at figuring out the sort of low-down Bowery* tough that that fellow was. Do you know what it is to shudder, in later life, for some small, stupid action—usually for some small, quite genuine piece of emotionalism—of your early life? Well, it was that sort of shuddering that came over Florence at the thought that she had surrendered to such a low fellow. I don't know that she need have shuddered. It was her footling old uncle's work; he ought never to have taken those two round the world together and shut himself up in his cabin for the greater part of the time. Anyhow, I am convinced that the sight of Mr. Bagshawe and the thought that Mr. Bagshawe—for she knew that unpleasant and toadlike personality—the thought that Mr. Bagshawe would almost certainly reveal to me that he had caught her coming out of Jimmy's bedroom at five o'clock in the morning on the 4th of August, 1900—that was the determining influence in her suicide.

And no doubt the effect of the date was too much for her superstitious personality. She had been born on the 4th of August; she had started to go round the world on the 4th of August; she had become a low fellow's mistress on the 4th of August. On the same day of the year she had married me; on that 4th she had lost Edward's love and Bagshawe had appeared like a sinister omen—like a grin on the face of Fate. It was the last straw. She ran upstairs, arranged herself decoratively upon her bed—she was a sweetly pretty woman with smooth pink and white cheeks, long hair, the eyelashes falling like a tiny curtain on her cheeks. She drank the little phial of prussic acid and there she lay.—O, extremely charming and clear-cut—looking with a puzzled expression at the electric-light bulb that hung from the ceiling, or perhaps through it, to the stars above. Who knows? Anyhow, there was an end of Florence.

You have no idea how quite extraordinarily for me that was the end of Florence. From that day to this I have never given her another thought; I have not bestowed upon her so much as a sigh. Of course, when it has been necessary to talk about her to Leonora or, when for the purpose of these writings I have tried to figure her out, I have thought about her as I might do about a problem in Algebra. But it has always been as a matter for study, not for remembrance. She just went completely out of existence, like yesterday's paper.

I was so deadly tired. And I dare say that my week or ten days of affaissement*—of what was practically catalepsy—was just the repose that my exhausted nature claimed after twelve years of the repression of my instincts, after twelve years of playing the trained poodle. For that was all that I had been. I suppose that it was the shock that did it—the several shocks. But I am unwilling to attribute my feelings at that time to anything so concrete as a shock. It was a feeling so tranquil. It was as if an immensely heavy—an unbearably heavy knapsack, supported upon my shoulders by straps, had fallen off and had left my shoulders themselves that the straps had cut into, numb and without sensation of life. I tell you, I had no regret. What had I to regret? I suppose that my inner soul—my dual personality— had realized long before that Florence was a personality of paper— that she represented a real human being with a heart, with feelings, with sympathies and with emotions only as a bank note represents a certain quantity of gold. I know that that sort of feeling came to the surface in me the moment the man Bagshawe told me that he had seen her coming out of that fellow's bedroom. I thought suddenly that she wasn't real; she was just a mass of talk out of guide-books, of drawings out of fashion-plates. It is even possible that, if that feeling had not possessed me, I should have run up sooner to her room and might have prevented her drinking the prussic acid. But I just couldn't do it; it would have been like chasing a scrap of paper—an occupation ignoble for a grown man.

And, as it began, so that matter has remained. I didn't care whether she had come out of that bedroom or whether she hadn't. It simply didn't interest me. Florence didn't matter.

I suppose you will retort that I was in love with Nancy Rufford and that my indifference was therefore discreditable. Well, I am not seeking to avoid discredit. I was in love with Nancy Rufford as I am in love with the poor child's memory, quietly and quite tenderly in my American sort of way. I had never thought about it until I heard Leonora state that I might now marry her. But, from that moment until her worse than death, I do not suppose that I much thought about anything else. I don't mean to say that I sighed about her or groaned; I just wanted to marry her as some people want to go to Carcassonne.

Do you understand the feeling—the sort of feeling that you must get certain matters out of the way, smooth out certain fairly negligible complications before you can go to a place that has, during all your life, been a sort of dream city? I didn't attach much importance to my superior years. I was forty-five, and she, poor thing, was only just rising twenty-two. But she was older than her years and quieter. She seemed to have an odd quality of sainthood, as if she must inevitably end in a convent with a white coif framing her face. But she had frequently told me that she had no vocation; it just simply wasn't there—the desire to become a nun. Well, I guess that I was a sort of convent myself; it seemed fairly proper that she should make her vows to me.

No, I didn't see any impediment on the score of age. I dare say no man does and I was pretty confident that, with a little preparation, I could make a young girl happy. I could spoil her as few young girls have ever been spoiled; and I couldn't regard myself as personally repulsive. No man can, or, if he ever comes to do so, that is the end of him. But, as soon as I came out of my catalepsy, I seemed to perceive that my problem—that what I had to do to prepare myself for getting into contact with her, was just to get back into contact with life. I had been kept for twelve years in a rarefied atmosphere; what I then had to do was a little fighting with real life, some wrestling with men of business, some travelling amongst larger cities, something harsh, something masculine. I didn't want to present myself to Nancy Rufford as a sort of an old maid. That was why, just a fortnight after Florence's suicide, I set off for the United States.

II

IMMEDIATELY after Florence's death Leonora began to put the leash upon Nancy Rufford and Edward. She had guessed what had happened under the trees near the Casino. They stayed at Nauheim some weeks after I went, and Leonora has told me that that was the most deadly time of her existence. It seemed like a long, silent duel with invisible weapons, so she said. And it was rendered all the more difficult by the girl's entire innocence. For Nancy was always trying to go off alone with Edward—as she had been doing all her life, whenever she was home for holidays. She just wanted him to say nice things to her again.

You see, the position was extremely complicated. It was as complicated as it well could be, along delicate lines. There was the complication caused by the fact that Edward and Leonora never spoke to each other except when other people were present. Then, as I have said, their demeanours were quite perfect. There was the complication caused by the girl's entire innocence; there was the further complication that both Edward and Leonora really regarded the girl as their daughter. Or it might be more precise to say that they regarded her as being Leonora's daughter. And Nancy was a queer girl; it is very difficult to describe her to you.

She was tall and strikingly thin; she had a tortured mouth, agonised eyes, and a quite extraordinary sense of fun. You might put it that at times she was exceedingly grotesque and at times extraordinarily beautiful. Why, she had the heaviest head of black hair that I have ever come across; I used to wonder how she could bear the weight of it. She was just over twenty-one and at times she seemed as old as the hills, at times not much more than sixteen. At one moment she would be talking of the lives of the saints and at the next she would be tumbling all over the lawn with the St. Bernard puppy. She could ride to hounds like a Mænad* and she could sit for hours perfectly still, steeping handkerchief after handkerchief in vinegar when Leonora had one of her headaches. She was, in short, a miracle of patience who could be almost miraculously impatient. It was no doubt the convent training that effected that. I remember that one of her letters to me, when she was about sixteen, ran something like:

"On Corpus Christi"*—or it may have been some other saint's day, I cannot keep these things in my head—"our school played Roehampton* at Hockey. And, seeing that our side was losing, being three goals to one against us at half-time, we retired into the chapel and prayed for victory. We won by five goals to three." And I remember that she seemed to describe afterwards a sort of saturnalia.* Apparently, when the victorious fifteen, or eleven, came into the refectory for supper, the whole school jumped upon the tables and cheered and broke the chairs on the floor and smashed the crockery—for a given time, until the Reverend Mother rang a hand-bell. That is of course the Catholic tradition—saturnalia that can end in a moment, like the crack of a whip. I don't of course like the tradition, but I am bound to say that it gave Nancy—or at any rate Nancy had, a sense of rectitude that I have never seen surpassed. It was a thing like a knife that looked out of her eyes and that spoke with her voice, just now and then. It positively frightened me. I suppose that I was almost afraid to be in a world where there could be so fine a standard. I remember when she was about fifteen or sixteen on going back to the convent I once gave her a couple of English sovereigns as a tip. She thanked me in a peculiarly heartfelt way, saying that it would come in extremely handy. I asked her why and she explained. There was a rule at the school that the pupils were not to speak when they walked through the garden from the chapel to the refectory. And, since this rule appeared to be idiotic and arbitrary, she broke it on purpose day after day. In the evening the children were all asked if they had committed any faults during the day, and every evening Nancy confessed that she had broken this particular rule. It cost her sixpence a time, that being the fine attached to the offence. Just for the information I asked her why she always confessed, and she answered in these exact words:

"Oh, well, the girls of the Holy Child have always been noted for their truthfulness. It's a beastly bore, but I've got to do it."

I dare say that the miserable nature of her childhood, coming before the mixture of saturnalia and discipline that was her convent life, added something to her queernesses. Her father was a violent madman of a fellow, a major in one of what I believe are called the Highland regiments. He didn't drink, but he had an ungovernable temper, and the first thing that Nancy could remember was seeing her father strike her mother with his clenched fist so that her mother fell over sideways from the breakfast table and lay motionless. The mother was no doubt an irritating woman and the privates of that regiment appeared to have been irritating, too, so that the house was a place of outcries and perpetual disturbance. Mrs. Rufford was Leonora's dearest friend and Leonora could be cutting enough at times. But I fancy she was as nothing to Mrs. Rufford. The Major would come in to lunch harassed and already spitting out oaths after an unsatisfactory morning's drilling of his stubborn men beneath a hot sun. And then Mrs. Rufford would make some cutting remark and pandemonium would break loose. Once, when she had been about twelve, Nancy had tried to intervene between the pair of them. Her father had struck her full upon the forehead a blow so terrible that she had lain unconscious for three days. Nevertheless Nancy seemed to prefer her father to her mother. She remembered rough kindnesses from him. Once or twice when she had been quite small he had dressed her in a clumsy, impatient, but very tender way. It was nearly always impossible to get a servant to stay in the family and, for days at a time, apparently, Mrs. Rufford would be incapable. I fancy she drank. At any rate she had so cutting a tongue that even Nancy was afraid of her—she so made fun of any tenderness, she so sneered at all emotional displays. Nancy must have been a very emotional child. . . .

Then one day, quite suddenly, on her return from a ride at Fort William,* Nancy had been sent, with her governess, who had a white face, right down South to that convent school. She had been expecting to go there in two months' time. Her mother disappeared from her life at that time. A fortnight later Leonora came to the convent and told her that her mother was dead. Perhaps she was. At any rate, I never heard until the very end what became of Mrs. Rufford.* Leonora never spoke of her.

And then Major Rufford went to India, from which he returned very seldom and only for very short visits; and Nancy lived herself gradually into the life at Branshaw Teleragh. I think that, from that time onwards, she led a very happy life, till the end. There were dogs and horses and old servants and the Forest.* And there were Edward and Leonora, who loved her.

I had known her all the time—I mean that she always came to the Ashburnhams' at Nauheim for the last fortnight of their stay, and I watched her gradually growing. She was very cheerful with me. She

always even kissed me, night and morning, until she was about eighteen. And she would skip about and fetch me things and laugh at my
tales of life in Philadelphia. But, beneath her gaiety, I fancy that there
lurked some terrors. I remember one day, when she was just eighteen, during one of her father's rare visits to Europe, we were sitting
in the gardens, near the iron-stained fountain. Leonora had one of
her headaches and we were waiting for Florence and Edward to come
from their baths. You have no idea how beautiful Nancy looked that
morning.

    We were talking about the desirability of taking tickets in lotter-
ies—of the moral side of it, I mean. She was all in white, and so tall
and fragile; and she had only just put her hair up, so that the carriage
of her neck had that charming touch of youth and of unfamiliarity.
Over her throat there played the reflection from a little pool of water,
left by a thunderstorm of the night before, and all the rest of her
features were in the diffused and luminous shade of her white para-
sol. Her dark hair just showed beneath her broad, white hat of
pierced, chip straw; her throat was very long and leaned forward,
and her eyebrows, arching a little as she laughed at some old-
fashionedness in my phraseology, had abandoned their tense line. And
there was a little colour in her cheeks and light in her deep blue eyes.
And to think that that vivid white thing, that saintly and swanlike
being—to think that . . . Why, she was like the sail of a ship, so white
and so definite in her movements. And to think that she will never . . .
Why, she will never do anything again. I can't believe it . . .

    Anyhow, we were chattering away about the morality of lotteries.
And then, suddenly, there came from the arcades behind us the over-
tones of her father's unmistakable voice; it was as if a modified fog-
horn had boomed with a reed inside it. I looked round to catch sight
of him. A tall, fair, stiffly upright man of fifty, he was walking away
with an Italian baron who had had much to do with the Belgian
Congo. They must have been talking about the proper treatment of
natives, for I heard him say:

    "Oh, hang humanity!"

    When I looked again at Nancy her eyes were closed and her face
was more pallid than her dress, which had at least some pinkish
reflections from the gravel. It was dreadful to see her with her eyes
closed like that.

    "Oh," she exclaimed, and her hand that had appeared to be

groping, settled for a moment on my arm. "Never speak of it. Promise never to tell my father of it. It brings back those dreadful dreams . . ." And, when she opened her eyes she looked straight into mine. "The blessed saints," she said, "you would think they would spare you such things. I don't believe all the sinning in the world could make one deserve them."

They say the poor thing was always allowed a light at night, even in her bedroom. . . . And yet, no young girl could more archly and lovingly have played with an adored father. She was always holding him by both coat lapels; cross-questioning him as to how he spent his time; kissing the top of his head. Ah, she was well-bred, if ever anyone was.

The poor, wretched man cringed before her—but she could not have done more to put him at his ease. Perhaps she had had lessons in it at her convent. It was only that peculiar note of his voice, used when he was overbearing or dogmatic, that could unman her—and that was only visible when it came unexpectedly. That was because the bad dreams that the blessed saints allowed her to have for her sins always seemed to her to herald themselves by the booming sound of her father's voice. It was that sound that had always preceded his entrance for the terrible lunches of her childhood . . .

I have reported, earlier in this chapter, that Leonora said, during that remainder of their stay at Nauheim, after I had left, it had seemed to her that she was fighting a long duel with unseen weapons against silent adversaries. Nancy, as I have also said, was always trying to go off with Edward alone. That had been her habit for years. And Leonora found it to be her duty to stop that. It was very difficult. Nancy was used to having her own way, and for years she had been used to going off with Edward, ratting, rabbiting, catching salmon down at Fordingbridge, district-visiting of the sort that Edward indulged in, or calling on the tenants. And at Nauheim she and Edward had always gone up to the Casino alone in the evenings—at any rate, whenever Florence did not call for his attendance. It shows the obviously innocent nature of the regard of those two that even Florence had never had any idea of jealousy. Leonora had cultivated the habit of going to bed at ten o'clock.

I don't know how she managed it, but, for all the time they were at Nauheim, she contrived never to let those two be alone together, except in broad daylight, in very crowded places. If a Protestant had done that it would no doubt have awakened a self-consciousness in the girl. But Catholics, who have always reservations and queer spots of secrecy, can manage these things better. And I dare say that two things made this easier—the death of Florence and the fact that Edward was obviously sickening. He appeared, indeed, to be very ill; his shoulders began to be bowed; there were pockets under his eyes; he had extraordinary moments of inattention.

And Leonora describes herself as watching him as a fierce cat watches an unconscious pigeon in a roadway. In that silent watching, again, I think she was a Catholic—of a people that can think thoughts alien to ours and keep them to themselves. And the thoughts passed through her mind; some of them even got through to Edward with never a word spoken. At first she thought that it might be remorse, or grief, for the death of Florence that was oppressing him. But she watched and watched, and uttered apparently random sentences about Florence before the girl, and she perceived that he had no grief and no remorse. He had not any idea that Florence could have committed suicide without writing at least a tirade to him. The absence of that made him certain that it had been heart disease. For Florence had never undeceived him on that point. She thought it made her seem more romantic.

No, Edward had no remorse. He was able to say to himself that he had treated Florence with gallant attentiveness of the kind that she desired until two hours before her death. Leonora gathered that from the look in his eyes, and from the way he straightened his shoulders over her as she lay in her coffin—from that and a thousand other little things. She would speak suddenly about Florence to the girl and he would not start in the least; he would not even pay attention, but would sit with bloodshot eyes gazing at the tablecloth. He drank a good deal, at that time—a steady soaking of drink every evening till long after they had gone to bed.

For Leonora made the girl go to bed at ten, unreasonable though that seemed to Nancy. She would understand that, whilst they were in a sort of half mourning for Florence, she ought not to be seen at public places, like the Casino; but she could not see why she should not accompany her uncle upon his evening strolls though the park. I don't know what Leonora put up as an excuse—something, I fancy, in the nature of a nightly orison* that she made the girl and herself perform for the soul of Florence. And then, one evening, about a fortnight later, when the girl, growing restive at even devotional exercises, clamoured once more to be allowed to go for a walk with Edward, and when Leonora was really at her wits' end, Edward gave himself into her hands. He was just standing up from dinner and had his face averted.

But he turned his heavy head and his bloodshot eyes upon his wife and looked full at her.

"Doctor von Hauptmann," he said, "has ordered me to go to bed immediately after dinner. My heart's much worse."

He continued to look at Leonora for a long minute—with a sort of heavy contempt. And Leonora understood that, with his speech, he was giving her the excuse that she needed for separating him from the girl, and with his eyes he was reproaching her for thinking that he would try to corrupt Nancy.

He went silently up to his room and sat there for a long time—until the girl was well in bed—reading in the Anglican prayer book. And about half past ten she heard his footsteps pass her door, going outwards. Two and a half hours later they came back, stumbling heavily.

She remained, reflecting upon this position until the last night of their stay at Nauheim. Then she suddenly acted. For, just in the same way, suddenly after dinner, she looked at him and said:

"Teddy, don't you think you could take a night off from your doctor's orders and go with Nancy to the Casino. The poor child has had her visit so spoiled."

He looked at her in turn for a long, balancing minute.

"Why, yes," he said at last. Nancy jumped out of her chair and kissed him.

Those two words, Leonora said, gave her the greatest relief of any two syllables she had ever heard in her life. For she realised that Edward was breaking up, not under the desire for possession, but from the dogged determination to hold his hand. She could relax some of her vigilance.

Nevertheless she sat in the darkness behind her half-closed jalousies,* looking over the street and the night and the trees until, very late, she could hear Nancy's clear voice coming closer and saying:

"You did look an old guy* with that false nose."

There had been some sort of celebration of a local holiday up in the Kursaal. And Edward replied with his sort of sulky good nature:

"As for you, you looked like old Mother Sideacher."*

The girl came swinging along, a silhouette beneath a gas-lamp; Edward, another, slouched at her side. They were talking just as they had talked any time since the girl had been seventeen; with the same tones, the same joke about an old beggar woman who always amused them at Branshaw. The girl, a little later, opened Leonora's door whilst she was still kissing Edward on the forehead as she had done every night.

"We've had a most glorious time," she said. "He's ever so much better. He raced me for twenty yards home. Why are you all in the dark?"

Leonora could hear Edward going about in his room, but, owing to the girl's chatter, she could not tell whether he went out again or not. And then, very much later, because she thought that if he were drinking again something must be done to stop it, she opened for the first time, and very softly, the never-opened door between their rooms. She wanted to see if he had gone out again. Edward was kneeling beside his bed with his head hidden in the counterpane. His arms, outstretched, held out before him a little image of the Blessed Virgin—a tawdry, scarlet and Prussian blue affair that the girl had given him on her first return from the convent. His shoulders heaved convulsively three times, and heavy sobs came from him before she could close the door. He was not a Catholic; but that was the way it took him.

Leonora slept for the first time that night with a sleep from which she never once started.

III

AND then Leonora completely broke down—on the day that they returned to Branshaw Teleragh. It is the infliction of our miserable minds—it is the scourge of atrocious but probably just destiny that no grief comes by itself. No, any great grief, though the grief itself may have gone, leaves in its place a train of horrors, of misery, and despair. For Leonora was, in herself, relieved. She felt that she could trust Edward with the girl and she knew that Nancy could be absolutely trusted. And then, with the slackening of her vigilance, came the slackening of her entire mind. This is perhaps the most miserable part of the entire story. For it is miserable to see a clear intelligence waver; and Leonora wavered.

You are to understand that Leonora loved Edward with a passion that was yet like an agony of hatred. And she had lived with him for years and years without addressing to him one word of tenderness. I don't know how she could do it. At the beginning of that relationship she had been just married off to him. She had been one of seven daughters in a bare, untidy Irish manor house to which she had returned from the convent I have so often spoken of. She had left it just a year and she was just nineteen. It is impossible to imagine such inexperience as was hers. You might almost say that she had never spoken to a man except a priest. Coming straight from the convent, she had gone in behind the high walls of the manor-house that was almost more cloistral than any convent could have been. There were the seven girls, there was the strained mother, there was the worried father at whom, three times, in the course of that year, the tenants took pot-shots from behind a hedge. The women-folk, upon the whole, the tenants respected. Once a week each of the girls, since there were seven of them, took a drive with the mother in the old basketwork chaise* drawn by a very fat, very lumbering pony. They paid occasionally a call, but even these were so rare that, Leonora has assured me, only three times in the year that succeeded her coming home from the convent did she enter another person's house. For the rest of the time the seven sisters ran about in the neglected gardens between the unpruned espaliers.* Or they played lawn-tennis or fives* in an angle of a great wall that surrounded the garden—an

angle from which the fruit trees had long died away. They painted in
water-colour; they embroidered; they copied verses into albums.
Once a week they went to Mass; once a week to the confessional
accompanied by an old nurse. They were happy since they had known
no other life.

It appeared to them a singular extravagance when, one day, a pho-
tographer was brought over from the county town and photographed
them standing, all seven, in the shadow of an old apple-tree with the
grey lichen on the raddled trunk.

But it wasn't an extravagance.

Three weeks before Colonel Powys had written to Colonel
Ashburnham:

"I say, Harry, couldn't your Edward marry one of my girls? It
would be a god-send to me, for I'm at the end of my tether and, once
one girl begins to go off, the rest of them will follow." He went on to
say that all his daughters were tall, upstanding, clean-limbed and
absolutely pure, and he reminded Colonel Ashburnham that, they
having been married on the same day, though in different churches,
since the one was a Catholic and the other an Anglican—they had
said to each other, the night before, that, when the time came, one of
their sons should marry one of their daughters. Mrs. Ashburnham
had been a Powys and remained Mrs. Powys' dearest friend. They
had drifted about the world as English soldiers do, seldom meeting,
but their women always in correspondence one with another. They
wrote about minute things such as the teething of Edward and of the
earlier daughters or the best way to repair a Jacob's ladder in a stocking. And, if they met seldom, yet it was often enough to keep each
other's personalities fresh in their minds, gradually growing a little
stiff in the joints, but always with enough to talk about and with a
store of reminiscences. Then, as his girls began to come of an age
when they must leave the convent in which they were regularly
interned during his years of active service, Colonel Powys retired
from the army with the necessity of making a home for them. It happened that the Ashburnhams had never seen any of the Powys girls,
though, whenever the four parents met in London, Edward
Ashburnham was always of the party. He was at that time twenty-
two and, I believe, almost as pure in mind as Leonora herself. It is
odd how a boy can have his virgin intelligence untouched in this
world.

That was partly due to the careful handling of his mother, partly to the fact that the house to which he went at Winchester had a particularly pure tone and partly to Edward's own peculiar aversion from anything like coarse language or gross stories. At Sandhurst* he had just kept out of the way of that sort of thing. He was keen on soldiering, keen on mathematics, on land-surveying, on politics and, by a queer warp of his mind, on literature. Even when he was twenty-two he would pass hours reading one of Scott's novels or the Chronicles of Froissart.*

Mrs. Ashburnham considered that she was to be congratulated, and almost every week she wrote to Mrs. Powys, dilating upon her satisfaction.

Then, one day, taking a walk down Bond Street with her son, after having been at Lord's,* she noticed Edward suddenly turn his head round to take a second look at a well-dressed girl who had passed them. She wrote about that, too, to Mrs. Powys, and expressed some alarm. It had been, on Edward's part, the merest reflex action. He was so very abstracted at that time owing to the pressure his crammer* was putting upon him that he certainly hadn't known what he was doing.

It was this letter of Mrs. Ashburnham's to Mrs. Powys that had caused the letter from Colonel Powys to Colonel Ashburnham—a letter that was half-humorous, half-longing. Mrs. Ashburnham caused her husband to reply, with a letter a little more jocular—something to the effect that Colonel Powys ought to give them some idea of the goods that he was marketing. That was the cause of the photograph. I have seen it, the seven girls, all in white dresses, all very much alike in feature—all, except Leonora, a little heavy about the chins and a little stupid about the eyes. I dare say it would have made Leonora, too, look a little heavy and a little stupid, for it was not a good photograph. But the black shadow from one of the branches of the apple tree cut right across her face, which is all but invisible.

There followed an extremely harassing time for Colonel and Mrs. Powys. Mrs. Ashburnham had written to say that, quite sincerely, nothing would give greater ease to her maternal anxieties than to have her son marry one of Mrs. Powys' daughters if only he showed some inclination to do so. For, she added, nothing but a love-match was to be thought of in her Edward's case. But the poor Powys couple had to run things so very fine that even the bringing together of the young people was a desperate hazard.

The mere expenditure upon sending one of the girls over from Ireland to Branshaw was terrifying to them; and whichever girl they selected might not be the one to ring Edward's bell. On the other hand, the expenditure upon mere food and extra sheets for a visit from the Ashburnhams to them was terrifying, too. It would mean, mathematically, going short in so many meals themselves, afterwards. Nevertheless, they chanced it, and all the three Ashburnhams came on a visit to the lonely manor-house. They could give Edward some rough shooting, some rough fishing and a whirl of femininity; but I should say the girls made really more impression upon Mrs. Ashburnham than upon Edward himself. They appeared to her to be so clean run and so safe. They were indeed so clean run that, in a faint sort of way, Edward seems to have regarded them rather as boys than as girls. And then, one evening, Mrs. Ashburnham had with her boy one of those conversations that English mothers have with English sons. It seems to have been a criminal sort of proceeding, though I don't know what took place at it. Anyhow, next morning Colonel Ashburnham asked on behalf of his son for the hand of Leonora. This caused some consternation to the Powys couple, since Leonora was the third daughter and Edward ought to have married the eldest. Mrs. Powys, with her rigid sense of the proprieties, almost wished to reject the proposal. But the Colonel, her husband, pointed out that the visit would have cost them sixty pounds, what with the hire of an extra servant, of a horse and car, and with the purchase of beds and bedding and extra tablecloths. There was nothing else for it but the marriage. In that way Edward and Leonora became man and wife.

I don't know that a very minute study of their progress towards complete disunion is necessary. Perhaps it is. But there are many things that I cannot well make out, about which I cannot well question Leonora, or about which Edward did not tell me. I do not know that there was ever any question of love from Edward to her. He regarded her, certainly, as desirable amongst her sisters. He was obstinate to the extent of saying that if he could not have her he would not have any of them. And, no doubt, before the marriage, he made her pretty speeches out of books that he had read. But, as far as he could describe his feelings at all, later, it seems that, calmly and without any quickening of the pulse, he just carried the girl off, there being no opposition. It had, however, been all so long ago that it seemed to him, at the end of his poor life, a dim and misty affair. He had the greatest admiration for Leonora.

He had the very greatest admiration. He admired her for her truthfulness, for her cleanness of mind, and the clean-run-ness of her limbs, for her efficiency, for the fairness of her skin, for the gold of her hair, for her religion, for her sense of duty. It was a satisfaction to take her about with him.

But she had not for him a touch of magnetism. I suppose, really, he did not love her because she was never mournful; what really made him feel good in life was to comfort somebody who would be darkly and mysteriously mournful. That he had never had to do for Leonora. Perhaps, also, she was at first too obedient. I do not mean to say that she was submissive—that she deferred, in her judgments, to his. She did not. But she had been handed over to him, like some patient medieval virgin; she had been taught all her life that the first duty of a woman is to obey. And there she was.

In her, at least, admiration for his qualities very soon became love of the deepest description. If his pulses never quickened she, so I have been told, became what is called an altered being when he approached her from the other side of a dancing floor. Her eyes followed him about full of trustfulness, of admiration, of gratitude, and of love. He was also, in a great sense, her pastor and guide—and he guided her into what, for a girl straight out of a convent, was almost heaven. I have not the least idea of what an English officer's wife's existence may be like. At any rate, there were feasts, and chatterings, and nice men who gave her the right sort of admiration, and nice women who treated her as if she had been a baby. And her confessor approved of her life, and Edward let her give little treats to the girls of the convent she had left, and the Reverend Mother approved of him. There could not have been a happier girl for five or six years.

For it was only at the end of that time that clouds began, as the saying is, to arise. She was then about twenty-three, and her purposeful efficiency made her perhaps have a desire for mastery. She began to perceive that Edward was extravagant in his largesses.* His parents died just about that time, and Edward, though they both decided that he should continue his soldiering, gave a great deal of attention to the management of Branshaw through a steward.

Aldershot* was not very far away, and they spent all his leaves there.

And, suddenly, she seemed to begin to perceive that his generosities were almost fantastic. He subscribed much too much to things connected with his mess, he pensioned off his father's servants, old or new, much too generously. They had a large income, but every now and then they would find themselves hard up. He began to talk of mortgaging a farm or two, though it never actually came to that.

She made tentative efforts at remonstrating with him. Her father, whom she saw now and then, said that Edward was much too generous to his tenants; the wives of his brother officers remonstrated with her in private; his large subscriptions made it difficult for their husbands to keep up with them. Ironically enough, the first real trouble between them came from his desire to build a Roman Catholic chapel at Branshaw. He wanted to do it to honour Leonora, and he proposed to do it very expensively. Leonora did not want it; she could perfectly well drive from Branshaw to the nearest Catholic Church as often as she liked. There were no Roman Catholic tenants and no Roman Catholic servants except her old nurse who could always drive with her. She had as many priests to stay with her as could be needed— and even the priests did not want a gorgeous chapel in that place where it would have merely seemed an invidious instance of ostentation. They were perfectly ready to celebrate mass for Leonora and her nurse, when they stayed at Branshaw, in a cleaned-up outhouse. But Edward was as obstinate as a hog about it.

He was truly grieved at his wife's want of sentiment—at her refusal to receive that amount of public homage from him. She appeared to him to be wanting in imagination—to be cold and hard. I don't exactly know what part her priests played in the tragedy that it all became; I dare say they behaved quite creditably but mistakenly. But then, who would not have been mistaken with Edward? I believe he was even hurt that Leonora's confessor did not make strenuous efforts to convert him. There was a period when he was quite ready to become an emotional Catholic.

I don't know why they did not take him on the hop; but they have queer sorts of wisdoms, those people, and queer sorts of tact. Perhaps they thought that Edward's too early conversion would frighten off other Protestant desirables from marrying Catholic girls. Perhaps they saw deeper into Edward than he saw himself and thought that he would make a not very creditable convert. At any rate they—and Leonora—left him very much alone. It mortified him very considerably. He has told me that if Leonora had then taken his aspirations seriously everything would have been different. But I dare say that was nonsense.

At any rate it was over the question of the chapel that they had their first and really disastrous quarrel. Edward at that time was not well; he supposed himself to be overworked with his regimental affairs—he was managing the mess at the time. And Leonora was not well—she was beginning to fear that their union might be sterile. And then her father came over from Glasmoyle to stay with them.

Those were troublesome times in Ireland, I understand. At any rate Colonel Powys had tenants on the brain—his own tenants having shot at him with shot-guns. And, in conversation with Edward's land-steward, he got it into his head that Edward managed his estates with a mad generosity towards his tenants. I understand also that those years—the nineties—were very bad for farming. Wheat was fetching only a few shillings the hundred; the price of meat was so low that cattle hardly paid for raising; whole English counties were ruined. And Edward allowed his tenants very high rebates.

To do both justice Leonora has since acknowledged that she was in the wrong at that time and that Edward was following out a more far-seeing policy in nursing his really very good tenants over a bad period. It was not as if the whole of his money came from the land; a good deal of it was in rails. But old Colonel Powys had that bee in his bonnet and, if he never directly approached Edward himself on the subject, he preached unceasingly, whenever he had the opportunity, to Leonora. His pet idea was that Edward ought to sack all his own tenants and import a set of farmers from Scotland. That was what they were doing in Essex. He was of opinion that Edward was riding hot-foot to ruin.

That worried Leonora very much—it worried her dreadfully; she lay awake nights; she had an anxious line round her mouth. And that, again, worried Edward. I do not mean to say that Leonora actually spoke to Edward about his tenants—but he got to know that some one, probably her father, had been talking to her about the matter. He got to know it because it was the habit of his steward to look in on them every morning about breakfast time to report any little happenings. And there was a farmer called Mumford who had only paid half his rent for the last three years. One morning the land-steward reported that Mumford would be unable to pay his rent at all that year. Edward reflected for a moment and then he said something like:

"O well, he's an old fellow and his family have been our tenants for over two hundred years. Let him off altogether."

And then Leonora—you must remember that she had reason for being very nervous and unhappy at that time—let out a sound that was very like a groan. It startled Edward, who more than suspected what was passing in her mind—it startled him into a state of anger. He said sharply:

"You wouldn't have me turn out people who've been earning money for us for centuries—people to whom we have responsibilities—and let in a pack of Scotch farmers?"

He looked at her, Leonora said, with what was practically a glance of hatred and then, precipitately, he left the breakfast-table. Leonora knew that it probably made it all the worse that he had been betrayed into a manifestation of anger before a third party. It was the first and last time that he ever was betrayed into such a manifestation of anger. The land-steward, a moderate and well-balanced man whose family also had been with the Ashburnhams for over a century, took it upon himself to explain that he considered Edward was pursuing a perfectly proper course with his tenants. He erred perhaps a little on the side of generosity, but hard times were hard times, and every one had to feel the pinch, landlord as well as tenants. The great thing was not to let the land get into a poor state of cultivation. Scotch farmers just skinned your fields and let them go down and down. But Edward had a very good set of tenants who did their best for him and for themselves. These arguments at that time carried very little conviction to Leonora. She was, nevertheless, much concerned by Edward's outburst of anger.

The fact is that Leonora had been practising economies in her department. Two of the under-housemaids had gone and she had not replaced them; she had spent much less that year upon dress. The fare she had provided at the dinners they gave had been much less bountiful and not nearly so costly as had been the case in preceding years, and Edward began to perceive a hardness and determination in his wife's character. He seemed to see a net closing round him—a net in which they would be forced to live like one of the comparatively poor county families of the neighbourhood. And, in the mysterious way in which two people, living together, get to know each other's thoughts without a word spoken, he had known, even before his outbreak, that Leonora was worrying about his managing of the estates. This appeared to him to be intolerable. He had, too, a great feeling of self-contempt because he had been betrayed into speaking harshly to Leonora before that land-steward. She imagined that his nerve must be deserting him, and there can have been few men more miserable than Edward was at that period.

You see, he was really a very simple soul*—very simple. He imagined that no man can satisfactorily accomplish his life's work without loyal and whole-hearted coöperation of the woman he lives with. And he was beginning to perceive dimly that, whereas his own traditions were entirely collective, his wife was a sheer individualist. His own theory—the feudal theory of an over-lord doing his best by his dependents, the dependents meanwhile doing their best for the over-lord—this theory was entirely foreign to Leonora's nature. She came of a family of small Irish landlords—that hostile garrison in a plundered country. And she was thinking unceasingly of the children she wished to have.

I don't know why they never had any children—not that I really believe that children would have made any difference. The dissimilarity of Edward and Leonora was too profound. It will give you some idea of the extraordinary naïveté of Edward Ashburnham that, at the time of his marriage and for perhaps a couple of years after, he did not really know how children are produced. Neither did Leonora. I don't mean to say that this state of things continued, but there it was. I dare say it had a good deal of influence on their mentalities. At any rate, they never had a child. It was the Will of God.

It certainly presented itself to Leonora as being the Will of God—as being a mysterious and awful chastisement of the Almighty. For she had discovered shortly before this period that her parents had not exacted from Edward's family the promise that any children she should bear should be brought up as Catholics. She herself had never talked of the matter with either her father, her mother, or her husband. When at last her father had let drop some words leading her to believe that that was the fact she tried desperately to extort the promise from Edward. She encountered an unexpected obstinacy. Edward was perfectly willing that the girls should be Catholic; the boys must be Anglican. I don't understand the bearings of these things in English society. Indeed, Englishmen seem to me to be a little mad in matters of politics or of religion. In Edward it was particularly queer because he himself was perfectly ready to become a Romanist.* He seemed, however, to contemplate going over to Rome himself and yet letting his boys be educated in the religion of their immediate ancestors. This may appear illogical, but I dare say it is not so illogical as it looks. Edward, that is to say, regarded himself as having his own body and soul at his own disposal. But his loyalty to the traditions of his family would not permit him to bind any future inheritors of his name or beneficiaries by the death of his ancestors. About the girls it did not so much matter. They would know other homes and other circumstances. Besides, it was the usual thing. But the boys must be given the opportunity of choosing—and they must have first of all the Anglican teaching. He was perfectly unshakable about this.

Leonora was in an agony during all this time. You will have to remember she seriously believed that children who might be born to her went in danger, if not absolutely of damnation at any rate of receiving false doctrine. It was an agony more terrible than she could describe. She didn't indeed attempt to describe it, but I could tell from her voice when she said, almost negligently, "I used to lie awake whole nights. It was no good my spiritual advisers trying to console me." I knew from her voice how terrible and how long those nights must have seemed and of how little avail were the consolations of her spiritual advisers. Her spiritual advisers seemed to have taken the matter a little more calmly. They certainly told her that she must not consider herself in any way to have sinned. Nay, they seem even to have extorted, to have threatened her, with a view to getting her out of what they considered to be a morbid frame of mind. She would just have to make the best of things, to influence the children when they came, not by propaganda, but by personality. And they warned her that she would be committing a sin if she continued to think that she had sinned. Nevertheless, she continued to think that she had sinned.

Leonora could not but be aware that the man whom she loved passionately and whom, nevertheless, she was beginning to try to rule with a rod of iron—that this man was becoming more and more estranged from her. He seemed to regard her as being not only physically and mentally cold, but even as being actually wicked and mean.

There were times when he would almost shudder if she spoke to him. And she could not understand how he could consider her wicked or mean. It only seemed to her a sort of madness in him that he should try to take upon his own shoulders the burden of his troop, of his regiment, of his estate and of half of his country. She could not see that in trying to curb what she regarded as megalomania she was doing anything wicked. She was just trying to keep things together for the sake of the children who did not come. And, little by little, the whole of their intercourse became simply one of agonised discussion as to whether Edward should subscribe to this or that institution or should try to reclaim this or that drunkard. She simply could not see it.

Into this really terrible position of strain, from which there appeared to be no issue, the Kilsyte case came almost as a relief. It is part of the peculiar irony of things that Edward would certainly never have kissed that nurse-maid if he had not been trying to please Leonora. Nurse-maids do not travel first-class and, that day, Edward travelled in a third-class carriage in order to prove to Leonora that he was capable of economies. I have said that the Kilsyte case came almost as a relief to the strained situation that then existed between them. It gave Leonora an opportunity of backing him up in a whole-hearted and absolutely loyal manner. It gave her the opportunity of behaving to him as he considered a wife should behave to her husband.

You see, Edward found himself in a railway carriage with a quite pretty girl of about nineteen. And the quite pretty girl of about nineteen, with dark hair and red cheeks and blue eyes was quietly weeping. Edward had been sitting in his corner thinking about nothing at all. He had chanced to look at the nurse-maid; two large, pretty tears came out of her eyes and dropped into her lap. He immediately felt that he had got to do something to comfort her. That was his job in life. He was desperately unhappy himself and it seemed to him the most natural thing in the world that they should pool their sorrows. He was quite democratic; the idea of the difference in their station never seems to have occurred to him. He began to talk to her. He discovered that her young man had been seen walking out with Annie of Number 54. He moved over to her side of the carriage. He told her that the report probably wasn't true; that, after all, a young man might take a walk with Annie from Number 54 without its denoting anything very serious. And he assured me that he felt at least quite half-fatherly when he put his arm around her waist and kissed her. The girl, however, had not forgotten the difference of her station.

All her life, by her mother, by other girls, by schoolteachers, by the whole tradition of her class she had been warned against gentlemen. She was being kissed by a gentleman. She screamed, tore herself away; sprang up and pulled a communication cord.

Edward came fairly well out of the affair in the public estimation; but it did him, mentally, a good deal of harm.

IV

IT is very difficult to give an all-round impression of any man. I wonder how far I have succeeded with Edward Ashburnham. I dare say
I haven't succeeded at all. It is even very difficult to see how such
things matter. Was it the important point about poor Edward that he
was very well built, carried himself well, was moderate at the table
and led a regular life—that he had, in fact, all the virtues that are usually accounted English? Or have I in the least succeeded in conveying
that he was all those things and had all those virtues? He certainly was
them and had them up to the last months of his life. They were the
things that one would set upon his tombstone. They will, indeed, be
set upon his tombstone by his widow.

And have I, I wonder, given the due impression of how his life was
portioned and his time laid out? Because, until the very last, the
amount of time taken up by his various passions was relatively small.
I have been forced to write very much about his passions, but you
have to consider—I should like to be able to make you consider—
that he rose every morning at seven, took a cold bath, breakfasted at
eight, was occupied with his regiment from nine until one; played
polo or cricket with the men when it was the season for cricket, till
tea-time. Afterwards he would occupy himself with the letters from
his land-steward or with the affairs of his mess, till dinner time. He
would dine and pass the evening playing cards, or playing billiards
with Leonora or at social functions of one kind or another. And the
greater part of his life was taken up by that—by far the greater part
of his life. His love-affairs, until the very end, were sandwiched in at
odd moments or took place during the social evenings, the dances
and dinners. But I guess I have made it hard for you, O silent listener,
to get that impression. Anyhow, I hope I have not given you the idea
that Edward Ashburnham was a pathological case. He wasn't. He
was just a normal man and very much of a sentimentalist. I dare say
the quality of his youth, the nature of his mother's influence, his
ignorances, the crammings that he received at the hands of army
coaches—I dare say that all these excellent influences upon his ado-
lescence were very bad for him. But we all have to put up with that
sort of thing and no doubt it is very bad for all of us. Nevertheless,

the outline of Edward's life was an outline perfectly normal of the life of a hard-working, sentimental and efficient professional man.

That question of first impressions has always bothered me a good deal—but quite academically. I mean that, from time to time I have wondered whether it were or were not best to trust to one's first impressions in dealing with people. But I never had anybody to deal with except waiters and chambermaids and the Ashburnhams, with whom I didn't know that I was having any dealings. And, as far as waiters and chambermaids were concerned I have generally found that my first impressions were correct enough. If my first idea of a man was that he was civil, obliging, and attentive, he generally seemed to go on being all those things. Once, however, at our Paris flat we had a maid who appeared to be charming and transparently honest. She stole, nevertheless, one of Florence's diamond rings. She did it, however, to save her young man from going to prison. So here, as somebody says somewhere, was a special case.

And, even in my short incursion into American business life—an incursion that lasted during part of August and nearly the whole of September—I found that to rely upon first impressions was the best thing I could do. I found myself automatically docketing and labelling each man as he was introduced to me, by the run of his features and by the first words that he spoke. I can't, however, be regarded as really doing business during the time that I spent in the United States. I was just winding things up. If it hadn't been for my idea of marrying the girl I might possibly have looked for something to do in my own country. For my experiences there were vivid and amusing. It was exactly as if I had come out of a museum into a riotous fancy-dress ball. During my life with Florence I had almost come to forget that there were such things as fashions or occupations or the greed of gain. I had, in fact, forgotten that there was such a thing as a dollar and that a dollar can be extremely desirable if you don't happen to possess one. And I had forgotten, too, that there was such a thing as gossip that mattered. In that particular, Philadelphia was the most amazing place I have ever been in in my life. I was not in that city for more than a week or ten days and I didn't there transact anything much in the way of business, nevertheless the number of times that I was warned by everybody against everybody else was simply amazing. A man I didn't know would come up behind my lounge chair in the hotel, and, whispering cautiously beside my ear, would warn me against some other man that I equally didn't know but who would be standing by the bar. I don't know what they thought I was there to do—perhaps to buy out the city's debt or get a controlling hold of some railway interest. Or, perhaps, they imagined that I wanted to buy a newspaper, for they were either politicians or reporters, which, of course, comes to the same thing. As a matter of fact, my property in Philadelphia was mostly real estate in the old-fashioned part of the city and all I wanted to do there was just to satisfy myself that the houses were in good repair and the doors kept properly painted. I wanted also to see my relations, of whom I had a few. These were mostly professional people and they were mostly rather hard up because of the big bank failure in 1907* or thereabouts. Still, they were very nice. They would have been nicer still if they hadn't, all of them, had what appeared to me to be the mania that what they called influences were working against them. At any rate, the impression of that city was one of old-fashioned rooms, rather English than American in type in which handsome but care-worn ladies, cousins of my own, talked principally about mysterious movements that were going on against them. I never got to know what it was all about; perhaps they thought I knew or perhaps there weren't any movements at all. It was all very secret and subtle and subterranean. But there was a nice young fellow called Carter who was a sort of second-nephew of mine, twice removed. He was handsome and dark and gentle and tall and modest. I understand also that he was a good cricketer. He was employed by the real-estate agents who collected my rents. It was he, therefore, who took me over my own property and I saw a good deal of him and of a nice girl called Mary, to whom he was engaged. At that time I did, what I certainly shouldn't do now,—I made some careful inquiries as to his character. I discovered from his employers that he was just all that he appeared, honest, industrious, high-spirited, friendly and ready to do anyone a good turn. His relatives, however, as they were mine too—seemed to have something darkly mysterious against him. I imagined that he must have been mixed up in some case of graft or that he had at least betrayed several innocent and trusting maidens. I pushed, however, that particular mystery home and discovered it was only that he was a Democrat. My own people were mostly Republicans. It seemed to make it worse and more darkly mysterious to them that young Carter was what they called a sort of a Vermont Democrat* which was the whole ticket and no mistake. But I don't know what it means. Anyhow, I suppose that my money will go to him when I die—I like the recollection of his friendly image and of the nice girl he was engaged to. May Fate deal very kindly with them.

I have said just now that, in my present frame of mind, nothing would ever make me make inquiries as to the character of any man that I liked at first sight. (The little digression as to my Philadelphia experiences was really meant to lead around to this.) For who in this world can give anyone a character? Who in this world knows anything of any other heart—or of his own? I don't mean to say that one cannot form an average estimate of the way a person will behave. But one cannot be certain of the way any man will behave in every case— and until one can do that a "character" is of no use to anyone. That, for instance, was the way with Florence's maid in Paris. We used to trust that girl with blank cheques for the payment of the tradesmen. For quite a time she was so trusted by us. Then, suddenly, she stole a ring. We should not have believed her capable of it; she would not have believed herself capable of it. It was nothing in her character. So, perhaps, it was with Edward Ashburnham.

Or, perhaps, it wasn't. No, I rather think it wasn't. It is difficult to figure out. I have said that the Kilsyte case eased the immediate tension for him and Leonora. It let him see that she was capable of loyalty to him; it gave her her chance to show that she believed in him. She accepted without question his statement that, in kissing the girl, he wasn't trying to do more than administer fatherly comfort to a weeping child. And, indeed, his own world—including the magistrates—took that view of the case. Whatever people say, one's world can be perfectly charitable at times . . . But, again, as I have said, it did Edward a great deal of harm.

That, at least, was his view of it. He assured me that, before that case came on and was wrangled about by counsel with all the sorts of dirty-mindedness that counsel in that sort of case can impute, he had not had the least idea that he was capable of being unfaithful to Leonora. But, in the midst of that tumult—he says that it came suddenly into his head* whilst he was in the witness-box—in the midst of those august ceremonies of the law there came suddenly into his mind the recollection of the softness of the girl's body as he had pressed her to him. And, from that moment, that girl appeared desirable to him—and Leonora completely unattractive.

He began to indulge in day-dreams in which he approached the nurse-maid more tactfully and carried the matter much further. Occasionally he thought of other women in terms of wary court-ship—or, perhaps, it would be more exact to say that he thought of them in terms of tactful comforting, ending in absorption. That was his own view of the case. He saw himself as the victim of the law. I don't mean to say that he saw himself as a kind of Dreyfus.* The law, practically, was quite kind to him. It stated that in its view Captain Ashburnham had been misled by an ill-placed desire to comfort a member of the opposite sex and it fined him five shillings for his want of tact, or of knowledge of the world. But Edward maintained that it had put ideas into his head.

I don't believe it, though he certainly did. He was twenty-seven then, and his wife was out of sympathy with him—some crash was inevitable. There was between them a momentary rapprochement; but it could not last. It made it, probably, all the worse that, in that particular matter Leonora had come so very well up to the scratch. For, whilst Edward respected her more and was grateful to her, it made her seem by so much the more cold in other matters that were near his heart—his responsibilities, his career, his tradition. It brought his despair of her up to a point of exasperation—and it riv-eted on him the idea that he might find some other woman who would give him the moral support that he needed. He wanted to be looked upon as a sort of Lohengrin.

At that time, he says, he went about deliberately looking for some woman who could help him. He found several—for there were quite a number of ladies in his set who were capable of agreeing with this handsome and fine fellow that the duties of a feudal gentleman were feudal. He would have liked to pass his days talking to one or other of these ladies. But there was always an obstacle—if the lady were mar-ried there would be a husband who claimed the greater part of her time and attention. If, on the other hand, it were an unmarried girl, he could not see very much of her for fear of compromising her. At that date, you understand, he had not the least idea of seducing any one of these ladies. He wanted only moral support at the hands of some female, because he found men difficult to talk to about ideals. Indeed, I do not believe that he had, at any time, any idea of making any one his mistress. That sounds queer; but I believe it is quite true as a statement of character.

It was, I believe, one of Leonora's priests—a man of the world—who suggested that she should take him to Monte Carlo. He had the idea that what Edward needed, in order to fit him for the society of Leonora was a touch of irresponsibility. For Edward, at that date, had much the aspect of a prig. I mean that, if he played polo and was an excellent dancer he did the one for the sake of keeping himself fit and the other because it was a social duty to show himself at dances, and, when there, to dance well. He did nothing for fun except what he considered to be his work in life. As the priest saw it, this must for ever estrange him from Leonora—not because Leonora set much store by the joy of life, but because she was out of sympathy with Edward's work. On the other hand, Leonora did like to have a good time, now and then, and, as the priest saw it, if Edward could be got to like having a good time now and then too, there would be a bond of sympathy between them. It was a good idea, but it worked out wrongly.

It worked out, in fact, in the mistress of the Grand Duke. In anyone less sentimental than Edward that would not have mattered. With Edward it was fatal. For, such was his honourable nature, that for him, to enjoy a woman's favours made him feel that she had a bond on him for life. That was the way it worked out in practice. Psychologically it meant that he could not have a mistress without falling violently in love with her. He was a serious person—and in this particular case it was very expensive. The mistress of the Grand Duke—a Spanish dancer of passionate appearance—singled out Edward for her glances at a ball that was held in their common hotel. Edward was tall, handsome, blond and very wealthy as she understood—and Leonora went up to bed early. She did not care for public dances, but she was relieved to see that Edward appeared to be having a good time with several amiable girls. And that was the end of Edward—for the Spanish dancer of passionate appearance wanted one night of him for his beaux yeux. He took her into the dark gardens and, remembering suddenly the girl of the Kilsyte case, he kissed her. He kissed her passionately, violently, with a sudden explosion of the passion that had been bridled all his life—for Leonora was cold, or, at any rate, well behaved. La Dolciquita liked this reversion, and he passed the night in her bed.

When the palpitating creature was at last asleep in his arms he discovered that he was madly, was passionately, was overwhelmingly in love with her. It was a passion that had arisen like fire in dry corn. He could think of nothing else; he could live for nothing else. But La Dolciquita was a reasonable creature without an ounce of passion in her. She wanted a certain satisfaction of her appetites and Edward had appealed to her the night before. Now that was done with and, quite coldly, she said that she wanted money if he was to have any more of her. It was a perfectly reasonable commercial transaction. She did not care two buttons for Edward or for any man and he was asking her to risk a very good situation with a Grand Duke. If Edward could put up sufficient money to serve as a kind of insurance against accident she was ready to like Edward for a time that would be covered, as it were, by the policy. She was getting fifty thousand dollars a year from her Grand Duke; Edward would have to pay a premium of two years' hire for a month of her society. There would not be much risk of the Grand Duke's finding it out and it was not certain that he would give her the keys of the street* if he did find out. But there was the risk—a twenty per cent. risk, as she figured it out. She talked to Edward as if she had been a solicitor with an estate to sell— perfectly quietly and perfectly coldly without any inflections in her voice. She did not want to be unkind to him; but she could see no reason for being kind to him. She was a virtuous business woman with a mother and two sisters and her own old age to be provided comfortably for. She did not expect more than a five years' further run. She was twenty-four and, as she said: "We Spanish women are horrors at thirty." Edward swore that he would provide for her for life if she would come to him and leave off talking so horribly; but she only shrugged one shoulder slowly and contemptuously. He tried to convince this woman, who, as he saw it, had surrendered to him her virtue, that he regarded it as in any case his duty to provide for her, and to cherish her and even to love her—for life. In return for her sacrifice he would do that. In return, again, for his honourable love she would listen for ever to the accounts of his estate. That was how he figured it out.

She shrugged the same shoulder with the same gesture and held out her left hand with the elbow at her side:

"Enfin, mon ami,"* she said, "put in this hand the price of that tiara at Forli's or . . ." And she turned her back on him.

Edward went mad; his world stood on its head; the palms in front of the blue sea danced grotesque dances. You see, he believed in the virtue, tenderness and moral support of women. He wanted more than anything to argue with La Dolciquita; to retire with her to an island and point out to her the damnation of her point of view and how salvation can only be found in true love and the feudal system. She had once been his mistress, he reflected, and by all the moral laws she ought to have gone on being his mistress or at the very least his sympathetic confidante. But her rooms were closed to him; she did not appear in the hotel. Nothing: blank silence. To break that down he had to have twenty thousand pounds. You have heard what happened.

He spent a week of madness; he hungered; his eyes sank in; he shuddered at Leonora's touch. I dare say that nine-tenths of what he took to be his passion for La Dolciquita was really discomfort at the thought that he had been unfaithful to Leonora. He felt uncommonly bad, that is to say—oh, unbearably bad, and he took it all to be love. Poor devil, he was incredibly naif. He drank like a fish after Leonora was in bed and he spread himself over the tables, and this went on for about a fortnight. Heaven knows what would have happened; he would have thrown away every penny that he possessed.

On the night after he had lost about forty thousand pounds and whilst the whole hotel was whispering about it, La Dolciquita walked composedly into his bedroom. He was too drunk to recognise her, and she sat in his armchair, knitting and holding smelling salts to his nose—for he was pretty far gone with alcoholic poisoning—and, as soon as he was able to understand her, she said:

"Look here, mon ami, do not go to the tables again. Take a good sleep now and come and see me this afternoon."

He slept till the lunch hour. By that time Leonora had heard the news. A Mrs. Colonel Whelen had told her. Mrs. Colonel Whelen seems to have been the only sensible person who was ever connected with the Ashburnhams. She had argued it out that there must be a woman of the harpy variety connected with Edward's incredible behaviour and mien; and she advised Leonora to go straight off to Town*—which might have the effect of bringing Edward to his senses—and to consult her solicitor and her spiritual adviser. She had better go that very morning; it was no good arguing with a man in Edward's condition.

Edward, indeed, did not know that she had gone. As soon as he awoke he went straight to La Dolciquita's room and she stood him his lunch in her own apartments. He fell on her neck and wept, and she put up with it for a time. She was quite a good-natured woman. And, when she had calmed him down with Eau de Melisse,* she said:

"Look here, my friend, how much money have you left? Five thousand dollars? Ten?" For the rumour went that Edward had lost two kings' ransoms a night for fourteen nights and she imagined that he must be near the end of his resources.

The Eau de Mélisse had calmed Edward to such an extent that, for the moment, he really had a head on his shoulders. He did nothing more than grunt:

"And then?"

"Why," she answered, "I may just as well have the ten thousand dollars as the tables. I will go with you to Antibes for a week for that sum."

Edward grunted: "Five." She tried to get seven thousand five hundred; but he stuck to his five thousand and the hotel expenses at Antibes. The sedative carried him just as far as that and then he collapsed again. He had to leave for Antibes at three; he could not do without it. He left a note for Leonora saying that he had gone off for a week with the Clinton Morleys, yachting.

He did not enjoy himself very much at Antibes. La Dolciquita could talk of nothing with any enthusiasm except money, and she tired him unceasingly, during every waking hour, for presents of the most expensive description. And, at the end of a week, she just quietly kicked him out. He hung about in Antibes for three days. He was cured of the idea that he had any duties towards La Dolciquita—feudal or otherwise. But his sentimentalism required of him an attitude of Byronic gloom—as if his court had gone into half-mourning. Then his appetite suddenly returned, and he remembered Leonora. He found at his hotel at Monte Carlo a telegram from Leonora, dispatched from London, saying: "Please return as soon as convenient." He could not understand why Leonora should have abandoned him so precipitately when she only thought that he had gone yachting with the Clinton Morleys. Then he discovered that she had left the hotel before he had written the note. He had a pretty rocky journey back to town; he was frightened out of his life—and Leonora had never seemed so desirable to him.

V

I CALL this the Saddest Story, rather than "The Ashburnham Tragedy," just because it is so sad, just because there was no current to draw things along to a swift and inevitable end. There is about it none of the elevation that accompanies tragedy; there is about it no nemesis, no destiny. Here were two noble people—for I am convinced that both Edward and Leonora had noble natures—here, then, were two noble natures, drifting down life, like fireships* afloat on a lagoon and causing miseries, heartaches, agony of the mind and death. And they themselves steadily deteriorated. And why? For what purpose? To point what lesson? It is all a darkness.

There is not even any villain in the story—for even Major Basil, the husband of the lady who next, and really, comforted the unfortunate Edward—even Major Basil was not a villain in this piece. He was a slack, loose, shiftless sort of fellow—but he did not do anything to Edward. Whilst they were in the same station in Burma he borrowed a good deal of money—though, really, since Major Basil had no particular vices, it was difficult to know why he wanted it. He collected—different types of horses' bits from the earliest times to the present day—but, since he did not prosecute even this occupation with any vigour, he cannot have needed much money for the acquirement, say, of the bit of Genghis Khan's charger—if Genghis Khan had a charger. And when I say that he borrowed a good deal of money from Edward I do not mean to say that he had more than a thousand pounds from him during the five years that the connection lasted. Edward, of course, did not have a great deal of money; Leonora was seeing to that. Still he may have had five hundred pounds a year English, for his menus plaisirs*—for his regimental subscriptions and for keeping his men smart. Leonora hated that; she would have preferred to buy dresses for herself or to have devoted the money to paying off a mortgage. Still, with her sense of justice, she saw that, since she was managing a property bringing in three thousand a year with a view to re-establishing it as a property of five thousand a year, and since the property really, if not legally, belonged to Edward, it was reasonable and just that Edward should get a slice of his own. Of course she had the devil of a job.

I don't know that I have got the financial details exactly right. I am a pretty good head at figures, but my mind, still, sometimes mixes up pounds with dollars and I get a figure wrong. Anyhow, the proposition was something like this: Properly worked and without rebates to the tenants and keeping up schools and things, the Branshaw estate should have brought in about five thousand a year when Edward had it. It brought in actually about four. (I am talking in pounds, not dollars.) Edward's excesses with the Spanish Lady had reduced its value to about three—as the maximum figure, without reductions. Leonora wanted to get it back to five.

She was, of course, very young to be faced with such a proposition—twenty-four is not a very advanced age. So she did things with a youthful vigour that she would, very likely, have made more merciful, if she had known more about life. She got Edward remarkably on the hop. He had to face her in a London hotel, when he crept back from Monte Carlo with his poor tail between his poor legs. As far as I can make out, she cut short his first mumblings and his first attempts at affectionate speech with words something like:

"We're on the verge of ruin. Do you intend to let me pull things together? If not I shall retire to Hendon on my jointure."* (Hendon represented a convent to which she occasionally went for what is called a "retreat" in Catholic circles.)

And poor dear Edward knew nothing—absolutely nothing. He did not know how much money he had, as he put it, "blued"* at the tables. It might have been a quarter of a million for all he remembered. He did not know whether she knew about La Dolciquita or whether she imagined that he had gone off yachting or had stayed at Monte Carlo. He was just dumb and he just wanted to get into a hole and not have to talk. Leonora did not make him talk and she said nothing herself.

I do not know much about English legal procedure—I cannot, I mean, give technical details of how they tied him up. But I know that, two days later, without her having said more than I have reported to you, Leonora and her attorney had become the trustees, as I believe it is called, of all Edward's property and there was an end of Edward as the good landlord and father of his people. He went out.

Leonora then had three thousand a year at her disposal. She occupied Edward with getting himself transferred to a part of his regiment that was in Burma—if that is the right way to put it. She herself had an interview, lasting a week or so—with Edward's land-steward. She made him understand that the estate would have to yield up to its last penny. Before they left for India she had let Branshaw for seven years at a thousand a year. She sold two Vandykes* and a little silver* for eleven thousand pounds and she raised, on mortgage, twenty-nine thousand. That went to Edward's money-lending friends in Monte Carlo. So she had to get the twenty-nine thousand back, for she did not regard the Vandykes and the silver as things she would have to replace. They were just frills to the Ashburnham vanity. Edward cried for two days over the disappearance of his ancestors and then she wished she had not done it; but it did not teach her anything and it lessened such esteem as she had for him. She did not also understand that to let Branshaw affected him with a feeling of physical soiling—that it was almost as bad for him as if a woman belonging to him had become a prostitute. That was how it did affect him; but I dare say she felt just as bad about the Spanish dancer.

So she went at it. They were eight years in India, and during the whole of that time she insisted that they must be self-supporting—they had to live on his Captain's pay, plus the extra allowance for being at the front.* She gave him the five hundred a year for Ashburnham frills, as she called it to herself—and she considered she was doing him very well.

Indeed, in a way, she did him very well—but it was not his way. She was always buying him expensive things which, as it were, she took off her own back. I have, for instance, spoken of Edward's leather cases. Well, they were not Edward's at all; they were Leonora's manifestations. He liked to be clean, but he preferred, as it were, to be threadbare. She never understood that and all that pigskin was her idea of a reward to him for putting her up to a little speculation by which she made eleven hundred pounds. She did, herself, the threadbare business. When they went up to a place called Simla,* where, as I understand, it is cool in the summer and very social—when they went up to Simla for their healths it was she who had him prancing around, as we should say in the United States, on a thousand-dollar horse with the gladdest of glad rags all over him. She herself used to go into "retreat." I believe that was very good for her health and it was also very inexpensive.

It was probably also very good for Edward's health, because he pranced about mostly with Mrs. Basil, who was a nice woman and very, very kind to him. I suppose she was his mistress, but I never heard it from Edward, of course. I seem to gather that they carried it on in a high romantic fashion, very proper to both of them—or, at any rate, for Edward; she seems to have been a tender and gentle soul who did what he wanted. I do not mean to say that she was without character; that was her job, to do what Edward wanted. So I figured it out, that for those five years, Edward wanted long passages of deep affection kept up in long, long talks and that every now and then they "fell," which would give Edward an opportunity for remorse and an excuse to lend the Major another fifty. I don't think that Mrs. Basil considered it to be "falling"; she just pitied him and loved him.

You see, Leonora and Edward had to talk about something during all these years. You cannot be absolutely dumb when you live with a person unless you are an inhabitant of the North of England or the State of Maine. So Leonora imagined the cheerful device of letting him see the accounts of his estate and discussing them with him. He did not discuss them much; he was trying to behave prettily. But it was old Mr. Mumford—the farmer who did not pay his rent—that threw Edward into Mrs. Basil's arms. Mrs. Basil came upon Edward in the dusk, in the Burmese garden, with all sorts of flowers and things. And he was cutting up that crop—with his sword, not a walk-ing-stick. He was also carrying on and cursing in a way you would not believe.

She ascertained that an old gentleman called Mumford had been ejected from his farm and had been given a little cottage rent-free, where he lived on ten shillings a week from a farmers' benevolent society, supplemented by seven that was being allowed him by the Ashburnham trustees. Edward had just discovered that fact from the estate accounts. Leonora had left them in his dressing room and he had begun to read them before taking off his marching kit. That was how he came to have a sword. Leonora considered that she had been unusually generous to old Mr. Mumford in allowing him to inhabit a cottage, rent-free, and in giving him seven shillings a week. Anyhow, Mrs. Basil had never seen a man in such a state as Edward was. She had been passionately in love with him for quite a time, and he had been longing for her sympathy and admiration with a passion as deep. That was how they came to speak about it, in the Burmese garden, under the pale sky, with sheafs of severed vegetation, misty and odor-ous, in the night around their feet. I think they behaved themselves with decorum for quite a time after that, though Mrs. Basil spent so many hours over the accounts of the Ashburnham estate that she got the name of every field by heart. Edward had a huge map of his lands in his harness-room and Major Basil did not seem to mind. I believe that people do not mind much in lonely stations.

It might have lasted for ever if the Major had not been made what is called a brevet-colonel* during the shuffling of troops that went on just before the South African War.* He was sent off somewhere else and, of course, Mrs. Basil could not stay with Edward. Edward ought, I suppose, to have gone to the Transvaal.* It would have done him a great deal of good to get killed. But Leonora would not let him; she had heard awful stories of the extravagance of the hussar regiment in war-time—how they left hundred-bottle cases of champagne, at five guineas a bottle, on the veldt* and so on. Besides, she preferred to see how Edward was spending his five hundred a year. I don't mean to say that Edward had any grievance in that. He was never a man of the deeds of heroism sort and it was just as good for him to be sniped at up in the hills of the North Western frontier,* as to be shot at by an old gentleman in a top hat at the bottom of some spruit.* Those are more or less his words about it. I believe he quite distinguished himself over there. At any rate, he had had his D. S. O. and was made a brevet-major.

Leonora, however, was not in the least keen on his soldiering. She hated also his deeds of heroism. One of their bitterest quarrels came after he had, for the second time, in the Red Sea, jumped overboard from the troopship and rescued a private soldier. She stood it the first time and even complimented him. But the Red Sea was awful, that trip, and the private soldiers seemed to develop a suicidal craze. It got on Leonora's nerves; she figured Edward, for the rest of that trip, jumping overboard every ten minutes. And the mere cry of "Man overboard" is a disagreeable, alarming and disturbing thing. The ship gets stopped and there are all sorts of shouts. And Edward would not promise not to do it again, though, fortunately, they struck a streak of cooler weather when they were in the Persian Gulf. Leonora had got it into her head that Edward was trying to commit suicide, so I guess it was pretty awful for her when he would not give the promise. Leonora ought never to have been on that troop-ship; but she got there somehow, as an economy.

Major Basil discovered his wife's relation with Edward just before he was sent to his other station. I don't know whether that was a blackmailer's adroitness or just a trick of destiny. He may have known of it all the time or he may not. At any rate, he got hold of, just about then, some letters and things. It cost Edward three hundred pounds immediately. I do not know how it was arranged; I cannot imagine how even a blackmailer can make his demands. I suppose there is some sort of way of saving your face. I figure the Major as disclosing the letters to Edward with furious oaths, then accepting his explanations that the letters were perfectly innocent if the wrong construction were not put upon them. Then the Major would say: "I say, old chap, I'm deuced hard up. Couldn't you lend me three hundred or so?" I fancy that was how it was. And, year by year, after that there would come a letter from the Major, saying that he was deuced hard up and couldn't Edward lend him three hundred or so.

Edward was pretty hard hit when Mrs. Basil had to go away. He really had been very fond of her, and he remained faithful to her memory for quite a long time. And Mrs. Basil had loved him very much and continued to cherish a hope of reunion with him. Three days ago there came a quite proper but very lamentable letter from her to Leonora, asking to be given particulars as to Edward's death. She had read the advertisement of it in an Indian paper. I think she must have been a very nice woman. . . .

And then the Ashburnhams were moved somewhere up towards a place or a district called Chitral.* I am no good at geography of the Indian Empire. By that time they had settled down into a model couple and they never spoke in private to each other. Leonora had given up even showing the accounts of the Ashburnham estate to Edward. He thought that that was because she had piled up such a lot of money that she did not want him to know how she was getting on any more. But, as a matter of fact, after five or six years it had penetrated to her mind that it was painful to Edward to have to look on at the accounts of his estate and have no hand in the management of it. She was trying to do him a kindness. And, up in Chitral, poor dear little Maisie Maidan came along. . . .

That was the most unsettling to Edward of all his affairs. It made him suspect that he was inconstant. The affair with the Dolciquita he had sized up as a short attack of madness like hydrophobia. His relations with Mrs. Basil had not seemed to him to imply moral turpitude of a gross kind. The husband had been complaisant; they had really loved each other; his wife was very cruel to him and had long ceased to be a wife to him. He thought that Mrs. Basil had been his soul-mate, separated from him by an unkind fate—something sentimental of that sort.

But he discovered that, whilst he was still writing long weekly letters to Mrs. Basil, he was beginning to be furiously impatient if he missed seeing Maisie Maidan during the course of the day. He discovered himself watching the doorways with impatience; he discovered that he disliked her boy husband very much for hours at a time. He discovered that he was getting up at unearthly hours in order to have time, later in the morning, to go for a walk with Maisie Maidan. He discovered himself using little slang words that she used and attaching a sentimental value to those words. These, you understand, were discoveries that came so late that he could do nothing but drift. He was losing weight; his eyes were beginning to fall in; he had touches of bad fever. He was, as he described it, pipped.*

And, one ghastly hot day, he suddenly heard himself say to Leonora:

"I say, couldn't we take little Mrs. Maidan with us to Europe and drop her at Nauheim?"

He hadn't had the least idea of saying that to Leonora. He had merely been standing, looking at an illustrated paper, waiting for dinner. Dinner was twenty minutes late or the Ashburnhams would not have been alone together. No, he hadn't had the least idea of framing that speech. He had just been standing in a silent agony of fear, of longing, of heat, of fever. He was thinking that they were going back to Branshaw in a month and that Maisie Maidan was going to remain behind and die. And then, that had come out.

The punkah* swished in the darkened room; Leonora lay exhausted and motionless in her cane-lounge;* neither of them stirred. They were both at that time very ill in indefinite ways.

And then Leonora said:

"Yes. I promised it to Charlie Maidan this afternoon. I have offered to pay her ex's* myself."

Edward just saved himself from saying: "Good God!" You see, he had not the least idea of what Leonora knew—about Maisie, about Mrs. Basil, or even about La Dolciquita. It was a pretty enigmatic situation for him. It struck him that Leonora must be intending to manage his loves as she managed his money affairs and it made her more hateful to him—and more worthy of respect.

Leonora, at any rate, had managed his money to some purpose. She had spoken to him, a week before, for the first time in several years—about money. She had made twenty-two thousand pounds out of the Branshaw land and seven by the letting of Branshaw furnished. By fortunate investments—in which Edward had helped her—she had made another six or seven thousand that might well become more. The mortgages were all paid off, so that, except for the departure of the two Vandykes and the silver, they were as well off as they had been before the Dolciquita had acted the locust. It was Leonora's great achievement. She laid the figures before Edward, who maintained an unbroken silence.

"I propose," she said, "that you should resign from the Army and that we should go back to Branshaw. We are both too ill to stay here any longer."

Edward said nothing at all.

"This," Leonora continued passionlessly, "is the great day of my life."

Edward said:

"You have managed the job amazingly. You are a wonderful woman." He was thinking that if they went back to Branshaw they would leave Maisie Maidan behind. That thought occupied him exclusively. They must, undoubtedly, return to Branshaw; there could be no doubt that Leonora was too ill to stay in that place. She said:

"You understand that the management of the whole of the expenditure of the income will be in your hands. There will be five thousand a year."

She thought that he cared very much about the expenditure of an income of five thousand a year and that the fact that she had done so much for him would rouse in him some affection for her. But he was thinking exclusively of Maisie Maidan—of Maisie, thousands of miles away from him. He was seeing the mountains between them—blue mountains and the sea and sunlit plains. He said:

"That is very generous of you." And she did not know whether that were praise or a sneer. That had been a week before. And all that week he had passed in an increasing agony at the thought that those mountains, that sea and those sunlit plains would be between him and Maisie Maidan. That thought shook him in the burning nights: the sweat poured from him and he trembled with cold, in the burning noons—at that thought. He had no minute's rest; his bowels turned round and round within him: his tongue was perpetually dry and it seemed to him that the breath between his teeth was like air from a pest-house.*

He gave no thought to Leonora at all; he had sent in his papers.* They were to leave in a month. It seemed to him to be his duty to leave that place and to go away, to support Leonora. He did his duty.

It was horrible, in their relationship at that time, that whatever she did caused him to hate her. He hated her when he found that she proposed to set him up as the Lord of Branshaw again—as a sort of dummy lord, in swaddling clothes. He imagined that she had done this in order to separate him from Maisie Maidan. Hatred hung in all the heavy nights and filled the shadowy corners of the room. So when he heard that she had offered to the Maidan boy to take his wife to Europe with him, automatically he hated her since he hated all that she did. It seemed to him, at that time, that she could never be other than cruel even if, by accident, an act of hers were kind. . . . Yes, it was a horrible situation.

But the cool breezes of the ocean seemed to clear up that hatred as if it had been a curtain. They seemed to give him back admiration for her, and respect. The agreeableness of having money lavishly at command, the fact that it had bought for him the companionship of Maisie Maidan—these things began to make him see that his wife might have been right in the starving and scraping upon which she had insisted. He was at ease; he was even radiantly happy when he carried cups of bouillon* for Maisie Maidan along the deck. One night, when he was leaning, beside Leonora, over the ship's side he said suddenly:

"By Jove, you're the finest woman in the world. I wish we could be better friends."

She just turned away, without a word and went to her cabin. Still, she was very much better in health.

*   *   *   *   *

And, now, I suppose I must give you Leonora's side of the case. . . .

That is very difficult. For Leonora, if she preserved an unchanged front, changed very frequently her point of view. She had been drilled—in her tradition, in her upbringing—to keep her mouth shut. But there were times, she said, when she was so near yielding to the temptation of speaking that afterwards she shuddered to think of those times. You must postulate that what she desired above all things was to keep a shut mouth to the world, to Edward and to the women that he loved. If she spoke she would despise herself.

From the moment of his unfaithfulness with La Dolciquita she never acted the part of wife to Edward. It was not that she intended to keep herself from him as a principle, for ever. Her spiritual advisers, I believe, forbade that. But she stipulated that he must, in some way, perhaps symbolical, come back to her. She was not very clear as to what she meant; probably she did not know herself. Or perhaps she did.

There were moments when he seemed to be coming back to her; there were moments when she was within a hair of yielding to her physical passion for him. In just the same way, at moments, she almost yielded to the temptation to denounce Mrs. Basil to her husband or Maisie Maidan to hers. She desired then to cause the horrors and pains of public scandals. For, watching Edward more intently and with more straining of ears than that which a cat bestows upon a bird overhead, she was aware of the progress of his passion for each of these ladies. She was aware of it from the way in which his eyes returned to doors and gateways; she knew from his tranquillities when he had received satisfactions.

At times she imagined herself to see more than was warranted. She imagined that Edward was carrying on intrigues with other women—with two at once; with three. For whole periods she imagined him to be a monster of libertinage and she could not see that he could have anything against her. She left him his liberty; she was starving herself to build up his fortunes; she allowed herself none of the joys of femininity—no dresses, no jewels—hardly even friendships, for fear they should cost money.

And yet, oddly, she could not but be aware that both Mrs. Basil and Maisie Maidan were nice women. The curious, discounting eye which one woman can turn on another did not prevent her seeing that Mrs. Basil was very good to Edward and Mrs. Maidan very good for him. That seemed to her to be a monstrous and incomprehensible working of Fate's. Incomprehensible! Why, she asked herself again

and again, did none of the good deeds that she did for her husband
ever come through to him, or appear to him as good deeds? By what
trick of mania could not he let her be as good to him as Mrs. Basil
was? Mrs. Basil was not so extraordinarily dissimilar to herself. She
was, it was true, tall, dark, with soft mournful voice and a great kindness of manner for every created thing, from punkah men to flowers
on the trees. But she was not so well read as Leonora, at any rate in
learned books. Leonora could not stand novels. But, even with all her
differences, Mrs. Basil did not appear to Leonora to differ so very
much from herself. She was truthful, honest and, for the rest, just a
woman. And Leonora had a vague sort of idea that, to a man, all
women are the same after three weeks of close intercourse. She
thought that the kindness should no longer appeal, the soft and
mournful voice no longer thrill, the tall darkness no longer give a
man the illusion that he was going into the depths of an unexplored
wood. She could not understand how Edward could go on and on
maundering* over Mrs. Basil. She could not see why he should continue to write her long letters after their separation. After that,
indeed, she had a very bad time.

She had at that period what I will call the "monstrous" theory of
Edward. She was always imagining him ogling at every woman that
he came across. She did not, that year, go into "retreat" at Simla
because she was afraid that he would corrupt her maid in her absence.
She imagined him carrying on intrigues with native women or
Eurasians. At dances she was in a fever of watchfulness. . . .

She persuaded herself that this was because she had a dread of
scandals. Edward might get himself mixed up with a marriageable
daughter of some man who would make a row or some husband who
would matter. But, really, she acknowledged afterwards to herself,
she was hoping that, Mrs. Basil being out of the way, the time might
have come when Edward should return to her. All that period she
passed in an agony of jealousy and fear—the fear that Edward might
really become promiscuous in his habits.

So that, in an odd way, she was glad when Maisie Maidan came
along—and she realised that she had not, before, been afraid of husbands and of scandals, since, then, she did her best to keep Maisie's
husband unsuspicious. She wished to appear so trustful of Edward
that Maidan could not possibly have any suspicions. It was an evil
position for her. But Edward was very ill and she wanted to see him

smile again. She thought that if he could smile again through her agency he might return, through gratitude and satisfied love—to her. At that time she thought that Edward was a person of light and fleeting passions. And she could understand Edward's passion for Maisie, since Maisie was one of those women to whom other women will allow magnetism.

She was very pretty; she was very young; in spite of her heart she was very gay and light on her feet. And Leonora was really very fond of Maisie, who was fond enough of Leonora. Leonora, indeed, imagined that she could manage this affair all right. She had no thought of Maisie's being led into adultery; she imagined that if she could take Maisie and Edward to Nauheim, Edward would see enough of her to get tired of her pretty little chatterings, and of the pretty little motions of her hands and feet. And she thought she could trust Edward. For there was not any doubt of Maisie's passion for Edward. She raved about him to Leonora as Leonora had heard girls rave about drawing masters in schools. She was perpetually asking her boy husband why he could not dress, ride, shoot, play polo, or even recite sentimental poems, like their major. And young Maidan had the greatest admiration for Edward, and he adored, was bewildered by and entirely trusted his wife. It appeared to him that Edward was devoted to Leonora. And Leonora imagined that when poor Maisie was cured of her heart and Edward had seen enough of her, he would return to her. She had the vague, passionate idea that, when Edward had exhausted a number of other types of women he must turn to her. Why should not her type have its turn in his heart? She imagined that, by now, she understood him better, that she understood better his vanities and that, by making him happier, she could arouse his love.

Florence knocked all that on the head. . . .

PART IV

I HAVE, I am aware, told this story in a very rambling way so that it may be difficult for anyone to find their path through what may be a sort of maze. I cannot help it. I have stuck to my idea of being in a country cottage with a silent listener, hearing between the gusts of the wind and amidst the noises of the distant sea, the story as it comes. And, when one discusses an affair—a long, sad affair—one goes back, one goes forward. One remembers points that one has forgotten and one explains them all the more minutely since one recognises that one has forgotten to mention them in their proper places and that one may have given, by omitting them, a false impression. I console myself with thinking that this is a real story and that, after all, real stories are probably told best in the way a person telling a story would tell them. They will then seem most real.

At any rate, I think I have brought my story up to the date of Maisie Maidan's death. I mean that I have explained everything that went before it from the several points of view that were necessary—from Leonora's, from Edward's and to some extent, from my own. You have the facts for the trouble of finding them; you have the points of view as far as I could ascertain or put them. Let me imagine myself back, then, at the day of Maisie's death—or rather at the moment of Florence's dissertation on the Protest, up in the old Castle of the town of M——. Let us consider Leonora's point of view with regard to Florence; Edward's, of course, I cannot give you, for Edward naturally never spoke of his affair with my wife. (I may, in what follows, be a little hard on Florence; but you must remember that I have been writing away at this story now for six months and reflecting longer and longer upon these affairs.)

And the longer I think about them the more certain I become that Florence was a contaminating influence—she depressed and deteriorated poor Edward; she deteriorated, hopelessly, the miserable Leonora. There is no doubt that she caused Leonora's character to deteriorate. If there was a fine point about Leonora it was that she was proud and that she was silent. But that pride and that silence broke when she made that extraordinary outburst, in the shadowy room that contained the Protest, and in the little terrace looking over the river. I don't mean to say that she was doing a wrong thing. She was certainly doing right in trying to warn me that Florence was making eyes at her husband. But, if she did the right thing, she was doing it in the wrong way. Perhaps she should have reflected longer; she should have spoken, if she wanted to speak, only after reflection. Or it would have been better if she had acted—if, for instance, she had so chaperoned Florence that private communication between her and Edward became impossible. She should have gone eaves-dropping; she should have watched outside bedroom doors. It is odi-ous; but that is the way the job is done. She should have taken Edward away the moment Maisie was dead. No, she acted wrongly. . . .

And yet, poor thing, is it for me to condemn her—and what did it matter in the end? If it had not been Florence, it would have been some other . . . Still, it might have been a better woman than my wife. For Florence was vulgar; Florence was a common flirt who would not, at the last, *lâcher prise*;* and Florence was an unstoppable talker. You could not stop her; nothing would stop her. Edward and Leonora were at least proud and reserved people. Pride and reserve are not the only things in life; perhaps they are not even the best things. But, if they happen to be your particular virtues you will go all to pieces if you let them go. And Leonora let them go. She let them go before poor Edward did even. Consider her position when she burst out over the Luther-Protest . . . Consider her agonies . . .

You are to remember that the main passion of her life was to get Edward back; she had never, till that moment, despaired of getting him back. That may seem ignoble; but you have also to remember that her getting him back represented to her not only a victory for herself. It would, as it appeared to her, have been a victory for all wives and a victory for her Church. That was how it presented itself to her. These things are a little inscrutable. I don't know why the getting back of Edward should have represented to her a victory for all wives, for Society and for her Church. Or, maybe, I have a glim-mering of it.

She saw life as a perpetual sex-battle between husbands who desire to be unfaithful to their wives, and wives who desire to recapture their husbands in the end. That was her sad and modest view of mat-rimony. Man, for her, was a sort of brute who must have his divaga-tions, his moments of excess, his nights out, his, let us say, rutting seasons. She had read few novels, so that the idea of a pure and constant love succeeding the sound of wedding bells had never been very much presented to her. She went, numbed and terrified, to the Mother Superior of her childhood's convent with the tale of Edward's infidelities with the Spanish dancer, and all that the old nun, who appeared to her to be infinitely wise, mystic and reverend, had done had been to shake her head sadly and to say:

"Men are like that. By the blessing of God it will all come right in the end."

That was what was put before her by her spiritual advisers as her programme in life. Or, at any rate, that was how their teachings came through to her—that was the lesson she told me she had learned of them. I don't know exactly what they taught her. The lot of women was patience and patience and again patience—*ad majorem Dei gloriam**—until upon the appointed day, if God saw fit, she should have her reward. If then, in the end, she should have succeeded in getting Edward back she would have kept her man within the limits that are all that wifehood has to expect. She was even taught that such excesses in men are natural, excusable—as if they had been children.

And the great thing was that there should be no scandal before the congregation. So she had clung to the idea of getting Edward back with a fierce passion that was like an agony. She had looked the other way; she had occupied herself solely with one idea. That was the idea of having Edward appear, when she did get him back, wealthy, glorious as it were, on account of his lands, and upright. She would show, in fact, that in an unfaithful world one Catholic woman had succeeded in retaining the fidelity of her husband. And she thought she had come near her desires.

Her plan with regard to Maisie had appeared to be working admirably. Edward had seemed to be cooling off towards the girl. He did not hunger to pass every minute of the time at Nauheim beside the child's recumbent form; he went out to polo matches; he played auction bridge in the evenings; he was cheerful and bright. She was certain that he was not trying to seduce that poor child; she was beginning to think that he had never tried to do so. He seemed in fact to be dropping back into what he had been for Maisie in the beginning—a kind, attentive, superior officer in the regiment, paying gallant attentions to a bride. They were as open in their little flirtations as the dayspring from on high.* And Maisie had not appeared to fret when he went off on excursions with us; she had to lie down for so many hours on her bed every afternoon, and she had not appeared to crave for the attentions of Edward at those times.

And Edward was beginning to make little advances to Leonora. Once or twice, in private—for he often did it before people—he had said: "How nice you look!" or "What a pretty dress!" She had gone with Florence to Frankfurt, where they dress as well as in Paris, and had got herself a gown or two. She could afford it, and Florence was an excellent adviser as to dress. She seemed to have got hold of the clue to the riddle.

Yes, Leonora seemed to have got hold of the clue to the riddle. She imagined herself to have been in the wrong to some extent in the past. She should not have kept Edward on such a tight rein with regard to money. She thought she was on the right tack in letting him—as she had done only with fear and irresolution—have again the control of his income. He came even a step towards her and acknowledged, spontaneously, that she had been right in husbanding, for all those years, their resources. He said to her one day:

"You've done right, old girl. There's nothing I like so much as to have a little to chuck away. And I can do it, thanks to you."

That was really, she said, the happiest moment of her life. And he, seeming to realise it, had ventured to pat her on the shoulder. He had, ostensibly, come in to borrow a safety pin of her.

And the occasion of her boxing Maisie's ears, had, after it was over, rivetted in her mind the idea that there was no intrigue between Edward and Mrs. Maidan. She imagined that, from henceforward, all that she had to do was to keep him well supplied with money and his mind amused with pretty girls. She was convinced that he was coming back to her. For that month she no longer repelled his timid advances that never went very far. For he certainly made timid advances. He patted her on the shoulder; he whispered into her ear little jokes about the odd figures that they saw up at the Casino. It was not much to make a little joke—but the whispering of it was a precious intimacy. . . .

And then—smash—it all went. It went to pieces at the moment when Florence laid her hand upon Edward's wrist, as it lay on the glass sheltering the manuscript of the Protest, up in the high tower with the shutters where the sunlight here and there streamed in. Or, rather, it went when she noticed the look in Edward's eyes as he gazed back into Florence's. She knew that look.

She had known—since the first moment of their meeting, since the moment of our all sitting down to dinner together—that Florence was making eyes at Edward. But she had seen so many women make eyes at Edward—hundreds and hundreds of women, in railway trains, in hotels, aboard liners, at street corners. And she had arrived at thinking that Edward took little stock in women that made eyes at him. She had formed what was, at that time, a fairly correct estimate of the methods of, the reasons for, Edward's loves. She was certain that hitherto they had consisted of the short passion for the Dolciquita, the real sort of love for Mrs. Basil, and what she deemed the pretty courtship of Maisie Maidan. Besides she despised Florence so haughtily that she could not imagine Edward's being attracted by her. And she and Maisie were a sort of bulwark round him.

She wanted, besides, to keep her eyes on Florence—for Florence knew that she had boxed Maisie's ears. And Leonora so desperately desired that her union with Edward should appear to be flawless. But all that went . . .

With the answering gaze of Edward into Florence's blue and uplifted eyes, she knew that it had all gone. She knew that that gaze meant that those two had had long conversations of an intimate kind—about their likes and dislikes, about their natures, about their views of marriage. She knew what it meant that she, when we all four walked out together, had always been with me ten yards ahead of Florence and Edward. She did not imagine that it had gone further than talks about their likes and dislikes, about their natures or about marriage as an institution. But, having watched Edward all her life, she knew that that laying on of hands, that answering of gaze with gaze, meant that the thing was unavoidable. Edward was such a serious person.

She knew that any attempt on her part to separate those two would be to rivet on Edward an irrevocable passion; that, as I have before told you, it was a trick of Edward's nature to believe that the seducing of a woman gave her an irrevocable hold over him for life. And that touching of hands, she knew, would give that woman an irrevocable claim—to be seduced. And she so despised Florence that she would have preferred it to be a parlour-maid. There are very decent parlour-maids.

And, suddenly, there came into her mind the conviction that Maisie Maidan had a real passion for Edward; that this would break her heart—and that she, Leonora, would be responsible for that. She went, for the moment, mad. She clutched me by the wrist; she dragged me down those stairs and across that whispering Rittersaal with the high painted pillars, the high painted chimney piece. I guess she did not go mad enough.

She ought to have said:

"Your wife is a harlot who is going to be my husband's mistress . . ." That might have done the trick. But, even in her madness she was afraid to go as far as that. She was afraid that, if she did, Edward and Florence would make a bolt of it and that, if they did that she would lose forever all chance of getting him back in the end. She acted very badly to me.

Well, she was a tortured soul who put her Church before the interests of a Philadelphia Quaker. That is all right—I daresay the Church of Rome is the more important of the two.

A week after Maisie Maidan's death she was aware that Florence had become Edward's mistress. She waited outside Florence's door and met Edward as he came away. She said nothing and he only grunted. But I guess he had a bad time.

Yes, the mental deterioration that Florence worked in Leonora was extraordinary; it smashed up her whole life and all her chances. It made her, in the first place, hopeless—for she could not see how, after that, Edward could return to her—after a vulgar intrigue with a vulgar woman. His affair with Mrs. Basil, which was now all that she had to bring, in her heart, against him, she could not find it in her to call an intrigue. It was a love affair—a pure enough thing in its way. But this seemed to her to be a horror—a wantonness, all the more detestable to her, because she so detested Florence. And Florence talked . . .

That was what was terrible, because Florence forced Leonora herself to abandon her high reserve—Florence and the situation. It appears that Florence was in two minds whether to confess to me or to Leonora. Confess she had to. And she pitched at last on Leonora, because if it had been me she would have had to confess a great deal more. Or, at least, I might have guessed a great deal more, about her "heart," and about Jimmy. So she went to Leonora one day and began hinting and hinting. And she enraged Leonora to such an extent that at last Leonora said:

"You want to tell me that you are Edward's mistress. You can be. I have no use for him."

That was really a calamity for Leonora, because, once started, there was no stopping the talking. She tried to stop—but it was not to be done. She found it necessary to send Edward messages through Florence; for she would not speak to him. She had to give him, for instance, to understand that if I ever came to know of his intrigue she would ruin him beyond repair. And it complicated matters a good deal that Edward, at about this time, was really a little in love with her. He thought that he had treated her so badly; that she was so fine. She was so mournful that he longed to comfort her, and he thought himself such a blackguard that there was nothing he would not have done to make amends. And Florence communicated these items of information to Leonora.

I don't in the least blame Leonora for her coarseness to Florence; it must have done Florence a world of good. But I do blame her for giving way to what was in the end a desire for communicativeness. You see that business cut her off from her Church. She did not want to confess what she was doing because she was afraid that her spiritual advisers would blame her for deceiving me. I rather imagine that she would have preferred damnation to breaking my heart. That is what it works out at. She need not have troubled.

But, having no priests to talk to she had to talk to someone and, as Florence insisted on talking to her, she talked back, in short, explosive sentences, like one of the damned. Precisely like one of the damned. Well, if a pretty period in hell on this earth can spare her any period of pain in Eternity—where there are not any periods—I guess Leonora will escape Hell fire.

Her conversations with Florence would be like this. Florence would happen in on her, whilst she was doing her wonderful hair, with a proposition from Edward, who seems about that time to have conceived the naïve idea that he might become a polygamist. I daresay it was Florence who put it into his head. Anyhow, I am not responsible for the oddities of the human psychology. But it certainly appears that at about that date Edward cared more for Leonora than he had ever done before—or, at any rate, for a long time. And, if Leonora had been a person to play cards and if she had played her cards well, and if she had had no sense of shame and so on, she might then have shared Edward with Florence until the time came for jerking that poor cuckoo out of the nest.

Well, Florence would come to Leonora with some such proposition.

I do not mean to say that she put it baldly, like that. She stood out that she was not Edward's mistress until Leonora said that she had seen Edward coming out of her room at an advanced hour of the night. That checked Florence a bit; but she fell back upon her "heart" and stuck out that she had merely been conversing with Edward in order to bring him to a better frame of mind. Florence had, of course, to stick to that story; for even Florence would not have had the face to implore Leonora to grant her favours to Edward if she had admitted that she was Edward's mistress. That could not be done. At the same time Florence had such a pressing desire to talk about something. There would have been nothing else to talk about but a rapprochement between that estranged pair. So Florence would go on babbling and Leonora would go on brushing her hair. And then Leonora would say suddenly something like:

"I should think myself defiled if Edward touched me now that he has touched you."

That would discourage Florence a bit; but after a week or so, on another morning she would have another try.

And, even in other things Leonora deteriorated. She had promised Edward to leave the spending of his own income in his own hands. And she had fully meant to do that. I daresay she would have done it too; though, no doubt, she would have spied upon his banking account in secret. She was not a Roman Catholic for nothing. But she took so serious a view of Edward's unfaithfulness to the memory of poor little Maisie that she could not trust him any more at all.

So, when she got back to Branshaw she started, after less than a month, to worry him about the minutest items of his expenditure. She allowed him to draw his own cheques, but there was hardly a cheque that she did not scrutinise—except for a private account of about five hundred a year which, tacitly, she allowed him to keep for expenditure on his mistress or mistresses. He had to have his jaunts to Paris; he had to send expensive cables in cipher to Florence about twice a week. But she worried him about his expenditure on wines, on fruit trees, on harness, on gates, on the account at his blacksmith's for work done to a new patent army stirrup that he was trying to invent. She could not see why he should bother to invent a new army stirrup and she was really enraged when, after the invention was mature, he made a present to the War Office of the designs and the patent rights. It was a remarkably good stirrup.

I have told you, I think, that Edward spent a great deal of time, and about two hundred pounds for law fees on getting a poor girl, the daughter of one of his gardeners, acquitted of a charge of murdering her baby. That was positively the last act of Edward's life. It came at a time when Nancy Rufford was on her way to India; when the most horrible gloom was over the household; when Edward, himself, was in an agony and behaving as prettily as he knew how. Yet even then Leonora made him a terrible scene about this expenditure of time and trouble. She sort of had the vague idea that what had passed with the girl and the rest of it ought to have taught Edward a lesson—the lesson of economy. She threatened to take his banking account away from him again. I guess that made him cut his throat. He might have stuck it out otherwise—but the thought that he had lost Nancy and that, in addition, there was nothing left for him but a dreary, dreary succession of days in which he could be of no public service . . . Well, it finished him.

It was during those years that Leonora tried to get up a love affair of her own with a fellow called Bayham—a decent sort of fellow. A really nice man. But the affair was no sort of success. I have told you about it already. . . .

II

WELL, that about brings me up to the date of my receiving, in Waterbury, the laconic cable from Edward to the effect that he wanted me to go to Branshaw and have a chat. I was pretty busy at the time and I was half minded to send him a reply cable to the effect that I would start in a fortnight. But I was having a long interview with old Mr. Hurlbird's attorneys and immediately afterwards I had to have a long interview with the Misses Hurlbird, so I delayed cabling.

I had expected to find the Misses Hurlbird excessively old—in the nineties or thereabouts. The time had passed so slowly that I had the impression that it must have been thirty years since I had been in the United States. It was only twelve years. Actually Miss Hurlbird was just sixty-one and Miss Florence Hurlbird fifty-nine and they were both, mentally and physically, as vigorous as could be desired. They were, indeed, more vigorous, mentally, than suited my purpose, which was to get away from the United States as quickly as I could. The Hurlbirds were an exceedingly united family—exceedingly united except on one set of points. Each of the three of them had a separate doctor, whom they trusted implicitly—and each had a separate attorney. And each of them distrusted the other's doctor and the other's attorney. And, naturally, the doctors and the attorneys warned one all the time—against each other. You cannot imagine how complicated it all became for me. Of course I had an attorney of my own—recommended to me by young Carter, my Philadelphia nephew.

I do not mean to say that there was any unpleasantness of a grasping kind. The problem was quite another one—a moral dilemma. You see, old Mr. Hurlbird had left all his property to Florence with the mere request that she would have erected to him in the city of Waterbury, Ill.,* a memorial that should take the form of some sort of institution for the relief of sufferers from the heart. Florence's money had all come to me—and with it old Mr. Hurlbird's. He had died just five days before Florence.

Well, I was quite ready to spend a round million dollars on the relief of sufferers from the heart. The old gentleman had left about a million and a half; Florence had been worth about eight hundred thousand—and as I figured it out, I should cut up at about a million myself. Anyhow, there was ample money. But I naturally wanted to consult the wishes of his surviving relatives and then the trouble really began. You see, it had been discovered that Mr. Hurlbird had had nothing whatever the matter with his heart. His lungs had been a little affected all through his life and he had died of bronchitis.

It struck Miss Florence Hurlbird that, since her brother had died of lungs and not of heart, his money ought to go to lung patients. That, she considered, was what her brother would have wished. On the other hand, by a kink, that I could not at the time understand, Miss Hurlbird insisted that I ought to keep the money all to myself. She said that she did not wish for any monuments to the Hurlbird family.

At the time I thought that that was because of a New England dislike for necrological ostentation. But I can figure out now, when I remember certain insistent and continued questions that she put to me, about Edward Ashburnham, that there was another idea in her mind. And Leonora has told me that, on Florence's dressing-table, beside her dead body, there had lain a letter to Miss Hurlbird—a letter which Leonora posted without telling me. I don't know how Florence had time to write to her aunt; but I can quite understand that she would not like to go out of the world without making some comments. So I guess Florence had told Miss Hurlbird a good bit about Edward Ashburnham in a few scrawled words—and that that was why the old lady did not wish the name of Hurlbird perpetuated. Perhaps also she thought that I had earned the Hurlbird money.

It meant a pretty tidy lot of discussing, what with the doctors warning each other about the bad effects of discussions, on the health of the old ladies, and warning me covertly against each other, and saying that old Mr. Hurlbird might have died of heart, after all, in spite of the diagnosis of *his* doctor. And the solicitors all had separate methods of arranging about how the money should be invested and entrusted and bound.

Personally, I wanted to invest the money so that the interest could be used for the relief of sufferers from the heart. If old Mr. Hurlbird had not died of any defects in that organ he had considered that it was defective. Moreover, Florence had certainly died of her heart, as I saw it. And when Miss Florence Hurlbird stood out that the money ought to go to chest sufferers I was brought to thinking that there ought to be a chest institution too, and I advanced the sum that I was ready to provide to a million and a half of dollars. That would have given seven hundred and fifty thousand to each class of invalid. I did not want money at all badly. All I wanted it for was to be able to give Nancy Rufford a good time. I did not know much about housekeeping expenses in England where, I presumed, she would wish to live. I knew that her needs at that time were limited to good chocolates, and a good horse or two and simple, pretty frocks. Probably she would want more than that later on. But even if I gave a million and a half dollars to these institutions I should still have the equivalent of about twenty thousand a year English, and I considered that Nancy could have a pretty good time on that or less.

Anyhow, we had a stiff set of arguments up at the Hurlbird mansion, which stands on a bluff over the town. It may strike you, silent listener, as being funny if you happen to be European. But moral problems of that description and the giving of millions to institutions are immensely serious matters in my country. Indeed, they are the staple topics for consideration amongst the wealthy classes. We haven't got peerage and social climbing to occupy us much, and decent people do not take interest in politics or elderly people in sport. So that there were real tears shed by both Miss Hurlbird and Miss Florence before I left that city.

I left it quite abruptly. Four hours after Edward's telegram came another from Leonora, saying: "Yes, do come. You could be so helpful." I simply told my attorney that there was the million and a half; that he could invest it as he liked, and that the purposes must be decided by the Misses Hurlbird. I was, anyhow, pretty well worn out by all the discussions. And, as I have never heard yet from the Misses Hurlbird, I rather think that Miss Hurlbird, either by revelations or by moral force, has persuaded Miss Florence that no memorial to their names shall be erected in the city of Waterbury, Conn. Miss Hurlbird wept dreadfully when she heard that I was going to stay with the Ashburnhams, but she did not make any comments. I was aware, at that date, that her niece had been seduced by that fellow Jimmy before I had married her—but I contrived to produce on her the impression that I thought Florence had been a model wife. Why, at that date I still believed that Florence had been perfectly virtuous after her marriage to me. I had not figured it out that she could have played it so low down as to continue her intrigue with that fellow under my roof. Well, I was a fool. But I did not think much about Florence at that date. My mind was occupied with what was happening at Branshaw.

I had got it into my head that the telegrams had something to do with Nancy. It struck me that she might have shown signs of forming an attachment for some undesirable fellow and that Leonora wanted me to come back and marry her out of harm's way. That was what was pretty firmly in my mind. And it remained in my mind for nearly ten days after my arrival at that beautiful old place. Neither Edward nor Leonora made any motion to talk to me about anything other than the weather and the crops.* Yet, although there were several young fellows about, I could not see that any one in particular was distinguished by the girl's preference. She certainly appeared illish and nervous, except when she woke up to talk gay nonsense to me. Oh, the pretty thing that she was. . . .

I imagined that what must have happened was that the undesirable young man had been forbidden the place and that Nancy was fretting a little.

What had happened was just Hell. Leonora had spoken to Nancy; Nancy had spoken to Edward; Edward had spoken to Leonora—and they had talked and talked. And talked. You have to imagine horrible pictures of gloom and half lights, and emotions running through silent nights—through whole nights. You have to imagine my beautiful Nancy appearing suddenly to Edward, rising up at the foot of his bed, with her long hair falling, like a split cone of shadow,* in the glimmer of a night-light that burned beside him. You have to imagine her, a silent, a no doubt agonised figure, like a spectre, suddenly offering herself to him—to save his reason! And you have to imagine his frantic refusal—and talk. And talk! My God!

And yet, to me, living in the house, enveloped with the charm of the quiet and ordered living, with the silent, skilled servants whose mere laying out of my dress clothes was like a caress—to me who was hourly with them they appeared like tender, ordered and devoted people, smiling, absenting themselves at the proper intervals; driving me to meets—just good people! How the devil—how the devil do they do it?

At dinner one evening Leonora said—she had just opened a telegram:—

"Nancy will be going to India, to-morrow, to be with her father."

No one spoke. Nancy looked at her plate; Edward went on eating his pheasant. I felt very bad; I imagined that it would be up to me to propose to Nancy that evening. It appeared to me to be queer that they had not given me any warning of Nancy's departure. But I thought that that was only English manners—some sort of delicacy that I had not got the hang of. You must remember that at that moment I trusted in Edward and Leonora and in Nancy Rufford, and in the tranquility of ancient haunts of peace,* as I had trusted in my mother's love. And that evening Edward spoke to me.

What in the interval had happened had been this:

Upon her return from Nauheim Leonora had completely broken down—because she knew she could trust Edward. That seems odd but, if you know anything about breakdowns, you will know that, by the ingenious torments that fate prepares for us, these things come as soon as, a strain having relaxed, there is nothing more to be done. It is after a husband's long illness and death that a widow goes to pieces; it is at the end of a long rowing contest that a crew collapses and lies forward upon its oars. And that was what happened to Leonora.

From certain tones in Edward's voice; from the long, steady stare that he had given her from his bloodshot eyes on rising from the dinner table in the Nauheim hotel, she knew that, in the affair of the poor girl, this was a case in which Edward's moral scruples, or his social code, or his idea that it would be playing it *too* low down, rendered Nancy perfectly safe. The girl, she felt sure, was in no danger at all from Edward. And, in that she was perfectly right. The smash was to come from herself.

She relaxed; she broke; she drifted, at first quickly, then with an increasing momentum, down the stream of destiny. You may put it that, having been cut off from the restraints of her religion, for the first time in her life, she acted along the lines of her instinctive desires. I do not know whether to think that, in that she was no longer herself; or that, having let loose the bonds of her standards, her conventions and her traditions, she was being, for the first time, her own natural self. She was torn between her intense, maternal love for the girl and an intense jealousy of the woman who realises that the man she loves has met what appears to be the final passion of his life. She was divided between an intense disgust for Edward's weakness in conceiving this passion, an intense pity for the miseries that he was enduring, and a feeling equally intense, but one that she hid from herself—a feeling of respect for Edward's determination to keep himself, in this particular affair, unspotted.

And the human heart is a very mysterious thing. It is impossible to say that Leonora, in acting as she then did, was not filled with a sort of hatred of Edward's final virtue. She wanted, I think, to despise him. He was, she realised, gone from her for good. Then let him suffer, let him agonise; let him, if possible, break and go to that Hell that is the abode of broken resolves. She might have taken a different line. It would have been so easy to send the girl away to stay with some friends; to have taken her away herself upon some pretext or other. That would not have cured things but it would have been the decent line . . . But, at that date, poor Leonora was incapable of taking any line whatever.

She pitied Edward frightfully at one time—and then she acted along the lines of pity; she loathed him at another and then she acted as her loathing dictated. She gasped, as a person dying of tuberculosis gasps for air. She craved madly for communication with some other human soul. And the human soul that she selected was that of the girl.

Perhaps Nancy was the only person that she could have talked to. With her necessity for reticences, with her coldness of manner, Leonora had singularly few intimates. She had none at all, with the exception of the Mrs. Colonel Whelen, who had advised her about the affair with La Dolciquita, and the one or two religious, who had guided her through life. The Colonel's wife was at that time in Madeira; the religious she now avoided. Her visitor's book had seven hundred names in it; there was not a soul that she could speak to. She was Mrs. Ashburnham of Branshaw Teleragh.

She was the great Mrs. Ashburnham of Branshaw and she lay all day upon her bed in her marvellous, light, airy bedroom with the chintzes and the Chippendale and the portraits of deceased Ashburnhams by Zoffany and Zucchero.* When there was a meet she would struggle up—supposing it were within driving distance—and let Edward drive her and the girl to the cross-roads or the country house. She would drive herself back alone; Edward would ride off with the girl. Ride Leonora could not, that season—her head was too bad. Each pace of her mare was an anguish.

But she drove with efficiency and precision; she smiled at the Gimmers and Ffoulkes and the Hedley Seatons. She threw with exactitude pennies to the boys who opened gates for her; she sat upright on the seat of the high dog-cart;* she waved her hands to Edward and Nancy as they rode off with the hounds, and every one could hear her clear, high voice, in the chilly weather, saying:

"Have a good time!"

Poor forlorn woman! . . .

There was, however, one spark of consolation. It came from the fact that Rodney Bayham, of Bayham, followed her always with his eyes. It had been three years since she had tried her abortive love-affair with him. Yet still, on the winter mornings he would ride up to her shafts and just say: "Good day," and look at her with eyes that were not imploring, but seemed to say: "You see, I am still, as the Germans say, A. D.—at disposition."

It was a great consolation, not because she proposed ever to take him up again but because it showed her that there was in the world one faithful soul in riding-breeches. And it showed her that she was not losing her looks.

And, indeed, she was not losing her looks. She was forty, but she was as clean run as on the day she had left the convent—as clear in outline, as clear coloured in the hair, as dark blue in the eyes. She thought that her looking-glass told her this; but there are always the doubts . . . Rodney Bayham's eyes took them away.

It is very singular that Leonora should not have aged at all. I suppose that there are some types of beauty and even of youth made for the embellishments that come with enduring sorrow. That is too elaborately put. I mean that Leonora, if everything had prospered, might have become too hard and, maybe, overbearing. As it was she was tuned down to appearing efficient—and yet sympathetic. That is the rarest of all blends. And yet I swear that Leonora, in her restrained way, gave the impression of being intensely sympathetic. When she listened to you she appeared also to be listening to some sound that was going on in the distance. But still, she listened to you and took in what you said, which, since the record of humanity is a record of sorrows, was, as a rule, something sad.

I think that she must have taken Nancy through many terrors of the night and many bad places of the day. And that would account for the girl's passionate love for the elder woman. For Nancy's love for Leonora was an admiration that is awakened in Catholics by their feeling for the Virgin Mary and for various of the saints. It is too little to say that the girl would have laid her life at Leonora's feet. Well, she laid there the offer of her virtue—and her reason. Those were sufficient instalments of her life. It would to-day be much better for Nancy Rufford if she were dead.

Perhaps all these reflections are a nuisance; but they crowd on me. I will try to tell the story.

You see—when she came back from Nauheim Leonora began to have her headaches—headaches lasting through whole days, during which she could speak no word and could bear to hear no sound. And, day after day, Nancy would sit with her, silent and motionless for hours, steeping handkerchiefs in vinegar and water, and thinking her own thoughts. It must have been very bad for her—and her meals alone with Edward must have been bad for her too—and beastly bad for Edward. Edward, of course, wavered in his demeanour. What else could he do? At times he would sit silent and dejected over his untouched food. He would utter nothing but monosyllables when Nancy spoke to him. Then he was simply afraid of the girl falling in love with him. At other times he would take a little wine; pull himself together; attempt to chaff Nancy about a stake and binder hedge* that her mare had checked at or talk about the habits of the Chitralis. That was when he was thinking that it was rough on the poor girl that he should have become a dull companion. He realised that his talking to her in the park at Nauheim had done her no harm.

But all that was doing a great deal of harm to Nancy. It gradually opened her eyes to the fact that Edward was a man with his ups and downs and not an invariably gay uncle like a nice dog, a trustworthy horse or a girl friend. She would find him in attitudes of frightful dejection, sunk into his armchair in the study that was half a gun-room. She would notice through the open door that his face was the face of an old, dead man, when he had no one to talk to. Gradually it forced itself upon her attention that there were profound differences between the pair that she regarded as her uncle and her aunt. It was a conviction that came very slowly.

It began with Edward's giving an oldish horse to a young fellow called Selmes. Selmes' father had been ruined by a fraudulent solicitor and the Selmes family had had to sell their hunters. It was a case that had excited a good deal of sympathy in that part of the county. And Edward, meeting the young man one day, unmounted, and seeing him to be very unhappy, had offered to give him an old Irish cob upon which he was riding. It was a silly sort of thing to do, really. The horse was worth from thirty to forty pounds and Edward might have known that the gift would upset his wife. But Edward just had to comfort that unhappy young man whose father he had known all his life. And what made it all the worse was that young Selmes could not afford to keep the horse even. Edward recollected this, immediately after he had made the offer and said quickly:

"Of course I mean that you should stable the horse at Branshaw until you have time to turn round or want to sell him and get a better."

Nancy went straight home and told all this to Leonora, who was lying down. She regarded it as a splendid instance of Edward's quick consideration for the feelings and the circumstances of the distressed. She thought it would cheer Leonora up—because it ought to cheer any woman up to know that she had such a splendid husband. That was the last girlish thought she ever had. For Leonora, whose headache had left her collected but miserably weak, turned upon her bed and uttered words that were amazing to the girl:

"I wish to God," she said, "that he was your husband, and not mine. We shall be ruined. We shall be ruined. Am I *never* to have a chance." And suddenly Leonora burst into a passion of tears. She pushed herself up from the pillows with one elbow and sat there— crying, crying, crying, with her face hidden in her hands and the tears falling through her fingers.

The girl flushed, stammered and whimpered as if she had been personally insulted.

"But if Uncle Edward . . ." she began.

"That man," said Leonora, with an extraordinary bitterness, "would give the shirt off his back and off mine—and off yours to any . . ." She could not finish the sentence.

At that moment she had been feeling an extraordinary hatred and contempt for her husband. All the morning and all the afternoon she had been lying there thinking that Edward and the girl were together—in the field and hacking it home at dusk. She had been digging her sharp nails into her palms.

The house had been very silent in the drooping winter weather. And then, after an eternity of torture, there had invaded it the sound of opening doors, of the girl's gay voice saying:

"Well, it was only under the mistletoe." . . . And there was

Edward's gruff undertone. Then Nancy had come in, with feet that had hastened up the stairs and that tiptoed as they approached the open door of Leonora's room. Branshaw had a great big hall with oak floors and tiger skins. Round this hall there ran a gallery upon which Leonora's doorway gave. And even when she had the worst of her headaches she liked to have her door open—I suppose so that she might hear the approaching footsteps of ruin and disaster. At any rate she hated to be in a room with a shut door.

At that moment Leonora hated Edward with a hatred that was like hell, and she would have liked to bring her riding-whip down across the girl's face. What right had Nancy to be young and slender and dark, and gay at times, at times mournful? What right had she to be exactly the woman to make Leonora's husband happy? For Leonora knew that Nancy would have made Edward happy.

Yes, Leonora wished to bring her riding-whip down on Nancy's young face. She imagined the pleasure she would feel when the lash fell across those queer features; the pleasure she would feel at drawing the handle at the same moment toward her, so as to cut deep into the flesh and to leave a lasting wheal.

Well, she left a lasting wheal, and her words cut deeply into the girl's mind. . . .

They neither of them spoke about that again. A fortnight went by—a fortnight of deep rains, of heavy fields, of bad scent.* Leonora's headaches seemed to have gone for good. She hunted once or twice, letting herself be piloted by Bayham, whilst Edward looked after the girl. Then, one evening, when those three were dining alone, Edward said, in the queer, deliberate, heavy tones that came out of him in those days (he was looking at the table):

"I have been thinking that Nancy ought to do more for her father. He is getting an old man. I have written to Colonel Rufford,* suggesting that she should go to him."

Leonora called out:

"How dare you? How dare you?"

The girl put her hand over her heart and cried out: "Oh, my sweet Saviour, help me!" That was the queer way she thought within her mind, and the words forced themselves to her lips. Edward said nothing.

And that night, by a merciless trick of the devil that pays attention to this sweltering hell of ours, Nancy Rufford had a letter from her

mother. It came whilst Leonora was talking to Edward, or Leonora
would have intercepted it as she had intercepted others. It was an
amazing and a horrible letter. . . .

I don't know what it contained. I just average out from its effects
on Nancy that her mother, having eloped with some worthless sort
of fellow, had done what is called "sinking lower and lower."
Whether she was actually on the streets I do not know, but I rather
think that she eked out a small allowance that she had from her
husband by that means of livelihood. And I think that she stated as
much in her letter to Nancy and upbraided the girl with living in
luxury whilst her mother starved. And it must have been horrible in
tone, for Mrs. Rufford was a cruel sort of woman at the best of times.
It must have seemed to that poor girl, opening her letter, for distrac-
tion from another grief, up in her bedroom, like the laughter of a
devil.

I just cannot bear to think of my poor dear girl at that moment. . . .

And, at the same time, Leonora was lashing, like a cold fiend, into
the unfortunate Edward. Or, perhaps, he was not so unfortunate;
because he had done what he knew to be the right thing, he may be
deemed happy. I leave it to you. At any rate, he was sitting in his deep
chair, and Leonora came into his room—for the first time in nine
years. She said:

"This is the most atrocious thing you have done in your atrocious
life." He never moved and he never looked at her. God knows what
was in Leonora's mind exactly.

I like to think that, uppermost in it was concern and horror at the
thought of the poor girl's going back to a father whose voice made her
shriek in the night. And, indeed, that motive was very strong with
Leonora. But I think there was also present the thought that she
wanted to go on torturing Edward with the girl's presence. She was,
at that time, capable of that.

Edward was sunk in his chair; there were in the room two candles,
hidden by green glass shades. The green shades were reflected in the
glasses of the book-cases that contained not books but guns with
gleaming brown barrels and fishing-rods in green baize over-covers.
There was dimly to be seen, above a mantelpiece encumbered with
spurs, hooves and bronze models of horses, a dark-brown picture of
a white horse.

"If you think," Leonora said, "that I do not know that you are in love with the girl . . ." She began spiritedly, but she could not find any ending for the sentence. Edward did not stir; he never spoke. And then Leonora said:

"If you want me to divorce you I will. You can marry her then. She's in love with you."

He groaned at that, a little, Leonora said. Then she went away.

Heaven knows what happened in Leonora after that. She certainly does not herself know. She probably said a good deal more to Edward than I have been able to report; but that is all that she has told me and I am not going to make up speeches. To follow her psychological development of that moment I think we must allow that she upbraided him for a great deal of their past life, whilst Edward sat absolutely silent. And, indeed, in speaking of it afterwards, she has said several times: "I said a great deal more to him than I wanted to, just because he was so silent." She talked, in fact, in the endeavour to sting him into speech.

She must have said so much that, with the expression of her grievance, her mood changed. She went back to her own room in the gallery, and sat there for a long time thinking. And she thought herself into a mood of absolute unselfishness, of absolute self-contempt, too. She said to herself that she was no good; that she had failed in all her efforts—in her efforts to get Edward back as in her efforts to make him curb his expenditure. She imagined herself to be exhausted; she imagined herself to be done. Then a great fear came over her.

She thought that Edward, after what she had said to him, must have committed suicide. She went out on to the gallery and listened; there was no sound in all the house except the regular beat of the great clock in the hall. But, even in her debased condition, she was not the person to hang about. She acted. She went straight to Edward's room, opened the door, and looked in.

He was oiling the breech action of a gun. It was an unusual thing for him to do, at that time of night, in his evening clothes. It never occurred to her, nevertheless, that he was going to shoot himself with that implement. She knew that he was doing it just for occupation—to keep himself from thinking. He looked up when she opened the door, his face illuminated by the light cast upwards from the round orifices in the green candle shades.

She said:

"I didn't imagine that I should find Nancy here." She thought that she owed that to him. He answered then:

"I don't imagine that you did imagine it." Those were the only words he spoke that night. She went, like a lame duck, back through the long corridors; she stumbled over the familiar tiger skins in the dark hall. She could hardly drag one limb after the other. In the gallery she perceived that Nancy's door was half open and that there was a light in the girl's room. A sudden madness possessed her, a desire for action, a thirst for self-explanation.

Their rooms all gave on to the gallery; Leonora's to the east, the girl's next, then Edward's. The sight of those three open doors, side by side, gaping to receive whom the chances of the black night might bring, made Leonora shudder all over her body. She went into Nancy's room.

The girl was sitting perfectly still in an arm-chair, very upright, as she had been taught to sit at the convent. She appeared to be as calm as a church; her hair fell, black and like a pall, down over both her shoulders. The fire beside her was burning brightly; she must have just put coals on. She was in a white silk kimono that covered her to the feet. The clothes that she had taken off were exactly folded upon the proper seats. Her long hands were one upon each arm of the chair that had a pink and white chintz back.

Leonora told me these things. She seemed to think it extraordinary that the girl could have done such orderly things as fold up the clothes she had taken off upon such a night—when Edward had announced that he was going to send her to her father, and when, from her mother, she had received that letter. The letter, in its envelope, was in her right hand.

Leonora did not at first perceive it. She said:

"What are you doing so late?" The girl answered:

"Just thinking." They seemed to think in whispers and to speak below their breaths. Then Leonora's eyes fell on the envelope, and she recognised Mrs. Rufford's handwriting.

It was one of those moments when thinking was impossible, Leonora said. It was as if stones were being thrown at her from every direction and she could only run. She heard herself exclaim:

"Edward's dying—because of you. He's dying. He's worth more than either of us. . . ."

The girl looked past her at the panels of the half-closed door.

"My poor father," she said, "my poor father."

"You must stay here," Leonora answered fiercely. "You must stay here. I tell you you must stay here."

"I am going to Glasgow," Nancy answered. "I shall go to Glasgow tomorrow morning. My mother is in Glasgow."

It appears that it was in Glasgow that Mrs. Rufford pursued her disorderly life. She had selected that city, not because it was more profitable, but because it was the natal home of her husband to whom she desired to cause as much pain as possible.

"You must stay here," Leonora began, "to save Edward. He's dying for love of you."

The girl turned her calm eyes upon Leonora.

"I know it," she said. "And I am dying for love of him."

Leonora uttered an "Ah," that, in spite of herself, was an "Ah" of horror and of grief.

"That is why," the girl continued, "I am going to Glasgow—to take my mother away from there." She added, "To the ends of the earth," for, if the last months had made her nature that of a woman, her phrases were still romantically those of a school-girl. It was as if she had grown up so quickly that there had not been time to put her hair up. But she added: "We're no good—my mother and I."

Leonora said, with her fierce calmness:

"No. No. You're not no good. It's I that am no good. You can't let that man go on to ruin for want of you. You must belong to him."

The girl, she said, smiled at her with a queer, faraway smile—as if she were a thousand years old, as if Leonora were a tiny child.

"I knew you would come to that," she said, very slowly. "But we are not worth it—Edward and I."

III

Nancy had, in fact, been thinking ever since Leonora had made that comment over the giving of the horse to young Selmes. She had been thinking and thinking, because she had had to sit for many days silent beside her aunt's bed. (She had always thought of Leonora as her aunt.) And she had had to sit thinking during many silent meals with Edward. And then, at times, with his bloodshot eyes and creased, heavy mouth, he would smile at her. And gradually the knowledge had come to her that Edward did not love Leonora and that Leonora hated Edward. Several things contributed to form and to harden this conviction.

She was allowed to read the papers in those days—or, rather, since Leonora was always on her bed and Edward breakfasted alone and went out early, over the estate, she was left alone with the papers. One day, in the paper, she saw the portrait of a woman she knew very well. Beneath it she read the words: "The Hon. Mrs. Brand, plaintiff in the remarkable divorce case reported on p. 8." Nancy hardly knew what a divorce case was. She had been so remarkably well brought up, and Roman Catholics do not practise divorce. I don't know how Leonora had done it exactly. I suppose she had always impressed it on Nancy's mind that nice women did not read these things, and that would have been enough to make Nancy skip those pages.

She read, at any rate, the account of the Brand divorce case—principally because she wanted to tell Leonora about it. She imagined that Leonora, when her headache left her, would like to know what was happening to Mrs. Brand, who lived at Christchurch,* and whom they both liked very well. The case occupied three days, and the report that Nancy first came upon was that of the third day. Edward, however, kept the papers of the week, after his methodical fashion, in a rack in his gun-room, and when she had finished her breakfast Nancy went to that quiet apartment and had what she would have called a good read. It seemed to her to be a queer affair. She could not understand why one counsel should be so anxious to know all about the movements of Mr. Brand upon a certain day; she could not understand why a chart of the bedroom accommodation at Christchurch Old Hall should be produced in court. She did not even see why they should want to know that, upon a certain occasion, the drawing-room door was locked. It made her laugh; it appeared to be all so senseless that grown people should occupy themselves with such matters. It struck her, nevertheless, as odd that one of the counsel should cross-question Mr. Brand so insistently and so impertinently as to his feelings for Miss Lupton. Nancy knew Miss Lupton of Ringwood* very well—a jolly girl, who rode a horse with two white fetlocks. Mr. Brand persisted that he did not love Miss Lupton. . . . Well, of course he did not love Miss Lupton; he was a married man. You might as well think of Uncle Edward loving . . . loving anybody but Leonora. When people were married there was an end of loving. There were, no doubt, people who misbehaved—but they were poor people—or people not like those she knew.

So these matters presented themselves to Nancy's mind.

But later on in the case she found that Mr. Brand had to confess to a "guilty intimacy" with someone or other. Nancy imagined that he must have been telling someone his wife's secrets; she could not understand why that was a serious offence. Of course it was not very gentlemanly—it lessened her opinion of Mr. Brand. But, since she found that Mrs. Brand had condoned that offence, she imagined that they could not have been very serious secrets that Mr. Brand had told. And then, suddenly, it was forced on her conviction that Mr. Brand—the mild Mr. Brand that she had seen a month or two before their departure to Nauheim, playing "Blind Man's Buff" with his children and kissing his wife when he caught her—Mr. Brand and Mrs. Brand had been on the worst possible terms. That was incredible.

Yet there it was—in black and white. Mr. Brand drank; Mr. Brand had struck Mrs. Brand to the ground when he was drunk. Mr. Brand was adjudged, in two or three abrupt words, at the end of columns and columns of paper, to have been guilty of cruelty to his wife and to have committed adultery with Miss Lupton. The last words conveyed nothing to Nancy—nothing real, that is to say. She knew that one was commanded not to commit adultery—but why, she thought, should one? It was probably something like catching salmon out of season—a thing one did not do. She gathered it had something to do with kissing, or holding some one in your arms. . . .

And yet the whole effect of that reading upon Nancy was mysterious, terrifying and evil. She felt a sickness—a sickness that grew as she read. Her heart beat painfully; she began to cry. She asked God how He could permit such things to be. And she was more certain that Edward did not love Leonora and that Leonora hated Edward. Perhaps, then, Edward loved some one else. It was unthinkable.

If he could love some one else than Leonora, her fierce, unknown heart suddenly spoke in her side, why could it not be herself? And he did not love her. . . . This had occurred about a month before she got the letter from her mother. She let the matter rest until the sick feeling went off; it did that in a day or two. Then, finding that Leonora's headaches had gone she suddenly told Leonora that Mrs. Brand had divorced her husband. She asked what, exactly, it all meant.

Leonora was lying on the sofa in the hall; she was feeling so weak that she could hardly find any words. She answered just:

"It means that Mr. Brand will be able to marry again."

Nancy said:

"But . . . but . . ." and then: "He will be able to marry Miss Lupton." Leonora just moved a hand in assent. Her eyes were shut.

"Then . . ." Nancy began. Her blue eyes were full of horror: her brows were tight above them; the lines of pain about her mouth were very distinct. In her eyes the whole of that familiar, great hall had a changed aspect. The andirons* with the brass flowers at the ends appeared unreal; the burning logs were just logs that were burning and not the comfortable symbols of an indestructible mode of life. The flame fluttered before the high fireback; the St. Bernard sighed in his sleep. Outside the winter rain fell and fell. And suddenly she thought that Edward might marry some one else; and she nearly screamed.

Leonora opened her eyes, lying sideways, with her face upon the black and gold pillow of the sofa that was drawn half across the great fireplace.

"I thought," Nancy said, "I never imagined. . . . Aren't marriages sacraments? Aren't they indissoluble? I thought you were married . . . and . . ." She was sobbing. "I thought you were married or not married as you are alive or dead."

"That," Leonora said, "is the law of the church. It is not the law of the land. . . ."

"Oh, yes," Nancy said, "the Brands are Protestants."

She felt a sudden safeness descend upon her, and for an hour or so her mind was at rest. It seemed to her idiotic not to have remembered

Henry VIII and the basis upon which Protestantism rests.* She almost laughed at herself.

The long afternoon wore on; the flames still fluttered when the maid made up the fire; the St. Bernard awoke and lolloped away towards the kitchen. And then Leonora opened her eyes and said almost coldly:

"And you? Don't you think you will get married?"

It was so unlike Leonora that, for the moment, the girl was frightened in the dusk. But then, again, it seemed a perfectly reasonable question.

"I don't know," she answered. "I don't know that anyone wants to marry me."

"Several people want to marry you," Leonora said.

"But I don't want to marry," Nancy answered. "I should like to go on living with you and Edward. I don't think I am in the way, or that I am really an expense. If I went you would have to have a companion. Or, perhaps, I ought to earn my living. . . ."

"I wasn't thinking of that," Leonora answered in the same dull tone. "You will have money enough from your father. But most people want to be married."

I believe that she then asked the girl if she would not like to marry me, and that Nancy answered that she would marry me if she were told to; but that she wanted to go on living there. She added:

"If I married anyone I should want him to be like Edward."

She was frightened out of her life. Leonora writhed on her couch and called out: "Oh, God! . . ."

Nancy ran for the maid; for tablets of aspirin; for wet handkerchiefs. It never occurred to her that Leonora's expression of agony was for anything else than physical pain.

You are to remember that all this happened a month before Leonora went into the girl's room at night. I have been casting back again; but I cannot help it. It is so difficult to keep all these people going. I tell you about Leonora and bring her up to date; then about Edward, who has fallen behind. And then the girl gets hopelessly left behind. I wish I could put it down in diary form. Thus: On the 1st of September they returned from Nauheim. Leonora at once took to her bed. By the 1st of October they were all going to meets together. Nancy had already observed very fully that Edward was strange in his manner. About the 6th of that month Edward gave the horse to young Selmes, and Nancy had cause to believe that her aunt did not love her uncle. On the 20th she read the account of the divorce case, which is reported in the papers of the 18th and the two following days. On the 23rd she had the conversation with her aunt in the hall—about marriage in general and about her own possible marriage. Her aunt's coming to her bedroom did not occur until the 12th of November. . . .

Thus she had three weeks for introspection—for introspection beneath gloomy skies, in that old house, rendered darker by the fact that it lay in a hollow crowned by fir trees with their black shadows. It was not a good situation for a girl. She began thinking about love, she who had never before considered it as anything other than a rather humorous, rather nonsensical matter. She remembered chance passages in chance books—things that had not really affected her at all at the time. She remembered someone's love for the Princess Badrulbadour;* she remembered to have heard that love was a flame, a thirst, a withering up of the vitals—though she did not know what the vitals were. She had a vague recollection that love was said to render a hopeless lover's eyes hopeless; she remembered a character in a book who was said to have taken to drink through love; she remembered that lovers' existences were said to be punctuated with heavy sighs. Once she went to the little cottage piano that was in the corner of the hall and began to play. It was a tinkly, reedy instrument, for none of that household had any turn for music. Nancy herself could play a few simple songs, and she found herself playing. She had been sitting on the window seat, looking out on the fading day. Leonora had gone to pay some calls; Edward was looking after some planting up in the new spinney.* Thus she found herself playing on the old piano. She did not know how she came to be doing it. A silly, lilting, wavering tune came from before her in the dusk—a tune in which major notes with their cheerful insistence wavered and melted into minor sounds, as, beneath a bridge the high lights on dark waters melt and waver and disappear into black depths. Well, it was a silly old tune. . . .

It goes with the words—they are about a willow tree, I think:

> Thou art to all lost loves the best
> The only true plant found*

—That sort of thing. It is Herrick, I believe, and the music with the reedy, irregular, lilting sound that goes with Herrick. And it was dusk; the heavy, hewn, dark pillars that supported the gallery were like mourning presences; the fire had sunk to nothing—a mere glow amongst white ashes. . . . It was a sentimental sort of place and light and hour. . . .

And suddenly Nancy found that she was crying. She was crying quietly; she went on to cry with long convulsive sobs. It seemed to her that everything gay, everything charming, all light, all sweetness, had gone out of life. Unhappiness; unhappiness; unhappiness was all around her. She seemed to know no happy being and she herself was agonising. . . .

She remembered that Edward's eyes were hopeless; she was certain that he was drinking too much; at times he sighed deeply. He appeared as a man who was burning with inward flame; drying up in the soul with thirst; withering up in the vitals. Then, the torturing conviction came to her—the conviction that had visited her again and again—that Edward must love some one other than Leonora. With her little, pedagogic sectarianism she remembered that Catholics do not do this thing. But Edward was a Protestant. Then Edward loved somebody. . . .

And, after that thought, her eyes grew hopeless; she sighed as the old St. Bernard beside her did. At meals she would feel an intolerable desire to drink a glass of wine, and then another and then a third. Then she would find herself grow gay. . . . But in half an hour the gaiety went; she felt like a person who is burning up with an inward flame; desiccating at the soul with thirst; withering up in the vitals. One evening she went into Edward's gun-room—he had gone to a meeting of the National Reserve Committee.* On the table beside his chair was a decanter of whiskey. She poured out a wine-glassful and drank it off.

Flame then really seemed to fill her body; her legs swelled; her face grew feverish. She dragged her tall height up to her room and lay in the dark. The bed reeled beneath her; she gave way to the thought that she was in Edward's arms; that he was kissing her on her face that burned; on her shoulders that burned, and on her neck that was on fire.

She never touched alcohol again. Not once after that did she have such thoughts. They died out of her mind; they left only a feeling of shame so insupportable that her brain could not take it in and they vanished. She imagined that her anguish at the thought of Edward's love for another person was solely sympathy for Leonora; she determined that the rest of her life must be spent in acting as Leonora's handmaiden—sweeping, tending, embroidering, like some Deborah,* some medieval saint—I am not, unfortunately, up in the Catholic hagiology.* But I know that she pictured herself as some personage with a depressed, earnest face and tightly closed lips, in a clear white room, watering flowers or tending an embroidery frame. Or, she desired to go with Edward to Africa and to throw herself in the path of a charging lion so that Edward might be saved for Leonora at the cost of her life. Well, along with her sad thoughts she had her childish ones.

She knew nothing—nothing of life, except that one must live sadly. That she now knew. What happened to her on the night when she received at once the blow that Edward wished her to go to her father in India and the blow of the letter from her mother was this. She called first upon her sweet Saviour—and she thought of Our Lord as her sweet Saviour!—that He might make it impossible that she should go to India. Then she realised from Edward's demeanour that he was determined that she should go to India. It must then be right that she should go. Edward was always right in his determinations. He was the Cid; he was Lohengrin; he was the Chevalier Bayard.

Nevertheless her mind mutinied and revolted. She could not leave that house. She imagined that he wished her gone that she might not witness his amours with another girl. Well, she was prepared to tell him that she was ready to witness his amours with another young girl. She would stay there—to comfort Leonora.

Then came the desperate shock of the letter from her mother. Her mother said, I believe, something like: "You have no right to go on living your life of prosperity and respect. You ought to be on the streets with me. How do you know that you are even Colonel Rufford's daughter?" She did not know what these words meant. She thought of her mother as sleeping beneath the arches whilst the snow fell.* That was the impression conveyed to her mind by the words "on the streets". A Platonic* sense of duty gave her the idea that she ought to go to comfort her mother—the mother that bore her, though she hardly knew what the words meant. At the same time she knew that her mother had left her father with another man—therefore she pitied her father, and thought it terrible in herself that she trembled at the sound of her father's voice. If her mother was that sort of woman it was natural that her father should have had accesses* of madness in which he had struck herself to the ground. And the voice of her conscience said to her that her first duty was to her parents. It was in accord with this awakened sense of duty that she undressed with great care and meticulously folded the clothes that she took off. Sometimes, but not very often, she threw them helter-skelter about the room.

And that sense of duty was her prevailing mood when Leonora, tall, clean-run, golden-haired, all in black, appeared in her doorway, and told her that Edward was dying of love for her. She knew then with her conscious mind what she had known within herself for months—that Edward was dying—actually and physically dying—of love for her. It seemed to her that for one short moment her spirit could say: "*Domine, nunc dimittis**. . . . Lord, now, lettest thou thy servant depart in peace." She imagined that she could cheerfully go away to Glasgow and rescue her fallen mother.

IV

AND it seemed to her to be in tune with the mood, with the hour, and with the woman in front of her to say that she knew Edward was dying of love for her and that she was dying of love for Edward. For that fact had suddenly slipped into place and become real for her as the niched marker on a whist tablet slips round with the pressure of your thumb. That rubber at least was made.*

And suddenly Leonora seemed to have become different and she seemed to have become different in her attitude towards Leonora. It was as if she, in her frail, white, silken kimono, sat beside her fire, but upon a throne. It was as if Leonora, in her close dress of black lace, with the gleaming white shoulders and the coiled yellow hair that the girl had always considered the most beautiful thing in the world—it was as if Leonora had become pinched, shrivelled, blue with cold, shivering, suppliant. Yet Leonora was commanding her. It was no good commanding her. She was going on the morrow to her mother who was in Glasgow.

Leonora went on saying that she must stay there to save Edward, who was dying of love for her. And, proud and happy in the thought that Edward loved her, and that she loved him, she did not even listen to what Leonora said. It appeared to her that it was Leonora's business to save her husband's body; she, Nancy, possessed his soul—a precious thing that she would shield and bear away up in her arms—as if Leonora were a hungry dog, trying to spring up at a lamb that she was carrying. Yes, she felt as if Edward's love were a precious lamb that she were bearing away from a cruel and predatory beast. For, at that time, Leonora appeared to her as a cruel and predatory beast. Leonora, Leonora with her hunger, with her cruelty, had driven Edward to madness. He must be sheltered by his love for her and by her love—her love from a great distance and unspoken, enveloping him, surrounding him, upholding him; by her voice speaking from Glasgow, saying that she loved, that she adored, that she passed no moment without longing, loving, quivering at the thought of him.

Leonora said loudly, insistently, with a bitterly imperative tone:

"You must stay here; you must belong to Edward. I will divorce him."

The girl answered:

"The Church does not allow of divorce. I cannot belong to your husband. I am going to Glasgow to rescue my mother."

The half-opened door opened noiselessly to the full. Edward was there. His devouring, doomed eyes were fixed on the girl's face; his shoulders slouched forward; he was undoubtedly half drunk and he had the whisky decanter in one hand, a slanting candlestick in the other. He said, with a heavy ferocity, to Nancy:

"I forbid you to talk about these things. You are to stay here until I hear from your father. Then you will go to your father."

The two women, looking at each other, like beasts about to spring, hardly gave a glance to him. He leaned against the door-post. He said again:

"Nancy, I forbid you to talk about these things. I am the master of this house." And, at the sound of his voice, heavy, male, coming from a deep chest, in the night, with the blackness behind him, Nancy felt as if her spirit bowed before him, with folded hands. She felt that she would go to India, and that she desired never again to talk of these things.

Leonora said:

"You see that it is your duty to belong to him. He must not be allowed to go on drinking."

Nancy did not answer. Edward was gone; they heard him slipping and shambling on the polished black oak of the stairs. Nancy screamed when there came the sound of a heavy fall. Leonora said again:

"You see!"

The sounds went on from the hall below; the light of the candle Edward held flickered up between the hand rails of the gallery. Then they heard his voice:

"Give me Glasgow . . . Glasgow, in Scotland . . . I want the number of a man called White, of Simrock Park, Glasgow . . . Edward White, Simrock Park, Glasgow . . . ten minutes . . . at this time of night . . ." His voice was quite level, normal, and patient. Alcohol took him in the legs, not the speech. "I can wait," his voice came again. "Yes, I know they have a number. I have been in communication with them before."

"He is going to telephone to your mother," Leonora said. "He will make it all right for her." She got up and closed the door. She came back to the fire, and added bitterly: "He can always make it all right for everybody, except me—excepting me!"

The girl said nothing. She sat there in a blissful dream. She seemed to see her lover, sitting as he always sat, in a round-backed chair, in the dark hall—sitting low, with the receiver at his ear, talking in a gentle, slow voice, that he reserved for the telephone—and saving the world and her, in the black darkness. She moved her hand over the bareness of the base of her throat, to have the warmth of flesh upon it and upon her bosom.

She said nothing; Leonora went on talking. . . .

God knows what Leonora said. She repeated that the girl must belong to her husband. She said that she used that phrase because, though she might have a divorce, or even a dissolution of the marriage by the Church, it would still be adultery that the girl and Edward would be committing. But she said that that was necessary; it was the price the girl must pay for the sin of having made Edward love her, for the sin of loving her husband. She talked on and on, beside the fire. The girl must become an adulteress; she had wronged Edward by being so beautiful, so gracious, so good. It was sinful to be so good. She must pay the price so as to save the man she had wronged.

In between her pauses the girl could hear the voice of Edward, droning on, indistinguishably, with jerky pauses for replies. It made her glow with pride; the man she loved was working for her. He at least was resolved; was malely determined; knew the right thing. Leonora talked on with her eyes boring into Nancy's. The girl hardly looked at her and hardly heard her. After a long time Nancy said— after hours and hours:

"I shall go to India as soon as Edward hears from my father. I cannot talk about these things, because Edward does not wish it."

At that Leonora screamed out and wavered swiftly towards the closed door. And Nancy found that she was springing out of her chair with her white arms stretched wide. She was clasping the other woman to her breast; she was saying:

"Oh, my poor dear; oh, my poor dear." And they sat, crouching together in each other's arms, and crying and crying; and they lay down in the same bed, talking and talking, all through the night. And all through the night Edward could hear their voices through the wall. That was how it went. . . .

Next morning they were all three as if nothing had happened.

Towards eleven Edward came to Nancy, who was arranging some Christmas roses in a silver bowl. He put a telegram beside her on the table. "You can uncode* it for yourself," he said. Then, as he went out of the door, he said:

"You can tell your aunt I have cabled to Mr. Dowell to come over. He will make things easier till you leave."

The telegram, when it was uncoded, read, as far as I can remember:

"Will take Mrs. Rufford to Italy. Undertake to do this for certain. Am devotedly attached to Mrs. Rufford. Have no need of financial assistance. Did not know there was a daughter, and am much obliged to you for pointing out my duty.—White." It was something like that.

Then the household resumed its wonted course of days until my arrival.

V

IT is this part of the story that makes me saddest of all. For I ask myself unceasingly, my mind going round and round in a weary, baffled space of pain—what should these people have done? What, in the name of God, should they have done?

The end was perfectly plain to each of them—it was perfectly manifest at this stage that, if the girl did not, in Leonora's phrase, "belong to Edward," Edward must die, the girl must lose her reason because Edward died—and, that after a time, Leonora, who was the coldest and the strongest of the three, would console herself by marrying Rodney Bayham and have a quiet, comfortable, good time. That end, on that night, whilst Leonora sat in the girl's bedroom and Edward telephoned down below—that end was plainly manifest. The girl, plainly, was half-mad already; Edward was half dead; only Leonora, active, persistent, instinct with her cold passion of energy, was "doing things." What then, should they have done? It worked out in the extinction of two very splendid personalities—for Edward and the girl *were* splendid personalities, in order that a third personality, more normal, should have, after a long period of trouble, a quiet, comfortable, good time.

I am writing this, now, I should say, a full eighteen months after the words that end my last chapter. Since writing the words "until my arrival," which I see end that paragraph, I have seen again, for a glimpse, from a swift train, Beaucaire with the beautiful white tower, Tarascon with the square castles, the great Rhone, the immense stretches of the Crau.* I have rushed through all Provence—and all Provence no longer matters. It is no longer in the olive hills that I shall find my Heaven; because there is only Hell. . . .

Edward is dead; the girl is gone—oh, utterly gone; Leonora is having her good time with Rodney Bayham, and I sit alone in Branshaw Teleragh. I have been through Provence; I have seen Africa; I have visited Asia to see, in Ceylon, in a darkened room, my poor girl, sitting motionless, with her wonderful hair about her, looking at me with eyes that did not see me, and saying distinctly: "*Credo in unum Deum omnipotentem**. . . . *Credo in unum Deum omnipotentem.*" Those are the only reasonable words she uttered; those are the only words, it appears, that she ever will utter. I suppose that they are reasonable words; it must be extraordinarily reasonable for her, if she can say that she believes in an Omnipotent Deity. Well, there it is. I am very tired of it all. . . .

For, I daresay, all this may sound romantic, but it is tiring, tiring, tiring to have been in the midst of it; to have taken the tickets; to have caught the trains; to have chosen the cabins; to have consulted the purser and the stewards as to diet for the quiescent patient who did nothing but announce her belief in an Omnipotent Deity. That may sound romantic—but it is just a record of fatigue.

I don't know why I should always be selected to be serviceable. I don't resent it—but I have never been the least good. Florence selected me for her own purposes, and I was no good to her; Edward called me to come and have a chat with him and I couldn't stop him cutting his throat.

And then, one day eighteen months ago, I was quietly writing in my room at Branshaw when Leonora came to me with a letter. It was a very pathetic letter from Colonel Rufford about Nancy. Colonel Rufford had left the army and had taken up the management of a tea-planting estate in Ceylon. His letter was pathetic because it was so brief, so inarticulate and so business-like. He had gone down to the boat to meet his daughter and had found his daughter quite mad. It appears that at Aden Nancy had seen in a local paper the news of Edward's suicide. In the Red Sea she had gone mad. She had remarked to Mrs. Colonel Luton, who was chaperoning her, that she believed in an Omnipotent Deity. She hadn't made any fuss; her eyes were quite dry and glassy. Even when she was mad Nancy could behave herself.

Colonel Rufford said the doctor did not anticipate that there was any chance of his child's recovery. It was, nevertheless, possible that, if she could see someone from Branshaw it might soothe her and it might have a good effect. And he just simply wrote to Leonora: "Please come and see if you can do it."

I seem to have lost all sense of the pathetic; but still, that simple, enormous request of the old colonel strikes me as pathetic. He was cursed by his atrocious temper; he had been cursed by a half-mad wife, who drank and went on the streets. His daughter was totally mad—and yet he believed in the goodness of human nature. He believed that Leonora would take the trouble to go all the way to

Ceylon in order to soothe his daughter. Leonora wouldn't. Leonora didn't ever want to see Nancy again. I daresay that that, in the circumstances, was natural enough. At the same time she agreed, as it were, on public grounds, that someone soothing ought to go from Branshaw to Ceylon. She sent me and her old nurse, who had looked after Nancy from the time when the girl, a child of thirteen, had first come to Branshaw. So off I go, rushing through Provence, to catch the steamer at Marseilles. And I wasn't the least good when I got to Ceylon; and the nurse wasn't the least good. Nothing has been the least good.

The doctors said, at Kandy,* that if Nancy could be brought to England, the sea air, the change of climate, the voyage, and all the usual sort of things, might restore her reason. Of course, they haven't restored her reason. She is, I am aware, sitting in the hall, forty paces from where I am now writing. I don't want to be in the least romantic about it. She is very well dressed; she is quite quiet; she is very beautiful. The old nurse looks after her very efficiently.

Of course you have the makings of a situation here, but it is all very humdrum, as far as I am concerned. I should marry Nancy if her reason were ever sufficiently restored to let her appreciate the meaning of the Anglican marriage service. But it is probable that her reason will never be sufficiently restored to let her appreciate the meaning of the Anglican marriage service. Therefore I cannot marry her, according to the law of the land.

So here I am very much where I started thirteen years ago. I am the attendant, not the husband, of a beautiful girl, who pays no attention to me. I am estranged from Leonora, who married Rodney Bayham in my absence and went to live at Bayham. Leonora rather dislikes me, because she has got it into her head that I disapprove of her marriage with Rodney Bayham. Well, I disapprove of her marriage. Possibly I am jealous.

Yes, no doubt I am jealous. In my fainter sort of way I seem to perceive myself following the lines of Edward Ashburnham. I suppose that I should really like to be a polygamist; with Nancy, and with Leonora, and with Maisie Maidan and possibly even with Florence. I am no doubt like every other man; only, probably because of my American origin I am fainter. At the same time I am able to assure you that I am a strictly respectable person. I have never done anything that the most anxious mother of a daughter or the most careful dean of a cathedral would object to. I have only followed, faintly, and in my unconscious desires, Edward Ashburnham. Well, it is all over. Not one of us has got what he really wanted. Leonora wanted Edward, and she has got Rodney Bayham, a pleasant enough sort of sheep. Florence wanted Branshaw, and it is I who have bought it from Leonora. I didn't really want it; what I wanted mostly was to cease being a nurse-attendant. Well, I am a nurse-attendant. Edward wanted Nancy Rufford and I have got her. Only she is mad. It is a queer and fantastic world. Why can't people have what they want? The things were all there to content everybody; yet everybody has the wrong thing. Perhaps you can make head or tail of it; it is beyond me.

Is there any terrestrial paradise* where, amidst the whispering of the olive-leaves, people can be with whom they like and have what they like and take their ease in shadows and in coolness? Or are all men's lives like the lives of us good people—like the lives of the Ashburnhams, of the Dowells, of the Ruffords—broken, tumultuous, agonised, and unromantic lives, periods punctuated by screams, by imbecilities, by deaths, by agonies? Who the devil knows?

For there was a great deal of imbecility about the closing scenes of the Ashburnham tragedy. Neither of those two women knew what they wanted. It was only Edward who took a perfectly clear line and he was drunk most of the time. But, drunk or sober, he stuck to what was demanded by convention and by the traditions of his house. Nancy Rufford had to be exported to India and Nancy Rufford hadn't to hear a word of love from him. She was exported to India and she never heard a word from Edward Ashburnham.

It was the conventional line; it was in tune with the tradition of Edward's house. I daresay it worked out for the greatest good of the body politic. Conventions and traditions I suppose work blindly but surely for the preservation of the normal type; for the extinction of proud, resolute and unusual individuals.

Edward was the normal man, but there was too much of the sentimentalist about him and society does not need too many sentimentalists. Nancy was a splendid creature but she had about her a touch of madness. Society does not need individuals with touches of madness about them. So Edward and Nancy found themselves steam-rolled out and Leonora survives, the perfectly normal type, married to a man who is rather like a rabbit. For Rodney Bayham is rather like a rabbit and I hear that Leonora is expected to have a baby in three months' time.

So those splendid and tumultuous creatures with their magnetism and their passions—those two that I really loved—have gone from this earth. It is no doubt best for them. What would Nancy have made of Edward if she had succeeded in living with him; what would Edward have made of her? For there was about Nancy a touch of cruelty—a touch of definite actual cruelty that made her desire to see people suffer. Yes, she desired to see Edward suffer. And, by God, she gave him hell.

She gave him an unimaginable hell. Those two women pursued that poor devil and flayed the skin off him as if they had done it with whips. I tell you his mind bled almost visibly. I seem to see him stand, naked to the waist, his forearms shielding his eyes, and flesh hanging from him in rags. I tell you that is no exaggeration of what I feel. It was as if Leonora and Nancy banded themselves together to do execution, for the sake of humanity, upon the body of a man who was at their disposal. They were like a couple of Sioux who had got hold of an Apache and had him well tied to a stake. I tell you there was no end to the tortures they inflicted upon him.

Night after night he would hear them talking; talking; maddened, sweating, seeking oblivion in drink, he would lie there and hear the voices going on and on. And day after day Leonora would come to him and would announce the results of their deliberations.

They were like judges debating over the sentence upon a criminal; they were like ghouls with an immobile corpse in a tomb beside them.

I don't think that Leonora was any more to blame than the girl—though Leonora was the more active of the two. Leonora, as I have said, was the perfectly normal woman. I mean to say that in normal circumstances her desires were those of the woman who is needed by society. She desired children, decorum, an establishment; she desired to avoid waste, she desired to keep up appearances. She was utterly and entirely normal even in her utterly undeniable beauty. But I don't mean to say that she acted perfectly normally in this perfectly abnormal situation. All the world was mad around her and she herself, agonised, took on the complexion of a mad woman; of a woman very wicked; of the villain of the piece. What would you have? Steel is a normal, hard, polished substance. But, if you put it in a hot fire it will become red, soft, and not to be handled. If you put it in a fire still more hot it will drip away. It was like that with Leonora. She was made for normal circumstances—for Mr. Rodney Bayham, who will keep a separate establishment, secretly, in Portsmouth, and make occasional trips to Paris and to Buda-Pesth.*

In the case of Edward and the girl Leonora broke and simply went all over the place. She adopted unfamiliar and therefore extraordinary and ungraceful attitudes of mind. At one moment she was all for revenge. After haranguing the girl for hours through the night she harangued for hours of the day the silent Edward. And Edward just once tripped up and that was his undoing. Perhaps he had had too much whiskey that afternoon.

She asked him perpetually what he wanted. What did he want? What did he want? And all he ever answered was: "I have told you." He meant that he wanted the girl to go to her father in India as soon as her father should cable that he was ready to receive her. But just once he tripped up. To Leonora's eternal question he answered that all he desired in life was that—that he could pick himself together again and go on with his daily occupations if—the girl, being five thousand miles away, would continue to love him. He wanted nothing more, He prayed his God for nothing more. Well, he was a sentimentalist.

And the moment that she heard that Leonora determined that the girl should not go five thousand miles away and that she should not continue to love Edward. The way she worked it was this:

She continued to tell the girl that she must belong to Edward; she was going to get a divorce; she was going to get a dissolution of marriage from Rome. But she considered it to be her duty to warn the girl of the sort of monster that Edward was. She told the girl of La Dolciquita, of Mrs. Basil, of Maisie Maidan, of Florence. She spoke of the agonies that she had endured during her life with the man, who was violent, overbearing, vain, drunken, arrogant, and monstrously a prey to his sexual necessities. And, at hearing of the miseries her aunt had suffered—for Leonora once more had the aspect of an aunt to the girl—with the swift cruelty of youth and, with the swift solidarity that attaches woman to woman, the girl made her resolves. Her aunt said incessantly: "You must save Edward's life; you must save his life. All that he needs is a little period of satisfaction from you. Then he will tire of you as he has of the others. But you must save his life."

And, all the while, that wretched fellow knew, by a curious instinct that runs between human beings living together—exactly what was going on. And he remained dumb; he stretched out no finger to help himself. All that he required to keep himself a decent member of society was, that the girl, five thousand miles away, should continue to love him. They were putting a stopper upon that.

I have told you that the girl came one night to his room. And that was the real hell for him. That was the picture that never left his imagination—the girl, in the dim light, rising up at the foot of his bed. He said that it seemed to have a greenish sort of effect as if there were a greenish tinge in the shadows of the tall bedposts that framed her body. And she looked at him with her straight eyes of an unflinching cruelty and she said: "I am ready to belong to you—to save your life."

He answered: "I don't want it; I don't want it; I don't want it."

And he says that he didn't want it; that he would have hated himself; that it was unthinkable. And all the while he had the immense temptation to do the unthinkable thing, not from the physical desire but because of a mental certitude. He was certain that if she had once submitted to him she would remain his for ever. He knew that.

She was thinking that her aunt had said he had desired her to love him from a distance of five thousand miles. She said: "I can never love you now I know the kind of man you are. I will belong to you to save your life. But I can never love you."

It was a fantastic display of cruelty. She didn't in the least know what it meant—to belong to a man. But, at that, Edward pulled himself together. He spoke in his normal tones; gruff, husky, overbearing, as he would have done to a servant or to a horse.

"Go back to your room," he said. "Go back to your room and go to sleep. This is all nonsense."

They were baffled, those two women.

And then I came on the scene.

VI

MY coming on the scene certainly calmed things down—for the whole fortnight that intervened between my arrival and the girl's departure. I don't mean to say that the endless talking did not go on at night or that Leonora did not send me out with the girl and, in the interval, give Edward a hell of a time. Having discovered what he wanted—that the girl should go five thousand miles away and love him steadfastly as people do in sentimental novels, she was determined to smash that aspiration. And she repeated to Edward in every possible tone that the girl did not love him; that the girl detested him for his brutality, his overbearingness, his drinking habits. She pointed out that Edward, in the girl's eyes, was already pledged three or four deep. He was pledged to Leonora herself, to Mrs. Basil and to the memories of Maisie Maidan and of Florence. Edward never said anything.

Did the girl love Edward, or didn't she? I don't know. At that time I daresay she didn't, though she certainly had done so before Leonora had got to work upon his reputation. She certainly had loved him for what I will call the public side of his record—for his good soldiering, for his saving lives at sea, for the excellent landlord that he was and the good sportsman. But it is quite possible that all those things came to appear as nothing in her eyes when she discovered that he wasn't a good husband. For, though women, as I see them, have little or no feeling of responsibility towards a county or a country or a career—although they may be entirely lacking in any kind of communal solidarity—they have an immense and automatically working instinct that attaches them to the interest of womanhood. It is, of course, possible for any woman to cut out and to carry off any other woman's husband or lover. But I rather think that a woman will only do this if she has reason to believe that the other woman has given her husband a bad time. I am certain that if she thinks the man has been a brute to his wife she will, with her instinctive feeling for suffering femininity, "put him back," as the saying is. I don't attach any particular importance to these generalisations of mine. They may be right, they may be wrong; I am only an ageing American with very little knowledge of life. You may take my generalisations or leave them. But I am pretty certain that I am right in the case of Nancy Rufford—that she had loved Edward Ashburnham very deeply and tenderly.

It is nothing to the point that she let him have it good and strong as soon as she discovered that he had been unfaithful to Leonora and that his public services had cost more than Leonora thought they ought to have cost. Nancy would be bound to let him have it good and strong then. She would owe that to feminine public opinion; she would be driven to it by the instinct for self-preservation, since she might well imagine that if Edward had been unfaithful to Leonora, to Mrs. Basil and to the memories of the other two he might be unfaithful to herself. And, no doubt, she had her share of the sex instinct that makes women be intolerably cruel to the beloved person. Anyhow, I don't know whether, at this point, Nancy Rufford loved Edward Ashburnham. I don't know whether she even loved him when, on getting, at Aden, the news of his suicide she went mad. Because that may just as well have been for the sake of Leonora as for the sake of Edward. Or it may have been for the sake of both of them. I don't know. I know nothing. I am very tired.

Leonora held passionately the doctrine that the girl didn't love Edward. She wanted desperately to believe that. It was a doctrine as necessary to her existence as a belief in the personal immortality of the soul. She said that it was impossible that Nancy could have loved Edward after she had given the girl her view of Edward's career and character. Edward, on the other hand, believed maunderingly that some essential attractiveness in himself must have made the girl continue to go on loving him—to go on loving him, as it were, in underneath her official aspect of hatred. He thought she only pretended to hate him in order to save her face and he thought that her quite atrocious telegram from Brindisi was only another attempt to do that—to prove that she had feelings creditable to a member of the feminine commonweal. I don't know. I leave it to you.

There is another point that worries me a good deal in the aspects of this sad affair. Leonora says that, in desiring that the girl should go five thousand miles away and yet continue to love him, Edward was a monster of selfishness. He was desiring the ruin of a young life. Edward on the other hand put it to me that, supposing that the girl's love was a necessity to his existence, and, if he did nothing by word or by action to keep Nancy's love alive, he couldn't be called selfish. Leonora replied that showed he had an abominably selfish nature even though his actions might be perfectly correct. I can't make out which of them was right. I leave it to you.

It is, at any rate, certain that Edward's actions were perfectly—were monstrously, were cruelly—correct. He sat still and let Leonora take away his character, and let Leonora damn him to deepest hell, without stirring a finger. I daresay he was a fool; I don't see what object there was in letting the girl think worse of him than was necessary. Still there it is. And there it is also that all those three presented to the world the spectacle of being the best of good people. I assure you that during my stay for that fortnight in that fine old house, I never so much as noticed a single thing that could have affected that good opinion. And even when I look back, knowing the circumstances, I can't remember a single thing any of them said that could have betrayed them. I can't remember, right up to the dinner, when Leonora read out that telegram—not the tremor of an eyelash, not the shaking of a hand. It was just a pleasant country house-party.

And Leonora kept it up jolly well, for even longer than that—she kept it up as far as I was concerned until eight days after Edward's funeral. Immediately after that particular dinner—the dinner at which I received the announcement that Nancy was going to leave for India on the following day—I asked Leonora to let me have a word with her. She took me into her little sitting-room and I then said—I spare you the record of my emotions—that she was aware that I wished to marry Nancy; that she had seemed to favour my suit and that it appeared to be rather a waste of money upon tickets and rather a waste of time upon travel to let the girl go to India if Leonora thought that there was any chance of her marrying me.

And Leonora, I assure you, was the absolutely perfect British matron. She said that she quite favoured my suit; that she could not desire for the girl a better husband; but that she considered that the girl ought to see a little more of life before taking such an important step. Yes, Leonora used the words "taking such an important step." She was perfect. Actually, I think she would have liked the girl to marry me well enough but my programme included the buying of the Kershaws' house, about a mile and a half away upon the Fordingbridge road, and settling down there with the girl. That didn't at all suit Leonora. She didn't want to have the girl within a mile and a half of Edward for the rest of their lives. Still, I think she might have managed to let me know, in some periphrasis or other, that I might have the girl if I would take her to Philadelphia or Timbuctoo. I loved Nancy very much—and Leonora knew it.

However, I left it at that. I left it with the understanding that Nancy was going away to India on probation. It seemed to me a perfectly reasonable arrangement and I am a reasonable sort of man. I simply said that I should follow Nancy out to India after six months' time or so. Or, perhaps, after a year. Well, you see, I did follow Nancy out to India after a year. . . .

I must confess to having felt a little angry with Leonora for not having warned me earlier that the girl would be going. I took it as one of the queer, not very straight methods that Roman Catholics seem to adopt in dealing with matters of this world. I took it that Leonora had been afraid I should propose to the girl or, at any rate, have made considerably greater advances to her than I did, if I had known earlier that she was going away so soon. Perhaps Leonora was right; perhaps Roman Catholics, with their queer, shifty ways, are always right. They are dealing with the queer, shifty thing that is human nature. For it is quite possible that, if I had known Nancy was going away so soon, I should have tried making love to her.* And that would have produced another complication. It may have been just as well.

It is queer the fantastic things that quite good people will do in order to keep up their appearance of calm poco-curantism.* For Edward Ashburnham and his wife called me half the world over in order to sit on the back seat of a dog-cart whilst Edward drove the girl to the railway station from which she was to take her departure to India. They wanted, I suppose, to have a witness of the calmness of that function. The girl's luggage had been already packed and sent off before. Her berth on the steamer had been taken. They had timed it all so exactly that it went like clockwork. They had known the date upon which Colonel Rufford would get Edward's letter and they had known almost exactly the hour at which they would receive his telegram asking his daughter to come to him. It had all been quite beautifully and quite mercilessly arranged, by Edward himself. They gave Colonel Rufford, as a reason for telegraphing, the fact that Mrs. Colonel Somebody or other would be travelling by that ship and that she would serve as an efficient chaperon for the girl. It was a most amazing business, and I think that it would have been better in the eyes of God if they had all attempted to gouge out each other's eyes with carving knives. But they were "good people."

After my interview with Leonora I went desultorily into Edward's gun-room. I didn't know where the girl was and I thought I might find her there. I suppose I had a vague idea of proposing to her in spite of Leonora. So, I presume, I don't come of quite such good people as the Ashburnhams. Edward was lounging in his chair smoking a cigar and he said nothing for quite five minutes. The candles glowed in the green shades; the reflections were green in the glasses of the book-cases that held guns and fishing-rods. Over the mantelpiece was the brownish picture of the white horse. Those were the quietest moments that I have ever known. Then, suddenly, Edward looked me straight in the eyes and said:

"Look here, old man, I wish you would drive with Nancy and me to the station to-morrow."

I said that of course I would drive with him and Nancy to the station on the morrow. He lay there for a long time, looking along the line of his knees at the fluttering fire, and then suddenly, in a perfectly calm voice, and without lifting his eyes, he said:

"I am so desperately in love with Nancy Rufford that I am dying of it."

Poor devil—he hadn't meant to speak of it. But I guess he just had to speak to somebody and I appeared to be like a woman or a solicitor. He talked all night.

Well, he carried out the programme to the last breath.

It was a very clear winter morning, with a good deal of frost in it. The sun was quite bright, the winding road between the heather and the bracken was very hard. I sat on the back seat of the dog-cart; Nancy was beside Edward. They talked about the way the cob went; Edward pointed out with the whip a cluster of deer upon a coombe* three-quarters of a mile away. We passed the hounds in the level bit of road beside the high trees going into Fordingbridge and Edward pulled up the dog-cart so that Nancy might say good-bye to the huntsman and cap* him a last sovereign. She had ridden with those hounds ever since she had been thirteen.

The train was five minutes late and they imagined that that was because it was market-day at Swindon or wherever the train came from. That was the sort of thing they talked about. The train came in; Edward found her a first-class carriage with an elderly woman in it. The girl entered the carriage, Edward closed the door and then she put out her hand to shake mine. There was upon those people's faces no expression of any kind whatever. The signal for the train's departure was a very bright red; that is about as passionate a statement as I can get into that scene. She was not looking her best; she had on a cap of brown fur that did not very well match her hair. She said:

"So long," to Edward.

Edward answered: "So long."

He swung round on his heel and, large, slouching, and walking with a heavy deliberate pace, he went out of the station. I followed him and got up beside him in the high dog-cart. It was the most horrible performance I have ever seen.

And, after that, a holy peace, like the peace of God which passes all understanding,* descended upon Branshaw Teleragh. Leonora went about her daily duties with a sort of triumphant smile—a very faint smile, but quite triumphant. I guess she had so long since given up any idea of getting her man back that it was enough for her to have got the girl out of the house and well cured of her infatuation. Once, in the hall, when Leonora was going out, Edward said, beneath his breath—but I just caught the words:

"Thou hast conquered, O pale Galilean."*

It was like his sentimentality to quote Swinburne.

But he was perfectly quiet and he had given up drinking. The only thing that he ever said to me after that drive to the station was:

"It's very odd. I think I ought to tell you, Dowell, that I haven't any feelings at all about the girl now it's all over. Don't you worry about me. I'm all right." A long time afterwards he said: "I guess it was only a flash in the pan." He began to look after the estates again; he took all that trouble over getting off the gardener's daughter who had murdered her baby. He shook hands smilingly with every farmer in the market-place. He addressed two political meetings; he hunted twice. Leonora made him a frightful scene about spending the two hundred pounds on getting the gardener's daughter acquitted. Everything went on as if the girl had never existed. It was very still weather.

Well, that is the end of the story. And, when I come to look at it I see that it is a happy ending with wedding bells and all. The villains—for obviously Edward and the girl were villains—have been punished by suicide and madness. The heroine—the perfectly normal, virtuous and slightly deceitful heroine—has become the happy wife of a perfectly normal, virtuous and slightly-deceitful husband. She will shortly become a mother of a perfectly normal, virtuous, slightly-deceitful son or daughter. A happy ending, that is what it works out at.

I cannot conceal from myself the fact that I now dislike Leonora. Without doubt I am jealous of Rodney Bayham. But I don't know whether it is merely a jealousy arising from the fact that I desired myself to possess Leonora or whether it is because to her were sacrificed the only two persons that I have ever really loved—Edward Ashburnham and Nancy Rufford. In order to set her up in a modern mansion, replete with every convenience and dominated by a quite respectable and eminently economical master of the house, it was necessary that Edward and Nancy Rufford should become, for me at least, no more than tragic shades.

I seem to see poor Edward, naked and reclining amidst darkness, upon cold rocks, like one of the ancient Greek damned, in Tartarus* or wherever it was.

And as for Nancy . . . Well, yesterday at lunch she said suddenly: "Shuttlecocks!"*

And she repeated the word "shuttlecocks" three times. I know what was passing in her mind, if she can be said to have a mind, for Leonora has told me that, once, the poor girl said she felt like a shuttlecock being tossed backwards and forwards between the violent personalities of Edward and his wife. Leonora, she said, was always trying to deliver her over to Edward, and Edward tacitly and silently forced her back again. And the odd thing was that Edward himself considered that those two women used *him* like a shuttlecock. Or, rather, he said that they sent him backwards and forwards like a blooming parcel that someone didn't want to pay the postage on. And Leonora also imagined that Edward and Nancy picked her up and threw her down as suited their purely vagrant moods. So there you have the pretty picture. Mind, I am not preaching anything contrary to accepted morality. I am not advocating free love in this or any other case. Society must go on, I suppose, and society can only exist if the normal, if the virtuous, and the slightly-deceitful flourish, and if the passionate, the headstrong, and the too-truthful are condemned to suicide and to madness. But I guess that I myself, in my fainter way, come into the category of the passionate, of the headstrong, and the too-truthful. For I can't conceal from myself the fact that I loved

Edward Ashburnham—and that I love him because he was just myself. If I had had the courage and the virility and possibly also the physique of Edward Ashburnham I should, I fancy, have done much what he did. He seems to me like a large elder brother who took me out on several excursions and did many dashing things whilst I just watched him robbing the orchards, from a distance. And, you see, I am just as much of a sentimentalist as he was. . . .

Yes, society must go on; it must breed, like rabbits. That is what we are here for. But then, I don't like society—much. I am that absurd figure, an American millionaire, who has bought one of the ancient haunts of English peace. I sit here, in Edward's gun-room, all day and all day in a house that is absolutely quiet. No one visits me, for I visit no one. No one is interested in me, for I have no interests. In twenty minutes or so I shall walk down to the village, beneath my own oaks, alongside my own clumps of gorse, to get the American mail. My tenants, the village boys and the tradesmen will touch their hats to me. So life peters out. I shall return to dine and Nancy will sit opposite me with the old nurse standing behind her. Enigmatic, silent, utterly well-behaved as far as her knife and fork go, Nancy will stare in front of her with the blue eyes that have over them strained, stretched brows. Once, or perhaps twice, during the meal her knife and fork will be suspended in mid-air as if she were trying to think of something that she had forgotten. Then she will say that she believes in an Omnipotent Deity or she will utter the one word "shuttle-cocks," perhaps. It is very extraordinary to see the perfect flush of health on her cheeks, to see the lustre of her coiled black hair, the poise of the head upon the neck, the grace of the white hands—and to think that it all means nothing—that it is a picture without a meaning. Yes, it is queer.

But, at any rate, there is always Leonora to cheer you up; I don't want to sadden you. Her husband is quite an economical person of so normal a figure that he can get quite a large proportion of his clothes ready-made. That is the great desideratum* of life, and that is the end of my story. The child is to be brought up as a Romanist.

It suddenly occurs to me that I have forgotten to say how Edward met his death.* You remember that peace had descended upon the house; that Leonora was quietly triumphant and that Edward said his love for the girl had been merely a passing phase. Well, one afternoon we were in the stables together, looking at a new kind of flooring that Edward was trying in a loose-box.* Edward was talking with a good deal of animation about the necessity of getting the numbers of the Hampshire territorials* up to the proper standard. He was quite sober, quite quiet, his skin was clear-coloured; his hair was golden and perfectly brushed; the level brick-dust red of his complexion went clean up to the rims of his eyelids; his eyes were porcelain blue and they regarded me frankly and directly. His face was perfectly expressionless; his voice was deep and rough. He stood well back upon his legs and said:

"We ought to get them up to two thousand three hundred and fifty."

A stable-boy brought him a telegram and went away. He opened it negligently, regarded it without emotion, and, in complete silence, handed it to me. On the pinkish paper in a sprawled handwriting I read: "Safe Brindisi. Having rattling good time. Nancy."

Well, Edward was the English gentleman; but he was also, to the last, a sentimentalist, whose mind was compounded of indifferent poems and novels. He just looked up to the roof of the stable, as if he were looking to Heaven, and whispered something that I did not catch.

Then he put two fingers into the waistcoat pocket of his grey, frieze suit;* they came out with a little neat pen-knife—quite a small pen-knife. He said to me:

"You might just take that wire to Leonora." And he looked at me with a direct, challenging, brow-beating glare. I guess he could see in my eyes that I didn't intend to hinder him. Why should I hinder him?

I didn't think he was wanted in the world, let his confounded tenants, his rifle-associations, his drunkards, reclaimed and unreclaimed, get on as they liked. Not all the hundreds and hundreds of them deserved that that poor devil should go on suffering for their sakes.

When he saw that I did not intend to interfere with him his eyes became soft and almost affectionate. He remarked:

"So long, old man, I must have a bit of a rest, you know."

I didn't know what to say. I wanted to say, "God bless you," for I also am a sentimentalist. But I thought that perhaps that would not be quite English good form, so I trotted off with the telegram to Leonora. She was quite pleased with it.

APPENDIX A

EMENDATIONS MADE TO UK FIRST EDITION FOR THIS EDITION

This edition	*UK first edition*
15	'That it was up to her to take it or leave it . . .'"	"That it was up to her to take it or leave it . . ."

(UK opens double inverted commas within the double inverted commas for Leonora's speech, and then only closes one set.)

| 25 | never, in all the years of her life, never | never, in all the years of her life never |

(UK has a space and a minuscule dot that might be the tail of a misprinted comma after 'life'; emended here as the grammar seems to require it.)

| 27 | isn't in the least | isn't—the least |

(Follows Stannard in restoring the MS and *Blast* reading.)

| 33 | the Ashburnhams' copy | the Ashburnham's copy |

| 44 | Mrs. Maidan—the woman | Mrs. Maidan, the woman |

| 45 | 'her playing with adultery, I suppose it was' | 'her playing with adultery. I suppose it was' it was' |

| 69 | an embrace of a warmth . . . | an embrace of a warmth. . . . |

(UK generally only uses four dots and no leading space after complete sentences; emended to three dots with leading space because Dowell's sentence is clearly incomplete.)

| 71 | ship's doctor | ship doctor |

(Follows Stannard in restoring MS reading.)

| 71 | the Hurlbirds' mysterious | the Hurlbird's mysterious |

(Follows Stannard in restoring MS reading.)

| 91 | impossible of me | impossible for me |

(Follows Stannard in restoring MS reading.)

| 104 | For Leonora made the girl go to bed at ten | For Florence made the girl go to bed at ten |

(Stannard, p. 207 (note to his p. 90) notes a comparable transposition of these names, though one Ford managed to correct.)

107 Branshaw Teleragh   Branshaw-Teleragh
    (The hyphen isn't used in other occurrences of the name.)

108 tall, upstanding   tall. upstanding

109 Froissart   Froisart

126 smelling salts to his nose   smelling salts to her nose
    (Follows Stannard who gives MS as reading 'his'.)

128 And they themselves steadily   And they themselves steadily
    deteriorated.   deteriorated?
    (The question mark is in the manuscript, but appears to be an error; perhaps uncaught because the passage is part of a long typescript insertion.)

154 to produce on her the   to produce on her the
    impression   impressions
    (Follows Stannard in restoring MS reading.)

159 unmounted, and   unmounted and
    (Following Stannard's emendation.)

183 the girl, being   the girl being
    (The comma seems required to make this ungainly sentence apprehensible. The phrase 'pick himself together' appears to conflate 'pick himself up' and 'pull himself together'; but there's no textual evidence for emending this relatively common mix-up.)

APPENDIX B

'ON IMPRESSIONISM'

[Ford's essay 'On Impressionism' was first published in the June and December 1914 issues of the magazine *Poetry and Drama*, edited by his friend Harold Monro, who also ran the Poetry Bookshop, and published some of Ford's poetry too—especially his best poem of the war, *Antwerp* (1915), strikingly illustrated by Wyndham Lewis. The essay was almost certainly written while Ford was writing *The Good Soldier*; and it not only serves as a manifesto for the novel, but also contains striking echoes and parallels with it (as indicated in the Explanatory Notes).

There is a nineteen-leaf typescript and manuscript of the first part only of the article in the Carl A. Kroch Library at Cornell University. The copy-text for the present edition is the version published in *Poetry and Drama*. Minor typographical errors have been corrected silently, and inconsistencies in the italicization of foreign words removed. Full-stops have been added after 'Mr' and 'Mrs' for consistency with the text of the novel.]

I.

These are merely some notes towards a working guide to Impressionism as a literary method.

I do not know why I should have been especially asked to write about Impressionism; even as far as literary Impressionism goes I claim no Papacy in the matter. A few years ago, if anybody had called me an Impressionist I should languidly have denied that I was anything of the sort or that I knew anything about the school, if there could be said to be any school. But one person and another in the last ten years has called me Impressionist with such persistence that I have given up resistance.* I don't know; I just write books, and if someone attaches a label to me I do not much mind.

I am not claiming any great importance for my work; I daresay it is all right. At any rate, I am a perfectly self-conscious writer; I know exactly how I get my effects, as far as those effects go. Then, if I am in truth an Impressionist, it must follow that a conscientious and exact account of how I myself work will be an account, from the inside, of how Impressionism is reached, produced, or gets its effects. I can do no more.

This is called egotism; but, to tell the truth, I do not see how Impressionism can be anything else. Probably this school differs from other schools, principally, in that it recognises, frankly, that all art must be the expression of an ego, and that if Impressionism is to do anything, it must, as the phrase is, go the whole hog. The difference between the description of a grass by the agricultural correspondent of the *Times** newspaper and the description of the same grass by Mr. W. H. Hudson* is just the difference—the measure of the difference between the egos of the two gentlemen. The difference between the description of any given book by a sound English reviewer and the description of the same book by some foreigner attempting Impressionist criticism is again merely a matter of the difference in the ego.

Mind, I am not saying that the non-Impressionist productions may not have their values—their very great values. The Impressionist gives you his own views, expecting you to draw deductions, since presumably you know the sort of chap he is. The agricultural correspondent of the *Times*, on the other hand—and a jolly good writer he is—attempts to give you, not so much his own impressions of a new grass as the factual observations of himself and of as many as possible other sound authorities. He will tell you how many blades of the new grass will grow upon an acre, what height they will attain, what will be a reasonable tonnage to expect when green, when sun-dried in the form of hay or as ensilage. He will tell you the fattening value of the new fodder in its various forms and the nitrogenous value of the manure dropped by the so-fattened beasts. He will provide you, in short, with reading that is quite interesting to the layman, since all facts are interesting to men of good will; and the agriculturist he will provide with information of real value. Mr. Hudson, on the other hand, will give you nothing but the pleasure of coming in contact with his temperament, and I doubt whether, if you read with the greatest care his description of false sea-buckthorn (*hippophae rhamnoides*) you would very willingly recognise that greenish-grey plant, with the spines and the berries like reddish amber, if you came across it.

Or again—so at least I was informed by an editor the other day—the business of a sound English reviewer is to make the readers of the paper understand exactly what sort of a book it is that the reviewer is writing about. Said the editor in question: "You have no idea how many readers your paper will lose if you employ one of those brilliant chaps who write readable articles about books. You will get yourself deluged with letter after letter from subscribers saying they have bought a book on the strength of articles in your paper; that the book isn't in the least what they expected, and that therefore they withdraw their subscriptions." What the sound English reviewer, therefore, has to do is to identify himself with the point of view of as large a number of readers of the journal for which he may be reviewing, as he can easily do, and then to give them as many facts about the book under consideration as his allotted space will hold. To do this he must sacrifice his personality, and the greater part of his readability. But he will probably very much help his editor, since the great majority of readers do not want to read anything that any reasonable person would want to read; and they do not want to come into contact with the personality of the critic, since they have obviously never been introduced to him.

The ideal critic, on the other hand—as opposed to the so-exemplary reviewer—is a person who can so handle words that from the first three phrases any intelligent person—any foreigner, that is to say, and any one of three inhabitants of these islands—any intelligent person will know at once the sort of chap that he is dealing with. Letters of introduction will therefore be unnecessary, and the intelligent reader will know pretty well what sort of book the fellow is writing about because he will know the sort of fellow the fellow is. I don't mean to say that he would necessarily trust his purse, his wife, or his mistress to the Impressionist critic's care. But that is not absolutely necessary. The ambition, however, of my friend the editor was to let his journal give the impression of being written by those who could be trusted with the wives and purses—not, of course, the mistresses, for there would be none—of his readers.

You will, perhaps, be beginning to see now what I am aiming at—the fact that Impressionism is a frank expression of personality; the fact that non-Impressionism is an attempt to gather together the opinions of as many reputable persons as may be and to render them truthfully and without exaggeration. (The Impressionist must always exaggerate.)

II.

Let us approach this matter historically—as far as I know anything about the history of Impressionism, though I must warn you that I am a shockingly ill-read man. Here, then, are some examples: do you know, for instance, Hogarth's drawing of the watchman with the pike over his shoulder and the dog at his heels going in at a door, the whole being executed in four lines? Here it is:

Now, that is the high-watermark of Impressionism; since, if you look at those lines for long enough you will begin to see the watchman with his slouch hat, the handle of the pike coming well down into the cobble-stones, the knee-breeches, the leathern garters strapped round his stocking, and the surly expression of the dog, which is bull-hound with a touch of mastiff in it.

You may ask why, if Hogarth saw all these things, did he not put them down on paper, and all that I can answer is that he made this drawing for a bet. Moreover why, if you can see all these things for yourself, should Hogarth bother to put them down on paper? You might as well contend that Our Lord ought to have delivered a lecture on the state of primary education in the Palestine of the year 32 or thereabouts, together with the statistics of rickets and other infantile diseases caused by neglect and improper feeding—a disquisition in the manner of Mrs. Sidney Webb. He preferred, however, to say: "It were better that a millstone were put about his neck and he were cast into the deep sea." The statement is probably quite incorrect; the statutory punishment either here or in the next world has probably nothing to do with millstones and so on, but our Lord was, you see, an Impressionist, and knew His job pretty efficiently. It is probable that He did not have access to as many Blue Books or white papers as the leaders of the Fabian Society, but, from His published utterances, one gathers that He had given a good deal of thought to the subject of children.

I am not in the least joking—and God forbid that I should be thought irreverent because I write like this. The point that I really wish to make is, once again, that—that the Impressionist gives you, as a rule, the fruits of his own observations and the fruits of his own observations alone. He should be in this as severe and as solitary as any monk. It is what he is in the world for. It is, for instance, not so much his business to quote as to state his impressions—that the Holy Scriptures are a good book, or a rotten book, or contain passages of good reading interspersed with dulness; or suggest gems in a cavern, the perfumes of aromatic woods burning in censers, or the rush of the feet of camels crossing the deep sands, or the shrill sounds of long trumpets borne by archangels—clear sounds of brass like those in that funny passage in "Aida."

The passage in prose, however, which I always take as a working model—and in writing this article I am doing no more than showing you the broken tools and bits of oily rag which form my brains, since once again I must disclaim writing with any authority on Impressionism—this passage in prose occurs in a story by de Maupassant called *La Reine Hortense*. I spent, I suppose, a great part of ten years in grubbing up facts about Henry VIII.* I worried about his parentage, his diseases, the size of his shoes, the price he gave for kitchen implements, his relation to his wives, his knowledge of music, his proficiency with the bow. I amassed, in short, a great deal of information about Henry VIII. I wanted to write a long book about him, but Mr. Pollard, of the British Museum, got the commission and wrote the book probably much more soundly. I then wrote three long novels* all about that Defender of the Faith. But I really know—so delusive are reported facts—nothing whatever. Not one single thing! Should I have found him affable, or terrifying, or seductive, or royal, or courageous? There are so many contradictory facts; there are so many reported interviews, each contradicting the other, so that really all that I *know* about this king could be reported in the words of Maupassant, which, as I say, I always consider as a working model. Maupassant is introducing one of his characters, who is possibly gross, commercial, overbearing, insolent; who eats, possibly, too much greasy food; who wears commonplace clothes—a gentleman about whom you might write volumes if you wanted to give the facts of his existence. But all that de Maupassant finds it necessary to say is: C'était un monsieur à favoris rouges qui entrait toujours le premier."

And that is all that I know about Henry VIII.*—that he was a gentleman with red whiskers who always went first through a door.

III.

Let us now see how these things work out in practice. I have a certain number of maxims, gained mostly in conversation with Mr. Conrad, which form my working stock-in-trade. I stick to them pretty generally; sometimes I throw them out of the window and just write whatever comes. But the effect is usually pretty much the same. I guess I must be fairly well drilled by this time and function automatically, as the Americans say. The first two of my maxims are these:

Always consider the impressions that you are making upon the mind of the reader, and always consider that the first impression with which you present him will be so strong that it will be all that you can ever do to efface it, to alter it or even quite slightly to modify it. Maupassant's gentleman with red whiskers, who always pushed in front of people when it was a matter of going through a doorway, will remain, for the mind of the reader, that man and no other. The impression is as hard and as definite as a tin-tack. And I rather doubt whether, supposing Maupassant represented him afterwards as kneeling on the ground to wipe the tears away from a small child who had lost a penny down a drain—I doubt whether such a definite statement of fact would ever efface the first impression from the reader's mind. They would think that the gentleman with the red whiskers was perpetrating that act of benevolence with ulterior motives– to impress the bystanders, perhaps.

Maupassant, however, uses physical details more usually as a method of introduction of his characters than I myself do. I am inclined myself, when engaged in the seductive occupation, rather to strike the keynote with a speech than with a description of personality, or even with an action. And, for that purpose, I should set it down, as a rule, that the first speech of a character you are introducing should always be a generalisation—since generalisations are the really strong indications of character. Putting the matter exaggeratedly, you might say that, if a gentleman sitting opposite you in the train remarked to you: "I see the Tories have won Leith Boroughs,"* you would have practically no guide to that gentleman's character. But, if he said: "Them bloody Unionists have crept into Leith because the Labourites, damn them, have taken away 1,100 votes from us," you would know that the gentleman belonged to a certain political party, had a certain social status, a certain degree of education and a certain amount of impatience.

It is possible that such disquisitions on Impressionism in prose fiction may seem out of place in a journal styled POETRY AND DRAMA. But I do not think they are. For Impressionism, differing from other schools of art, is founded so entirely on observation of the psychology of the patron—and the psychology of the patron remains constant. Let me, to make things plainer present you with a quotation. Sings Tennyson:

> "And bats went round in fragrant skies,
>   And wheeled or lit the filmy shapes
>   That haunt the dusk, with ermine capes
> And woolly breasts and beady eyes."

Now that is no doubt very good natural history, but it is certainly not Impressionism, since no one watching a bat at dusk could see the ermine, the wool or the beadiness of the eyes. These things you might read about in books, or observe in the museum or at the Zoological Gardens. Or you might pick up a dead bat upon the road. But to import into the record of observations of one moment the observations of a moment altogether different is not Impressionism. For Impressionism is a thing altogether momentary.

I do not wish to be misunderstood. It is perfectly possible that the remembrance of a former observation may colour your impression of the moment, so that if Tennyson had said:

> "And we remembered they have ermine capes,"

he would have remained within the canons of Impressionism. But that was not his purpose, which, whatever it was, was no doubt praiseworthy in the extreme, because his heart was pure.* It is, however, perfectly possible that a piece of Impressionism should give a sense of two, of three, of as many as you will, places, persons, emotions, all going on simultaneously in the emotions of the writer. It is, I mean, perfectly possible for a sensitised person, be he poet or prose writer, to have the sense, when he is in one room, that he is in another, or when he is speaking to one person he may be so intensely haunted by the memory or desire for another person that he may be absent-minded or distraught. And there is nothing in the canons of Impressionism, as I know it, to stop the attempt to render those super-imposed emotions. Indeed, I suppose that Impressionism exists to render those queer effects of real life that are like so many views seen through bright glass—through glass so bright that whilst you perceive through it a landscape or a backyard, you are aware that, on its surface, it reflects a face of a person behind you. For the whole of life is really like that; we are almost always in one place with our minds somewhere quite other.

And it is, I think, only Impressionism that can render that peculiar effect; I know, at any rate, of no other method. It has, this school, in consequence, certain quite strong canons, certain quite rigid unities that must be observed. The point is that any piece of Impressionism, whether it be prose, or verse, or painting, or sculpture, is the record of the impression of a moment; it is not a sort of rounded, annotated record of a set of circumstances—it is the record of the recollection in your mind of a set of circumstances that happened ten years ago—or ten minutes. It might even be the impression of the moment—but it is the impression, not the corrected chronicle. I can make what I mean most clear by a concrete instance.

Thus an Impressionist in a novel, or in a poem, will never render a long speech of one of his characters verbatim, because the mind of the reader would at once lose some of the illusion of the good faith of the narrator. The mind of the reader will say: "Hullo, this fellow is faking this. He cannot possibly remember such a long speech word for word." The Impressionist, therefore, will only record his impression of a long speech. If you will try to remember what remains in your mind of long speeches you heard yesterday, this afternoon or five years ago, you will see what I mean. If to-day, at lunch at your club, you heard an irascible member making a long speech about the fish, what you remember will not be his exact words. However much his proceedings will have amused you, you will not remember his exact words. What you will remember is that he said that the sole was not a sole, but a blank, blank, blank plaice; that the cook ought to be shot, by God he ought to be shot. The plaice had been out of the water two years, and it had been caught in a drain: all that there was of Dieppe about this Sole Dieppoise was something that you cannot remember. You will remember this gentleman's starting eyes, his grunts between words, that he was fond of saying "damnable, damnable, damnable." You will also remember that the man at the same table with you was talking about morals, and that your boots were too tight, whilst you were trying, in your under mind, to arrange a meeting with some lady. . . . .

So that, if you had to render that scene or those speeches for purposes of fiction, you would not give a word for word re-invention of sustained sentences from the gentleman who was dissatisfied; or if you were going to invent that scene, you would not so invent those speeches and set them down with all the panoply of inverted commas, notes of exclamation. No, you would give an impression of the whole thing, of the snorts, of the characteristic exclamation, of your friend's disquisition on morals, a few phrases of which you would intersperse into the monologue of the gentleman dissatisfied with his sole. And you would give a sense that your feet were burning, and that the lady you wanted to meet had very clear and candid eyes. You would give a little description of her hair. . . . .

In that way you would attain to the sort of odd vibration that scenes in real life really have; you would give your reader the impression that he was witnessing something real, that he was passing through an experience. . . . . You will observe also that you will have produced something that is very like a Futurist picture—not a Cubist picture, but one of those canvases that show you in one corner a pair of stays, in another a bit of the foyer of a music hall, in another a fragment of early morning landscape, and in the middle a pair of eyes, the whole bearing the title of "A Night Out." And, indeed, those Futurists are only trying to render on canvas what Impressionists *tel que moi* have been trying to render for many years. (You may remember Emma's love scene at the cattle show in *Madame Bovary*.)*

Do not, I beg you, be led away by the English reviewer's cant phrase to the effect that the Futurists are trying to be literary and the plastic arts can never be literary. Les Jeunes of to-day are trying all sorts of experiments, in all sorts of media. And they are perfectly right to be trying them.

(To be continued.)

SECOND ARTICLE

[I.]

I have been trying to think what are the objections to Impressionism as I understand it—or rather what alternative method could be found. It seems to me that one is an Impressionist because one tries to produce an illusion of reality—or rather the business of Impressionism is to produce that illusion. The subject is one enormously complicated and is full of negatives. Thus the Impressionist author is sedulous to avoid letting his personality appear in the course of his book. On the other hand, his whole book, his whole poem is merely an expression of his personality. Let me illustrate exactly what I mean. You set out to write a story, or you set out to write a poem, and immediately your attempt becomes one creating an illusion. You attempt to involve the reader amongst the personages of the story or in the atmosphere of the poem. You do this by presentation and by presentation and again by presentation. The moment you depart from presentation, the moment you allow yourself, as a poet, to introduce the ejaculation:

"O Muse Pindarian, aid me to my theme;"*

or the moment that, as a story-teller, you permit yourself the luxury of saying:

"Now, gentle reader, is my heroine not a very sweet and oppressed lady?"—*

at that very moment your reader's illusion that he is present at an affair in real life or that he has been transported by your poem into an atmosphere entirely other than that of his arm-chair or his chimney-corner—at that very moment that illusion will depart. Now the point is this:

The other day I was discussing these matters with a young man whose avowed intention is to sweep away Impressionism.* And, after I had energetically put before him the views that I have here expressed, he simply remarked: "Why try to produce an illusion?" To which I could only reply: "Why then write?"

I have asked myself frequently since then why one should try to produce an illusion of reality in the mind of one's reader. Is it just an occupation like any other—like postage-stamp collecting, let us say—or is it the sole end and aim of art? I have spent the greater portion of my working life in preaching that particular doctrine: is it possible, then, that I have been entirely wrong?

Of course it is possible for any man to be entirely wrong; but I confess myself to being as yet unconverted. The chief argument of my futurist friend was that producing an illusion causes the writer so much trouble as not to be worth while. That does not seem to me to be an argument worth very much because—and again I must say it seems to me—the business of an artist is surely to take trouble, but this is probably doing my friend's position, if not his actual argument, an injustice. I am aware that there are quite definite æsthetic objections to the business of producing an illusion. In order to produce an illusion you must justify;* in order to justify you must introduce a certain amount of matter that may not appear germane to your story or to your poem. Sometimes, that is to say, it would appear as if for the purpose of proper bringing out of a very slight Impression-ist sketch the artist would need an altogether disproportionately enor-mous frame; a frame absolutely monstrous. Let me again illustrate exactly what I mean. It is not sufficient to say: "Mr. Jones was a gentleman who had a strong aversion to rabbit-pie." It is not sufficient, that is to say, if Mr. Jones's dislike for rabbit-pie is an integral part of your story. And it is quite possible that a dislike for one form or other of food might form the integral part of a story. Mr. Jones might be a hard-worked coal-miner with a well-meaning wife, whom he disliked because he was developing a passion for a frivolous girl. And it might be quite possible that one evening the well-meaning wife, not knowing her husband's peculiarities, but desiring to give him a special and extra treat, should purchase from a stall a couple of rabbits and spend many hours in preparing for him a pie of great succulence, which should be a solace to him when he returns, tired with his labours and rendered nervous by his growing passion for the other lady. The rabbit-pie would then become a symbol—a symbol of the whole tragedy of life. It would symbolize for Mr. Jones the whole of his wife's want of sympathy for him and the whole of his distaste for her; his reception of it would symbolize for Mrs. Jones the whole hopelessness of her life, since she had expended upon it inventiveness, sedulous care, sentiment, and a good will. From that position, with the rabbit-pie always in the centre of the discussion, you might work up to the murder of Mrs. Jones, to Mr. Jones's elopement with the other lady—to any tragedy that you liked. For indeed the position contains, as you will perceive, the whole tragedy of life.

And the point is this, that if your tragedy is to be absolutely convincing, it is not sufficient to introduce the fact of Mr. Jones's dislike for rabbit-pie by the bare statement. According to your temperament you must sufficiently account for that dislike. You might do it by giving Mr. Jones a German grandmother, since all Germans have a peculiar loathing for the rabbit and regard its flesh as unclean. You might then find it necessary to account for the dislike the Germans have for these little creatures; you might have to state that this dislike is a self-preservative race instinct, since in Germany the rabbit is apt to eat certain poisonous fungi, so that one out of every ten will cause the death of its consumer, or you might proceed with your justification of Mr. Jones's dislike for rabbit-pie along different lines. You might say that it was a nervous aversion caused by having been violently thrashed when a boy by his father at a time when a rabbit-pie was upon the table. You might then have to go on to justify the nervous temperament of Mr. Jones by saying that his mother drank or that his father was a man too studious for his position. You might have to pursue almost endless studies in the genealogy of Mr. Jones; because, of course, you might want to account for the studiousness of Mr. Jones's father by making him the bastard son of a clergyman, and then you might want to account for the libidinous habits of the clergyman in question. That will be simply a matter of your artistic conscience.

You have to make Mr. Jones's dislike for rabbits convincing. You have to make it in the first place convincing to your reader alone; but the odds are that you will try to make it convincing also to yourself, since you yourself in this solitary world of ours will be the only reader that you really and truly know. Now all these attempts at justification, all these details of parentage and the like, may very well prove uninteresting to your reader. They are, however, necessary if your final effect of murder is to be a convincing impression.

But again, if the final province of art is to convince, its first province is to interest. So that, to the extent that your justification is uninteresting, it is an artistic defect. It may sound paradoxical, but the truth is that your Impressionist can only get his strongest effects by using beforehand a great deal of what one may call non-Impressionism. He will make, that is to say, an enormous impression on his reader's mind by the use of three words. But very likely each one of those three words will be prepared for by ten thousand other words. Now are we to regard those other words as being entirely unnecessary, as being, that is to say, so many artistic defects? That I take to be my futurist friend's ultimate assertion.

Says he: "All these elaborate conventions of Conrad or of Maupassant give the reader the impression that a story is being told—all these meetings of bankers and master-mariners in places like the Ship Inn at Greenwich,* and all Maupassant's dinner-parties, always in the politest circles, where a countess or a fashionable doctor or someone relates a passionate or a pathetic or a tragic or a merely grotesque incident—as you have it, for instance, in the '*Contes de la Bécasse*'*—all this machinery for getting a story told is so much waste of time. A story is a story; why not just tell it anyhow? You can never tell what sort of an impression you will produce upon a reader. Then why bother about Impressionism? Why not just chance your luck?"

There is a good deal to be said for this point of view. Writing up to my own standards is such an intolerable labour and such a thankless job, since it can't give me the one thing in the world that I desire—that for my part I am determined to drop creative writing for good and all. But I, like all writers of my generation, have been so handicapped that there is small wonder that one should be tired out. On the one hand the difficulty of getting hold of any critical guidance was, when I was a boy, insuperable. There was nothing. Criticism was non-existent; self-conscious art was decried; you were supposed to write by inspiration; you were the young generation with the vine-leaves in your hair, knocking furiously at the door.* On the other hand, one writes for money, for fame, to excite the passion of love, to make an impression upon one's time. Well, God knows what one writes for. But it is certain that one gains neither fame nor money; certainly one does not excite the passion of love, and one's time continues to be singularly unimpressed.

But young writers to-day have a much better chance, on the æsthetic side at least. Here and there, in nooks and corners, they can find someone to discuss their work, not from the point of view of goodness or badness or of niceness or of nastiness, but from the simple point of view of expediency. The moment you can say: "Is it expedient to print *vers libre* in long or short lines, or in the form of prose, or not to print it at all, but to recite it?"—the moment you can find someone to discuss these expediences calmly, or the moment that you can find someone with whom to discuss the relative values of justifying your character or of abandoning the attempt to produce an illusion of reality—at that moment you are very considerably helped; whereas an admirer of your work might fall down and kiss your feet and it would not be of the very least use to you.

II.

This adieu, like Herrick's, to poesy,* may seem to be a digression. Indeed it is; and indeed it isn't. It is, that is to say, a digression in the sense that it is a statement not immediately germane to the argument that I am carrying on. But it is none the less an insertion fully in accord with the canons of Impressionism as I understand it. For the first business of Impressionism is to produce an impression, and the only way in literature to produce an impression is to awaken interest. And, in a sustained argument, you can only keep interest awakened by keeping alive, by whatever means you may have at your disposal, the surprise of your reader. You must state your argument; you must illustrate it, and then you must stick in something that appears to have nothing whatever to do with either subject or illustration, so that the reader will exclaim: "What the devil is the fellow driving at?" And then you must go on in the same way—arguing, illustrating and startling and arguing, startling and illustrating—until at the very end your contentions will appear like a ravelled skein. And then, in the last few lines, you will draw towards you the master-string of that seeming confusion, and the whole pattern of the carpet,* the whole design of the net-work will be apparent.

This method, you will observe, founds itself upon analysis of the human mind. For no human being likes listening to long and sustained arguments. Such listening is an effort, and no artist has the right to call for any effort from his audience. A picture should come out of its frame and seize the spectator.

Let us now consider the audience to which the artist should address himself. Theoretically a writer should be like the Protestant angel, a messenger of peace and goodwill towards all men. But, inasmuch as the Wingless Victory appears monstrously hideous to a Hottentot, and a beauty of Tunis* detestable to the inhabitants of these fortunate islands, it is obvious that each artist must adopt a frame of mind, less Catholic possibly, but certainly more Papist, and address himself, like the angel of the Vulgate, only *hominibus bonae voluntatis.** He must address himself to such men as be of goodwill; that is to say, he must typify for himself a human soul in sympathy with his own; a silent listener* who will be attentive to him, and whose mind acts very much as his acts. According to the measure of this artist's identity with his species, so will be the measure of his temporal greatness. That is why a book, to be really popular, must be either extremely good or extremely bad. For Mr. Hall Caine* has millions of readers; but then Guy de Maupassant and Flaubert have tens of millions.

I suppose the proposition might be put in another way. Since the great majority of mankind are, on the surface, vulgar and trivial—the stuff to fill graveyards—the great majority of mankind will be easily and quickly affected by art which is vulgar and trivial. But, inasmuch as this world is a very miserable purgatory for most of us sons of men—who remain stuff with which graveyards are filled—inasmuch as horror, despair and incessant strivings are the lot of the most trivial of humanity, who endure them as a rule with commonsense and cheerfulness—so, if a really great master strike the note of horror, of despair, of striving, and so on, he will stir chords in the hearts of a larger number of people than those who are moved by the merely vulgar and the merely trivial. This is probably why *Madame Bovary* has sold more copies than any book ever published, except, of course, books purely religious. But the appeal of religious books is exactly similar.

It may be said that the appeal of *Madame Bovary** is largely sexual. So it is, but it is only in countries like England and the United States that the abominable tortures of sex—or, if you will, the abominable interests of sex—are not supposed to take rank alongside of the horrors of lost honour, commercial ruin, or death itself. For all these things are the components of life, and each is of equal importance.

So, since Flaubert is read in Russia, in Germany, in France, in the United States, amongst the non-Anglo-Saxon population, and by the immense populations of South America, he may be said to have taken for his audience the whole of the world that could possibly be expected to listen to a man of his race. (I except, of course, the Anglo-Saxons who cannot be confidently expected to listen to anything other than the words produced by Mr. George Edwardes,* and musical comedy in general.)

My futurist friend again visited me yesterday, and we discussed this very question of audiences. Here again he said that I was entirely wrong. He said that an artist should not address himself to *l'homme moyen sensuel*,* but to intellectuals, to people who live at Hampstead and wear no hats.* (He withdrew his contention later.)

I maintain on my own side that one should address oneself to the cabmen round the corner, but this also is perhaps an exaggeration. My friend's contention on behalf of the intellectuals was not so much due to his respect for their intellects. He said that they knew the A B C of an art, and that it is better to address yourself to an audience that knows the A B C of an art than to an audience entirely untrammelled by such knowledge. In this I think he was wrong, for the intellectuals are persons of very conventional mind, and they acquire as a rule simultaneously with the A B C of any art the knowledge of so many conventions that it is almost impossible to make any impression upon their minds. Hampstead and the hatless generally offer an impervious front to futurisms, simply because they have imbibed from Whistler* and the Impressionists the convention that painting should not be literary. Now every futurist picture tells a story; so that rules out futurism. Similarly with the cubists. Hampstead has imbibed, from God knows where, the dogma that all art should be based on life, or should at least draw its inspiration and its strength from the representation of nature, so there goes cubism, since cubism is non-representational, has nothing to do with life, and has a quite proper contempt of nature.

When I produced my argument that one should address oneself to the cabmen at the corner, my futurist friend at once flung to me the jeer about Tolstoi and the peasant. Now the one sensible thing in the long drivel of nonsense with which Tolstoi misled this dull world was the remark that art should be addressed to the peasant.* My futurist friend said that that was sensible for an artist living in Russia or Roumania, but it was an absurd remark to be let fall by a critic living on Campden Hill.* His view was that you cannot address yourself to the peasant unless that peasant have evoked folk-song or folk-lores. I don't know why that was his view, but that was his view.

It seems to me to be nonsensical, even if the inner meaning of his dictum was that art should be addressed to a community of practising artists. Art, in fact, should be addressed to those who are not preoccupied. It is senseless to address a Sirventes* to a man who is going mad with love, and an Imagiste* poem will produce little effect upon another man who is going through the bankruptcy court.

It is probable that Tolstoi thought that in Russia the non-preoccupied mind was to be found solely amongst the peasant class, and that is why he said that works of art should be addressed to the peasant. I don't know how it may be in Russia, but certainly in Occidental Europe the non-preoccupied mind—which is the same thing as the peasant intelligence—is to be found scattered throughout every grade of society. When I used just now the instances of a man mad for love, or distracted by the prospect of personal ruin, I was purposely misleading.* For a man mad as a hatter for love of a worthless creature, or a man maddened by the tortures of bankruptcy, by dishonour or by failure,* may yet have, by the sheer necessity of his nature, a mind more receptive than most other minds. The mere craving for relief from his personal thoughts may make him take quite unusual interest in a work of art. So that is not preoccupation in my intended sense, but for a moment the false statement crystallised quite clearly what I was aiming at.

The really impassible mind is not the mind quickened by passion, but the mind rendered slothful by preoccupation purely trivial. The "English gentleman" is, for instance, an absolutely hopeless being from this point of view. His mind is so taken up by considerations of what is good form, of what is good feeling, of what is even good fellowship; he is so concerned to pass unnoticed in the crowd; he is so set upon having his room like everyone else's room, that he will find it impossible to listen to any plea for art which is exceptional, vivid, or startling. The cabman, on the other hand, does not mind being thought a vulgar sort of bloke; in consequence he will form a more possible sort of audience. On the other hand, amongst the purely idler classes it is perfectly possible to find individuals who are so firmly and titularly gentle folk that they don't have to care a damn what they do. These again are possible audiences for the artist. The point is really, I take it, that the preoccupation that is fatal to art is the moral or the social preoccupation. Actual preoccupations matter very little. Your cab-man may drive his taxi through exceedingly difficult streets; he may have half-a-dozen close shaves in a quarter of an hour. But when those things are over they are over, and he has not the necessity of a cabman. His point of view as to what is art, good form, or, let us say, the proper relation of the sexes; is unaffected. He may be a hungry man, a thirsty man, or even a tired man, but he will not necessarily have his finger upon his moral pulse, and he will not hold as æsthetic dogma the idea that no painting must tell a story, or the moral dogma that passion only becomes respectable when you have killed it.

It is these accursed dicta that render an audience hopeless to the artist, that render art a useless pursuit and the artist himself a despised indi-vidual.

So that those are the best individuals for an artist's audience who have least listened to accepted ideas—who are acquainted with deaths at street corners, with the marital infidelities of crowded courts, with the goodness of heart of the criminal, with the meanness of the undetected or the sinless, who know the queer odd jumble of negatives that forms our miserable and hopeless life. If I had to choose as reader I would rather have one who had never read anything before but the Newgate Calendar,* or the records of crime, starvation and divorce in the Sunday paper—I would rather have him for a reader than the man who had discovered the song that the sirens sang,* or had by heart the whole of the *Times* Literary Supplement, from its inception to the present day. Such a peasant intelligence will know that this is such a queer world that anything may be possible. And that is the type of intelligence that we need.

Of course, it is more difficult to find these intelligences in the town than in the rural districts. A man thatching all day long has time for many queer thoughts; so has a man who from sunrise to sunset is trimming a hedge into shape with a bagging hook. I have, I suppose, myself thought more queer thoughts when digging potatoes than at any other time during my existence. It is, for instance, very queer if you are digging potatoes in the late evening, when it has grown cool after a very hot day, to thrust your hand into the earth after a potato and to find that the earth is quite warm—is about flesh-heat.* Of course, the clods would be warm because the sun would have been shining on them all day, and the air gives up its heat much quicker than the earth. But it is none the less a queer sensation.

Now, if the person experiencing that sensation have what I call a peasant intelligence, he will just say that it is a queer thing and will store it away in his mind along with his other experiences. It will go along with the remembrance of hard frost, of fantastic icicles, the death of rabbits pursued by stoats, the singularly quick ripening of corn in a certain year, the fact that such and such a man was overlooked by a wise woman and so died because, his wife, being tired of him, had paid the wise woman five sixpences which she had laid upon the table in the form of a crown; or along with the other fact that a certain man murdered his wife by the use of a packet of sheep dip which he had stolen from a field where the farmer was employed at lamb washing. All these remembrances he will have in his mind, not classified under any headings of social reformers, or generalized so as to fulfil any fancied moral law.

But the really dangerous person for the artist will be the gentleman who, chancing to put his hand into the ground and to find it about as warm as the breast of a woman, if you could thrust your hand between her chest and her stays, will not accept the experience as an experience, but will start talking about the breast of mother-nature. This last man is the man whom the artist should avoid, since he will regard phenomena not as phenomena, but as happenings, with which he may back up preconceived dogmas—as, in fact, so many sticks with which to beat a dog.

No, what the artist needs is the man with the quite virgin mind—the man who will not insist that grass must always be painted green, because all the poets, from Chaucer till the present day, had insisted on talking about the green grass, or the green leaves, or the green straw.

Such a man, if he comes to your picture and sees you have painted a haycock bright purple* will say:

"Well, I have never myself observed a haycock to be purple, but I can understand that if the sky is very blue and the sun is setting very red, the shady side of the haycock might well appear to be purple." That is the kind of peasant intelligence that the artist needs for his audience.

And the whole of Impressionism comes to this: having realized that the audience to which you will address yourself must have this particular peasant intelligence, or, if you prefer it, this particular and virgin openness of mind, you will then figure to yourself an individual, a silent listener, who shall be to yourself the *homo bonæ voluntatis*—man of goodwill. To him, then, you will address your picture, your poem, your prose story, or your argument. You will seek to capture his interest; you will seek to hold his interest. You will do this by methods of surprise, of fatigue, by passages of sweetness in your language, by passages suggesting the sudden and brutal shock of suicide. You will give him passages of dulness, so that your bright effects may seem more bright; you will alternate, you will dwell for a long time upon an intimate point; you will seek to exasperate so that you may the better enchant. You will, in short, employ all the devices of the prostitute. If you are too proud for this you may be the better gentleman or the better lady, but you will be the worse artist. For the artist must always be humble and humble and again humble, since before the greatness of his task he himself is nothing. He must again be outrageous, since the greatness of his task calls for enormous excesses by means of which he may recoup his energies. That is why the artist is, quite rightly, regarded with suspicion by people who desire to live in tranquil and ordered society.

But one point is very important. The artist can never write to satisfy himself—to get, as the saying is, something off the chest.* He must not write propaganda which it is his desire to write; he must not write rolling periods, the production of which gives him a soothing feeling in his digestive organs or wherever it is. He must write always so as to satisfy that other fellow—that other fellow who has too clear an intelligence to let his attention be captured or his mind deceived by special pleadings in favour of any given dogma. You must not write so as to improve him, since he is a much better fellow than yourself, and you must not write so as to influence him, since he is a granite rock, a peasant intelligence, the gnarled bole of a sempiternal oak, against which you will dash yourself in vain. It is in short no pleasant kind of job to be a conscious artist. You won't have any vine-leaves in your poor old hair; you won't just dash your quill into an inexhaustible ink-well and pour out fine frenzies.* No, you will be just the skilled workman doing his job with drill or chisel or mallet. And you will get precious little out of it. Only, just at times, when you come to look again at some work of yours that you have quite forgotten, you will say, "Why, that is rather well done." That is all.

APPENDIX C

A CHRONOLOGY OF THE NOVEL

'I have, I am aware, told this story in a very rambling way so that it may be difficult for anyone to find their path through what may be a sort of maze', says Dowell. The following chronological thread is provided to make more visible some of the implications and inconsistencies of Ford's elaborate time-scheme. It attempts to give dates for the main events, as far as these can be established from the text. Several critics have commented on some of the inconsistencies; notably R. W. Lid, Arthur Mizener, Frank Kermode, Thomas Moser, Vincent Cheng, Roger Poole, and Martin Stannard. What follows is indebted to their research, but gives a fuller picture of the novel's structure and its difficulties.

When he looked back at *The Good Soldier* in the 'Dedicatory Letter' Ford was struck by its 'intricate tangle of references and cross-references'. Given Dowell's uncertainty about some of the chronology, we cannot be sure all the confusions were Ford's and not his narrator's. But given the complexity of the story's interconnections, uncertainty about one date destabilizes many others, and makes disentangling them an intriguing challenge. Rather than trying to conceal any temporal confusions, Ford tangles the time-line so intricately as to make it impossible to tease out definitively. He makes the task of figuring out the chronology so mind-bending it stops readers from trying; which is why so few have noticed any problems, and why they do not detract from the novel's power.

(Page references given in brackets are to the relevant passages from the novel.)

1868   John Dowell born.

1870/71   Edward Ashburnham born.

1873   Leonora born.

4 August 1874   Florence Hurlbird born.

These birthdates are based on the ages Dowell gives for the two couples when they met in Nauheim in 1904: Dowell is 36, Edward 33, Leonora 31, Florence 30 (p. 11). Martin Stannard (ed.), *The Good Soldier*, Norton Critical Edition (New York and London: W. W. Norton & Company, 1995), 195–6, shows that some revisions to these ages were made but not all implemented, and plausibly suggests this shows Ford 'struggling to adjust the relative ages of his characters at a late stage of composition'. The revisions make Edward and Leonora older by two or three years; it is possible they were an attempt to resolve the confusions identified below concerning the early years of the Ashburnham marriage: see 1892–8 below. Alternatively, they may be explained by the revision of the year of the fateful excursion to 'M——' from 1906 to 1904, as discussed in the Introduction.

1891   Nancy Rufford born. (Nancy first came to Branshaw when 'a child of thirteen' (pp. 77, 180); by 1913 she had been with the Ashburnhams 'for eight years or so' (p. 78); that is, since about 1905. Thus she is about 21 then, and has lived with them for most of the time they knew the Dowells.) When Dowell thinks of marrying her after Florence's suicide in August 1913, he says 'I was forty-five, and she, poor thing, was only just rising twenty-two' (p. 97).

1892/93   Edward Ashburnham marries Leonora Powys; he is at least 22 (p. 108); she is at least 19 (p. 107). Edward is prepared to become a Roman Catholic, but insists that any male offspring be raised Anglican. They live at Branshaw Teleragh after the deaths of Edward's parents. Dowell says that Leonora 'could not have been a happier girl for five or six years. For it was only at the end of that time that clouds began, as the saying is, to arise' (p. 111). But these 'clouds' surely include the 'Kilsyte case' and Edward's affair with 'La Dolciquita', below, the dating for which is unclear. Dowell gives Leonora's age here as about 23, which suggests a date of 1896; whereas 5 or 6 years after her marriage she'd be 24 or 25, and the year 1897/98.

1895 or before [or 1898?]   The 'Kilsyte case': Edward 'kissed a servant girl in a railway train'. He is tried, faces jail, but is fined five shillings. Dowell says this episode 'came at the very beginning of [Edward's] finding Leonora cold and unsympathetic' (p. 44). Dowell's statement that 'He was twenty-seven then, and his wife was out of sympathy with him' (p. 123) would date the court-case and period just after it to 1897/98. But see below:

1895[/98?]   Edward's affair with the Spanish dancer, 'La Dolciquita'— 'a cosmopolitan harpy who passed for the mistress of a Russian Grand Duke', in Monte Carlo; he takes her to Antibes for a week. Dowell dates this 'in 1895, about nine years before the date of which I am talking— the date of Florence's getting her hold over Leonora' (p. 48); the latter definitely refers to 1904, and 9 years before is indeed 1895. But on p. 129 he gives Leonora's age as 24 at the time of the affair with 'La Dolciquita', pointing to a date of around 1897. And, as stated above, Dowell gives Edward's age at the time of the Kilsyte case, which precedes this affair, as 27; which would also entail a later date of 1897/98. Edward runs up enormous gambling debts. Leonora takes over the management of the estate.

1896 The Ashburnhams lease out Branshaw, and go to India. Dowell says
when they met in 1904, Edward was 'home on sick leave from an India
to which he was never to return' (p. 11), and that they spent 'eight years
in India' (p. 130).

Some time between 1896 and 1899 Edward has a love affair with Mrs.
Basil, lasting 'several years' (p. 49), and ending when Major Basil is sent off
'just before the South African War' (p. 132) that began in October 1899.

4 August 1899 On her birthday, Florence Hurlbird sets out with her
uncle John and his factotum Jimmy on a tour around the world—'a
birthday present to celebrate her coming of age' (p. 65). This would
probably have been her 21st birthday. But if she is 30 in 1904 (p. 11),
she'd be 25 in 1899.

4 August 1900 Florence begins a love affair with Jimmy in England, at
the Bagshawes' house in Ledbury: 'on the fourth of August, 1900, she
yielded to an action that certainly coloured her whole life' (p. 65). But
she is discovered coming out of Jimmy's bedroom at five in the morning
by Bagshawe (p. 82).

4 August 1901 Despite the Hurlbird family's attempts to discourage
him, Dowell elopes with and marries Florence (on her 27th birthday).
They set sail for Europe from America; Florence begins her deception
of Dowell, pretending to have a 'heart'.

1901–03/04 Florence resumes her affair with Jimmy in Europe, but tires
of him. Dowell places the end of the relationship in 1903 (p. 73). But
he also says here that by then Florence had taken on Edward, which is
impossible since he was in India until 1904. See 'December 1904' below,
for the reason why the affair is more likely to have ended in 1904.

Soon before August 1904 The Ashburnhams meet the Maidans in India.
Edward begins affair with Maisie Maidan, who is about 23 (p. 45).

1904 Edward and Leonora return from India with Maisie Maidan.
Edward is 'home on sick leave from an India to which he was never to
return' (p. 11). Dowell says Edward has a 'heart'; but that may have
more to do with Maisie than with his health, which otherwise does not
seem a problem: 'whereas a yearly month or so at Nauheim tuned him
up to exactly the right pitch for the rest of the twelvemonth, the two
months or so were only just enough to keep poor Florence alive from
year to year' (p. 11).

[July?]/4 August 1904 At Nauheim that summer, Florence witnesses
Leonora boxing Maisie's ears; the Ashburnhams become acquainted
with the Dowells later that evening at dinner. Dowell gives the date as
4 August; but he gives the same date for the two couples making a joint
excursion to the town of M—— in the afternoon, and it is impossible

both events happened on the same day. Ford appears originally to have had the couples meeting in July, but then moved the date to August without making all the required alterations. For example, Dowell says of Maisie: 'We saw plenty of her for the first month of our acquaintance, then she died'; the death on 4 August points to the meeting occurring in July. This major inconsistency is discussed in the Introduction.

4 August 1904   The 'Protest' scene. The Dowells and Ashburnhams take a trip to the town of M—— (Marburg). Florence acts as tour guide, pointing out the Protest document, and lays a finger on Edward's wrist. Leonora realizes they are having, or are on the verge of having, an affair; but Dowell appears not to have noticed. The four return to Nauheim that evening. Maisie, having overheard a conversation between Edward and Florence, writes Leonora a letter, then dies of a heart attack (pp. 55, 65).

Dowell says: 'Then nothing happened until the 4th of August, 1913' (p. 65). But, though he was not aware of it until later, Edward and Florence have an affair throughout those nine years from 1904 to 1913. Leonora catches Florence coming out of Edward's room a week after Maisie's death (p. 148). Dowell gives the following details from his diaries, but doesn't give dates for any events between 1906 and 1913:

4–21 September 1904   Edward accompanies Florence and Dowell to Paris (p. 79). But Dowell has said that the Ashburnhams were due to stay with a Colonel Hervey in Scotland 'for the month of September', but that Leonora 'did not know whether the date fixed would be the eleventh or the eighteenth' (p. 47).

December 1904   Edward visits them again. This is the occasion when he 'knocked Mr. Jimmy's teeth down his throat' (p. 79); which indicates that the end of Florence's affair with Jimmy should be dated to 1904 instead of 1903.

1905   Edward visits the Dowells in Paris three times, once with Leonora (p. 79).

1906   'In 1906 we spent the best part of six weeks together at Mentone, and Edward stayed with us in Paris on his way back to London' (p. 79).

1905   Nancy Rufford comes to live with the Ashburnhams at Branshaw— soon after the death of Maisie Maidan.

1907   Dowell is convinced Edward had tired of Florence 'within three years' (p. 79).

1910   When Nancy is 18 (p. 102), her father, Major Rufford, arrives at Nauheim, and the sound of his voice panics Nancy.

1910   Leonora attempts an affair of her own, with Rodney Bayham (pp. 14–15, 151, 158).

Feb? 1912   (Assuming Dowell has begun writing in Feb. 1914). Dowell
and Florence 'motored from Biarritz to Las Tours, which is in the Black
Mountains' (p. 18).

Summer 1913   Nancy Rufford is at Nauheim with Ashburnhams for 'the
whole of our last stay' (p. 76). She usually joined them for only the last
two weeks (p. 101).

30 July 1913   Death of Florence's uncle John Hurlbird.

4 August 1913   Outside the casino at Nauheim, Florence overhears
Edward declare his love to Nancy Rufford. Then she sees Dowell talking
to Bagshawe, and probably guesses that Bagshawe, who has recognized
her, is revealing her affair with Jimmy to Dowell. Florence commits
suicide. Dowell thinks she died of a heart attack. In shock, he says, 'Now
I can marry the girl' (pp. 81–2, 85, 88).

*c.*18 August 1913   Dowell goes back to America to settle the financial problems of the Hurlbird estate: 'just a fortnight after Florence's suicide, I
set off for the United States' (p. 98). His 'short incursion into American
business life [. . .] lasted during part of August and nearly the whole of
September' (p. 120). Given that he was not summoned to Branshaw till
mid-November, his activities from October to then are unaccounted for;
unless he meant he saw to his own business in August–September, and
the Hurlbird inheritance afterwards.

1 September 1913   Edward, Leonora and Nancy return to Branshaw
(p. 169). Leonora breaks down, and 'at once took to her bed'; the tension
is intolerable; but by

1 October 1913   Edward, Leonora, and Nancy are 'all going to meets
together' (p. 169). Perhaps because by then Edward has decided that
Nancy is to go to her father in India.

'About' 6 October 1913   Edward gives a horse to Selmes (p. 169).

*c.*20 October 1913   'A fortnight went by' after Edward gives Selmes the
horse. One evening he announces that he has written to Nancy's father
suggesting she should join him in India (p. 161).

20 October 1913   Nancy reads about the Brand divorce case in the papers
(p. 170).

23 October 1913   Leonora and Nancy discuss marriage (p. 169). Dowell says
'You are to remember that all this happened a month before Leonora went
into the girl's room at night'; which would place the discussion around
12 October instead. Nancy realizes Edward is 'dying—actually and physically dying—of love' for her (p. 173).

12 November 1913   Leonora goes to Nancy's bedroom: 'her aunt's coming to her bedroom did not occur until the 12th of November' (p. 170);

tells her 'you must belong to Edward' (p. 174). Nancy receives a letter from her mother, Mrs Rufford, who was supposed to have committed suicide years before, saying something like: 'You ought to be on the streets with me. How do you know that you are even Colonel Rufford's daughter?' (p. 172).[1]

13 November 1913 Edward then Leonora send telegrams to Dowell to come and stay to ease the situation (pp. 154–5, 176–7).

November 1913 Nancy goes to Edward's bedroom to offer herself to him (p. 184).

'Then the household resumed its wonted course of days until my arrival' (p. 177).

mid-November 1913 or later Dowell arrives at Branshaw. From this point on—effectively after Edward's death—Dowell gives few definite dates, and mainly time-intervals between events. Mid-November seems the earliest possible date for him to have made the transatlantic crossing, if the telegrams inviting him were sent on 13 November. But Dowell's departure, and all the subsequent events, could occur at later dates— hence the queries.

For 'nearly ten days' (p. 155) Dowell stays at Branshaw, living tranquilly with Edward, Leonora, and Nancy, unaware why he has been summoned: 'Neither Edward nor Leonora made any motion to talk to me about anything other than the weather and the crops' (p. 155).

end of November/early December 1913? Then, 'nearly ten days' (p. 155) after Dowell's arrival, Leonora announces at dinner Nancy's imminent departure for Ceylon. Dowell writes of 'the whole fortnight that intervened between my arrival and the girl's departure' (p. 185), implying she left about four days after this announcement.

early to mid-December 1913? Edward's 'final outburst' (pp. 28, 89, 189) to Dowell, the night before Nancy leaves for Ceylon. On the day of Nancy's departure, Edward and Dowell drive her to the train station. Dowell witnesses their parting.

mid-December 1913? Edward gets 'a poor girl, the daughter of one of his gardeners, acquitted of a charge of murdering her baby. That was positively the last act of Edward's life. It came at a time when Nancy Rufford was on her way to India' (p. 151). (Dowell is slightly misleading here, since the last act of Edward's life was his suicide.)

---

[1] Thomas C. Moser, *The Life in the Fiction of Ford Madox Ford* (Princeton; Princeton University Press, 1980), 162, cites as an inconsistency that on p. 155 'Ford has Dowell be present by the night that Leonora goes into Nancy's bedroom'. But this seems to misread Dowell's phrase 'to me who was hourly with them' to refer to that night, whereas he more probably means that when he was with them later they were still keeping up the performance of being 'just good people' (p. 155).

end of 1913?   Nancy sends a telegram saying that she is having a 'rattling good time' in Brindisi (p. 193). Edward takes this to mean she is not continuing to love him at a distance, as he had dreamed. He commits suicide. Nancy reads of his death in the paper when she reaches Aden, and goes mad (p. 179). She would presumably have taken the cross-channel packet to France, then trains through France and Italy; then the (probably P&O) steamer from Brindisi that passed through the Suez canal and stopped at Aden before heading for Bombay. The Hampshire–Brindisi journey might have taken about three or four days; Brindisi to Aden another two.

end of 1913?   Edward's funeral. Dowell dates his revelatory conversation with Leonora 'eight days' (p. 187) or 'about a week after the funeral' (p. 85); during it she says Edward has been dead 'ten days' (p. 86); thus the funeral took place about two or three days after his death.

[November 1913]/[4 January/]4 February 1914   About a week after Edward's funeral (p. 85), Leonora begins a long conversation with Dowell, in which she 'let me into her full confidence' (p. 86). This is probably the period Dowell refers to as the 'four crashing days' in which he learns that his apparently happy life had been an illusion. He has been cuckolded by his best friend (p. 85); his wife committed suicide (p. 86). The 4 February date assumes these days come nine years and six months (not six weeks, for reasons explained below) after their meeting. The 4 January date is where these four days would fall if the first meeting is understood to have occurred in July instead of August (for reasons explained above: see '[July?]/4 August 1904'). Just to complicate things further, Dowell/Ford also places this conversation on 'a windy November evening' (p. 86).

Dowell refers twice to this crucial four-day period in the first few pages of the novel. First he says: 'that long, tranquil life, which was just stepping a minuet, vanished in four crashing days at the end of nine years and six weeks' (p. 13); then he writes: 'If for nine years I have possessed a goodly apple that is rotten at the core and discover its rottenness only in nine years and six months less four days [. . .]' (p. 13). Which four days does he mean? And is the discrepancy between 'six weeks' and 'six months' significant, and if so, of what? Neither instance has been revised in the manuscript. One could argue that Ford placed the conflicting versions close together so they'd be noticed as an early signal of Dowell's cavalier way with time, but previous editors or commentators seem not to have spotted it. The novel begins with the information that the Dowells had known the Ashburnhams for 'nine seasons' of Nauheim, so the nine years must begin when they meet.

The 'four days' might be thought to relate to the 'three or four days' (p. 88; though p. 96 says a 'week or ten days') Dowell says he was 'in a state just simply cataleptic' after Florence's death, and when he blurts out that he can now marry Nancy. But Florence's death is on 4 August 1913; exactly nine years (not plus six weeks or months) after the two couples meet. And since Dowell says he did not remember the rest of the cataleptic four days he is unlikely to have thought of them as 'crashing'. The 'four crashing days' mark the end of his 'long, tranquil life'; the point when he discovers his 'goodly apple' is 'rotten at the core'. There are two candidates for such phases of traumatic disabusal. The first is when Dowell witnesses the station parting, Edward tells him he is dying for love of Nancy, kills himself, and she reads of his death and goes mad—if all that could occur within four days, which might just be possible. In that case the rottenness would refer to the passion between guardian and ward, showing Edward as monstrous and shattering Dowell's hopes of marrying Nancy. The second is set about a week after Edward's funeral, when Leonora begins telling Dowell the truth about Florence's suicide and her affair with Edward, and the details of Edward's passion for Nancy. This seems the more likely candidate: the rottenness in this case would refer to the shock news about the adultery, deception, and Florence's suicide; and the tragedy of Edward's fatal attempt to renounce Nancy.

If we follow the published text's date for their meeting, 4 August 1904, nine years and six *weeks* later would be 16 September 1913. This is too early, since Dowell was still in the USA then (till at least around the end of September), and says he reached Branshaw in mid-November. Unless that date is a trace of a superseded time-scheme: given that Dowell also places the devastating conversation with Leonora on 'a windy November evening' (p. 86) it's possible at one stage he meant Dowell to have returned earlier than November, to allow time for the fortnight before Nancy leaves, then her telegram, Edward's suicide, and the funeral. But if Dowell's return date of mid-November stands, then 'six weeks' must be an error, whether Dowell's or Ford's. Nine years and six *months* from 4 August 1904 would take us to 4 February 1914. (Or 4 January 1914 if their meeting is dated from July 1904.) Either date is long enough after Dowell's arrival in mid-November to make it clear that the 'four crashing days' cannot refer to the station parting, suicide, and madness, but must mean the conversation in which Leonora reveals Florence's suicide and adultery.

February 1914?/mid-May 1914? Dowell begins to compose his narrative. He says he is writing the start of Part III about five weeks after
Edward's funeral (he writes: 'a month ago, about a week after the funeral', p. 85). This would require Parts I and II to have been begun soon
after the funeral—presumably after the conversation with Leonora—
and to have taken a month.

However: in the first paragraph of the novel Dowell says 'Six months ago I had never been to England' (presumably because he could not make the trip while Florence was alive, because it was thought her heart might not survive sea-crossings). Some critics have understood Dowell to be saying here that he is beginning the novel six months after his arrival; and that, if he arrives in November 1913, summoned by the Ashburnhams' telegrams, then he starts composing six months later, around mid-May 1914.[2] According to this reading, for the February start-date to be plausible, he would have had to have arrived in England in September. But Dowell dates too many events in October and November as taking place before his arrival. Since Ford repeats the 'six months' at the start of Part IV (see next entry), it is possible that he started with the idea that Dowell would be writing the story six months later; but didn't think of the writing as a protracted sequence till afterwards, when his own delays in completing it may have led him to thematize Dowell's delays in detail.

This reading thus generates another serious contradiction in his chronology here. Whenever it is that Dowell arrives at Branshaw, the length of time between his arrival and Edward's death is fixed at between two and three weeks (there is a fortnight between his arrival and Nancy's departure; then the few days it takes her to get to Brindisi). The claim that Dowell begins Part I six months after arriving in Britain is irreconcilable with his giving the date of beginning Part III as five weeks after Edward's funeral; thus about two months after his arrival at Branshaw. This claim renders the chronological sequence of the narration as problematic as that of the events Dowell narrates.

However, Dowell's comment on his first page about never having been to England 'Six months ago' is preceded by his remark about 'English people of whom, till to-day, when I sit down to puzzle out what I know of this sad affair, I knew nothing whatever' (p. 11). This makes little sense if 'to-day' is understood as being in May, six months after his arrival in England. It is perhaps possible that he means that, even four months after Leonora's revelations during the 'four crashing days' of January or February, he is

---

[2] Arthur Mizener, *The Saddest Story: A Biography of Ford Madox Ford* (New York: Harper & Row, 1971; London: The Bodley Head, 1972), 568 n. 22, thinks Ford has made a mistake here. 'Dowell says he is writing down this part of the story [Part III] about a month after his conversation with Leonora [. . .], that is about Feb. 1, 1914. Ford could not have intended to suggest that; I believe he meant us to think of Dowell's writing Parts III and IV continuously, in a single stretch from October to December, 1914.' This is because, Mizener says on p. 268, the novel's opening implies a lapse of six months after Edward's death before Dowell starts writing, which implies a May start. At the start of Part IV Dowell says he has been writing for six months, which takes us to mid-November. But Dowell takes an eighteen-month break when he travels to Nancy in India; so it is not impossible Ford thought of him as interrupting the composition earlier too.

still only beginning to understand the full implications. But it makes more sense if 'to-day' refers to the period immediately after the 'four crashing days', when he learns that the Ashburnhams had been concealing from him Edward's adultery with Florence, and their own unhappiness, for years. According to this reading, Dowell's phrase 'Six months ago' is not Ford's mistake, but refers not to when Dowell arrives in England, but when he last saw the Ashburnhams, and indeed Florence, in Nauheim in August 1913; in other words, when he last had dealings with the English. This reading is supported by Dowell's comment on p. 27: 'And that was absolutely all that I knew of him until a month ago'; again indicating that, *pace* Mizener, Ford did indeed intend Dowell to begin writing soon after the 'four crashing days'. Thus in what follows I assume he has begun by February. Readers opting for a May start can add three months to the remaining tentative dates.

[The opening of 'The Saddest Story' appears in *Blast* in June 1914.]

June/July/August 1914?   Dowell begins Part IV. Exactly when depends on earlier decisions about when he meets the Ashburnhams, when he arrives in England, and when he starts writing. He dates the start of Part IV as six months into the writing: '(I may, in what follows, be a little hard on Florence; but you must remember that I have been writing away at this story now for six months and reflecting longer and longer upon these affairs.)' (p. 143). That means that Dowell has been living with Leonora alone at Branshaw for six months, while writing the first three Parts.

mid–late 1914   (Probably late 1914, since Dowell would be unlikely to wait half a year before setting off to India.) Then, Leonora and Dowell receive a letter from Colonel Rufford with the information that Nancy, having learned in Aden of Edward's suicide, has gone mad; he requests Leonora to come and see Nancy. Dowell agrees to go instead.

c.December 1914?   Dowell goes to India, accompanied by Nancy's old nurse. 'I did follow Nancy out to India after a year. . . .' (p. 188). He travels through Europe, Africa, and Asia; finds Nancy and brings her back to Branshaw Teleragh.

Eighteen-month break (p. 178) between the writing of IV.iv and the last two chapters (IV.v and IV.vi).

Why does Dowell stop writing for so long? Was he travelling all that time? It seems unlikely. He would surely have wanted to get to Nancy as quickly as possible; and having found what state she was in, would not have taken a grand tour back with her. He says 'I wasn't the least good when I got to Ceylon; and the nurse wasn't the least good' (p. 180), indicating that the plan was that they should spend time with Nancy in India to see if that would help her; and it is only after that fails that it is decided to take her back to Branshaw. But his comment: 'Well, you see, I did follow Nancy out to India after a year. . . .' (p. 188) points to a departure date of late 1914, and a lacuna in his writing of up to six months. Perhaps it was the shock of hearing of her madness that made him unable to continue before he leaves for Ceylon. Nor can he resume the narrative till he gets back. It is as if he can only write the story at Branshaw.

1915? Leonora 'married Rodney Bayham in my absence and went to live at Bayham' (p. 180). When Dowell returns, she is pregnant: 'For Rodney Bayham is rather like a rabbit, and I hear that Leonora is expected to have a baby in three months' time' (p. 182). Dowell would have been living with Leonora for over a year by the time he left, and decides he is jealous (pp. 180, 191). Dowell buys Branshaw from her, and lives there with Nancy, who never recovers.

mid-1916? Dowell now finishes writing *The Good Soldier*. He begins IV.v: 'I am writing this, now, I should say, a full eighteen months after the words that end my last chapter.' If Part IV was begun some time between June and August 1914, he could have finished IV.iv a few months later; say between August and December 1914. The eighteen-month interval would thus give a start-date for the last two chapters of February–June 1916. Which is odd, given the fact that *The Good Soldier* was published on 17 March 1915.

EXPLANATORY NOTES

THE following annotations are indebted to the work of other Ford scholars, especially Thomas Moser's previous edition for Oxford World's Classics, and Martin Stannard's Norton critical edition: *The Good Soldier* (New York and London: W. W. Norton & Company, 1995; second edition, 2012).

DEDICATORY LETTER

3 *To Stella Ford*: the first edition in 1915 carried no dedication or preface. Ford added the Dedicatory Letter for the second American edition (New York: Boni, 1927) and it was also included in the second English edition (London: John Lane, 1928). Stella Bowen (1893–1947) lived with Ford from 1919 to 1927, and was the mother of his third child, Julia (1920–85). Bowen was an Australian-born painter, who had sailed to London in the spring of 1914 and enrolled at the Westminster School of Art, studying under Walter Sickert. She was staying in a hostel in Kensington when she met a neighbour, Ezra Pound, who soon introduced her to Ford and Violet Hunt. Hunt invited Bowen to her cottage at Selsey on the Sussex coast in October 1917, and that was when she met Ford. They corresponded and a romance developed, but were only able to be together after Ford was demobilized from the Army in the spring of 1919, and had separated from Hunt. Ford was not able to marry Bowen—his wife Elsie Hueffer still refused to divorce him—so naming her publicly as 'Stella Ford' was a fiction, presumably designed to spare her and especially Julia from any resulting stigma. Dedicating *The Good Soldier* to her as they were about to separate—as amicably as such things can be managed—was a gesture of affection, and gratitude for helping him to recover after the war.

my best book: Ford may truly have thought of *The Good Soldier* as his 'best book'. It is certainly a masterpiece surpassing anything he had written earlier. But critics who accept that valuation do not always attend to his qualification: 'at any rate as the best book of mine of a pre-war period'. To the first readers of this 'Dedicatory Letter' in 1927, Ford would have been known not as the author of *The Good Soldier*—which had sunk with little trace during the war, when people had other sadnesses on their mind. What he was known for were the first three 'Tietjens novels', not yet known collectively as *Parade's End*, but which had appeared to increasing acclaim from 1924 to 1926, giving Ford the best reviews and best sales he had ever achieved. So his singling out of *The Good Soldier* needs to be read in this context. He knew it was still one of the best things he had ever done. He wanted people to read it; and the implied modesty about the other sixty books he had published by 1927 is in part strategic. He was using the meteoric reception of the war novels to re-launch the other book on which his claim to fame would rest. He also referred to *The Good Soldier* as his 'one novel' four years later in *Return to Yesterday* in 1931 (pp. 417, 429). That might appear to confirm the judgement of *The Good Soldier* as in a different league. By then the final volume of *Parade's End*, *Last Post* (1928), had appeared; and Ford occasionally expressed doubts about whether he should have added it. At such moments *The Good Soldier* may have seemed the better piece of work. On the other hand, it was still true in 1931 that the Tietjens novels were much better known; the second edition of *The Good Soldier* seemed to have done little to raise its standing. (It was only with the paperback versions after the Second World War, in Penguin in 1948 and Vintage in 1951, that it acquired a following among the formalists of the New Criticism.) Even in 1931 readers would still have remembered the acclaim of the *Parade's End* volumes as amongst the best of modern novels and war books. For Ford to talk of his 'one novel' was not so much to denigrate the others, as to say that *The Good Soldier* was at least as good, if not better. It was thus paradoxically an attempt to persuade his readers precisely that he *wasn't* a one-work novelist (or at least, that *Parade's End* wasn't the one work), by teasing them with the suggestion: if you think *Parade's End* is good, try this one!

3 *Conrad*: Joseph Conrad (1857–1924), Polish-born novelist who settled in England after a career in the Merchant Marine. Conrad was introduced to Ford by the literary agent Edward Garnett in 1898, and collaborated with Ford on three books. Their close friendship cooled in 1909, but Ford wrote a moving tribute to it as soon as he heard of Conrad's death: *Joseph Conrad: A Personal Remembrance* (London: Duckworth, 1924).

4 *Cubists, Vorticists, Imagistes*: members of three Modernist art movements. Cubism, developed by Pablo Picasso and Georges Braque from 1907 and continuing into the 1920s, reinvented the pictorial representation of space, fragmenting traditional three-dimensional perspective, presenting its objects from multiple angles and composing them from geometric forms. Vorticism was founded by the painter and writer Percy Wyndham Lewis (1882–1957), and combined a cubist angularity with the dynamism and violence of the Italian Futurists. Its main literary manifestation was the magazine *Blast*, the first issue of which carried the opening of *The Good Soldier* (under its original title of 'The Saddest Story') in 1914. Imagism or Imagisme was a poetic movement, named and led by Ford's friend the American poet Ezra Pound (1885–1972), at first in combination with two poets who took dictation of parts of *The Good Soldier*, Richard Aldington and 'H.D.' (Hilda Doolittle), but later including a larger number of British and American poets. Imagism sought to escape what it saw as the self-indulgence, excessive symbolism, and imprecision of the literary language of the late nineteenth century, and to aim instead for direct, concrete presentation of the object, verbal clarity and exactness, and a return to a pre-Romantic, classical sense of formal beauty. It also advocated 'vers libre' or free verse, written according to musical cadence rather than conventional metrical forms.

tapageur: noisy, showy. Stannard emends to '*tapageux*'.

Jeunes: the Young; Ford's term for the younger generation of avant-garde writers, several of whom he discovered and nurtured, discussing their work with them and publishing them in his magazines—the *English Review* before the war, and the *transatlantic review* after it.

Great Auk: a flightless seabird, with a large body and small wings, the auk became extinct in 1844. Anatole France's novel *Penguin Island* (1908; French: *L'Île des Pingouins*) invents an island of great auks. Conrad had reviewed it for the first number of Ford's *English Review*.

Thrush: Ford had published an essay in this short-lived poetry magazine in December 1909; but he is thought not to have taken this 'formal farewell of literature' till December 1914, when he wrote—in the magazine called *Poetry and Drama*: 'for my part I am determined to drop creative writing for good and all'; 'On Impressionism' see Appendix B, p. 207.

Ezra . . . H.D.: Ezra Pound. See note to p. 4. Ford met Pound in 1909 soon after he had arrived in London, and they became lifelong friends. Ford gave Pound his first major publication, taking nine poems for the *English Review*. Eliot: T. S. Eliot (1888–1965), American poet and critic who also lived in London from 1914; Wyndham Lewis: Ford had published three of his essays in the *English Review*; H.D.: Hilda Doolittle (1886–1961), another American expatriate poet. H.D. had been Pound's lover but in 1914 was married to the English poet and later novelist Richard Aldington.

translate it into French: Ford, who spoke excellent French, said he began translating *The Good Soldier* in 1916 during the Battle of the Somme: see *Return to Yesterday*, p. 429. He apparently worked on it in Paris in 1924. When Sondra J. Stang and Maryann De Julio described it in 'The Art of Translation: Ford's "Le bon soldat"', *Contemporary Literature*, 30:2 (Summer 1989), 263–79, only 37 leaves of the handwritten translation were known, and Ford's comments about getting the translation published made it sound possible it had been completed. However, a thirty-eighth leaf was subsequently discovered, which appears to be the last (and is now reunited with the others at Cornell University Library's Division of Rare and Manuscript Collections). Two complete French translations of the novel have been published; the first, by Jacques Papy, appeared under the imaginative title of *Quelque chose au cœur* (Paris: Le Club Français du Livre, 1953).

5 *Maupassant*: Guy de Maupassant (1850–93), French writer of short stories and novels, was one of the authors Ford most admired, seeing him as a pioneer of literary impressionism. *Fort Comme la Mort* (*Strong as Death*) appeared in 1889, and is discussed in the Introduction.

John Rodker: (1894–1955) English poet, essayist, novelist, publisher, and translator from the French; one of the 'Whitechapel Boys' group of Jewish intellectuals and artists, including Mark Gertler, David Bomberg, and Isaac Rosenberg.

5 *finest French novel in the English language*: Rodker may have known Arthur
Ransome's recent description of *The Picture of Dorian Gray* as 'the first
French novel to be written in the English language': *Oscar Wilde: A
Critical Study* (London: Secker, 1912), 95. I'm indebted to Sara Haslam
for this possible source.

Mr. Lane: John Lane (1854–1926), English publisher; founder, in 1887, of
The Bodley Head press.

other pursuits: Ford enlisted in the Army in late July 1915, four months
after the novel's publication. Since finishing it, he had been writing
propaganda for the British government.

gentlemen with red hatbands: staff officers.

THE GOOD SOLDIER

7 [*Title*]: see the Introduction, p. xxvi, for the story of the change of title
from 'The Saddest Story'. The eventual title has been thought to allude to
several possible sources. Beatrice in *Much Ado About Nothing* puns on 'a
good soldier'—the version Ford proposed to John Lane:

Messenger: And [Benedick is] a good soldier too, lady.
Beatrice: And a good soldier to a lady, but what is he to a lord?

(I. i. 51–3).

In the King James Version of the Bible, 2 Timothy 2: 3 says: 'Thou therefore endure hardness, as a good soldier of Jesus Christ.' Heinrich Heine,
one of Ford's favourite poets, wrote: 'You may lay a sword on my coffin,
I was a good soldier in the warfare for humanity' (Heine, 'Journey from
Munich to Genoa', *Reisebilder*, Part III, chapter XXXI, last paragraph;
see *Heinrich Heines Sämtliche Werke* (Leipzig, 1912), iv. 305–6). The
translation is from the epigraph to Lucy Masterman's biography of her
husband, *C. F. G. Masterman*. The book wasn't published till 1939, but
Ford's friendship with the Mastermans—Lucy was a fellow-poet—suggests that Ford may well have been familiar with the quotation. Matthew
Arnold used it at the start of his essay on Heine, though his translation
says 'brave soldier'. However, given that the novel almost appeared under
a different title, it would be rash to assume such allusions were intended,
especially during the process of composition. The phrase is anyway common enough not to derive from a specific source. Compare, for example,
The Good Soldier Schwejk by Jaroslav Hašek. On the other hand, Ford's
subsequent echoes of the phrase may be more telling. In *Great Trade
Route* (London: Allen and Unwin, 1937), he wrote: 'let it be remembered
that even amongst murderers there is honour and the definition of a good
soldier is not merely that he is one who wins battles, or even one who
wins battles at all. A good soldier is one who wins or loses battles with
the least possible loss of the men entrusted to him' (p. 366). This chimes
with Dowell's comment that Leonora loved Edward 'for what I will call

the public side of his record—for his good soldiering, for his saving lives at sea, for the excellent landlord that he was and the good sportsman' (p. 185).

"Beati Immaculati": Psalm 119: 1 in the Latin Vulgate Bible; translated in the King James Version as: 'Blessed are the undefiled [in the way, who walk in the law of the Lord].' Latin remained the traditional liturgical language in the Roman Catholic Church until the second Vatican Council of the 1960s, so such allusions would have been familiar to Ford, who had been received into the Catholic Church when he was 19.

11 *Nauheim*: Bad Nauheim, a well-known spa and holiday resort near Frankfurt, in the grand duchy of Hesse-Darmstadt on the north-east slopes of the Taunus Mountains. Its saline springs are recommended for people with heart problems.

Nice . . . Bordighera: Nice, leading resort city on the French Riviera; Bordighera, winter resort town on the north-eastern Ligurian coast of Italy, near the French border.

12 *Ashburnham*: the historical Ashburnham family had lived in Ashburnham House or Place in the village of Ashburnham, about 6 miles from Battle in (what is now East) Sussex, since the twelfth century, but came to prominence when John Ashburnham was knighted by James I. His son, another John, became Groom of the Bedchamber to Charles I in 1628 and was a loyal supporter of the Royalist cause during the Civil War. After the Restoration he served Charles II as a diplomat, and he represented his home county of Sussex in the House of Commons between 1661 and 1667. His grandson John was ennobled as Baron Ashburnham in 1689, and his great-grandson as Earl of Ashburnham, a title that became extinct in 1924. See: http://www.nationalarchives.gov.uk/A2A/records.aspx?cat =179-ashburnham&cid=-1#-1 accessed 23 September 2011. Ford may have known of the Ashburnhams from his grandfather's friend, the poet Algernon Charles Swinburne, whose mother was the daughter of the third Earl of Ashburnham. As W. G. Sebald explains in *The Rings of Saturn* (London: Harvill, 1999, p. 161), 'As long as anyone could remember, the Swinburnes and the Ashburnhams had been members of the royal entourage, prominent commanders and warriors, lords of vast estates, and explorers.' Ford had written about the house in 1900 in *The Cinque Ports*: 'Ashburnham House is a rather uninteresting modern building, but the lands around it have been in possession of the Ashburnham family from time immemorial. The library used to be famous the world over, and the relics of Charles I. are still preserved in the place' (p. 57). On pp. 36–7 he tells the story of Ashburnham getting a ship ready which was supposed to carry Charles abroad to safety. When Ford moved to Winchelsea in 1901, he was only about 15 miles away from the village. In *The Good Soldier* he not only moves the house to Hampshire, but says Florence's family used to own it (p. 55).

12 *Cranford*: allusion to Elizabeth Gaskell's novel *Cranford* (1853) about a quiet, old-fashioned, country town near Manchester.

Chestnut and Walnut Streets: two fashionable streets in downtown Philadelphia.

wampum: sacred shell beads used by indigenous North Americans. Wampum was sometimes woven into belts to commemorate treaties, so could record an agreement about land transfer.

William Penn: (1644–1718), English entrepreneur and Quaker leader, the founder of the state of Pennsylvania.

Fordingbridge: market town in Hampshire, where Ford had gone to recover during his breakdown of 1904. The historical Ashburnham Place was in Sussex, not Hampshire, as Ford well knew: see note to p. 12.

Some one has said . . . Goths: Violet Hunt—Ford's partner while he was composing *The Good Soldier*—had written in a novel two decades earlier: 'Lauder Brunton says that "the death of a mouse from anthrax may be compared with the destruction of the Roman Empire by the Barbarians" ': *The Maiden's Progress: A Novel in Dialogue* (London: Osgood, McIlvaine and Co., 1894), 134. Gervaise Maskelyne is patronizing his daughter, 'Moderna', saying that 'Women always want a romantic basis to their science—don't take it in unless it's popularised'; and cites this as an example. I am grateful to Venetia Abdalla for pointing me towards this reference, which is to the Scottish physician Sir Thomas Lauder Brunton (1844–1916). What he actually wrote was: 'we see that a likeness may be observed between the body corporeal and the body corporate, and that the death of a mouse from anthrax may be compared with the destruction of the Roman Empire by the savage hordes who invaded it': *An Introduction to Modern Therapeutics* (London and New York: Macmillan, 1892), 13–14. His use of amyl nitrite to treat angina pectoris is also relevant to *The Good Soldier*. See note to p. 87.

Homburg: Bad Homburg, another German spa town also in the Taunus Mountains; famous for its mineral springs and Casino.

13 *minuet*: stately dance in triple measure. Maupassant's story 'The Minuet' was included in the volume of translations by Ford's wife, Elsie: *Stories from De Maupassant* (London: Duckworth, 1903), for which Ford contributed a Preface. Ford's imagery here and in the preceding paragraph perhaps draws upon the comparably conflicted narration at the end of the first chapter of Henry James's 'The Turn of the Screw', in which the governess writes of music, dance, a castle, a ship, the colour blue, and the contrast between innocence and knowledge.

nine years and six weeks: two paragraphs further on, Dowell refers to the same period as 'nine years and six months'. The inconsistency may be Ford's, or he may have planted it to cast doubt on Dowell's reliability. See Appendix C.

Kur orchestra: *Kur* is German for 'cure'; thus the sanatorium orchestra.

favours: ribbons worn as decorations at a party.

Trianon . . . Hessian . . . Nirvana: Trianon is the name for two villas in the royal park at Versailles, sacked by the mob during the French Revolution. 'Hessian' pertains to Hesse, grand duchy of south-west Germany, split by a narrow strip of Prussian territory. (See note to p. 36 on Prussia.) Nirvana is the state of release from suffering sought by Indian religions including Buddhism and Hinduism, involving the transcendence of self and desire.

Taunus Wald: the forests of the Taunus mountain region.

14 *Swedish exercises*: system of therapeutic muscular exercises.

county family: a provincial family belonging to the gentry with an ancestral estate in a county.

15 *in saeculum saeculorum*: more commonly *in saeculo saeculorum* or *in saeculo saeculi*; Latin expression from the Vulgate common in the liturgy; literally 'the age of the ages'; usually translated as 'for ever and ever'.

16 *smoking-room . . . stories*: Ford asked around 1930: 'what has become of the piquant—the smoking room—story that could *just* be told over the dinner table': untitled essay, published as 'This Extraordinary Riot of Obscenities', in Sara Haslam and Seamus O'Malley (eds.), *Ford Madox Ford and America* (Amsterdam and New York: Rodopi, 2012), 203–14.

the Field: magazine founded in 1853, as its current website explains, 'for those who loved shooting, fishing, hunting and could sniff out a decent claret at 1,000 paces'.

neighing after his neighbour's womenkind: cf. Jeremiah 5: 8: 'They were *as* fed horses in the morning: every one neighed after his neighbour's wife.'

18 *Provence*: Ford's father, Francis Hueffer, was an authority on the literature and history of Provence. Ford lived in Provence for some of the late 1920s and much of the 1930s, in or near the port of Toulon.

Peire Vidal: (*c*.1180?–*c*.1205), Provençal troubadour. Francis Hueffer discusses him at length in his scholarly survey *The Troubadours: A History of Provençal Life and Literature in the Middle Ages* (London: Chatto and Windus, 1878), as does Ford in his more personal book *Provence* (1935).

Biarritz . . . Las Tours . . . Black Mountains: Biarritz: fashionable French seaside resort on the Bay of Biscay. Las Tours is just north of Carcassonne. Black Mountains: Montagne Noire, in south-western France.

mistral: strong regional wind in the south of France; the mistral can occur throughout the year, but especially in the winter or spring; it blows from the north or north-west, and is generally cold but dry. It can cause storms in the Mediterranean, as at the start of Ford's 1933 novel *The Rash Act*.

Poughkeepsie: the exclusive women's college of Vassar is in Poughkeepsie, New York.

William the Silent . . . Gustave the Loquacious . . . Fantin Latour: William the Silent (1533–84), Prince of Orange, led the revolt of the Netherlands against Spain. 'Gustave the Loquacious' probably refers to Gustavus I

Vasa (1496–1560), king of Sweden (1523–60), founder of the modern Swedish state, a prolific letter-writer and a theatrical orator; though the nickname seems to be Ford's joke. Henri Fantin Latour (1836–1904) was a French painter, printmaker, and illustrator, best known for his delicate flower compositions.

19 *Tarascon . . . Beaucaire*: picturesque pair of medieval towns on either bank of the river near the mouth of the Rhône.

Flatiron: early New York skyscraper (1902) on Fifth Avenue and Broadway, so called because of its triangular shape.

Heidelberg . . . Hamelin . . . Verona . . . Mont Majour: famous picturesque medieval towns. Heidelberg: seat of an ancient university in south-west Germany; Hamelin: another German town, on the river Weser in Lower Saxony, known for the 'Pied Piper' legend. Verona, in north-east Italy, is the setting for Shakespeare's *Romeo and Juliet*. Montmajour, near Tarascon and Beaucaire, is best known for its medieval abbey.

Carcassonne: medieval hilltop fortress town, extensively restored in the nineteenth century. See Paul Skinner, ' "Speak up, Fordie!": How Some People Want to Go to Carcassonne', in Sara Haslam (ed.), *Ford Madox Ford and the City* (Amsterdam and New York: Rodopi, 2005), 197–210.

crowstepped gables . . . palazzi: gables with stepped rather than sloping edges. Palazzi are Italian mansions, palaces.

Leghorn: Italian town of Livorno on the Tuscan coast.

modistes: milliners or dressmakers.

plages: beaches.

20 *Browning tea*: social event held to discuss the life and works of the popular English poet Robert Browning (1812–89).

Fourteenth Street: major New York thoroughfare in lower Manhattan.

spelling bee: a spelling contest.

Stuyvesant crowd: Dowell later says he first met Florence 'at the Stuyvesants' (p. 65); so this might be their social 'set' or possibly people who live near Stuyvesant Square in Manhattan; named after Peter Stuyvesant (1592–1672), the last Dutch governor of New York.

a Frantz Hals and a Woovermans: Franz Hals (1580?–1666), Dutch portrait and genre painter. Philips Wooverman (1619–68), pupil of Hals who became a successful Dutch landscape painter.

Pre-Mycenaic: pertaining to Greek civilization of the Middle Bronze Age (about 2000–1550 BC). The ancient Greek town of Mycenae had been excavated by Heinrich Schliemann from 1876.

Gnossos: or Knossos, city in ancient Crete excavated by Sir Arthur Evans between 1900 and 1908; legendary site of the palace and labyrinth of King Minos.

Walter Pater: (1839–94), English essayist, critic, aesthetician, and leading advocate of impressionism.

"things": see Introduction, pp. xxiv-xxv.

chatelaine Blanche Somebody-or-other: a chatelaine is the mistress of a château. This love of Vidal's, as Ford's father relates in his book *The Troubadours*, pp. 176–7, was Loba de Peinautier, of Carcassonne. Her name, which translates as La Louve in French, or 'she-wolf', inspired Vidal to call himself a wolf, and even wear a wolfskin and get the shepherds to hunt him.

Troubadour: one of the poet-singers of southern France who composed intricate romantic lyrics in the Old Occitan or Provençal language between the eleventh and fourteenth centuries.

21 *Holy Sepulchre*: the Church of the Holy Sepulchre in Jerusalem, said to be built on the site of Christ's crucifixion, burial, and resurrection.

Misses Hurlbird: in *Return to Yesterday*, p. 270, Ford tells how he met 'two adorably old-maidish maiden ladies from Stamford, Conn.' named Hurlbird in November 1904 in the Marienberg Kaltwasser Heilanstalt at Boppard, the last of several sanatoria visited for treatment after his breakdown that summer. The chapter of *Return to Yesterday*, 'Some Cures', pp. 266–87, gives a striking account of this fraught period which gave Ford much of the material for the rendering of German spa life in *The Good Soldier*. In 1906 Ford and Elsie Hueffer visited the Hurlbirds in their American home. He described the Hurlbird sisters in greater detail in 'The Passing of Toryism', *McNaught's Monthly*, 5:6 (June 1926), 174–6. The name may have been recalled by that of Charles Hurlburt, director of the Africa Inland Mission. Theodore Roosevelt persuaded the Belgian king to allow AIM to work in the Congo. Roosevelt visited Hurlburt in his mission station in Kenya on 4 August 1909.

Waterbury: industrial town in the state of Connecticut famous for the manufacture of clocks and watches.

liveries: uniforms worn by a person's servants.

Democrat . . . Republican: members of the two main US political parties, the former associated with social reform and the latter with business and financial interests. Abraham Lincoln had been a Republican: after the Civil War, white Southerners were generally Democrats and Republicans were more likely to be Northerners and opposed to slavery. The Democrats elected only one president (Grover Cleveland) between 1860 and the election of Woodrow Wilson in 1912, the year before Ford began the novel.

22 *North Cape*: there are several North Capes, but the Hurlbirds' route from California to the South Seas makes the most probable the northern tip of New Zealand's North Island.

23 *Branshaw Teleragh*: as discussed in the Note on the Text, the manuscript originally read 'Bramshaw'. Bramshaw is a small village in the New Forest, close to the village of Brockenhurst where Ford stayed during his 1904 breakdown. He may well have known Bramshaw, and even had Bramshaw

House in mind when thinking of the Ashburnhams' seat (which Dowell calls 'Branshaw House' when he first names it on p. 26; though his other five references are to 'Branshaw Manor'). However, Ford appears to have invented the unusual 'Teleragh' part of the name; and has Dowell place Branshaw in another town, Fordingbridge, about 10 miles away from Bramshaw.

23 *New Forest*: large woodland area in Hampshire, established as a royal forest by William the Conqueror; now parkland, and famous for its wild ponies.

24 *nakedness . . . open space*: Ford had suffered a severe agoraphobic break-down in 1904, and was unable to cross open spaces without holding on to someone.

Englischer Hof . . . châlets . . . hot rooms . . . douche . . . Hotel Regina: Stannard identifies the Englischer Hof ('English hotel') as probably the Hotel Angleterre, which was subsequently renamed the Deutsches Hof. Dowell's uncertainty about the châlets reflects the fact that the old half-timbered facilities were replaced with the Sprudelhof (fountain court) between 1905 and 1912—one of the major works of German *art nouveau* or *Jugendstil*. As the Dowells have returned to Nauheim annually since 1904, they would, like Ford, have known both. The hot rooms were Turkish baths or steam rooms. A douche is a shower. The Hotel Regina is a real Nauheim hotel on the same street as the Englischer Hof.

lefthanded this time: as the previous direction is also 'lefthanded', one is likely to be an error; but there is no textual evidence to warrant emendation.

25 *Leghorn hat*: straw hat.

Chapeau de Paille of Rubens: *The Straw Hat*, by Flemish painter Peter Paul Rubens (1577–1640). A portrait of the artist's sister-in-law, Susanna Fourment, now in the National Gallery, London.

Hotel Excelsior: another actual Nauheim hotel, close by the Regina and Englischer Hof.

26 *Fourteenth Hussars*: light cavalry regiment.

27 *Martingales, Chiffney bits*: martingales are straps for restraining or steady-ing the upward movement of horses' heads. The jockey Samuel Chiffney (1753?–1807) invented a horse's bit.

plater . . . Khyber: a 'plater' is a horse that usually runs in 'selling' races, after which the winner is auctioned. The Khyber Pass linked India (and now Pakistan) to Afghanistan.

Burlington Arcade: Regency period covered passageway off London's Piccadilly; famous for its small shops; a prototype of the larger glazed shopping arcades of the nineteenth century.

Caledonian Deferred: Scottish railway stock which doesn't pay dividends until a prescribed time.

Gadarene swine: see Matthew 8: 28–32, Mark 5: 1–13, and Luke 8: 26–33. When Jesus visits the Gadarenes, he casts devils out from a madman (two in Matthew's version), and they enter a herd of pigs who immediately drown themselves.

28 *that fatal Brindisi*: it is from Brindisi that Nancy sends the telegram that seals Edward's fate in Part IV. P&O Steamers went from Brindisi, in Puglia, Italy, to Bombay, via the Suez Canal and Aden. See Jules Verne, *Around the World in Eighty Days* (1873), chapter 6.

Assizes: sessions of the High Court of Justice, held periodically in English counties.

29 *Wiesbaden*: elegant German town and spa in the Prussian province of Hesse-Nassau; near Mainz and the river Rhine.

Bonner Hussaren: hussars (light cavalry regiment) of Bonn, in Germany.

Lelöffel: in her memoir describing her life with Ford, *The Flurried Years* (London: Hurst and Blackett, 1926), Violet Hunt mentions their knowing a polo-playing German lieutenant she calls Count Lelöffel in Nauheim in 1910. However, as many of her characters appear under pseudonyms she may have been using the name from Ford's novel—especially as she describes him as a 'card'.

31 *plastron*: a man's starched shirt front—the name taken from breastplate armour.

corsage: the bodice (upper part) of a woman's dress.

tailor-made: a woman's garment such as a suit, made by a tailor rather than a dressmaker, and characterized by simple, straight lines.

32 *round table*: an allusion to the legendary King Arthur's Knights of the Round Table; the archetypal heroes of medieval chivalric romance, as retold in the fifteenth century by Thomas Malory in *Le Morte d'Arthur*. In *Rossetti* (1902), Ford quotes the painter's comment on the breaking-up of the Pre-Raphaelite Brotherhood: 'So now the whole Round Table is dissolved', slightly misquoting line 234 of Alfred Tennyson's poem 'Morte d'Arthur' (published in 1842).

Avanti!: forward! (Italian).

33 *Fachingen water*: a German mineral spring water, effective against excess stomach acid.

Grand Duke: according to Hunt's *The Flurried Years*, p. 134, she and Ford met the Grand Duke of Hesse-Darmstadt, who 'expected to be asked out to dinner' every night. Though 'Nassau Schwerin' appears not to exist as a title or a place, the town of Nassau on the river Lahn (about 15 miles north-east of Boppard on the Rhine, where Ford stayed in 1904) faces the town of Scheuern across the river, and there is a Bergnassau-schauern nearby.

34 *bonne bouche*: delicacy or special treat.

34 *traps*: luggage.

   a lire: Stannard, p. 31, corrects Dowell's Italian to 'a lira'; the manuscript
   and first edition reading is retained here as we cannot be sure the mistake
   is Ford's.

   Kummel: kümmel is a sweet, cumin-flavoured German liqueur.

35 *Æsculapius*: Greek god of medicine. In Plato's *Phaedo*, Socrates' last words
   are to tell Crito they owe a cock to Æsculapius. This would normally have
   been a sacrifice to the god for a cure; having just drunk poison Socrates is
   ironically suggesting that the only cure for life is death.

   archæological exceptions: this reading is in all the witnesses; Stannard suggests it might have been a scribal mishearing for 'excavations'; 'expeditions'
   has also been suggested. But Ford/Dowell may have meant unusual
   finds.

   Baedeker: famous series of nineteenth-century German guidebooks; first
   English edition in 1861.

36 *M——*: This is clearly Marburg, ancient German university town in the
   Prussian province of Hesse-Nassau. Marburg was the site of a crucial
   theological conference in 1529 between Luther and Zwingli on the subject of Transubstantiation. Ford's decision to have Dowell identify it only
   by its initial appears to be part of the novel's metafictional play, transpos-
   ing an actual historical site into what looks like a fictional location.

   St. Elizabeth of Hungary: (1207–31), princess who built a hospice for the
   poor in Marburg. As Martin Stannard points out, the present castle was
   not built in her time.

   Prussia: at the unification of Germany under Bismarck in 1871, and the
   proclamation of the German Empire that year, Prussia included nearly
   two-thirds of its land and people, so became the dominant element. Its
   territory covered most of the north of today's Germany, and also reached
   as far east as Russia, including part of Poland. Ford, especially in the two
   propaganda books he wrote during the war, contrasted the predominantly
   northern and Protestant Prussia with the southern and more Catholic
   Germany he knew from his visits of 1904 and 1910–11. Disparagement of
   Prussia for the militarism, conservatism, academicism, and professional-
   ism of its 'Junker' class of aristocratic landowners was common in Britain,
   especially as the German empire was perceived as increasingly threatening to the British Empire in the years before the First World War.

   Lahn: a tributary of the Rhine.

   pour le bon motif: with the best of intentions (French).

   Ludwig the Courageous: Dowell means Philip the Magnanimous, Landgrave
   of Hesse (1504–67). (As he says later: 'I may have got some of the names
   wrong', p. 40.) A zealous protector of German Protestants, Philip insti-
   gated the Marburg Conference of 1529. Later he persuaded Luther to
   allow him to enter a bigamous marriage. Philip had a son and a grandson
   named Ludwig.

37 *muffs*: people useless at sports; specifically, who drop a catch in a ball-game.

one of the dark places of the earth: echoes Conrad's 'Heart of Darkness': ' "And this also," said Marlow suddenly, "has been one of the dark places of the earth".' *Heart of Darkness and Other Tales*, ed. Cedric Watts (Oxford: Oxford University Press, 2002), 105.

Armenians . . . Erastians: 'Armenians' is Dowell's mistake for 'Arminians'; followers of a seventeenth-century progressive theological movement based on the ideas of Dutch theologian Jacobus Arminius (1560–1609), seen as a rival version of Calvinism. Ford's later references to Arminianism in *Some Do Not . . .* show the mistake is very unlikely to have been his, so should not be emended. Erastians: the Swiss theologian Thomas Erastus (1524–83) argued that Christian sinners should be punished by the state rather than the Church; 'Erastian' has also come to designate those supporting state supremacy in Church affairs.

Mrs. Markham: pseudonym of Elizabeth Penrose (1780–1837), English author of history books for children. She is best known for *A History of England from the First Invasion by the Romans to the End of the Reign of George III* (1823).

Schloss: castle (German).

History of the Popes . . . Table Talk: Leopold von Ranke (1795–1886) is considered a founding figure of modern empirical or source-based historiography. His multi-volume *History of the Popes* (1834–6) introduced the term 'Counter-Reformation'. John Addington Symonds (1840–93) was a poet, critic, and biographer best known for his seven-volume study of the *Renaissance in Italy* (1875–86). *Rise of the Dutch Republic* (1856): a classic three-volume work by the American historian John Lothrop Motley (1814–77); it celebrates the triumph of Dutch independence and Protestantism over Catholic despotism. *Table Talk*: Luther's sayings, compiled by Johannes Mathesius and published in 1566.

38 *purple in the shadows*: this might sound like an allusion to Monet's famous series of paintings of haystacks with purple or indigo shadows; but as Ford explained, his grandfather Madox Brown had anticipated this technique: 'It was Madox Brown who first painted bright purple haycocks—yes, bright purple ones—upon a bright green field. But he painted them like that because he happened to notice that when sunlight is rather red and the sky very blue, the shadowy side of green-grey hay is all purple. He noticed it, and he rendered it' (*Ancient Lights*, p. 213). See Angela Thirlwell, 'From Paint to Print—Grandfather's Legacy', in Laura Colombino (ed.), *Ford Madox Ford and Visual Culture* (Amsterdam and New York: Rodopi, 2009), 293–8; and note to p. 212 below.

stomachers: ornamental chest coverings worn by women under the lacing of the bodice.

meadow-sweet: a white-flowered plant.

38 *Hessen*: Hesse.

student corps: university student society.

39 *droschka*: low four-wheeled open carriage for hire.

Pennsylvania Duitsch: more commonly 'Pennsylvania Dutch', but referring to people living mostly in south-eastern Pennsylvania whose seventeenth- and eighteenth-century ancestors came from Germany or Switzerland.

trinkgeld: tip, gratuity (from German: 'drink-money').

firebacks: decorated iron sheet for the back wall of open fireplaces.

Rittersaal: stateroom, from the German 'knight's hall'.

the Reformer: Martin Luther (1483–1546), German priest, professor of theology, and leading figure of the Reformation. His doctrine of salvation by faith rather than works challenged the papacy, and led to his excommunication and the rise of Protestantism.

presses: cupboards.

I believe . . . wrong: it is Dowell who is wrong: according to Stannard, p. 36, Luther stayed in the Schloss for three nights as a guest of Philip the Magnanimous.

the Protest: the document at Marburg, which Ford and Hunt saw in 1910, was not the 'Protest'—the formal declaration of dissent from the Diet of Spires, which had excommunicated Luther. It was a statement of fifteen doctrinal points, known as 'the protocol' or the 'Articles of Marburg', drawn up at the conference, also known as the 'Marburg Colloquy', in the castle in 1529. Rather than being the pencil draft Dowell describes, it is a large document in ink, indeed signed by Luther, Bucer, and Zwingli, but not of course 'Ludwig the Courageous'.

40 *Bucer . . . Zwingli*: Martin Bucer (1491–1551), German Protestant reformer based in Strasbourg who mediated the doctrinal disagreements between Luther and Huldrych Zwingli (1484–1531), an important Swiss religious reformer. It was the last of the fifteen points, concerning the interpretation of the Eucharist, that caused greatest disagreement between the two men: whether the bread and wine were to be understood as literally or metaphorically the body and blood of Christ.

42 *"By hammer . . . stand"*: a favourite quotation of Ford's, used for example in *The Rash Act*.

"thank'ee-marms": potholes or bumps in the road that give travellers a rough ride.

43 *Free City*: cities that had the status of sovereign states; as for example Bremen, Hamburg, and Lübeck after the unification of Germany.

Spa: town in north-east Belgium known for its mineral springs, said to be the oldest in Europe.

44 *Kursaal*: the main building provided for the use of visitors at a German health resort.

Burma: the British conquered Burma between 1824 and 1886, after which it was run as a province of British India until it became a self-governing colony in 1937.

45 *Chitral*: the name of both a princely state and its capital town, and the site of a British outpost, in the extreme north-west of colonial India (in today's Pakistan), near the border with Afghanistan.

access: sudden attack.

47 *my small household cockle-shell*: Dowell is perhaps thinking of Sir Walter Raleigh's poem 'His Pilgrimage', beginning 'Give me my scallop-shell of quiet'.

Maisie Maidan: Ford's naming of Maisie Maidan is richly suggestive. Maidan is a word used in India for a public square or park where games are played; but the pun on 'maiden' emphasizes her innocence; which strengthens the allusion to one of Ford's favourite novels of Henry James, *What Maisie Knew* (1897), with its adolescent central consciousness negotiating the world of adult sexual intrigue and scandal.

Linlithgowshire: county in south-east Scotland; now West Lothian.

48 *pipped*: annoyed; hurt.

five hundred thousand dollars: about £100,000 then, but it would make the Ashburnhams millionaires in today's equivalent—about £10,000,000 or $16,000,000 in 2011.

forty thousand pounds: about $200,000 in 1895; nowadays equivalent to £4,000,000 or $6,400,000 in 2011. Even if Ford had been thinking of what these sums meant in 1913, the equivalents today would be much the same.

Circe . . . Antibes: Circe is a sorceress in Greek mythology who turned Odysseus' companions into animals. Antibes is a smart French resort between Nice and Cannes on the Côte d'Azur.

General Trochu: (1815–96) was appointed governor of Paris and President of the Government of National Defence, effectively the French head of state during the Franco-Prussian War, but resigned when the Prussian army took the city in 1871 after the Siege of Paris.

51 *Scarlet Woman*: i.e. the Roman Catholic Church, as denounced by Protestants, alluding to Revelation 17: 1–18.

Friends' Meeting House in Arch Street: Quaker meeting house in Philadelphia; the largest in the world, and the oldest still in use.

Nonconformist: member of a Protestant sect dissenting from the Anglican Church.

52 *Tory caucus, or whatever it is*: local political party association managing election campaigns.

degraded: lowered in rank.

little stations in Chitral and Burma: not railway stations, but places where the colonial officials or military officers lived; often purpose-built Victorian towns in the hills to avoid the heat.

53 *rook*: swindle.

54 *ballyragged*: intimidated, harassed.

56 *pellitory*: low bushy plant, growing upon or at the foot of walls. See Ford's fine 1936 poem 'Coda'.

57 *the girl*: it is usually Nancy whom Dowell refers to as 'the girl'; perhaps he means Maisie Maidan here, or he intends to wrong-foot us by implying that Nancy dies.

58 *"Requiem . . . aeternam erit"*: from the Mass for the Dead. But Dowell wrongly inserts 'per', and omits the last word, 'justus'. The complete translation is: 'Eternal rest give to them, O Lord; and let perpetual light shine upon them. The just shall be in everlasting remembrance.'

    some picture . . . somewhere: Ford or Dowell may be thinking of *The Plains of Heaven* (1851–3) by the popular painter of dramatic biblical scenes, John Martin (1789–1854); one of a trio of paintings of the Apocalypse now at Tate Britain, the others being *The Last Judgement* and *The Great Day of His Wrath*.

59 *northern light*: *aurora borealis*, a luminous atmospheric phenomenon best seen in Arctic regions.

    district visiting: a district visitor was a female worker in the Church of England who gave voluntary assistance to the rector, such as visiting the poor and the sick; with a pejorative sense of officious interference.

61 *Reiseverkehrsbureau*: tourist office.

    Schreibzimmer, the winter garden: writing room (German); that Dowell calls the winter garden a public room suggests a glass-house to protect plants through the winter, rather than an outdoor garden of winter-hardy plants.

66 *Rialto*: covered sixteenth-century bridge across the Grand Canal in Venice.

    Strathpeffer: Scottish Highland village and former spa whose sulphurous springs attracted sufferers from anaemia, rheumatism, etc.

    Ledbury: market town in Herefordshire, England.

67 *1688*: the year of the 'Glorious Revolution' which ousted Catholic James II in favour of William and Mary of Orange. This suggests that Florence's ancestor who owned Branshaw may have been Catholic.

    General Braddock to General Washington: Edward Braddock (1695–1755), British commander in North America in the early stages of the French and Indian War (1755–63), who was killed in a massacre while trying to attack Fort Duquesne. George Washington (1732–99) served with Braddock, and survived to become the first president of the United States.

68 *"Pocahontas"*: named after the Native American princess (1595–1617), who married an Englishman and died on a visit to England. Ford and his wife returned to England from New York in 1906 aboard the *Minnetonka*, named after the home of princess Minnehaha, the fictional Native

American lover of the protagonist of Henry Wadsworth Longfellow's *The Song of Hiawatha*.

tracked out: found out by following her trail.

Rye Station: reference to Rye, a residential suburb of New York City, with both trolley-cars and commuter trains.

71 *Sandy Hook*: a barrier spit off the New Jersey coast enclosing the southern part of the entrance to Lower New York Bay; a landmark passed by passengers bound to or from New York City.

72 *Julien's*: the Académie Julian was a famous private art school established at the Passage des Panoramas, off the Boulevard Montmartre, in Paris in 1868, and popular with Americans.

cinque cento: sixteenth century (Italian).

73 *as fresh as Venus . . . legends*: Venus, the Roman goddess of love, beauty, and sexuality, had lovers including the god Mars, Aeneas' father Anchises, and Adonis.

74 *Hoboken*: city in north-eastern New Jersey on the Hudson river, opposite Manhattan, and forming part of the Port of New York and New Jersey.

75 *"a pure woman"*: Thomas Hardy used the phrase as the subtitle for his novel *Tess of the D'Urbervilles* (1891).

76 *scullion*: cook's servant; dishwasher.

77 *D. S. O.*: Distinguished Service Order, awarded to officers for meritorious service in war, typically but not necessarily in combat.

the Royal Humane Society: a charity that grants awards for acts of bravery in the saving or resuscitation of human lives.

V.C.: Victoria Cross, the highest military honour awarded for valour 'in the face of the enemy' to members of the British armed forces of any rank.

Beefeaters: the Yeomen of the Guard, rather than the better-known Warders of the Tower of London.

Lohengrin: hero of German Arthurian legend, the son of Parsifal, and a knight of the Round Table, he is sent to rescue a maiden in distress, makes her promise never to ask about his identity, and then leaves her when she breaks the promise. Lohengrin is the subject of the opera first performed in 1850 by Richard Wagner (1813–83)—the composer especially championed by Ford's father.

Chevalier Bayard: Pierre Terrail LeVieux, seigneur de Bayard (1473–1524), was a French soldier generally known as the Chevalier de Bayard, and considered the epitome of chivalry: *le chevalier sans peur et sans reproche*—'the knight without fear and beyond reproach'. His contemporaries called him 'le bon chevalier', or 'the good knight'.

78 *the Cid*: the Castilian nobleman Rodrigo Diaz de Bivar (1043–99) became a Spanish national hero. Exiled by the Emperor Alfonso VI, he fought first for the Moors, but then against them after Alfonso recalled him. He became known as *El Cid Campeador*—'the master of military arts'.

79 *got hold of a Tartar . . . sucking kid*: he had got someone more violent-tempered than he had bargained for; compared to whom, Leonora was as soft as a baby goat.

80 *put him at it*: made him do it (a riding term, for making a horse take a jump).

86 *au mieux*: on the best of terms, i.e. intimate.

87 *Nitrate of amyl . . . angina pectoris*: amyl nitrate is a reagent used, for example, as an additive in diesel fuel, where it enhances ignition. It is amyl nitrite, a powerful vasodilator, which is used medically to treat heart diseases such as angina and also as an antidote to cyanide poisoning. Angina pectoris, commonly known as angina, is severe chest pain; sometimes a prelude to a heart attack. Myocardial infarction (heart attack) only became a separate diagnosis from angina around 1912. I'm grateful to David Stone for cardiological advice.

prussic acid: hydrocyanic acid; an extremely poisonous volatile liquid; the solution in water of hydrogen cyanide. Ford's father-in-law, the pharmacologist William Martindale, had committed suicide in 1902 by poisoning himself with prussic acid.

88 *"Zum Befehl, Durchlaucht"*: 'very good, Serene Highness.'

89 *Casino*: Stannard, p. 76, says the Nauheim Kurhaus Casino closed in 1872, but that the mirrored room was possibly still known by this name.

if it's the business of a novelist . . . clearly: one of Ford's many echoes of Conrad's Preface to *The Nigger of the 'Narcissus'*: 'My task which I am trying to achieve is, by the power of the written word, to make you hear, to make you feel—it is, before all, to make you *see*.' See pp. xiii–xiv.

Rakocsy march: the 'Rákóczi March' has the status of Hungary's unofficial national anthem. It probably originated in the eighteenth century, and its composer is unknown. The Romani violinist János Bihari used to perform it in the early nineteenth century. The most famous version is the Hungarian Rhapsody No. 15 for piano by Franz Liszt (1811–86); but Dowell is more likely to mean the orchestral version Hector Berlioz (1803–69) included in his opera *The Damnation of Faust* (1846).

91 *impeccable*: incapable of sinning.

94 *bolt*: to run off suddenly; often used of animals such as foxes or horses. A 'bolter' was a slang term for a woman running away to elope or leave her husband.

all for love . . . lost: *All for Love; or, the World Well Lost* is John Dryden's imitation of Shakespeare's *Antony and Cleopatra*.

95 *the last time I shall mention Florence's name*: it is not, of course.

Bowery: the Bowery is both a street and a neighbourhood in the southern part of Manhattan. At the turn of the century it was known for prostitution and alcohol. Ford's friend Stephen Crane set some of his fiction there, such as *Maggie: A Girl of the Streets* (1893).

96 *affaissement*: nervous collapse; depression.

99 *Mænad*: female followers of the Greek god Dionysus. In Euripides' play *The Bacchae* (405 BC) they tear King Pentheus limb from limb in an orgiastic frenzy.

100 *Corpus Christi*: ('the body of Christ': Latin). Roman Catholic moveable feast celebrating the Eucharist, and falling between late May and late June.

Roehampton: the Convent of the Sacred Heart School was established on French lines in Roehampton in 1850. Ford had moved his daughters Christina and Katharine from a convent school in Rye to the Sacred Heart School in Hammersmith in 1906. See Introduction, p. xxix, on a passage deleted from the manuscript in which Edward sends his illegitimate daughters to 'the convent at Roehampton'.

saturnalia: scene of wild revelry: in *Provence*, pp. 42, 44, Ford says the girls of the convent schools in Tarascon were permitted, 'even encouraged, to perform every kind of excess from dancing on the desks to smashing inexpensive articles of furniture. A regular pandemonium will at times ensue. But, at the ringing of the Mother Superior's bell, suddenly absolute silence and order must at once obtain. That is supposed to be good discipline.'

101 *Fort William*: town in Inverness-shire in western Scotland, with strong Catholic associations.

Perhaps she was . . . what became of Mrs. Rufford: another point where Dowell's narrative intentionally misleads us. See pp. 161–2.

Forest: the New Forest.

104 *orison*: prayer.

105 *jalousies*: blinds or shutters with adjustable horizontal slats.

guy: someone of grotesque appearance or dress: resembling one of the effigies of Guy Fawkes traditionally burnt (to commemorate the foiling of the Catholic 1605 'Gunpowder Plot') on 5 November.

106 *old Mother Sideacher*: this might just be the unfortunate name of the 'old beggar woman who always amused them at Branshaw' (p. 106); or might be their nickname for her, perhaps from a game involving Old Mother Witch. (Witches may be like elves, who traditionally shoot arrows into people's sides causing stitches.) 'Side-acher' is also uncommon slang for something so funny you laugh till it hurts; so they may have called her that because she amused them.

107 *chaise*: light open one-horse carriage.

espaliers: fruit trees or plants trained to grow flat against a wall or framework.

fives: a school game (associated especially with the public schools of Eton and Rugby) in which a ball is struck with a bare or gloved hand against the wall of an enclosed court.

109 *Sandhurst*: the Royal Military College (now Academy) on the borders of
     Berkshire and Surrey, where cadets train before receiving commissions as
     officers in the British Army.

     Scott's novels . . . Froissart: Sir Walter Scott (1771–1832), the foremost
     writer of historical romances such as *Ivanhoe* (1819). Jean Froissart
     (*c*.1337–*c*.1405), historian whose French *Chronicles* are the classic history
     of western Europe from 1325 to 1400, covering the first part of the
     Hundred Years War. They are seen as a key document of the chivalric
     revival of the fourteenth century.

     Lord's: Lord's cricket ground in St John's Wood, London, is owned by the
     Marylebone Cricket Club (MCC), and known as 'the home of cricket'.

     crammer: tutor or school concentrating on preparing pupils for examin-
     ations. The reference on p. 119 to 'the crammings that he received at the
     hands of army coaches' suggests he needs extra help either to get into
     Sandhurst, or to pass the exams there. Either way, there's a suggestion of
     irony about the 'good soldier'.

111 *largesses*: extravagant generosities.

112 *Aldershot*: garrison town in Hampshire.

115 *a very simple soul*: in Flaubert's story, 'A Simple Heart', from his *Three
     Tales* (1877), Félicité like Edward has a succession of passionate attach-
     ments to love objects (though in her case unrequited) which leads to her
     death.

116 *Romanist*: Roman Catholic (as described by someone who is not).

121 *big bank failure in 1907*: financial crisis of October 1907, known as 'The
     Panic of 1907' or 'The 1907 Banker's Panic', during which the New York
     Stock Exchange fell by almost 50 per cent of its peak the previous year.

     Vermont Democrat: Vermont had a progressive Jeffersonian history—its
     1777 constitution was the first to provide for the abolition of slavery. But
     its Democrats started voting against Andrew Jackson during his presi-
     dency (1829–37), and turned towards the Republicans. So Dowell's family
     seem rather behind the times; 'the whole ticket' refers to the election of all
     the candidates nominated by a single party in a state election; hence the
     expression here implies that for Dowell's people you cannot be more
     Democrat than a Vermont Democrat.

122 *he says that it came suddenly into his head*: the switch into the present tense
     here is strange. It might be an error of Ford's (according to Stannard, pp.
     208–9, Ford was typing a section to replace part of H.D.'s dictation at this
     point); but—especially given that the effect is repeated on p. 123 ('At that
     time, he says')—it might be intended to signal Dowell's difficulty in
     accepting Edward's death.

123 *Dreyfus*: Alfred Dreyfus (1859–1935), Franco-Jewish army officer wrongly
     accused and convicted of treason in 1894 in the most famous trial in mod-
     ern French history. He was sentenced to deportation for life to Devil's
     Island, but was released in 1906.

125 *give her the keys of the street*: throw her out.

"*Enfin, mon ami*": 'Well, my friend' (French).

126 *Town*: London.

127 *Eau de Melisse*: medicinal cordial of herbs (including Melissa) in alcohol, dating from the time of Louis XIV.

128 *fireships*: ships freighted with combustibles and explosives, and sent among the enemy's ships to set them alight.

menus plaisirs: little luxuries.

129 *Hendon on my jointure*: Hendon is a north-west London suburb notable for a number of Roman Catholic institutions. A jointure is property settled on a wife.

"*blued*": squandered.

130 *Vandykes*: Anthony van Dyck (1599–1641) was a Flemish artist in the Baroque manner who came to Britain and became the dominant court painter to Charles I; famous for his portraits of the Royal Family and other aristocrats.

silver: the Ashburnham family silver was sold in March 1914—while Ford was writing the novel—the sale being widely reported; the centrepiece was bought by an American collector but later acquired by the Victoria and Albert Museum.

the front: the North-Western frontier; where Edward is described as being 'sniped at up in the hills' (p. 132).

Simla: (now 'Shimla'), town in Punjab, India; located high in the north-west Himalayas, it became the summer capital and social centre of the British Raj.

132 *brevet-colonel*: a brevet is a military document conferring a higher rank on an officer without extra pay.

South African War: the second of the two Boer Wars, though more commonly known now as the Boer War, 1899–1902, between Great Britain and the two Boer Republics of the Transvaal and the Orange Free State. Early British victories in open warfare gave way to a prolonged and bitter guerrilla campaign which inflicted heavy losses on the British.

Edward ought . . . Transvaal: despite the blasé words Dowell attributes to Edward (on p. 132) about it being 'just as good for him' to be shot at on the North-Western Frontier as in Africa, there is perhaps a suggestion that he is staying in India as the less dangerous option, whether at Leonora's instigation or his own; a suggestion which casts further ironic light on the idea of him as a 'good soldier'.

veldt: South African open pasture-land.

North Western Frontier: province of British India on the Afghanistan border; now a province in Pakistan.

spruit: small stream or watercourse in South Africa, usually dry outside the wet season.

133 *Chitral*: see note to p. 45.

134 *pipped*: exhausted (cf. p. 48).

  punkah: an Anglo-Indian term for a large fan, probably hanging from the ceiling and requiring an Indian servant (a punkah-wallah) to operate it by pulling a cord.

  cane-lounge: a reclining chair or chaise-longue made of cane.

  ex's: expenses.

136 *pest-house*: hospital for patients suffering from infectious diseases.

  sent in his papers: resigned his Army commission.

  bouillon: soup, broth.

138 *maundering*: doting.

144 *lâcher prise*: let go. Stannard corrects silently to '*lâcher prise*', but Dowell's French is not emended for this edition on the grounds of the impossibility of deciding whether the error is his or Ford's.

145 *ad majorem Dei gloriam*: 'for the greater glory of God': the Latin motto of the Society of Jesus, whose members are known as Jesuits.

  dayspring from on high: 'dayspring' is dawn; ironic echo of Zechariah's prophecy about his son John (the Baptist): 'the dayspring from on high hath visited us': see Luke 1: 76–9.

152 *Waterbury, Ill.*: Waterbury is in fact in Connecticut, as Dowell says on p. 154.

155 *the weather and the crops*: Ford used this expression for the content of talk where the important issues are being suppressed.

  like a split cone of shadow: the image suggests Pre-Raphaelite portraits with striking hair, as for example John Everett Millais' 1851 *The Bridesmaid*, or 1857 *Portrait of a Girl (Sophie Gray)*.

156 *ancient haunts of peace*: in 1901 the Poet Laureate, Alfred Austin (1835–1913), travelled through Britain and wrote about its past in *Haunts of Ancient Peace* (London: A. and C. Black, 1902).

157 *Zoffany and Zucchero*: Johann Zoffany (1733–1810), German painter who came to England in 1860, became known for his theatrical and society portraits (including some of George III and Queen Charlotte), and was a founding member of the Royal Academy. Federico (or Federigo) Zucchero (or Zuccari or Zuccaro) (*c*.1541–1609), Italian Mannerist painter, who came to England in 1574 and painted portraits of Queen Elizabeth I, Mary Queen of Scots, and various courtiers; though some of the attributions have been challenged.

158 *dog-cart*: light one-horse two-wheeled carriage.

159 *stake and binder hedge*: a fence made from brushwood woven between stakes, used as an obstacle for horses to jump over, especially in fox hunting.

161 *bad scent*: trail left by hunted animal that is difficult to follow.

  Colonel Rufford: at the last mention (p. 101) he was Major Rufford; but that was before he went to India, around the time Nancy joins the Ashburnhams, so he has presumably been promoted since then.

166 *Christchurch*: Hampshire coastal town about 20 miles south of Fordingbridge.

167 *Ringwood*: ancient town on the border of the New Forest; about 10 miles south of Fordingbridge.

168 *andirons*: a pair of raised horizontal supports for burning logs in a large fireplace.

169 *Henry VIII . . . Protestantism rests*: it was because Henry VIII wanted to divorce Catherine of Aragon to marry Anne Boleyn that he broke away from the Roman Catholic Church and established the Church of England, with himself at its Head. Compare p. 36, contrasting Henry VIII and 'Ludwig the Courageous' as polygamists.

170 *Princess Badrulbadour*: the beloved of the hero of the *Arabian Nights* 'Story of Aladdin; or, the Wonderful Lamp'.

spinney: small wood, often kept for game-birds.

The only true plant found: from 'To the Willow-Tree', by English clergyman and Cavalier poet Robert Herrick (1591–1674). Ford had composed a setting for the lyric in about 1895: see Sondra J. Stang and Carl Smith, ' "Music for a While": Ford's Compositions for Voice and Piano', *Contemporary Literature*, 30:2 (Summer 1989), 183–223.

171 *National Reserve Committee*: the National Reserve was a register kept by Territorial Force County Associations of men with military experience who were not already in the Army, Special, or Territorial Force Reserves.

172 *Deborah*: as Dowell suspects, he has made a mistake here. Deborah was an Old Testament prophet; a judge and warrior, rather than the handmaiden type; and not a saint.

hagiology: literature about the lives of the saints.

She thought . . . the snow fell: the fallen woman sheltering from the cold under the arches was a familiar composition in Victorian painting. See *Past and Present, No. 3*, 1858 by Augustus Egg (1816–63), Tate Britain; and *Found Drowned*, 1867, by George Frederic Watts (1817–1904), The Watts Gallery, Compton.

Platonic: i.e. abstract and universal, rather than based on any family-feeling for her mother.

173 *Domine, nunc dimittis . . .*: Luke 2: 29. The first words of the Song of Simeon, used in evening prayer.

174 *That rubber at least was made*: a rubber in whist is a set of three games; 'made' by the player who wins the best of three.

177 *uncode*: telegraph messages needed to be encoded (probably into Morse code here) to be transmitted as electrical signals. Normally they would be decoded at the receiving post office.

178 *Crau*: generally arid plain of the river Rhône in the south of France,

between Tarascon and Marseilles. In the 'Protest' scene Dowell comments on the 'immense plain' of the valley of the Lahn, and he uses the phrase again, twice, in describing an image of God's judgement (see p. 58 and note). The suggestion of agoraphobia reflects Ford's 1904 memories of Salisbury Plain during his breakdown.

178 *Credo in unum Deum Omnipotentem*: 'I believe in one God Almighty' (Latin); from the Nicene Creed, though Nancy omits the word 'Patrem' (Father) after Deum.

180 *Kandy*: former capital of Ceylon (now Sri Lanka), island by the south-eastern tip of India.

181 *terrestrial paradise*: this is the subject of one of Ford's best-known poems, 'On Heaven', published in *Poetry* (Chicago) in June 1914, just before *The Good Soldier*. In it, Ford imagines Heaven as a café in Provence where adulterers unhappy in life can be reunited under the blessing of a kind God.

183 *Buda-Pesth*: originally twin cities Buda and Pesth, on either side of the River Danube, Budapest is the capital city of Hungary, and had a louche reputation in the period.

188 *making love to her*: courting, flirting.

poco-curantism: indifference.

189 *coombe*: hollow or valley on the side of a hill.

cap: cap-money is a tip collected for the huntsman (the man in charge of the hounds).

190 *the peace of God which passes all understanding*: Epistle to the Philippians 4: 7.

"Thou hast conquered, O pale Galilean": line 25 of 'Hymn to Proserpine' by Algernon Charles Swinburne (1837–1909), the Pre-Raphaelite poet and friend of Ford's grandfather, Ford Madox Brown. The 'pale Galilean' is Christ.

191 *Tartarus*: in Greek mythology, the deepest part of Hades; the place of punishment for the wicked. As Stannard notes (p. 160), the description of the tortures there in *Aeneid* 6 influenced Dante and Christian concepts of Hell; '*Aeneid* 6 specifically mentions adulterers (612) and those who lust after their daughters (623).'

"Shuttlecocks": the pieces of cork fitted with a crown of feathers and hit across the net in the game of badminton; figuratively, people knocked back and forth by external forces. Another allusion to James's *What Maisie Knew*. In his *Henry James* (1914), p. 160, Ford quotes appreciatively James's use of the term in the Preface to describe his young heroine.

192 *desideratum*: thing to be desired.

how Edward met his death: though Dowell says here he's forgotten to tell us, he has already told us on p. 151: 'I guess that made him cut his throat.'

193 *loose-box*: stall in which a horse can move about freely.

territorials: the Territorial Force of local volunteer reserve troops was formed in 1907–8, at a time of fear of a possible German invasion.

grey, frieze suit: frieze is 'A kind of coarse woollen cloth, with a nap, usually on one side only; now *esp.* of Irish manufacture' (*Oxford English Dictionary*).

'ON IMPRESSIONISM'

197 *But one person . . . resistance*: Ford may have had in mind Ezra Pound in particular, who repeatedly defined his own practice against Fordian impressionism.

Times: Ford's father, Francis Hueffer, was the music correspondent for *The Times*.

198 *W. H. Hudson*: William Henry Hudson (1841–1922) was a naturalist, ornithologist, and author. Born in Argentina, he moved to England in 1874, writing books on British natural history and rural life such as *Afoot in England* (1909) and *A Shepherd's Life* (1910), as well as books about South America such as the novel *Green Mansions: A Romance of the Tropical Forest* (1904). Ford knew him in the years before the First World War, published his essay on Stonehenge in the first number of the *English Review*, and often wrote about him admiringly as an impressionist: see *Thus to Revisit* (London: Chapman and Hall, 1921), 77–8, and *Mightier Than the Sword* (London: Allen and Unwin, 1938), 70–1.

200 *I spent . . . Henry VIII*: Ford told this story in greater detail in *Return to Yesterday* (London: Gollancz, 1931), 170–6. A. F. Pollard's biography, *Henry VIII*, appeared in 1902.

three long novels: the individual volumes of Ford's trilogy *The Fifth Queen* are: *The Fifth Queen: And How She Came to Court* (London: Alston Rivers, 1906); *Privy Seal* (Alston Rivers, 1907); and *The Fifth Queen Crowned* (Eveleigh Nash, 1908).

201 *And that is all that I know about Henry VIII*: compare *The Good Soldier*, p. 27: 'And that was absolutely all that I knew of him until a month ago.'

202 *Tories . . . Leith Boroughs*: the Conservative Party; the parliamentary seat for Leith Boroughs no longer exists; Leith, the port area of Edinburgh, was merged with the city in 1920.

his heart was pure: Tennyson, 'Sir Galahad' (in *Poems*, 1842): 'His strength was as the strength of ten, | Because *his heart was pure*': lines 3–4.

204 *tel que moi . . . Madame Bovary*: 'such as I' (French). In Gustave Flaubert's *Madame Bovary* (1857), Emma meets her lover Rodolphe at an agricultural show in chapter 8. Their romantic talk is interspersed ironically with unromantic speeches about servants, prizes for farm animals, and manure.

205 *"O Muse . . . theme"*: possibly Ford's pastiche of a Miltonic invocation.

205 *"Now, gentle reader . . . lady?"*: probably Ford's pastiche of novelists such as Thackeray. In *The English Novel* (London: Constable, 1930), p. 78, he wrote: 'I imagine that the greatest literary crime ever committed was Thackeray's sudden, apologetic incursion of himself into his matchless account of the manoeuvres of Becky Sharp on Waterloo day in Brussels.'

young man . . . Impressionism: almost certainly Wyndham Lewis. Ford elaborated this important story several times. See for example *Thus to Revisit*, 139–40; *Return to Yesterday*, 417–19; *Mightier Than the Sword*, 282–3; *The March of Literature* (London: Allen and Unwin, 1939), 583.

justify: Ford gives an extensive explanation of what he calls 'the mystic word "justification"' in *Joseph Conrad*, 204–5, as part of the discussion of 'Structure': 'Before everything a story must convey a sense of inevitability: that which happens in it must seem to be the only thing that could have happened. Of course a character may cry, "If I had then acted differently how different everything would now be." The problem of the author is to make his then action the only action that character could have taken. It must be inevitable, because of his character, because of his ancestry, because of past illness or on account of the gradual coming together of the thousand small circumstances by which Destiny, who is inscrutable and august, will push us into one certain predicament.'

207 *Ship Inn at Greenwich*: several of Conrad's fictions begin with a group of men sitting together and someone telling a story; sometimes round a dinner-table, as in 'Youth'. Though he doesn't use the Ship Inn as a setting, it was a famous pub, destroyed in the Second World War; the site is where the *Cutty Sark* now stands.

'Contes de la Bécasse': a collection of short stories by Guy de Maupassant, published in 1883. A preface describes how the stories were told by a group of friends who enjoy hunting (*la bécasse* is the French for woodcock) and who meet regularly over dinner.

vine-leaves . . . door: two allusions to Henrik Ibsen (1828–1906). In *Hedda Gabler* (1890), Hedda idealizes her former lover Lovborg as having (Dionysian) vine-leaves in his hair; in *The Master Builder* (1892), the young Hilda Wangel's destructive entrance into Solness's life is announced by her knocking at the door.

208 *adieu, like Herrick's, to poesy*: 'Mr. Robert Herrick: His Farewell Unto Poetry'. See note to p. 170 on Herrick, whose poem 'To the Willow Tree' is quoted in *The Good Soldier*.

pattern of the carpet: Ford is probably alluding to Henry James's story 'The Figure in the Carpet' (1896).

Wingless Victory . . . Hottentot . . . Tunis: contrasting icons of feminine beauty. The Greek goddess of Victory, Nike, was usually depicted with wings (as in the *Winged Victory of Samothrace*, in the Louvre). The Temple of Athena Nike on the Acropolis in Athens used to house a statue of Athena as goddess of victory, but without wings. Athenians came to describe her as the 'wingless victory'. Hence a classical ideal of feminine form. 'Hottentot' was a name for the Khoisan tribe of hunter-gatherers who lived in the southernmost tip of Africa. Ford's allusion is to Saarti Baartman, who became known as the 'Hottentot Venus' for her pronounced buttocks and genitals. In 1810 a British ship's doctor took her to London, exhibiting her to a paying audience as a freak of nature. She was then sold to a French businessman, and died in Paris in 1816. She was dissected as a scientific specimen and displayed in a Paris museum until the 1970s. Her remains were returned to South Africa in 2002. 'The Beauty of Tunis' was the billing given to Rachel Ben-Eny when she performed at the Royal Aquarium in October 1887. She was a regular at the Folies Bergères in Paris, where she was billed as 'La Belle Fatma'.

Vulgate . . . hominibus bonae voluntatis: the Vulgate is a fourth-century Latin translation of the Bible, mostly by St Jerome; 'to men of good will'.

209 *silent listener*: also see p. 213, and compare Dowell's use of this phrase on pp. 44, 119, 143, and 154.

Hall Caine: Sir Thomas Henry Hall Caine (1853–1931), immensely popular and prolific Manx novelist and playwright of the Victorian and Edwardian eras.

Madame Bovary: unitalicized in the published essay, so it is possible that Ford is being playful about the sex-appeal of the character; but the preceding discussion of the appeal of books suggests he means here the title of Flaubert's novel.

George Edwardes: (1855–1915), successful theatre-manager, who produced several Gilbert and Sullivan operas, and later popularized the musical comedy form.

l'homme moyen sensual: the averagely sensual man (French).

Hampstead and wear no hats: Hampstead village in north-west London has been known for its bohemian intellectual community since the late nineteenth century.

210 *Whistler*: the painter James Abbott McNeill Whistler (1834–1903) was born in America and moved to London in 1859. His work has been seen as anticipating French Impressionism, and he became a leading figure in the Aesthetic Movement.

art . . . peasant: see for example Tolstoy's *What is Art?* (1898), in *Tolstoy on Art*, ed. Aylmer Maude (London: Oxford University Press [*c*.1924]), 226: 'A good and lofty work of art may be incomprehensible, but not to simple, unperverted peasant labourers (all that is highest is understood by them)—it may be and often is unintelligible to erudite, perverted people destitute of religion.' What Ford objected to in Tolstoy was his linking of art to just such moral positions. As he says here, 'the preoccupation that is fatal to art is the moral or the social preoccupation'.

Campden Hill: Ford was living at the time with Violet Hunt in her house 'South Lodge', on Campden Hill Road, Kensington. See Douglas

Goldring, *South Lodge: Reminiscences of Violet Hunt, Ford Madox Ford and the English Review Circle* (London: Constable, 1943).

210 *Sirventes*: a genre of Occitan lyric poetry used by the Troubadours, written from the perspective of a paid soldier. Its most famous exponent was Bertran de Born (1140s–by 1215), whom Ford thought Pound resembled.

Imagiste: the term 'Imagiste' (later 'Imagist') was coined when Pound met H.D. and Richard Aldington in the British Museum tea room in 1912. Ford knew all three well; he had published Pound for the first time in a British magazine in his *English Review*; and the other two both took dictation for parts of *The Good Soldier*. Ford wrote favourable reviews of Imagism, such as: 'Literary Portraits—XXXV. Les Jeunes and *Des Imagistes*', *Outlook*, 33 (9 May 1914), 636, 653; 'Literary Portraits—XXXVI. Les Jeunes and *Des Imagistes* (Second Notice)', *Outlook*, 33 (16 May 1914), 682–3; and 'A Jubilee' (review of *Some Imagist Poets*), *Outlook*, 36 (10 July 1915), 46–8: see Ford, *Critical Essays*, ed. Max Saunders and Richard Stang (Manchester: Carcanet Press, 2002), 150–8, 178–82.

When . . . purposely misleading: see Introduction, pp. xiv, xvi on Dowell's mention of having 'unintentionally misled' us.

a man mad . . . failure: whatever Ford thought of Brigit Patmore, he was at the time in love with her, had recently experienced bankruptcy, dishonour in the *Throne* case, and a lack of success for his books.

211 *Newgate Calendar*: the Newgate Calendar began as a bulletin of executions published from Newgate Prison, then the name was used for pamphlet biographies of famous criminals, which were collected into book form from the eighteenth century, and remained extremely popular into the nineteenth.

song that the sirens sang: according to the *Oxford Companion to Classical Literature* ' "What song the Sirens sang" is said by Suetonius to be one of the impossible questions with which the emperor Tiberius used to tease the scholars at his court.' The best-known English version is Sir Thomas Browne's, who wrote: 'What song the Sirens sang, or what name Achilles assumed when he hid himself among women, though puzzling questions, are not beyond all conjecture' (*Urn-Burial*, ch. 5).

212 *It is . . . flesh-heat*: Ford had described this experience in *The Heart of the Country* (London: Alston Rivers, 1906), 94–5.

painted a haycock bright purple: allusion to Ford Madox Brown. See *The Good Soldier*, p. 38 and note.

213 *The artist . . . off the chest*: compare Dowell, p. 12: 'You may well ask why I write [. . .] it is not unusual in human beings who have witnessed the sack of a city or the falling to pieces of a people to desire to set down what they have witnessed [. . .] or, if you please, just to get the sight out of their heads.'

fine frenzies: allusion to Shakespeare's *A Midsummer Night's Dream*, V.i:

> The poet's eye, in fine frenzy rolling,
> Doth glance from heaven to earth, from earth to heaven;
> And as imagination bodies forth
> The forms of things unknown [. . .]

American Literature

British and Irish Literature

Children's Literature

Classics and Ancient Literature

Colonial Literature

Eastern Literature

European Literature

Gothic Literature

History

Medieval Literature

Oxford English Drama

Poetry

Philosophy

Politics

Religion

The Oxford Shakespeare

A complete list of Oxford World's Classics, including Authors in Context, Oxford English Drama, and the Oxford Shakespeare, is available in the UK from the Marketing Services Department, Oxford University Press, Great Clarendon Street, Oxford OX2 6DP, or visit the website at www.oup.com/uk/worldsclassics.

In the USA, visit www.oup.com/us/owc for a complete title list.

Oxford World's Classics are available from all good bookshops. In case of difficulty, customers in the UK should contact Oxford University Press Bookshop, 116 High Street, Oxford OX1 4BR.